THE MERMAID

AVONSTOW

R.E. LOTEN

CASTLE PRIORY PRESS

First published in Great Britain in 2024 by Castle Priory Press, Brightlingsea

978-1-915970-08-4

Copyright © R.E. Loten, 2024
Cover Design: Olivia Reilly

For Dad, whose war this was

WORLD WAR TWO TIMELINE OF KEY EVENTS

3rd September 1939: Britain and France declare war on Germany
September 1939 – May 1940: 'Phoney' War
26th May – 4th June 1940: Operation Dynamo (Dunkirk evacuation)
10th July – 31st October 1940: Battle of Britain
22nd June 1941: Hitler attacks Russia
7th December 1941: Pearl Harbour attacked
August 1942: Allies invade North Africa
23rd October 1942: Battle of El Alamein
November 1942: Battle of Stalingrad
July 1943: Allies invade Siciliy
6th June 1944: D-Day
8th May 1945: V.E. Day
2nd September 1945: Japan surrenders

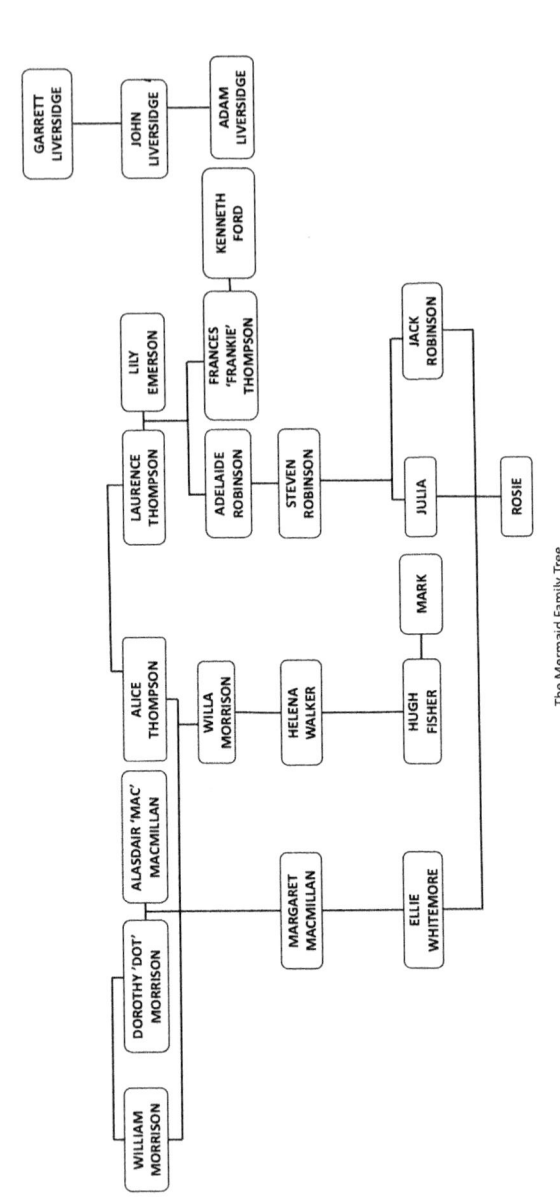

The Mermaid Family Tree

CONTENTS

1935	1
July 2017	3
Christmas 1939	17
March 1940	25
April 1940	32
July 2017	51
April 1940	60
May 1940	64
John - 1940	101
July 2017	103
John - 1940	105
July 1940	107
September 1940	124
October 1940	126
Adam - 1940	135
July 2017	137
November 1940	141
December 1940	144
August 2017	149
Adam - 1940	159
January 1941	161
Adam - 1941	170
August 2017	172
February 1941	177
August 2017	186
March 1941	195
August 2017	200
February 1943	209
Adam - 1943	212
August 2017	214
June 1943	222
August 2017	227
March 1944	229

August 2017	231
John - 1944	250
August 2017	253
May 1944	265
August 2017	282
September 2017	285
May 1944	289
September 2017	290
June 1944	301
September 2017	306
June 1944	313
October 2017	317
June 1944	321
October 2017	325
John - 1944	329
October 2017	331
John 1944	334
October 2017	343
John - 1944	350
October 2017	352
John - 1944	355
New Year's Eve 1944	357
October 2017	360
February 1945	366
Notes	369
Author's Notes and Acknowledgments	371
About the Author	375
Also by R.E. Loten	376
As Henrietta Edwards	377

1935

*T*he young man sat awkwardly on the chair. It was his first time modelling and he felt ridiculous. His sister was the class teacher and her usual model had let her down.

'Please,' she'd begged him. 'It's only an hour and nobody will see anything.'

'Nobody will see anything?' He stared at her, aghast. 'You're asking me to pose naked in front of an art room full of strangers and you think no-one will see anything?'

His sister laughed. 'Alright so they'll see something. But they won't be looking at you like that. It's a life drawing class. They'll only be looking at you as an object, not a person.'

'Oh well, that's alright then. That makes it so much better!'

That had been two weeks ago. He'd never been able to refuse her anything and so there he was, doing his best to keep still while a room full of people attempted to capture his likeness.

It hadn't been too bad so far. Most of them only glanced up at him, then their eyes fell immediately to their sketches.

Except for her. She studied him for long periods at a time, her face thoughtful. She was older than many of the others, but he didn't think the lines on her face were just age. This was a woman who had known pain. Deep pain.

At the end of the class, she was the last one to pack up. Seeing his sister growing impatient, he told her to go to lunch. He would lock the room as he left. He slipped behind the screen to put his clothes on, expecting the woman to be gone when he emerged. She was still there. Still looking at him. He swallowed nervously.

'Was there something else you wanted?'

'I wondered if you did private work?'

'Private work?'

'Private modelling.'

He stared at her. She sighed.

'I'd like you to come to my house and model for me. Just me. Hence, the 'private'.'

'For a picture?'

Her laugh was husky. 'A sculpture. I'd like to capture you in clay. I can pay for your time.'

The price she named was outrageous. It would pay for his college fees many times over.

'Why me? For that money you could get a professional model.'

She ran an appraising eye over him, her finger tracing a line down his chest.

'I couldn't get what I need from a professional. Your inexperience makes you look… apprehensive. It's an expression I want to capture. The naivety of youth is exactly what I need.'

He held out his hand. 'It's a deal.'

JULY 2017

*H*annah looked out of the café window. At the far end of the Lido, perched on his lifeguard's chair, sat Clem, seemingly unaware of the effect he was having on the occupants of the pool. There was a chuckle from behind her.

'Makes quite the picture, doesn't he?'

Hannah turned to see Frankie Ford grinning at her and laughed at the expression on the older lady's face. 'I was just thinking about those poor girls trying so desperately to get his attention.'

'Can't say I blame them. I was having a good old gawp myself. If I was fifty years younger, I'd have conveniently forgotten how to swim this morning. You'd have found me flailing around in trouble down at the deep end.'

'Wouldn't be the first time you'd employed that tactic either, would it?' Ken Ford laughed at the indignant expression on his wife's face.

'If it's not broke, don't fix it,' Frankie smiled, reaching out for his hand. 'It worked on you, didn't it?'

Ken laughed again. 'He's not in love with you already though, is he?'

Hannah hurriedly excused herself and returned to the kitchen. She shouldn't have been embarrassed. The couple came in every day: she swam while he read the newspaper and then they shared a toasted teacake with their coffees. Both were in their nineties, but the affectionate exchanges and loving looks showed they were as much in love as they had ever been and Hannah envied them. No one in her family had ever made it past 10 years of marriage and even at 25, her own love life was already a catalogue of disasters. She slammed the door on the thought. She told people she was happily single. It was better that way. She could never tell them the truth, not if she wanted to keep them as friends. Just her and Monty was the way she liked it and even he had been an accidental acquisition.

A few weeks after Hannah had started working at the Lido, Clem had turned up for work with the dog in tow.

'Sorry,' he said sheepishly, as a string of sausages slithered off the counter. 'This is Monty and apparently he's usually better behaved than this.'

'He's gorgeous.' Kate, the café manager and Clem's sister-in-law, bent to stroke the silky head. 'But I have to ask why he's here? I know we're dog-friendly, but the pool isn't and you're working today, aren't you?'

Clem sighed. 'I am. I was hoping maybe you could have him in here.'

'And how do you propose we manage that? You know how busy we get at lunchtime.'

'I know, I know. I wouldn't ask unless I was desperate.'

'How come you've got him anyway? Who does he belong to?'

'You know my aunt's next-door neighbour went into hospital and she agreed to look after Monty for a few days?

4

Well, the neighbour's family have decided she has to go into care, so they need a more permanent solution for poor Monty. None of them want a dog, so we're not sure what's going to happen to him. I agreed to dog-sit today as I was meant to be in the office, but one of the lifeguards called in sick so I've got to cover the shift.'

'Poor boy,' Hannah said, crouching down and petting him. She knew what it felt like to be unwanted. 'If you can have him in the office over the lunchtime rush, I'm sure we could manage the rest of the day. Couldn't we?' She looked at Kate.

Her boss shook her head with a resigned smile. 'Oh, alright then.' She fixed a glare on her brother-in-law. 'But if he eats any more sausages I'm coming after you for payment.'

Clem grinned and hugged her. 'Thanks Kate.'

'Thank Hannah.'

Clem turned his grin on Hannah, who laughed. 'I've always been a sucker for hard luck cases.'

Monty licked her hand and she looked down into the wide brown eyes. He really was a beautiful creature. Before she'd even finished forming the idea in her head, Hannah found herself offering to take him permanently. Clem arranged for her to meet Monty's owner and the old lady was so relieved he wasn't going to end up in a rescue centre that she'd agreed immediately and Monty had moved in with Hannah. Had she known what a sociable activity walking him would turn out to be, she wasn't sure she would have been so quick to offer him a home. She had no desire to get close to anyone again, but Monty gave her no choice. He loved being made a fuss of and everyone in Avonstow seemed to be a dog lover.

One day when he'd been in the café with her, Maisie, the local celebrity cat, had wandered in and curled up next to him. Kate, ever quick to spot a promotional opportunity, took a photo of the pair and put it on the café's Facebook page. By the end of the week, Hannah found herself being stopped by every other person they met.

'Oh, what a gorgeous boy. He was in that photo with Maisie, wasn't he?' Their words were accompanied by much stroking of Monty's head and he played up to them every single time, turning adoring eyes on them and licking their hands.

'He's an old fraud,' Hannah assured them, smiling politely before hurrying away.

Since then, Monty had accompanied her to work most days, sitting quietly in his basket beneath the counter, only getting up to say hello to the other dogs who were regular visitors to the café. He was loved by all the staff and even the lifeguards often came in to say hello to him before they started their shifts. Reluctantly, Hannah had found herself being drawn into the social circle of the staff and she had been out for drinks with colleagues after work, but still she held herself back. The rest of them gossiped happily about their lives outside the Lido, but Hannah always found a way to turn their questions back to them. She didn't want to talk about herself. There was no point: the job was only temporary. She'd taken it as a stop gap while she decided what to do after being made redundant.

Following the trauma of her final year at school, Hannah's father had allowed her to leave and do her A-levels through the local night school, rather than suffer a further two years of everyone around her knowing what had happened. She'd aced the exams but chose to stay living at home and study for a remote degree in Accountancy, while working part-time at Morgan Peters, a local firm. Nobody there knew about her past and it had felt like a fresh start. Her boss, Andy, had taken an interest in her and encouraged her studies. With his support she'd done her exams and qualified as an accountant, but then the firm had been sold and

Richard had happened. It wasn't long afterwards that the accounts department was told it was being 'streamlined' by the new owners. Roughly translated, they'd known that meant redundancies and when they'd asked for volunteers, Hannah had put herself forward immediately. She was keen to get away, to put it all behind her. Besides, she'd reasoned, many of the people she worked with had families and mortgages to pay: she was single and only renting. If the worst came to the worst, she could always ask her dad if she could move back home. They offered her a generous package and thanks to the local Facebook page she had a few private clients, so if she was careful with her money, she could afford to take a few months to decide what she wanted to do with her life.

When she saw the advert for the Lido café, she decided on the spur of the moment to apply. The money wasn't much but it would give her a bit more time to consider her options. Andy had floated the idea of going into business on her own as a private accountant and it wasn't wholly unappealing.

'What happened wasn't your fault, Hannah. They knew that and that's why they gave you such a good settlement. You're an excellent accountant. Don't let that weasel put you off the job.'

Hannah didn't believe him. Of course it had been her fault, it always was. But perhaps he had a point about the job. It was Andy who had responded to the Facebook inquiries, tagging her as a potential candidate. Once he'd suggested it though, the idea wouldn't leave her alone. The thought of being her own boss was appealing and it would mean she didn't have to go through the rigmarole of office politics and this time all her relationships would be professional, not personal.

. . .

'HANNAH? HANNAH?' Kate's voice cut across her thoughts and she turned to face her manager. 'The bacon!'

Hannah swore under her breath, raced into the kitchen to pull the smoking pan out from under the grill.

'Sorry.' She grimaced as she tipped the burnt pieces into the bin and quickly replaced them with fresh slices.

Kate waved her hand furiously under the smoke detector and grinned. 'Don't worry. I saw you watching Clem earlier. He has that effect on a lot of people.'

Hannah blushed. Kate had made it very clear she thought her employee and her brother-in-law would make a good pair and even though Hannah had told her she wasn't interested in a relationship, Kate enjoyed teasing her about it.

'Emmy must be mental,' Kate continued. 'But then I always knew she was.'

Hannah kept quiet, knowing Kate's feelings on the subject of Clem's soon-to-be ex-wife. According to Kate, she'd had an affair with her boss the previous year, but the relationship had ended and she'd spent the past few months begging Clem to stop divorce proceedings and take her back.

Kate sighed. 'Why would you want someone else if that was waiting for you at home? I probably shouldn't say it being married to his brother, but he's a decent bloke and nicely packaged to boot.'

'You never know what goes on behind closed doors though, do you?'

'True, but then I'm biased. I love Clem to bits and I never liked her. She reckoned she was better than the rest of us and she's exactly the sort to have an affair. That one doesn't care about anyone but herself.'

Hannah shrugged, concentrating on not burning the bacon again. Tears collected in her eyes and she blinked them back furiously.

'Hannah? What is it?' Kate turned her away from the grill.

Should have known she'd notice. Kate notices everything. 'It's nothing, honestly. I'm fine.'

Kate raised an eyebrow and waited.

Hannah sighed. 'It's nothing.' She gave her boss a weak grin. 'Promise.'

Kate harrumphed but didn't push her further. Hannah knew it was only a temporary reprieve though. From the moment she'd arrived for her first shift, Kate had taken her under her wing and decided they were going to be friends. Hannah had been given no choice in the matter. She didn't mind. Not really. Kate was lovely. It was just…Hannah sighed inwardly. Her past was always there hovering at her shoulder. Kate had definite views and that was why Hannah could never tell her about Ethan and Richard.

Sliding the now cooked bacon into the waiting roll, Hannah added a sachet of ketchup to the side of the plate and hurried out with it, handing it over to the customer who'd been drumming their fingers on the table. That done, she cleared the dirty cups and plates from Ken and Frankie's table, almost dropping them as Clem suddenly appeared in the doorway from the pool.

'Any chance of a cuppa?'

Hannah nodded. 'Sit down, I'll bring one over.'

As she brought the tea to his table, she passed two giggling teenagers who sashayed past her to order milkshakes. Clem rolled his eyes and she smiled.

'They been giving you trouble?'

He motioned to the seat and she slid in opposite him; when the café was quiet Kate didn't mind her taking five minutes.

'Not trouble so much as inappropriate flirting. I'm almost old enough to be their father but that doesn't stop them suggesting they need mouth to mouth resuscitation. It's embarrassing. I don't think I'd have dared at their age.'

'I don't think age has anything to do with confidence,' Hannah said thoughtfully, remembering Frankie's earlier remarks. 'Some people are just born with it.' She smiled 'The older members of the community share their appreciation of your lifeguarding skills.'

'Frankie Ford, by any chance?'

'Did she ask to be resuscitated as well?'

'Not today.'

Hannah laughed. It was good that she could relax in his company now. Before Monty she'd been unable to even say good morning, but their shared experience had loosened her tongue enough to have a conversation without worrying he'd think she was interested in him. That Clem himself was so laid back also helped. If she had been looking for a relationship, he would have been perfect. She silenced the thought. Relationships were for people like Frankie and Ken Ford, good people who deserved to be happy together. They weren't for people like her. All she did was destroy them. That it was unintentional, didn't matter. The end result was always the same and she would not risk it happening again.

THE FOLLOWING SATURDAY, Hannah spent the day running from till to kitchen to tables and back again until eventually, the queue grew shorter and Kate told her to take five minutes while she could. Frankie Ford was at a table on her own and she beckoned Hannah over.

'You look cream crackered,' she said, patting the younger girl's hand. 'It been busy today?'

'Like you wouldn't believe. We've not stopped since about 10 o'clock.' Hannah frowned. 'Where's Ken?'

A cloud shadowed Frankie's face. 'He's not feeling too

good. I told him to stay home and rest while I came for a swim.'

Hannah glanced at Frankie's dry hair.

'I'll run some water through it before I go home. I didn't really come to swim today. I'm meeting the family.' She swallowed, tears collecting in the corners of her eyes. 'It's time they knew.'

'Oh, Frankie!' Hannah reached out and took her hand, surprised at the depth of her own emotion. 'I'm so sorry. Is there anything we can do?'

Frankie shook her head. 'Just keep me supplied with coffee and friendship.'

Hannah's surprise must have shown because Frankie continued. 'You'll find as you get older that friendship comes in very unlikely forms and this place has always been a huge part of my life, so anyone who works here becomes a friend.' She hesitated, a slight frown deepening her wrinkles. 'Well… almost everyone, anyway.'

Hannah squeezed her hand but looked down. 'Not everyone deserves your friendship,' she mumbled.

'That's true enough,' Frankie agreed, with a wry grin. 'But that was a long time ago.'

'Not necessarily.' Hannah risked looking up. 'You know nothing about me, for example. I could be an awful person.'

Frankie laughed gently. 'I don't think so, my dear. I like to think I've proved a good judge of character over the years and I've seen enough of you to know I like you.' She tilted her head slightly, giving Hannah an appraising look. 'You give away far more of yourself than you think, you know.'

Hannah was alarmed. 'What do you mean?'

'Everyday things: the way you speak, the way you carry yourself. All of that gives clues to your personality. You don't even know you're doing it. Nobody does really. I just happen to be better than most at reading the signals.'

'I wish I had your confidence in myself.' Hannah found herself unexpectedly amused.

'The training never leaves you.'

Hannah frowned, but Frankie smiled mysteriously and refused to elaborate further.

Hannah sighed. 'There are things I've done that you can't tell from watching me. Maybe I'm not the person you think I am.'

'Oh, I think you are,' Frankie assured her. 'You might have secrets in your past, Hannah, who doesn't? But over the years, you learn that they don't define you. They make you who you are, but even someone with the most terrible things in their past can be a good person. Trust me. No one is determined by their past, only by their future.'

Hannah shook her head. 'And what about the people who keep making the same mistakes over and over again?'

'They're not destined to keep doing it. They learn from them and keep going. Our best is all any of us can do. In my lifetime I've kept more secrets than I care to remember and many of them hurt people I loved, but I've learnt to live with that. I had to. Otherwise, I wouldn't have had the life I have. I wouldn't have lived at all.' Frankie narrowed her eyes. 'Perhaps you should do the same. You can't hide from life forever, Hannah. Eventually it comes looking for you whether you want it to or not. My advice would be to let it find you.'

Frankie looked up as a shadow fell over them. 'Ellie!'

The woman bent to kiss Frankie's cheek, then sat down as the men behind her did the same.

'Hannah, this is my great-nephew, Jack and his partner, Ellie. And this is Hugh, my cousin – I forget how many times removed – and his partner, Mark. Everyone, Hannah.'

Jack laughed. 'We know Hannah, Aunt Frankie. We come in here almost as often as you do, remember!'

Frankie shook her head and smiled ruefully. 'Of course you do. Perils of old age.'

Ellie snorted. 'Don't make me laugh. The Thompson women stay as sharp as ever, regardless of age.'

Frankie looked wistful for a moment. 'Alice certainly did, didn't she? And I'm sure Addie would have done if the cancer hadn't got her first.' Her eyes filled with tears again.

'I'll get you some fresh coffee.'

As she waited for the machine to whirr into life, Hannah watched the family group out of the corner of her eye. As Jack had said, they were all regulars in the café. Ellie and Mark were the swimmers of the group and their partners were happy to sit in the café and chat while they counted off the lengths. Jack had recently retired, but Ellie still lectured part-time at the university. Hugh was a freelance journalist and Mark was the fundraising officer for a local charity. Ellie, a native Australian, had moved to Avonstow for work and Hannah envied the outsider who had found a way in. It was something Hannah was still trying to accomplish, but her desire to fit in warred with her need to avoid complicating her life. The feeling of being adrift had been her lifelong companion and community was a frightening concept. It didn't stop a part of her leaning towards it though. *They're not your friends,* she reminded herself. *Not when they don't know the real you.* She was still reminding herself of this when she put Frankie's coffee down in front of her, wishing she could join them and vicariously experience their closeness.

When she returned to the kitchen to start loading the dishwasher, Kate gestured to the group. 'Is Frankie telling them about Ken?'

'It's so sad, isn't it? Is he really unwell?'

Kate nodded, her face solemn. 'Cancer. He's been having treatment, but I think it's stopped working.'

'That's awful, poor Frankie. What will she do?'

'Wait and hope, I guess. There's not much else she can do at this stage. At least she's got her family around her and I know she gets a lot from coming here.' Kate grinned. 'She's always telling me about what a water baby she was when she was younger and apparently her and Ken got together here. You should get her to tell you the story one day. If half of what I've been told is true, she was a force to be reckoned with, especially when she was teaching.'

'She'll have to make the most of the Lido while it's still here,' Hannah said sadly.

'What do you mean?' Kate's voice was suddenly sharp.

'You don't know?' Hannah looked puzzled. 'I assumed it was common knowledge. My next-door neighbour works for the council and she reckons they're talking of closing it for good at the end of the season.'

Kate looked horrified. 'Nobody's said anything to us. Is it definite?'

Hannah shrugged. 'I don't know. She only mentioned it in passing when I said I was going to be working here.'

Kate scowled. 'They've kept that bloody quiet. If they close this place, then bang go our plans. We're so close to buying the lease for the campsite. We might have to reconsider if the Lido won't be here. It's a good site, but it needs a lot of work doing and if the Council close this whole building it'll become an eyesore – all boarded up and covered in graffiti, or concreted over and ugly. No one will want to visit with that on the doorstep. Could you ask your neighbour if it's definite??'

Hannah nodded. 'Of course.' She finished loading the dishwasher, then went back out to serve a customer, keeping a watchful eye on Frankie's table and wondering what the old lady would do if she couldn't swim every day. Surely the council couldn't have made a decision already. There must be a consultation period or something first. She didn't know much about how local government worked, but there had to be an opportunity for them to argue against the decision.

'Will she be okay, do you think?'

Kate nodded. 'She's a tough old thing is our Frankie, ask anyone who was taught by her. She might look like a fluffy old lady, but there's steel running through every bone in her body. Twenty years ago, when the live animal exports were happening, her and her sister, Jack's grandmother, were out on the streets every day. They might have had their knitting in their bags for when they were waiting, but you could guarantee there'd be a pair of bolt cutters, or handcuffs or something, hidden underneath. I was a few years behind Jack's niece, Rosie, at school but I got to know her after we left and I remember her telling me about when she and her mum got arrested on the same day and they were released without charge because Jack's boss was so terrified of Adelaide Robinson. Mark told me the same kind of thing – she harangued the inspector into letting him go as well. Frankie's like her sister. She's got a heart of gold but under-estimate her at your peril!'

'I know,' Hannah laughed. 'She was telling me the other day about what Avonstow was like during the war. I know it must have been awful at times, but she said the sense of community was even stronger than it is today. Did you know she ran away to join the Land Army? Apparently, they found out she was underage and sent her straight back home again. She was furious!'

'I worry for her though.' Kate looked sombre. 'She and Ken have been together for so long. I don't know how she'll cope without him. I haven't been with Harry half that time and the thought of losing him is awful.'

'Did they get together in the war then?'

'Towards the end of it,' Frankie called over. 'I may be old but I'm not completely deaf! I can hear you two, you know.'

'Sorry Frankie.' Kate came out of the kitchen looking sheepish. 'We're concerned about you, that's all.'

'I've survived loss before,' she told them sharply. 'I can do it again.'

Jack put a hand on her arm. 'No one's saying you can't, Aunt Frankie. But Kate and Hannah care about you. It's natural they'd worry.'

Frankie rolled her eyes at him. 'Sorry girls.' She gave them an apologetic smile. 'I know you mean well. It's only that *some* people,' she directed a glare at her great-nephew, 'Seem to think that when you get old you lose the ability to look after yourself.'

'Jack didn't say that, Frankie.' Ellie cut in. 'He just asked if you could manage on your own. There was no implication that you couldn't.'

Frankie harrumphed and folded her arms. 'I've been making decisions for myself since I was seventeen. I've been married twice, contributed to a war effort and taught hundreds of children over the years. I think I can manage a few days at home on my own!'

'You've been married twice?' Hugh sat forward in his chair. 'I didn't know that.'

Frankie glanced at Ellie and bit her lip. 'I don't talk about it much.'

CHRISTMAS 1939

*F*rankie sat in the corner of the Lido café, hands wrapped around a steaming mug of tea, her mood at odds with the festive atmosphere. Children laughed and giggled as they played games; brightly coloured decorations hung from the ceiling and the rousing *Santa Claus Is Coming To Town* came from the gramophone in the corner. Tears pricked at her eyes. *It's not fair. Just because Addie's a few years older, doesn't mean she's more capable than me.*

Thinking about her sister only brought more tears to her eyes. This time they were about more than the injustice of her situation. She missed Addie. It was nice having a bedroom to herself for once, but it felt odd waking up and not seeing her sister's face across the room. *They could at least have given me a chance to prove myself. They didn't have to send me home straight away.*

As soon as war had been declared, Addie had announced she was joining the newly re-formed Women's Land Army.

'We're going to need to grow as much food as we can,' she

17

told them over dinner. 'And if the men are all going to be off fighting, they're going to need women to grow it.'

'But Addie, there are plenty of farms around here,' their mother argued. 'Why can't you go and work up at the Warburton's place? I'm sure they'd appreciate an extra pair of hands and it would mean you'd still be close to Eric.'

Adelaide scowled. 'Eric Warburton is no concern of mine and I'd not work on that farm if you paid me!'

Lily opened her mouth to continue the argument but her husband's hand on her arm was enough for her to change her mind. Laurence Thompson rarely put his foot down, but when he did, his word was final. She glanced at him and he smiled gently before patting her arm. She stabbed the potato on her plate, her frustration clear.

Frankie looked at her father and saw he was now smiling sympathetically at his eldest daughter. *He knows. He must do. But how?* Frankie was sure her proud sister would not have breathed a word about what had happened, so was at a loss to explain how their father had found out Addie had ended her relationship with Eric Warburton. She wondered if he also knew why and found herself fervently praying that their mother remained in ignorance. Frankie and Addie adored their mother. She might have unconventional ideas, but she was a good person.

Frankie squeezed her sister's knee under the table and was rewarded with a rub of acknowledgement on her ankle. She knew why Addie didn't want to talk about it with her mother. Eric had pushed his luck and Addie had told him what he could do with his wandering hands. When Addie had told her the story, Frankie wasn't sure if her sister was angrier about his presumption, or what had come next.

'And then,' Addie had declared, hands on hips, 'Do you know what he had the gall to say?' She dropped her voice a tone. 'With a mother like yours I thought you'd have less pride. She wasn't too choosy when she was younger from what I've heard.'

'How dare he?' Frankie sprang to her feet. 'I'll knock the cheeky sod out.'

Addie grabbed her hand. 'Don't. It'll only upset Mum.'

Frankie subsided. Their mother was not typical when it came to social norms. She didn't hold with having different values of behaviour for men and women and where other mothers – which they knew from talking to their peers – held the view that sex was something only to be encouraged after marriage, Lily had told her girls simply to be careful not to fall for a baby. They'd assumed she spoke from her own experience, though they'd never dared to ask.

'The worst of it is, I'd probably have said yes if he'd been polite enough to ask,' Addie remarked. 'I liked him, Frankie. I mean, *really* liked him.'

Frankie bit her tongue. She'd never believed Eric was good enough for her beloved older sister, but Addie had fallen for the veneer of charm. Frankie didn't like seeing her sister upset but couldn't help feeling pleased Addie had finally seen Eric for what he really was.

'Forget him, sis. You're going to go and work on a farm somewhere and you'll meet a handsome farmhand and live happily ever after.' She flashed her sister a cheeky grin. 'Or at the very least have a roll in the hay with him.'

Adelaide swatted Frankie's arm but grinned in spite of herself. 'You're incorrigible. Mum's going to have her hands full with you once the uniforms start turning up.'

Frankie's humour disappeared. 'Is that what you think of me? That I'll throw myself at anyone?'

Adelaide shook her head and took her sister's hand. 'No. But you're so passionate about everything you do, I worry you'll have your head turned and get yourself into trouble. I remember what I was like at your age. I don't want you to get hurt and it's easy to mistake the physical stuff for love, especially at your age.'

Frankie smiled. 'Ever the big sister. Don't worry about me, I'm not daft.'

THE PARTY FRANKIE was sulking in the corner of had been Lily's idea. Her initial suggestion had been to have it at their hotel, The Mermaid, but when the Royal Navy had commandeered it to use as their onshore base, the Lido café had been suggested as an alternative. It would be far too cold to swim of course, but the children would enjoy watching the crabs and eels swimming around in the water.

'I'd have hated it if you two had been small and I'd had to send you away,' she told Frankie. 'Those poor little mites must be missing their families dreadfully. I want to do something to help cheer them up a bit. Christmas is a horrible time to be away from the people you love. Who knows when we'll be able to have proper parties again, so let's make the most of it while we're still able to.'

There had been no talk of a quick end to the war in the Thompson house. Lily and Laurence had lived through the 1914-18 War and Laurence's younger brother had lost his life on the first day of the Battle of the Somme – two years into a war that was meant to be over by Christmas. The newspapers might have christened this one the Phoney War, but Laurence insisted it wouldn't stay phoney for long.

'Cheer up Frankie, it might never happen.' Kenneth Ford slid into the empty chair next to her and he nudged his shoulder against hers.

'It already did,' she said glumly, aware she was being unfair. He was only trying to help. It wasn't his fault the Land Army had found out she'd lied about her age.

'Didn't you try crying?'

His reference to their shared secret earned him half a smile. They had avoided much trouble in their younger years because of Frankie's ability to cry on demand and he was still the only person who could distinguish the fake and the real.

'You can always apply again when you're old enough.' He pulled a face in an attempt to make her smile.

She grinned in spite of her foul mood. Ken always made her feel better and she'd missed him while he'd been away. He'd joined the RAF and was based in Blackpool for his basic training. Unlike her sister, he'd managed to wangle a few days leave to come home for Christmas.

'You will carry on writing to me while I'm away, won't you?' he said suddenly. 'I don't know where I'll end up but I'll want all the news from home still. Avonstow never seems so far away when I read your letters. There's a few poor blokes who've come from Australia and Eastern Europe and they're terribly envious of them.'

'Of course I will,' Frankie said. 'I doubt there'll be anything interesting to tell though. I expect my life will be very boring once you've gone back to do your bit.'

'You do miss us then?'

'Every day! I sit by my window pining away until you come home again.' She laughed, suddenly feeling much better.

Getting up from her chair, she put her mug to one side and headed towards her mother. Eric Warburton might have described Lily as no better than she ought to be, but as far as Frankie was concerned, there was no finer woman in the world and if Lily wanted to give the evacuees a party to remember, then her daughter would do her best to make sure it happened.

. . .

WHEN THE LAST plate had been washed up and put away, Lily packed the gramophone into the back of the car and turned expectantly to her daughter. 'You coming?'

'I'll walk Frankie home, if that's alright, Auntie Lil?'

She kissed Ken's cheek. 'Of course it is, love. Pop in for a cuppa before you go home? I've knitted you a scarf to keep you warm while you're up north.'

Ken smiled and nodded. Waving Lily off, he tucked Frankie's arm through his, noting the frown had returned to her face.

'Come on,' he said, squeezing her arm. 'That's a face that needs to throw stones.'

A reluctant smile tugged at the corners of her lips. 'I'm not a child to be pacified.'

'You know it will make you feel better.' Letting her arm go, Ken took off, laughing. 'Race you.'

Frankie hared after him, never able to resist a challenge. Skidding to a halt on the pebbles, she stooped, grabbed a stone and hurled it into the sea, watching with grim satisfaction as it sent the water splashing up.

'Be reasonable, kiddo.' Ken's stone followed a less aggressive trajectory. 'What did you expect them to do? You're underage. They had to send you back.'

'I can lift just as much as Addie can. They should have let me stay.'

'The government says you have to be 18. You're 17. Even if they wanted to, they wouldn't have been allowed. How did they find out anyway?'

Frankie kicked out at the waves that lapped around her shoes. 'Someone obviously told them. I do wish people would mind their own business!'

Ken slipped an arm around her shoulders. 'Cheer up. I hate seeing you like this.'

For the first time in their conversation, Frankie's head

dropped and she lost the angry scowl she'd been wearing since they'd left the Lido. 'What's there to be cheerful about?' she said mournfully. 'Addie's gone. You're gone. I'm the only one left behind. Just like always.'

Ken pulled her up the steps and made her sit down on a nearby bench. 'I wanted to talk to you about that.' Taking a seat next to her, he took her cold hand in his. 'Promise you'll write to me?'

Frankie smiled. 'I said I would, don't be daft.'

'You'll miss me then?'

'You know I will.'

He lifted his free hand and brushed the wisps of hair away from her face. 'I'm going to really miss you, you know.' He paused. 'Frankie, I...' He lowered his head and brushed his lips against hers.

Startled, Frankie pulled back, her eyes wide. 'What are you doing?'

Ken flushed. 'I'm sorry... I...I thought... that is, I hoped... I'm sorry...'

Frankie laid a hand on his chest. 'Don't be sorry. You took me by surprise, that's all. I like you, Ken, but... I always assumed if you were going to be interested in any of us, it would be Addie.'

'It's you. It's always been you.'

Frankie ignored the tears gathering in her eyes. 'I'm so sorry, Ken. I... we're friends you and me. That's all we've ever been.'

'Is that all we could ever be?'

Frankie looked at her lap, where his hand still covered hers and nodded. 'I'm sorry.'

'Don't be.' Ken tilted her chin up gently, forcing her to make eye contact. 'You can't help how you feel. Will you still write to me though? As friends?'

Frankie threw her arms around him. 'How could you think I wouldn't?'

For a moment, Ken allowed himself to enjoy the sensation of holding her in his arms, then reluctantly he let her go. *I had to try*, he told himself. *I couldn't leave again without asking.*

AFTER KEN HAD WALKED her home, Frankie sat cross-legged on her bed. What on earth had possessed him? He was more like a brother than a friend, part of their gang from school, a group of them who'd always stuck together. They'd grown up within a few streets of each other and had naturally gravitated towards each other for company. Addie and Frankie bookended the group in terms of age, but somehow the age difference had never mattered to any of them until now. Tears filled her eyes again. *It's bad enough they're all going and leaving me behind. Why did he have to make it worse by spoiling our friendship like that? Should I have lied? What if he doesn't come back?* She threw herself down and allowed the tears to soak her pillowcase until she fell into an exhausted sleep.

MARCH 1940

'*H*ey kiddo! Ease off.' Ken detached Frankie's arms from around his neck. 'Anyone would think you were pleased to see me.'

'I am pleased, you idiot.' Frankie punched him on the arm and grinned. 'It's been so boring around here without you and Addie.'

She looked at the man standing slightly behind Ken. A slight smiled played across his face, as though her greeting amused him in some way.

'You must be Frankie,' he said, moving forward and extending his arm. 'Ken's told me all about you.'

He was Australian. And younger than she'd first thought. *Probably not much older than Ken. But he looks tired.* She nodded as Ken made the introductions.

'Mac, this is indeed Frankie. Frankie, this is Mac. He did some of his training with me and we're both going up to Debden. His family's all in Australia, so I suggested he came home with me for his leave as he had nowhere else to go.'

'You make me sound like a lost dog,' Mac laughed, his

eyes creasing at the corners. 'I could have gone to a hotel somewhere.'

'Mum would have killed me.'

Frankie nodded. 'He's right. When we were kids, we were all told that if anyone was lonely, we should bring them home with us. My mum's even worse than his for it. She didn't have the best childhood, so she can't stand the idea of anyone being alone if she can do something about it.' She tilted her head to one side as she studied him. 'What's Mac short for anyway?'

'It's my surname. Alastair MacMillan is a bit of a mouthful so everyone calls me Mac.'

'What family did you leave behind?'

His smile fell away and he hesitated for a moment. 'My parents and my sister. My dad was over here in the last war and I flew a fair bit at home, so it seemed only right to use the skills I have.'

'Your dad was in Britain during the first war?'

'Not just in Britain. Here in Avonstow. He was attached to the Australian Engineers Training Division and they were based in the village. In fact, I was born here. Well, in Britain, anyway. He married my mum at the beginning of the war and had my sister, Molly. I was born at the end of 1916. When the war ended, he went back to Australia and we all went with him.'

'How did your family feel about you signing up?' Frankie asked. 'You're a long way from home.'

'My dad understood. Mum and Molly less so, but once I'd explained I think they knew I didn't really have a choice. They worry though. My dad lost a lot of friends and now it's all happening again.'

'There's a plaque on the Rec for all the ANZAC[1] troops who died. You could put some flowers there, maybe? I'd be happy to show you where it is.' Frankie rested her hand on Mac's arm for a moment.

'Thanks. I think my dad would appreciate it.'

'Maybe take a photo to send to him.' Ken gestured to the case slung across Mac's chest. 'In the meantime, lets drop our things at home and we can give you the grand tour of Avonstow.'

He led the way out of the train station, Frankie and Mac following on behind him, chatting as though they'd been friends for years. He smiled to himself. It was good to be home and Frankie seemed perfectly normal, as though he'd never embarrassed them both by declaring his love for her. The last time he'd been home on leave she'd still been a little stilted with him. This time, their old easiness had returned and she was behaving more like herself again. Whatever the cause he was grateful.

MAC KNELT to lay the flowers at the base of the wall, before standing and running his finger over the names on the brass plaque.

'Are you alright?' Frankie laid a gentle hand on his shoulder. He sprang to his feet and nodded but didn't speak, so she continued, needing to fill the silence that had sprung up between them. 'Does your dad ever talk about any of them?'

Mac shook his head. 'He's told me stories of being here, but of his time at the front, nothing. He never charges veterans who call him out though. Says they had a far worse time of it than he did and treating them is his way of saying thank-you.'

'He sounds like a wonderful man.'

'He is. I wish I could be half the father he is.'

'You will be, I'm sure.'

He gave her an odd look and turned back to the plaque, resting his hand on it again. 'I wonder if they knew they were going to die, or if it came out of nowhere. I think if death was coming, I'd rather it was quick.'

'Don't say that. Don't ever wish for death.'

Mac smiled at the anxious expression on her face. 'I'm sorry, I didn't mean to offend you.'

Frankie shivered. 'You haven't. I…'

Instead of continuing with what she'd been about to say, she stretched on her tiptoes and pressed her cold lips against his. For a moment, they softened against her, then he gently pushed her away.

'Don't, Frankie. Please.'

She dropped her gaze. 'I'm sorry, I didn't mean…'

He tilted her chin up, forcing her to look at him. 'You're so young, I–'

'I'm 18. I'm not a child.'

Mac laughed gently at her petulant expression. 'Maybe not, but I'm 24 and I've seen far more of life than you. More than I would ever want you to. Find someone your own age, Frankie. Find someone who deserves you.'

'Meaning you don't?'

'You deserve more than damaged goods. You've only known me a few days and I'm not right for you. You're worth more than a quick fling. Besides, Ken would kill me if I messed with you.'

'Ken isn't in charge of me,' Frankie said through gritted teeth. 'Who I see has nothing to do with him.'

'I'm not sure he sees it that way,' Mac said. 'He cares a great deal about you. This can't happen.' He tucked her hair behind her ear, letting his fingers linger a moment on her cheek. 'However tempted I might be.'

'WHAT THE HELL are you playing at, Frankie?'

She'd never seen Ken so angry. 'What are you talking about?'

'You. Mac. I saw you.'

'We took some flowers to the ANZAC plaque. We did tell you we were going, but you said you were busy.'

'So were you apparently! You've only known him a few days and you're kissing him in public?'

'Don't you dare pass judgement on me, Kenneth Ford. You're only jealous because I turned you down.'

Frankie turned to walk away but was surprised when a strong hand fastened around her wrist.

'Do you really think so little of me?'

Even in the midst of her anger, she could hear the hurt in his voice and she shook her head, her temper cooling instantly.

'You know I don't. I'm sorry.'

'Frankie, first and foremost, you're my friend and I love you because of that. I don't want you to get hurt and I don't want you to… to… damage your reputation. And especially not with someone I introduced you to. Your parents would never forgive me.'

'So it's okay as long as I'm discreet?' She quickly smothered the mischievous grin that had crept across her face. 'I'm teasing, don't look so serious.' She reached up and smoothed the frown away from his forehead. 'He turned me down, so don't worry your head about it.'

'If that's true, he's a fool, but I'm glad of it.' He smiled down at her. 'You alright?'

Frankie nodded. 'I feel like an idiot, but yes. I don't know what came over me. I'm not in the habit of throwing myself at men, you know. How did you see us anyway?'

'I walked up to meet you once I'd finished the jobs Mum

asked me to do. I saw you kiss him so I left. There was no one else around, don't worry.'

ALL TOO SOON, Ken and Mac's leave was over and it was time for them to join their squadron. For the most part, Mac had avoided being alone with Frankie, but she knew he'd spent much of their time together watching her. At the station, he drew her to one side.

'I wanted to say thank-you. These last few days have been wonderful.'

'You told me you were damaged goods. I'm not giving up on you though.' She brushed her hand against his. 'I don't know what the damage is, but I'd like the chance to try to repair it.'

Mac cupped her face in his hand. 'Frankie, I–'

'Don't say it. If you weren't interested, I'd leave you alone, but I've seen how you look at me when you think I'm not watching. I know what those looks mean.'

'Experienced it often, have you?'

She flushed. 'I've seen how men look at my sister.' She turned and stalked away to where Ken stood, half-turned away from them. She touched his arm gently and he turned to her, a half-smile on his face.

'I wish you didn't have to go.'

'I know, kiddo, but this war isn't going to fight itself you know. I'll make time soon for a sneaky trip home, don't worry.' He kissed her cheek and swung himself up onto the train to find their compartment.

Frankie glanced at Mac who had moved to re-join them. 'And you?'

'I'm not sure it's a good idea. I don't know how welcome I'd be.'

'Nobody should have to spend their leave alone.'

Mac nodded but said nothing. Frankie bit back the tears that sprang to her eyes. She jabbed her hands into the pocket of her coat, her shoe grinding the stones on the platform.

'Will you at least write? Let me know you're okay?'

He looked at her gravely for a moment. 'Would you like me to?'

She nodded.

'Very well.' He bent and brushed his lips against her cheek. Frankie closed her eyes, feeling the slight scratch of his stubble against her cheek. She breathed in the woody lemon scent of his soap and clenched her fists.

I will not cry. I am not in love with him. It's like he said. He's not right for me.

RELEASING HER, Mac stepped slowly onto the train. As it pulled out of the station, he watched her figure become smaller and smaller as the distance between them grew ever wider. *For God's sake man, the last thing your life needs is more complications.* There could never be anything between them. So why was he even considering it? He didn't want to answer that. Frances Thompson was a dangerous young woman and his heart was best kept close. *So why do I think it may already be too late? Why does it feel like I've left it behind on that platform?*

APRIL 1940

'I thought you weren't coming back?' Frankie hugged Mac as he stepped off the train.

'If I was more sensible, or less polite, I wouldn't have done.' He stepped back, needing to put some distance between them. Frankie raised an eyebrow. 'Ken told his parents I got banged up when I crashed the kite and they wrote and asked me if I'd like to come here while I was grounded. I didn't feel I could refuse when they'd made me so welcome last time. What?'

Frankie was laughing at him. 'When you wrote, you said you'd crashed your plane and hurt your shoulder and weren't allowed to fly until it heals. What you just came out with was so incredibly British it sounded funny with your accent.'

'I guess the language rubs off on you after a while.' He hurried towards the station exit and Frankie had to run to catch up with him.

'And what about us?'

Mac had been careful not to allow his letters to stray beyond the boundaries he'd set, but Frankie wasn't stupid, he knew she'd have sensed what he was feeling when he wrote them.

'Just stop for a second, will you?' She caught his arm. 'I know what you said last time, but I'm telling you I don't care. Your letters–'

'Frankie, you're such a child!'

Her face crumpled. Dropping his arm, she spun around, running towards the seafront. Still not fully fit after his accident, Mac eventually caught up with her by the boating lake.

'Please don't cry.'

'I'm not a child.'

'Believe me, I am well aware of that.'

'Then why did you call me one?'

'Partly because you're behaving like one, wheedling for something you've been told isn't good for you and...'

'And?'

'And partly to stop myself doing this.' He bent his head to hers and kissed her softly. 'This isn't fair to either of us.'

'I know what I'm doing,' Frankie whispered against his neck.

He moved her firmly away. 'No. You don't. You're 18.'

'I'd be old enough to fight if I was a boy.'

'But you're not. You're a young girl who's never left the village she was born in. You think you know everything and war's made you feel as though everything has to happen now. Trust me, it doesn't. I don't want you to do something we'll both regret. I've spent years trying to do the right thing and it's not always been easy. I wish I could abandon my principles and take what you're offering. But I can't.'

'Do you know how pompous you sound?' Frankie scoffed. 'Abandon your principles?' Then she looked apologetic. 'Sorry. Are you really religious or something?'

Mac shook his head wearily. 'No, I'm not religious.'

Her expression brightened and she leant in to kiss him

again, but he pushed her away. 'Dammit, Frankie. I don't want to hurt you, but I will. It's inevitable.'

'You've warned me often enough. Surely now it's my choice whether or not to take the risk?'

Mac's jaw twitched. 'I'm all wrong for you.'

'I disagree.' Frankie leant in and kissed him again. For a moment, he allowed himself to enjoy the freedom and sense of release it brought him, then gently pushed her away.

'Stop it, Frankie. I mean it.' He trailed his fingers across her damp cheeks. 'You know Ken's in love with you, don't you? He'd be a far better choice.'

'But I don't love him.'

Drawing her into his arms, he kissed the top of her head. 'I know.' He murmured the words against her hair. 'I'd hate it if you did, but it would make it easier to let you go.'

'How long are you here for?'

'Doc gave me three days.'

He took her hand in his and she rested her head against his chest. Even this was wrong, but if it brought her some comfort, how could he deny her? He was strong enough to put a stop to it when he needed to. He'd had plenty of practice, after all.

Over the next few days, he swung between trying to keep his distance from Frankie and finding himself walking past The Mermaid, hoping for a glimpse of her. Her parents had been welcoming but cautious and he understood why. They knew nothing about him – if they did, they'd have banned him from coming anywhere near her – and Frankie, in spite of what she said, was still little more than a child. He loved that she was so open about what she wanted, but he kept reminding himself it was nothing more than a crush. He was older and foreign and in uniform, nothing more. And yet…

when she smiled at him, he felt a glow inside which he thought had forever been extinguished. Perhaps if he wrote home. If he explained. Perhaps. He shook his head. It could never be. Too much had happened. He talked himself in and out of various actions but no sooner had he convinced himself to leave Avonstow and stay away, he would see a glint of red hair in the sun and know he couldn't.

'GIVE KEN MY LOVE,' Frankie said, as she handed Mac his bag. He raised an eyebrow and she grinned. He knew she wanted to kiss him again and he was struggling not to pull her into his arms to say a proper goodbye, but he had promised himself he wouldn't.

Mac had done his best not to overstep the boundary he had set for himself, but there had been the occasional moment of weakness. A stolen kiss at the cinema. Hands brushed together in a crowded room. Wordless promises made across packed concert halls. Frankie had freely admitted she was doing everything in her power to make him break his vow not to give in to his feelings and a part of him was glad of it. He felt loved. Wanted. He had struggled not to take advantage of their being alone so frequently, to stop himself reaching for her every time they met. His conscience warned they were heading towards broken hearts, but he silenced it with a vow that he was in control. He would not let things go too far. The last thing he wanted was to cause her pain. But neither could he bring himself to tell her the truth.

THE DRONE OF THE PLANES' engines filled Frankie's ears as she carried the bins to the back of the hotel. The breeze caught her hair, still damp from her morning swim, and chilled the back of her neck. Peering up into the spring sunshine, she wasn't surprised to see a group of fighters heading out over the coast. As two of the planes gave a slight waggle of their wings, she grinned to herself. Mac and Ken were among them. She waved. There was no way they could see her, but she'd promised to wave them off nonetheless. She tried not to think about what they were flying towards and focused instead on the pleasure of having seen them.

More and more planes filled the sky as the day wore on and once her chores were done, there was little for her to do but wait, anxiously scanning the skies for any sign of the planes returning. Every time a group flew over, she watched for the tell-tale dip of the wing, but it never came.

As she collected the empty glasses in the bar area, a young seaman came racing up to her.

'Have you seen Mr. Portis?'

Frankie nodded her head towards the corner of the room, where an elderly man sat slumped against the wall, drool collecting in the folds of his chin.

'No use trying to wake him. He's been in here all afternoon. What's the hurry?'

'There's a plane gone down somewhere off Clacton. The pilot was reported ejecting but the message has only just come through and it's getting dark. We need to get the boat out now.'

'Well, he's in no fit state to pilot it. Isn't there anyone else who could do it?'

The seaman shrugged. 'He's the pilot. He's meant to do it. We're not allowed to touch the boat.'

'For God's sake! Wait there.'

Frankie hurried from the room and returned a few moments later wearing one of her father's thick woollen jumpers.

'Come on,' she said, heading for the door. 'I'll do it.'

'You? But you're a woman!'

'10 out of 10 for observation, sailor. I've also been sailing since I was big enough to reach the wheel. If the Navy aren't allowed to touch his boat, I will. I'll deal with him when he sobers up. Do we know who we're looking for?'

The man frowned. 'Some Aussie chap, I think they said.'

Frankie stopped abruptly. 'Alastair MacMillan.' Her voice sounded hollow above the rushing in her ears.

'Yeah, that's right. Know him, do you?'

Frankie shook her head to clear it. 'He's a friend.'

She swallowed the bile rising in her throat. She would find him. She would bring him home. She would not lose him. Jumping into the launch that was kept tied up at the end of the jetty, she ignored the incredulous looks and protestations from the waiting sailors and started the engine, directing the boat out into the channel. As they chugged out, two thundering crashes rang out from the direction of the town and when she glanced back, startled out of her fear by the noise, two plumes of smoke were rising. One from somewhere near the church on the hill above the town and one from somewhere behind The Mermaid. A single twin engine bomber roared overhead.

'Reckon he got lost?'

'Prob'ly. Either that or it was a recon of the base.'

'Nah. Recons don't carry bombs. He must have got lost. If they'd been targeting the base, there'd have been more of 'em.'

Frankie turned to the front of the boat again, pushing this latest worry aside. Whatever had happened in Avonstow would have to wait. He had to be safe. He had to be.

. . .

'MY GOD! Frankie, where have you been? I've been worried sick!' Lily raced down the steps of The Mermaid to gather her daughter in her arms.

Relieved of their burden, the two sailors who had helped the shivering girl home, followed them into the building.

'She's been out with us, Mrs T. Plane came down up the coast and Mr Portis weren't in a fit state to pilot the launch, so she took us out. She could have come back once we got out to the other boats but she wouldn't. Insisted on staying to help look for him.'

'Mum, it's Mac.' Frankie spoke through chattering teeth and blinked back the tears. 'He's still out there somewhere.'

Lily's gaze shifted from her daughter to the men and they looked away. She tightened her grip around Frankie.

'Thank you for seeing her home safely.' The two men nodded and turned to leave.

As they reached the door, the elder of the two turned back. 'Don't be too hard on her Mrs T. We picked up a couple of bodies from *The Pullman.* It's a week since she sank, so they weren't a pretty sight for anyone, least of all an 18-year-old girl, but you should be proud of her. She was the one who spotted them and kept her nerve. She held the boat steady while we got them in. There's two families who'll get their sons back for burial thanks to her.'

Lily nodded, a tight smile on her face. Wordlessly, she ushered Frankie upstairs and helped her out of her wet clothes, towelling her hair before putting her into bed with a hot water bottle and strict instructions to stay where she was until she had warmed up. Eventually, Frankie waved her away and lay back, closing her eyes and trying to block out the pain. She knew her mother was angry and she had every right to be, but Frankie knew she would do the same thing again if there was even the slightest chance of finding the man she loved.

She jolted upright, the hot water bottle crashing to the floor. The man she loved. Did she love Mac? He was attractive, certainly, but suddenly she knew there was more to it than that. She had teased and flirted her way into loving him and now she might never be able to tell him.

Putting her dressing gown on, she went in search of her mother, finding her in the hotel's bar.

'May I have one?' She nodded at the drink clutched in Lily's hand.

'I'll put some hot water in it. You still look half frozen.'

Her hand shaking, Lily poured some of the whisky into the mug and handed it to her daughter. 'Do you want to talk about it?'

Frankie shook her head. 'Every time I close my eyes, I see their faces and then they turn into Mac's face.' She took a sip from the mug, feeling the warmth of the alcohol take effect.

'I didn't realise you were so close,' Lily said carefully.

'We're not. I… He…' Frankie trailed off. How could she describe their relationship? Whatever she said would be inadequate to convey what he'd been. What he was. *What he is,* she thought. *Is. Present tense.*

Lily drained her glass and set it down on the table. 'You liked him, didn't you?'

Frankie looked at the sympathetic expression on her mother's face and nodded.

'My poor darling.' Lily opened her arms and Frankie fell into them, no longer bothering to hold back the tears. 'Did he know?'

Frankie nodded, feeling her tears smear across her mother's blouse.

'Were you…?'

Frankie shook her head. 'But I know he loved me, Mum.' She glanced up at Lily, who said nothing. 'He did, I know it. He just couldn't say so.'

'Why not?'

'He said he was too old. Too damaged.'

'Or maybe he was trying to gain your trust. Your sympathy.'

'Why would he do that and then not take advantage of it? It makes no sense.'

'I don't know. darling. Perhaps he liked the idea of you begging him.' Lily paused and something in her face had changed when she spoke again. 'Some men like the power, the control. They need to feel they're wanted. Needed.'

Again, Frankie shook her head. 'Mac's not like that.'

Lily refilled her glass and drained it. 'How do you know? You've known him, what? A few months? And in that time, you've spent only a matter of hours with him. He seemed nice, but people can hide who they really are.'

'How would you know? You've known Dad all your life. How could you know anything about whether it's possible to fall in love with someone as soon as you meet them?'

'I know a good deal more than you think, Frances Thompson!' With a shaking hand, Lily filled her glass again. 'So don't you dare tell me I know nothing of love!'

Shaken by the raised voice, Frankie laid a hand on her mother's arm. 'I'm sorry, Mum. I know you love Dad, I only meant that you and he took ages to get together. You can't dismiss the possibility of falling instantly in love just because you've never experienced it.'

Lily shook her hand off. 'I do know it's possible, especially in wartime. But I also know it leads to nothing but heartbreak.' She dashed a hand across her face. 'I don't want that for you.'

'Mum? Was there... Did you...? Did you love someone before Dad?'

To Frankie's growing alarm, Lily didn't reply immediately. The longer her mother remained mute, the more outlandish the possibilities racing through her head became.

'Was it John Liversidge? It was, wasn't it? That's why you've always been so angry when his name's mentioned. Did he reject you? That's why you warned me off Adam –'

'No!'

Lily's glass shattered against the far wall and Frankie stared at the pieces as they glinted in the dim lights.

'Mum? What's going on? You're scaring me.'

Lily looked at her daughter's white face and wrapped a hand around the one that trembled on Frankie's lap.

'I'm sorry,' she said quietly. 'I'm not thinking straight tonight and when you said... when you thought... I loathe that man, Frankie. I've never been in love with him.' She swayed slightly in her seat, then pulled Frankie's half-finished drink towards her.

Frankie took the mug away from her mother. 'Talk to me Mum. What happened today? You never drink like this and by the state of you, I reckon you'd already had a few by the time I got home. It's not simply because you were worried about me: let's be honest, it's not the first scrape I've got myself into.' She forced a laugh. 'Is it Dad? Where is he? Or Addie? Has something happened to them?'

Lily shook her head. 'As far as I know, your sister's fine. Dad is... out. There was... an incident. Two actually.'

A memory of smoke plumes flashed through Frankie's mind. 'The smoke,' she whispered. 'Bombs.' The blood drained from her face and the whisky surged up to meet it. She swallowed it down again. 'Dad?'

'Dad's fine. He's helping with the rubble. Lionel and Meredith's house was hit, along with the one next door.'

'Oh god,' Frankie moaned. 'Has someone telephoned Ken?'

'They're okay, love. Meredith is asleep upstairs and

Lionel's with your dad. Next door took the brunt of it and they think the neighbours might be under the rubble somewhere. They put the fire out quite quickly, but it's all a bit unstable and they're worried more might come down as they're moving bricks.'

'There was a second one, wasn't there? Up near the church. Was anyone hurt?'

Lily went over to the bar and collected two glasses. She poured them a large measure each then sat down again, her drink clutched tightly to her chest.

'That wasn't a bomb. It was one of those mines they put in the fields to stop tanks going across them. For some reason Nate Parker and his crowd decided to ignore the warning signs and go and play in there.'

Frankie's hand flew to her mouth. 'Are they...' She couldn't finish the question.

'Nate and Johnny.'

Frankie knew both boys. Had gone to school with their older siblings. She shivered. 'Oh Mum. What a waste. Their poor families.'

'It's been such a day. And then when I got home and you were gone, I –'

'You were out of your mind with worry. I'm sorry, Mum. I had to do something to help though.'

'You take after me, love. Too impulsive by half. That's why I worry so much.'

'Addie's just as stubborn. Admittedly she takes time to think things through first though.'

Lily smiled sadly. 'She takes after –'

Frankie looked at her mother. The sentence had been cut off abruptly and Lily's lips were clamped together. She narrowed her eyes suspiciously.

'Who does she take after, Mum? What were you going to say?'

Lily met her gaze, her expression fierce. 'She takes after her father.'

'Mum?' Frankie tried to keep her voice steady. 'Dad's the least stubborn person I've met.'

'He isn't Addie's father. I married him when Addie was a toddler.'

'Then who?'

'Officially, she's John's.'

'John? John Liversidge?' Frankie choked on a mouthful of her drink.

'We were married once. A long time ago.'

'But, you said…'

'I married him. I never loved him.'

'Why?'

Lily shook her head, her face white in the pale light from the lamps.

'And unofficially?' Frankie pressed. 'Who is Addie's father really? Did John know? Does Addie know?'

'His name was Bert. He was an Australian, over here for training. I fell for him the minute I saw him. I'd never have said anything – I had a reputation in those days and I'd have been too afraid of rejection – but I saw a chance and I took it before I could talk myself out of it. A friend set us up.' Lily smiled wistfully. 'You look a lot like her, actually. Anyway, she put in a good word for me and I got lucky. He was wonderful. We only had a few months together, but it was the first time I'd felt truly loved since my parents died. We made plans for after the war – he was going to come back and if we still felt the same, I was going to go to Australia with him. I found out I was pregnant after I got the news he'd been killed.' Lily broke off. 'I was beside myself with worry. There was a lot going on at the time and I couldn't think straight. Alice – my friend – lost her husband at the same time and then she left the village and I married John.

'He'd been obsessed with Alice since we were kids and he didn't take her marriage well. He married me thinking he could turn me into her. I was sent for elocution lessons to make me sound like her, made to dye my hair so I looked more like her. He even called me by her name sometimes. By the time I realised what a mess my life was in, Addie had been born and I couldn't risk anything happening to her. It was a relief when he said he wanted a divorce so he could marry Penny. Even being on my own seemed a better option than what I'd endured in the years we'd been married. When the divorce came through, your father immediately proposed. Claimed he'd been in love with me for years. Maybe I was his sister's friend and he just felt sorry for me, but I was in no position to argue. I had no money, no house and no husband and I had a daughter to support.'

'Do you love him now?' Frankie's voice wavered.

'I do. Your father is one of the kindest, gentlest men I've ever known. I've never regretted marrying him and I hope I've never made him regret taking us on. He treated Addie as his own from the beginning, he brought me you and I love all three of you very, very much. Everything I am today, is because of him.'

Lily closed her eyes and rested her head against the back of the chair. The outer door opened and Laurence Thompson and Lionel Ford entered the room. Both were covered in dust and looked exhausted.

'Alright love?' Laurence greeted his daughter with a smile.

Frankie nodded and moved to hug him. 'I'm sorry I ran off without telling anyone where I was going. They needed someone to pilot the boat and I didn't think.'

'I heard about Mac, love and I'm sorry. I know you were friends.'

'They might still find him.' Frankie gritted her teeth at the assumption Mac was dead.

Her father pulled her towards him and kissed the top of her head. 'I'm glad you're home. How's Mum?'

'Tired.' Frankie nodded at the chair beside her.

'She is awake.' Lily's voice floated up to them. Getting unsteadily to her feet, she hugged her daughter. 'Not a word,' she whispered, 'Especially not to Addie. And don't give up on Mac yet. There's still hope.'

Frankie returned the embrace, nodding into her mother's shoulder. 'I love you, Mum.'

'Love you too, sweetheart. Now get yourself off to bed.' She looked at her husband and his friend. 'Same goes for you two. Bed. Now.'

Frankie turned the lights off before following them upstairs. She pulled the covers up to her chin and lay in the dark thinking of Mac. She'd just drifted into an uneasy sleep when there was a pounding on the door. She tried to leap out of bed, got tangled in the sheets and hit her head on the corner of the table as she fell to the floor. Consequently, it was her father who reached the door first and opened it.

'Sorry, Mr Thompson, this was the nearest place to bring him. Doc's on his way. All hell's breaking loose. There's another ship gone down out past the Folly. *The Pandora* this time. It found that bloody mine we've been searching for all week. Beggin' your pardon Miss.' The sailor transferred the weight of the figure in his arms to Laurence.

'Do you need me on the boat again?' Frankie asked wearily.

'I reckon you might want to stay here, Miss.' The sailor nodded at the man leaning limply against her father. 'That's the chap we was looking for earlier. That airman that went in the drink. Anyway, it's Mr Nelson's watch now and he's sober. 'Night all.'

With that, he raced back out of the hotel and through the window, Frankie saw his bobbing torch as he sprinted along the jetty to the waiting boat. She stooped to look at Mac's face.

'Hello you,' she whispered, touching her fingers to his cheek.

'If he's been in the sea all this time, we need to get him into bed and get him warmed up.' Her father was already moving towards the stairs. 'If I take him upstairs, can you get the water heated and we'll put some bottles in his bed.'

By the time the bottles were ready, the Navy's doctor had arrived and Frankie led him up the stairs.

'We've put him in the family wing,' she said, 'We thought it might be quieter for him than the Navy side. Plus, he's a friend of Frankie's.'

The doctor nodded. He looked grave as he pressed the stethoscope to Mac's chest.

'Not much I can do at this stage,' he said eventually. 'Keep him warm and we'll see if he develops a fever. He needs someone with him tonight. I don't have a spare nurse though, not with them bringing men off *The Pandora*. Can you manage or do you need me to send a nurse?'

Frankie didn't look at her father. 'I'll sit with him. I'll call if I need anything. I'll get my book and a blanket from my room.'

By the time she returned, the doctor had returned to his more pressing duties and her father had lined the hot water bottles around Mac's body.

'Are you sure you're up to this?'

'I am. Go back to bed. I'll get some sleep tomorrow once you and Mum are up.'

A few hours later, Frankie's attention was drawn from her book by a slight noise from the bed.

'Mac?

'Frankie? Where am I?'

She leant forward and gently brushed the hair away from

his forehead. 'You're in The Mermaid. Do you remember what happened?'

'Wrote the bloody kite off.'

She laughed quietly. 'In spectacular style. You were in the water for a while, we couldn't find you.'

He coughed. 'We?'

'The launch pilot was drunk so I took the Navy lads out.'

'That sounds like my girl. Bloody reckless.' A low chuckle spilled over the pale lips. 'You got any more blankets there? I'm freezing.'

Frankie touched his forehead again. It was blazing. Pulling the sheets back, she pushed at him. 'Move over, will you. You're too heavy for me to shift.'

Obediently, he made space for her and she slipped into the bed next to him. Wrapping her arms around, she covered as much of his body as she could with her own.

'Frankie, what are you doing?' Weakly, he tried to move, but she pinned him down.

'Shh. Go back to sleep. It would be better if we were naked – the heat transfer would be quicker – but this will have to do.'

'How am I supposed to sleep now?'

She smothered a giggle and kissed the base of his throat. 'Now I know you're delirious.'

There was no answer other than a soft snore. Within minutes, she was also asleep. When she awoke, it was to find his arms wrapped tightly around her and his eyes watching her. She smiled sleepily at him.

'What time is it?'

'I don't know, but it's still dark. Why are you in my bed?'

'I knew you weren't quite yourself last night.' She reached up and stroked his face. 'They fished you out of the sea and brought you here. The Doctor said we had to keep you warm, but the bottles weren't working, so I got into bed with you.'

'Ah.'

Frankie ran her tongue over her lips. They suddenly felt very dry.

'Don't do that.' Mac's voice was hoarse.

She kissed him.

'Definitely don't do that.'

She kissed him again.

'Frankie–'

She cut him off. 'Why are you doing this, Mac? Last night, when you had less, I don't know – control – over yourself, you called me your girl. Look me in the eye and tell me you don't feel this too. That you don't want me.'

'It isn't that, Frankie. I can barely lift my head off the pillow.'

Instantly, she was contrite. 'I'm sorry, I didn't think.' She kissed his forehead, then slid out of the bed. 'Go back to sleep, I'll leave you to rest.'

A couple of days later, the doctor came for his daily visit and pronounced that with another night of rest, Mac would be fit enough to return to duty. Frankie, who had been hovering anxiously in the corridor, hurried in as soon as the man had left.

'So you're off tomorrow?'

'It's for the best.'

'I don't agree.'

'I didn't expect you to.'

She glared at him, then swung out of the room.

IN THE MIDDLE of the night, Mac woke to find Frankie sliding into the bed beside him.

'Frankie…' She kissed him, silencing his protest. For a

moment, he allowed himself to yield to the gentle pressure of her lips, then, remembering himself, tried to pull away.

She clung to him and kissed him again, harder this time, more insistent, pressing her body against his. His hand moved, almost of its own accord, to cup the soft curve of her bottom, pulling her closer still. He tried again to remind himself why this was not a good idea. She was so young. He was... who he was. He tried to speak between kisses. 'Stop it.' Another kiss. 'I'm not strong enough for this.'

Frankie pulled her head back and raised an eyebrow. 'That was sort of my point.'

'Taking advantage of my weakness?'

'Only a little. I'm not asking for anything from you beyond this, now. Not everything has to be thought through and analysed. Sometimes you have to take what life offers and enjoy it.'

'I care too much about you to take what you're offering and walk away.'

She leant over and kissed him. 'I know you want me and this feels right. Stop doing what you think society says you should and just be yourself.'

Mac groaned. 'I can't keep walking away. God knows I didn't want this, but I do. I want you.'

She stared at him, not daring to speak.

'For the first time in years, I feel as though I'm living again and I'm tired of trying to do the right thing, so yes, I'll admit it. I want you. Is that what you wanted to hear?'

Frankie glanced at the clock on the bedside table. It would be hours until her parents woke. Keeping her gaze fixed on him, she sat up and slowly undid the buttons on her nightdress, letting it fall from her shoulders. Mac's eyes darkened and he touched the exposed flesh almost reverentially. She shivered as his fingers danced across her skin.

'It's almost morning. I'll have to get up soon if I'm to catch the early train back to base.'

'Then make the most of the time we've got.' She bent to kiss him again. 'Unless you're not feeling well enough?' She drew back, her face anxious.

A chuckle rumbled deep in his throat. 'I'm not at my most athletic, but I think I'll cope.' He studied her face, as she bit her lip. He realised with a jolt that for the first time since he'd known her, she suddenly looked shy. 'Frankie? Is this...? I mean, you have...?' He stammered to a halt as her eyes met his and he knew the truth without having to ask. His arms pulled her closer, before gently rolling her onto her back.

'I'll be gentle,' he promised.

Threading her fingers through his hair, she arched her back, as he pulled loose the drawstring of his borrowed pyjamas and lifted the skirt of her nightdress.

JULY 2017

'*H*ave you given any consideration to what I said the other day?' Frankie caught hold of Hannah's hand as the younger girl placed the coffee on the table.

'The teacake won't be a minute.'

'Ellie knows what I'm talking about.' Frankie nodded at the other occupant of the table. 'Keeping secrets eats you up inside, it's always best to give them some air every now and again.'

Hannah smiled awkwardly.

Ellie rolled her eyes. 'Leave the poor girl alone, Frankie. Anyway, there's no chance of you keeping any secrets – your face gives you away.'

Frankie looked indignant. 'What do you mean?'

'I can always tell when people are irritating you. You get a certain look on your face every time, even though you think you're concealing it well.'

Frankie scoffed. 'That's not a proper secret!'

'Actually, I did have something to tell you,' Hannah said quickly, anxious to avoid an argument. 'But you're not going to like it. The council are definitely thinking of closing the Lido because it's not making any money – actually they reckon it's costing them a fortune – so they're considering writing it off altogether and selling the site.'

Frankie waved a dismissive arm. 'Rubbish. This place was built by the community. They'll never close it. There's too much history here. It's all just hot air.' She narrowed her eyes. 'And don't try and change the subject. Everyone has things they'd like to be different, but you make the best of what you're offered.'

'Stop trying to interfere.'

'I'm not. I'm merely trying to show young Hannah that life is never as straightforward as you think. Look at you and Jack. He had to work really hard to persuade you to give things a go with him, but I think you'd agree it was worth it in the end.'

Ellie smiled and raised her coffee cup in acknowledgement.

'Same with me and Ken,' Frankie continued, looking at Hannah. 'He loved me long before I did him and I never deserved him, but we've been together more than seventy years now.' Frankie's voice caught in her throat and she took Ellie's hand. 'There are things I've never told anyone, so much to be sorry for, so much hurt, but he stood by me through everything.'

'Because he loves you,' Ellie said gently.

Frankie nodded. 'He wanted children, but and I couldn't have them, but he said he wanted me more than them, so it didn't matter. We talked about adopting, but there was so much that I…' she trailed off.

'You didn't know if you could ever love them as you would have done your own,' Hannah prompted quietly.

Frankie shook her head. 'I knew what my mother went through. Having children gives people the power to hurt you in ways you can't imagine. When I married Ken, I'd been through enough to know I wasn't prepared to make myself vulnerable like that. Not again. By the time I realised how foolish I'd been, it was too late and we were too old. My sister's boy and his children were as close as I'd ever get to being a proper mother or grandmother.'

Ellie smiled. 'I never had an issue with being a mother, I just didn't want to get married. I had to work to get the respect I knew I deserved from my colleagues and I wasn't prepared to throw it all away for a man. Even one as lovely as Jack.' She patted a seat, encouraging Hannah to sit down for a moment. 'He wanted a relationship, you see, but I wasn't prepared to throw up my life back home for someone I'd only known a few weeks. It wasn't until after I got the job here that we got together. Marriage is an institution and that's all as far as I'm concerned. My mum and dad are happy enough, but my grandfather died when my mum was a kid and my grandmother never wanted to talk about him.'

'Does it not bother you?' Hannah asked, her eyes wide.

'What do you mean?'

'Your family history. Doesn't it make you worry you'll end up the same way?'

'Is that what you're worried about?'

'Partly.' Hannah swallowed nervously. 'Nobody in my family has ever stayed with anyone more than 10 years. After my mum walked out on us, my dad swore off women. They were more trouble than they were worth, he said. He didn't stick to it though and there were plenty of girlfriends over the years, but none of them lasted. Dad wasn't interested in commitment. Not after mum.'

Ellie sighed. 'I'm sorry you had a rough time. Like I said, I don't think my grandparents were particularly happily married, but Mum and Dad did okay together. Jack and I have been together twenty years more or less, but the feminist in me objects to the idea of belonging to someone, so marriage was never an option for me.'

'You'd be surprised at what holds a marriage together,' Frankie put in quietly. 'It's not always a good thing to stay together no matter what. Sometimes it's best to let a person go and start again. Oh, I don't mean me and Ken,' she said waspishly, waving a dismissive hand as Ellie and Hannah turned startled eyes on her. 'I meant in general terms. Maybe your mum did what she thought was best at the time.'

'By abandoning us?'

'If she believed you'd have a better life without her.'

Hannah's temper flared. 'How could she possibly have known that? What kind of parent leaves their child?'

'One who perhaps feels they don't have a choice.'

Hannah's anger vanished as quickly as it had arisen and sadness welled inside her. 'I don't understand.'

Frankie glanced at Ellie. 'Would it genuinely not trouble you to learn your grandparents were unhappy?'

Ellie frowned but shook her head. 'I never knew my grandfather and I don't really remember my grandmother. From what mum told me, she was an odd lady, remote one minute, smothering the next and always angry at life.'

Frankie took a deep breath. 'Do you remember when you first came to Avonstow and you showed us the photo of your grandfather at the ANZAC memorial up at the Rec?'

Ellie nodded.

'I was the one who took it. As soon as I realised who you were I wanted to tell you who I was, but I couldn't find the words. And the longer I left it, the harder it became, until eventually I decided you were better off not knowing.'

'You knew my grandfather?'

Frankie nodded. 'I…' She trailed off as she caught sight of Hannah's expression. 'Hannah? Is everything alright?'

Hannah didn't respond. She was staring, white-faced at

the man who had just walked through the door. He had his back to them, but she would have known him anywhere. Scraping her chair back, she fled into the kitchen, leaving the other two staring after her. Her throat constricted, leaving her gasping for air and she sank to the floor before crawling under the counter and pressing her back against the wall, her knees drawn tightly to her chest. *What is he doing here?* White noise surrounded her and she closed her eyes against the onslaught, clamping her hands over her ears. *It can't be him. It can't be.* She had no idea how long she sat there, but the next thing she knew, Clem was sitting beside her, his arm around her shoulders.

'How are you feeling?'

She stared at him. She didn't know. 'Embarrassed?' she offered.

'No need.'

She tried to get to her feet. 'I have to get back to work.'

Clem put a restraining hand on her arm. 'It's fine, it's not busy. Kate's having a cuppa with Ellie and Frankie.'

'It was just a panic attack.'

'I know. Kate recognised the symptoms. That's why she called me in. I had them when I first found out about Emmy's affair. Not so much anymore.' He stood up and helped her to her feet. 'It's nothing to be embarrassed about.'

'I thought I was over them. I'm fine to go back to work though, honest. Is Kate angry?'

'She is, but not because of you. I'll let her tell you.'

Hannah stepped out into the main part of the café and offered a smile to the wan faces that greeted her. 'Sorry to worry you,' she said, forcing herself to sound cheerful.

'Are you okay?' Kate jumped up to usher her to a seat.

'I'm fine. I've not had one in ages. I didn't mean to worry everyone.'

'You're sure you're alright?' Ellie sounded dubious. 'What prompted it?'

'I promise I'm okay. You're obviously not though, Kate. What's happened?' Hannah could feel Frankie's eyes boring into her and she focused her attention on the other two.

'A man came from the council to tell us they're definitely closing the Lido at the end of the summer season,' Kate said, her hands twisting in her lap. 'It's like you said: it's in a massive deficit and the council can't justify subsidising it anymore. It will only get worse over the winter months so they won't even keep it open until the end of the year.'

'Surely there has to be a consultation period? They can't just decide to close it. Can they?'

Clem placed a cup on the table in front of Hannah. 'You sure you're okay if I get back to the pool?

She smiled and nodded and he left them to talk.

Ellie shrugged. 'I'll ask Hugh to look into it – he understands more about all that kind of stuff than I do, but even if they consult on it, they don't have to listen to us. I hate to admit it, but in winter, sometimes Frankie and I are the only people here. The café does okay, but the pool can be deserted and yet there always has to be a lifeguard here in case someone wants to swim.'

'There's ways around that though,' Frankie said. 'If you trained a lifeguard to work in here, they could be in here the rest of the day and only go out to the pool if someone wanted to come in. It's the chlorine and whatnot that's expensive.'

'That and operating the pump every day, I suppose.'

'Well, they've certainly not spent anything on the rest of it, have they? I can't remember the last time those changing rooms were decorated and I bet the pump's nearly as old as I am. Great, noisy thing it is too.' Frankie pulled a face.

'I didn't realise you could go in there. I wouldn't mind a tour myself,' Hannah said. 'I bet it's fascinating.'

Frankie hesitated. 'It was a long time ago… before all the health and safety came in. It's not…' she shuddered. 'It's not a nice place.' She fell silent for a moment, then continued. 'I don't suppose their plans will come to anything. They wanted to close it during the war, but if murder couldn't keep it closed, I don't suppose a few penny-pinching councillors will be able to either. We'll fight it, like we always do.'

Ellie, Kate and Hannah looked at each other, seeing their confusion reflected on the others' faces.

'Aunt Frankie? What do you mean, a murder?'

Frankie stared at Ellie. 'What? Oh.' She shook her head. 'I don't know. I'm probably getting muddled with somewhere else. There's been a few around here over the years.'

Ellie frowned but didn't question her any further. 'So do you think we could fight it then? I'd hate to think what the alternative would be for this place, but I don't know what we could do.'

'Offer to run it yourselves,' Frankie said. 'It's been used for purposes other than leisure swimming in the past. No reason why it couldn't be again. You need to put a proposal together and prove you could make it work.'

Kate's expression brightened. 'If we go ahead with the campsite, that will bring more visitors in surely?'

Ellie nodded slowly. 'It's an idea, certainly. We'd need to get people together though. Think it through properly.'

Kate darted into the kitchen and returned with a notepad and pen. 'No time like the present.'

As she and Ellie started throwing ideas at each other, Frankie leant towards Hannah. 'He's not worth it, you know.'

Hannah glanced at her then down at her hands. 'Who?'

'The man who came in earlier. Whoever he is, or was, to you, he's not worth that much pain. No man is, trust me.'

Hannah looked sceptical. Frankie smiled gently.

'I once considered ending my life because of a man, but then another man showed me that in spite of what I'd suffered, my life could still have purpose.'

'Ken?'

Frankie grinned. 'No. Ken was my friend then, nothing more. No, this was another man – and it wasn't a romantic interest before you ask – he was more of a father figure. Not that I needed another one – my father was a wonderful man. But this man offered me a job. It wasn't as thrilling or exciting as it sounded, but it was important and it gave me something else to focus on rather than what I'd lost.'

Hannah smiled sadly. 'I don't hate him, but I hate that he made a fool of me and that I allowed him to.'

'We don't always see clearly when we're young and in love. I certainly didn't, but I got there in the end.'

'Not everyone is lucky enough to find a Ken.' Hannah blinked away her tears and Frankie patted her hand.

'There's plenty of time.'

'What are you two whispering about?' Kate laughed, turning their way suddenly.

'Just gossiping about the unreliability of men,' Frankie smiled.

'Speaking of which,' Ellie said. 'That reminds me. Earlier on, you were about to tell me what you knew about my grandfather.'

'Ah,' Frankie nodded and took a deep breath. 'That.'

'Well?' Ellie prompted.

'Are you sure you want to know?'

Ellie raised her eyebrows and Frankie sat up straighter, her eyes anxious.

'I loved him once upon a time.'

Ellie stared at her. 'What do you mean, you loved him? Are you sure we're talking about the same man?'

'Alasdair Macmillan, son of Doctor Macmillan of Melbourne, Australia. I promise you, it's the same man, dear.'

'I don't understand.' Ellie frowned. 'My mother was born in 1936. Was my grandfather married when you met?'

'It's a complicated story and one I should have told you a long time ago. Are you sure you're ready to hear it?'

Ellie shrugged. 'Like I said, I never knew him and I have almost no memories of my grandmother.'

Frankie nodded, appearing satisfied with the answer. 'Very well.'

APRIL 1940

'*I* want to marry you.'

Frankie stared at him in surprise. 'What happened to "I'm all wrong for you"?'

Mac gave her a lopsided grin and traced a finger across her collarbone and down into the hollow between her breasts.

'Let's just say you make a very persuasive case for being right for me.'

'I hate to say I told you so…' Frankie trailed off as his lips found hers.

'There's no rush. There's lots to sort out, but at least we'd be official.'

Frankie tilted her head back. It had the double advantage of allowing him easier access to continue kissing her exposed skin, while enabling her to study his expression.

'Is that important?'

'What?' He kissed her nipple and she shivered, her mind immediately leaping back to the events of the previous night. There had been some pain the first time, but the subsequent pleasure had all but erased it from her mind.

'Stop trying to distract me. Is being official important to you? Are you proposing because we had sex?'

Mac raised his head. 'Partly. But mostly because I love you.' He sighed. 'Frankie, I can't help who I am. I need time to make the arrangements, but yes, I feel a certain responsibility towards you now. You may not think it's important, but it is to me. Last night shouldn't have happened, but I'm glad it did. And I know what I need to do to make it right.'

She gulped. 'Once you decide to do something, you don't hold back, do you?'

'I wouldn't be doing this if I wasn't serious about you. It's not too late to change your mind though, if I've scared you off.'

Frankie shook her head. 'You haven't. Alasdair, I –'

He flinched. 'Don't call me that. That's what my... my parents call me.'

'You still want me to use your nickname?'

'What's wrong with my nickname?'

'It's what everyone else calls you. I thought it would be nice to call you something different, that's all.'

'Only if I get to call you Frances.'

Frankie pulled a face.

'Or a different nickname?'

'I warn you, I'm not a "sugar plum" kind of girl.'

Mac laughed. 'Oh god no, I can't think of anything worse!'

Frankie giggled. 'How about "Goggles"?'

'Goggles?'

'You wear them when you're flying, don't you?'

Mac snorted.

'Harry?'

He raised an eyebrow.

'Your plane. Harry Cane.'

61

Mac groaned. 'What have I let myself in for? Is it too late to change my mind?'

Frankie beamed at him. 'Far too late.'

'Maybe we should stick with the names we have.'

Frankie poked her tongue out at him, then swung her legs out of bed and picked up her discarded nightgown. Mac stretched out an arm and pulled her back into bed with a growl.

'Wicked girl.'

She kissed him. 'That's why you love me.' She murmured the words against his lips.

'Temptress.'

Frankie ran a hand down his side and Mac sighed. 'I don't want to go, but I need to get my things together if I'm to catch that train.'

'Want some company?' Frankie's hands were cool against his warm skin.

'No.' He pulled her against him, kissed her deeply, then pushed her away with a smile. 'Go find someone else to bother.'

Frankie grinned. 'See you downstairs then.'

She sauntered casually out of the room, returning to her own to dress. By the time Mac had located his uniform and got dressed, Frankie had finished her breakfast and was cleaning out the Navy offices. He waited for her in the corridor outside Admiral Ashton's room.

'I've got to go, or I'll miss my train. Don't come to the station with me. I'll come again as soon as I can. Here.' He pulled the signet ring from his little finger and handed it to her. 'Until I can buy you a proper one.'

Frankie slipped the ring into the pocket of her overalls, stretched up and kissed him.

'Fly safe.'

She watched him leave, blushing as Admiral Ashton passed her on his way into his office. 'Miss Thompson.'

Did he see? So what if he did? I'm sure he's seen people kissing before. She picked up her cleaning things and headed to the next job on her list. At least she'd be able to set her mother's mind at rest about Mac's intentions. She smiled to herself, her hand drifting to the pocket. He loved her.

MAY 1940

'I've written home and told them about you,' Mac said, putting an arm around Frankie's shoulders. "I'm expecting a telegram in the next few weeks offering congratulations and I thought we could maybe start thinking about what kind of wedding we want. There's no rush, but you know how much longer everything takes to organise these days.'

Frankie sighed happily. 'I hope your family approve.'

Mac's face became suddenly serious. 'So do I.'

He laid a cheek on her hair and fell silent.

'What if they don't?' Frankie asked, alarmed by his response. 'Will it make a difference to how you feel about me?'

Mac drew her closer. 'No. Never. It would make things more difficult, but we'd find a way to get around it. I won't give you up, Frankie. Not for anyone.'

She settled back into his side. For a moment, she tilted her face towards the spring sunshine and closed her eyes, enjoying the feeling of being loved.

'If you ignore the Navy boats and the barbed wire on the

beach, you could almost forget we were at war, couldn't you? It's so peaceful and the war seems very far away.'

Mac nodded. 'It's like a little haven.' He laughed and turned to kiss her gently. 'Or maybe it's the effect of being near you.'

Frankie grinned. 'That's not what you normally say. And I don't think my parents would ever describe living with me as peaceful. I just meant that everything was calm today. It's not always so pleasant.' Her mind drifted back to the awful day when Mac had been missing and the bombs had exploded.

'Hey,' Mac gave her a gentle shake. 'Don't dwell on it. Make the most of the calm.'

She smiled, loving that he understood her well enough to know what she'd been thinking about.

'When you're up there with Jerry on your tail, I promise you it feels very much like we're at war. I've learnt to find peace whenever and wherever I can.'

Frankie laid a hand on his thigh. 'When it gets too bad, think of me down here waiting for you.'

Mac laughed. 'If I start thinking of you while I'm flying, I'd almost certainly get myself shot down. Either that or crash the plane of my own accord. When you're up there you have to forget everything except where the enemy is. You especially have to forget beautiful and distracting girls. I'll save thinking of you for when my feet are firmly on the ground, if that's okay.'

'And what about Ken? Is there a girl to distract him? He never mentions anyone in his letters.'

'I couldn't say. He doesn't say much to me these days.'

'Because of me, I suppose. I'm sorry.'

'Don't be. I understand how he feels. I wouldn't want to talk to him if our roles were reversed.'

Frankie sighed. 'So many lives in upheaval because of us. Mum and Dad like you but I know they're worried what will happen. They've lived through war before, they know what it's like. And if we come through safely, what happens then? Where will we live, for example?'

'How would you feel about moving to Australia? It's a long way from Avonstow.'

Frankie considered it for a moment. 'I don't know. I'd miss my family, but so would you if we stayed here. Do we have to decide right now though?'

Mac took her hand. 'We may not need to talk about it all. There's a lot can happen in war.'

'Don't say that!' She flung herself into his arms. 'I can't bear it!'

He allowed her a few minutes, then patted her back. 'Enough now. It's no use pretending it's not a possibility. The Navy base is a target and you're pretty much next door to it and even when I'm not up in the air, the airfield is a target. We've got off fairly lightly so far, but that won't always be the case. They've had us training to defend it from the ground now as well.'

Frankie stared at him. 'From the ground? Why?'

'Frankie, what do you think is going on over there?'

She shook her head, looking confused. 'I don't understand.'

'The army are getting a pasting. Jerry's moving too fast for them and we're pulling back. It won't be too long until we've got our backs to the channel and when that happens, unless there's a miracle and we can somehow keep them out of the skies, it's only a matter of time until they come knocking on our door. If they land troops, we've got instructions to defend the airfield to the last man. The planes won't be much use if we can't get them in the air, so they've issued us all with guns and if there's an invasion, we all have our instructions.'

Frankie chewed her bottom lip and looked away from

him. When she turned back her eyes were glistening but her face was composed. She nodded.

'That makes sense I suppose. We have bicycle patrols around here now at night, watching for an invasion. I'm not sure what they'll do if they do see anything though. None of them are armed with anything more than a pitchfork and unless Dad's got a secret stash of weapons hidden away somewhere in the hotel, we've nothing to defend it with beyond the odd kitchen knife.'

Mac put his arm around her again. 'We'll do our best to make sure you never need to use them,' he promised. 'They've got to get past us first.'

Frankie settled her head against his shoulder and sighed. 'One day at a time, that's what Dad says.'

'He's right. For the likes of us, that's all there is to it. Worry about today and let tomorrow take care of itself.'

'That's why we have to make the most of every minute we have together,' Frankie said, lifting her face to his.

He brushed his lips against hers. 'Anyone could see,' he murmured.

'I don't care. Shut up and kiss me.'

He grinned and did as he was told.

'WHEN DO YOU LEAVE?' Frankie leant against the side of the *Jenny B*, smiling at the young sailor who was getting it ready.

'First light tomorrow.' He puffed out his chest as he spoke and Frankie smothered a grin. 'Don't you worry, Miss. We'll bring our boys home.'

'I know you will.' Frankie gave him her sweetest smile before pushing herself off the boat and strolling back down the jetty. Feeling his eyes on her, she gave him a jaunty wave and a swish of her hips as she walked. 'I intend to make sure of it,' she added under her breath.

She felt no guilt at the mild flirtation it had taken to get the information she wanted. *Mac would understand*, she told herself. *It was all in a good cause.* She smiled at the thought of him. In the month that had passed since he'd admitted he was in love with her, she'd seen as much of him as she was able to. Using his rest time to travel meant he'd be in trouble if he got caught, but he'd declared her worth the risk. She reasoned this was no different. This was worth the risk too.

She'd been expecting to see him the next day, but he'd telephoned to say not to expect him. Something big was happening, so he couldn't get away. There was increased activity at the harbour too and this had piqued her curiosity further, prompting her to go information gathering.

FRANKIE OPENED the heavy front door of the hotel then paused, remembering her mother's terror the last time she'd left without a word. Turning back, she hastily scribbled a note for her parents.

GONE TO HELP AT DUNKIRK. BACK SOON. DON'T WORRY. F x

It wasn't enough but it would have to do. There'd be a fearful row when she got back but that couldn't be helped. If it was Alasdair or Ken over there, she'd be praying for someone to rescue them. If she could bring home someone's sweetheart, brother or son, it would be worth the argument.

There was no one in sight as she crept down the jetty and stepped carefully into the waiting boat. Pulling a heavy tarpaulin over herself, she lay down and waited for the dawn to break over the horizon. When she woke, cautiously poking her head out, the sun was high in the sky. Greys, blues and greens blurred together at the point of meeting between the sky and the sea, the washed-out landscape punctuated only by the other boats bobbing along beside them.

'Miss Thompson!' An angry shout made her jump and she spun round, the colour rushing to her cheeks.

'I can sail as well as any of you. I can be useful.' She crossed her arms, the defiant pose matching her tone.

'When we get to Ramsgate you will get off this boat and you will return yourself to Avonstow on the train, young lady.'

'I will not. If you don't let me come with you, I'll simply hide on another boat and go anyway. I know I can help.'

'Miss Thompson, do you have the first idea what it's going to be like over there? There'll be people shooting at us. How can I go home and tell your parents I let you get yourself killed?'

Frankie stared defiantly at him. 'You'll tell them I died trying to serve my country, same as everyone else.'

Leading Hand Dawson looked at her. He could handle any number of disorderly able seamen but a stubborn 18-year-old girl terrified him. Short of physically putting her on the train himself, he wasn't sure how he could enforce his instruction. A satisfied smirk played at one corner of her mouth. Damn her. She'd out manoeuvred him and she knew it.

'Get in the cabin.' At least there he'd know where she was and she'd be out of the direct line of fire when the strafing started. Frankie did as she was told, but her lack of argument warned him she'd made no promises to remain in there. With any luck someone more senior would come on board and he'd be able to pass the responsibility on to them.

Unfortunately for him, when they finally arrived at Ramsgate, he was given his orders, the boat was refuelled and they set sail for the French coastline almost immediately.

He'd missed the opportunity to have Frankie thrown from the boat when she was discovered in the cabin by the Lieutenant in charge of their sector of the port. With little more than a smart salute, she'd disarmed the officer before he'd had chance to say anything.

'Sir! Frances Thompson, shore to sea pilot at HMS Dory.'

The man had expressed his surprise at her youth and gender, but without even the faintest tell-tale blush, Frankie covered her tracks.

'Always been told I look young for my age, Sir. Bit of a nuisance, but my mother assures me I'll be grateful when I'm her age. Not many younger men left in Avonstow and the older ones like a drink or two. Admiral Ashton needed someone he could rely on.'

Behind the Lieutenant, Leading Hand Dawson gaped at her. *How can she use the Admiral's name so lightly? If they ring him to check...* The thought trailed away and he snapped to attention as the Lieutenant left the boat. Frankie flashed Dawson a cheeky grin.

'Piece of cake.'

He shook his head. He couldn't help admiring her audacity. 'You know I'll have to report to the Admiral that you took his name in vain?'

'By then it won't matter. I'll have done my bit.'

'Why are you so desperate? Anyone with any sense would run a mile in the other direction and you're here lying through your teeth to get over there. Have you someone at Dunkirk?'

'No. My sister's in the Land Army and my fiancé and my best friend are both RAF. I've always been the youngest in our group and I'm tired of being left out. I tried to do things properly but they sent me home again, so I'm doing it my own way now.

'I'll do my best to get you home safely, Miss, but I

wouldn't want to be in your shoes when the Admiral hears about all this. Or your parents, for that matter. Or are they used to your hairbrained ideas?'

Frankie grinned ruefully. 'You'd think they would be by now, but no. There'll be hell to pay when I get home, but I don't care.'

'Frances Thompson!'

Frankie jumped and her face paled at the sight of the figure on the boat that had pulled alongside them. 'Mr Nelson? What are you doing here?'

'What am I….' he spluttered. 'How your mother has any hair left is beyond me, young lady. How did you get here?'

'She stowed away on our boat. Leading Hand Dawson.' The sailor snapped to attention.

'No need for that,' Mr Nelson said. 'I'm not your commanding officer. I'll take young Frances off your hands. She can come on the boat with us.' He sighed and shook his head. The younger Thompson girl was a handful, no question. He didn't want the responsibility, but he knew if he tried to leave her behind, she'd only get herself into more trouble.

'Thank you, Sir.'

Mr Nelson tried not to laugh at the look of relief on the other man's face. He could imagine the chaos Frankie had caused already. He turned to the girl.

'You. On board. Now.' The firm grip on her arm as she briefly straddled the two boats left her in no doubt as to his feelings, but on reflection, she considered, it could have been much worse. *Thank goodness he didn't see me earlier when there might still have been time to call home.* 'I hope you know what you're letting yourself in for.' His face was grim.

'You know I'm a good sailor,' she countered. 'They asked anyone who could help to do so.'

'How in God's name do you know that? I'm only here

71

because I happened to be on the boat when they came to requisition it.'

'I was outside the Admiral's office when he gave the order last night. I'm here to help not be a burden. You've sailed with me before, you know I'm capable.'

'This isn't a pleasure cruise, Frankie.'

'I know.'

'I won't expect any less of you than I do of my own men.'

'I'd be disappointed if you did.'

He nodded. 'Get to it then. You know the drill.'

SMOKE BILLOWED in thick clouds over the foaming grey sea. It stung Frankie's eyes as she leant over the side of the boat, hauling exhausted men onboard.

'I'm so sorry,' she said to the next man in line, as Mr Nelson yelled that they couldn't take any more and stay afloat. 'We'll be back, I promise.'

As the skipper swung the boat around, there was a scream overhead and the occupants of the boat flinched as yet more bombs fell on either side of them, sending waves of saltwater splashing over them. Frankie forced herself to keep looking forwards as they headed away from the beach and out to where the bigger boats waited in deeper water. She didn't need to witness it to know that the remains of the men they'd left behind would now be floating face down. She'd seen more than enough already. Pushing her exhausted limbs into action, she moved as best she could between the bodies in the boat, offering a smile or a word of comfort. More practical help could only be given once they'd been loaded onto the ships taking them home. There they'd be given food and water. The most she could do was to reassure them they were almost in sight of safety now.

It was their second day of ferrying men from beach to boat and she'd lost count of the number of trips they'd done, or how many men she'd helped to climb into the boat.

WHEN THE FIRST wave of men had expressed their surprise at being pulled aboard by a woman, she'd made the mistake of telling them that Mac and Ken were RAF pilots and she was doing it because she hoped someone might do the same for them if they were shot down. The vitriol and invectives that had poured forth at her mention of the Airforce had stunned her.

'Fucking cowards! Why aren't they over here protecting us? The only sodding Spitfire we've seen is one that bloody Jerry captured. We thought the flyboys had finally showed up to give us some help and then it came down low and strafed the beach. Killed a load of silly buggers who were stood cheering it on.'

After that she'd kept quiet about her true motivation for being there. By the fourth trip it didn't matter anymore. The men didn't care who got them off the Dunkirk beach, as long as someone did. By the time they got into the boat, they wanted to be left in peace. There was no obvious sense of relief, just weariness and dejection. On their last trip of the day, she'd had to push aside the dead bodies floating in the water to allow the boat to carve a way through to the waiting men. The boatload they'd picked up that trip stayed with them all the way back to Ramsgate. At the end of a gruelling first day, Mr Nelson had offered her the option of remaining on shore the following day.

'There's no shame in it, Frankie,' he said. 'No one would think any less of you.'

'I'd think less of me. I'm coming.'

Over a hasty dinner that evening, they heard the *Jenny B*

had been hit and sunk. Some of the men on board had been fished out of the water, but many had been lost.

Frankie paled. 'It's a good job you said you'd take me with you, otherwise...'

'Now do you understand why I'm asking you again to stay here?'

'I do, but the answer is still no. Was I helpful today?'

'You know you were.'

'There you go then.'

'Up you come,' Frankie gasped as the next man came over the gunwales and tumbled to the deck. The *Amelia Emerence* was on her second beach to ship mission of the day.

Moments later, she ducked as bullets sent splinters of wood spitting into the air. The first time the Messerschmitts had appeared, machine guns sputtering, she'd thrown herself to the deck, arms clamped over her head. Now, she barely even flinched, continuing to pull men onto the boat.

'Last one for this trip,' she called to Mr Nelson.

There was no response. Frankie turned towards the wheel and one of the soldiers made a weak gesture to the prone figure by his feet.

Frankie muttered an unladylike oath under her breath and pushed her way through the soldiers crammed together. Taking the wheel, she swung the boat around, keeping an anxious eye on both sky and sea. *It's no good picking these men up if I then hit debris and put them all back in the water, or let us get sunk by one of those bloody planes.*

Mr Nelson had stirred by the time the last of the men went up the ladder of the waiting destroyer. He touched a hand to his head and it came away red. Frankie handed him a bandage to wrap round it.

'What happened?'

'Either you got hit by a large splinter or a bullet grazed you. I didn't see. You were breathing though, so I just kept going.'

Mr Nelson shook his head. 'Does nothing phase you?'

Frankie moved to one side as he took the wheel again and they turned back towards the beach.

'I'm terrified.'

'AT LEAST I left a note this time,' Frankie attempted a weak smile.

Laurence Thompson waved the note in question at her. 'Do you really think this made us any less concerned about your safety?'

Frankie blanched. Her father rarely raised his voice and even less frequently was his anger directed at her.

'I'm sorry you were worried, but I'm not sorry I went.'

'You might think differently by the time everyone's finished with you.' Her father's expression was grim.

'What do you mean?'

He handed her an envelope. 'That arrived from Debden while you were away. Mac rang and Admiral Ashton wants to speak to you.'

'The Admiral?' Frankie gulped as her father nodded. 'What did you tell Mac?'

'The truth, of course. What else did you expect?' He sighed. 'You must be exhausted. Go up to bed. We'll talk later.'

At the door, she turned and looked at her mother who had remained silent throughout this exchange.

'I really am sorry, Mum.'

Her mother still didn't speak, a brief nod of her head the only acknowledgement that she'd heard.

In her room, Frankie flopped onto the bed. Now the last of the adrenaline had left her, she wanted nothing more than to sleep. Putting the envelope on her dressing table, she lay down and closed her eyes. Within minutes, soft snores were the only sound in the room.

When she eventually opened her eyes, the envelope was the first thing she saw. Someone had been in while she slept and propped it up against her cold cream pot. It stared reproachfully at her and she closed her eyes against its accusing gaze. She could still feel it through her eyelids and she groaned. *Alright, alright, I'll read it*, she thought crossly. *Although, I can guess what Ken has to say.*

DEAR FRANKIE,

After Mac rang and you weren't there, he told me what you'd done. The man was beside himself with worry. You probably think this is going to be an angry letter full of recriminations and you're quite correct to think I'm furious with you. You'd also be correct if you told me there are others who have a greater right than I to give you the telling off you deserve. However, I've known you all your life and I think that buys me some liberties.

What on earth were you thinking? By now, you'll be well aware of the danger you put yourself in, so I won't dwell on that beyond asking how you think those of us who care about you would have felt if anything had happened to you? You can't play with your life like this, Frankie. It was a risk you didn't need to take. Every time I take the kite up I know it's likely I won't come down again, but that's my job. It's what I signed up for and I believe it's my duty to help defend this country. You don't have that same responsibility, but you do have a responsibility to the people who care for you. Even without your family, what about Mac? He's worried sick and he doesn't need to be thinking about you instead of concentrating on flying his machine.

I may not like it (and I freely admit I'm jealous as hell of him, but first and foremost you're my friend and I want you to be happy) but the man is so in love with you he's prepared to leave his family and move halfway across the world to be with you if that's what you want. You don't throw away that kind of love, kiddo. So, if you won't do it for me, or Addie, or your parents, then for his sake, stop doing such hair-brained things. Pause for a moment and think of the consequences, or one day you're going to get yourself into more trouble than you can handle.

Telling off is done, now onto other news. All is good here – we've been in the same part of the world as you recently and had a few close calls, but we're both well. I'd expect a phone call, or maybe even a flying visit once you're home – if you'll allow me to offer one more piece of advice, I'd telephone as soon as you can. Partly to put us out of our misery and partly to get the inevitable out of the way sooner.

I'm on duty in a few minutes so I'll sign off for now but expect more of the same when I get some leave.

Love you kiddo. Take care.
Ken

FRANKIE FOLDED the thin paper and placed it carefully back in its envelope. Sliding her feet into her slippers, she padded down the stairs to her parents' office. Poking her head around the open door, she tapped quietly on it.

'Can I come in?'

Laurence Thompson looked up from the paperwork strewn across the desk and nodded. Frankie moved to stand behind her mother and put a hand on her shoulder.

'I'm sorry I ran off. I didn't think about anything other

than what I wanted to do. At the very least, I should have talked to you first and told you what I was planning.'

'Even if you then ignored what we said.' Laurence raised an eyebrow and gave her a wry smile.

Frankie blushed and hung her head, knowing he was right.

'I understand, love. More than most I reckon. I couldn't join up for the last one because of my leg and I watched every other bloke in the village go off. I felt less of a man because of it an' all. You'll get your chance, just stop being so hair-brained about it all the time.'

'That's exactly what Ken said.' Frankie smiled.

'That boy knows you well,' Lily said quietly. 'And he cares a great deal for you.'

'I know, Mum. I care for him too and I promise I will try to think before I act in future.'

Lily drew her daughter towards her. 'We heard the *Jenny B* was gone and we thought... When we got Mr Nelson's telegram saying you were with him...'

Frankie threw her arms around her mother. 'I am sorry. I promise I'll try to think things through more. I wish I was more like Addie.'

'We don't want you to change too much, love, otherwise you wouldn't be you. Just try to cause fewer grey hairs, that's all we ask.'

The telephone on the desk rang sharply, making them all jump. Laurence picked it up.

'Good afternoon, Mermaid Hotel.' His face softened. 'Yes, she's here.' He handed the receiver to his daughter.

'Hello? Yes. No, no injuries. Not to me anyway.' Lily tapped her husband's arm and they crept out of the room. 'Mac, stop, please. Everything you're saying is absolutely right. I'm well aware of how worried you've all been and I promise I will try not to be so reckless in future. I've apologised to Mum and Dad and I'm telling you I'm sorry too. I also owe Ken an apology, but there's only so many times I can say it. Please don't be cross with me.'

She listened for a moment. 'I know... I've said I'm sorry... Don't say that, of course I do. How can you ask? Oh...Yes...I'm a terrible trial to you. I don't mean to be though.' She smiled as his tone changed. 'I promise. Oh, could you? That would be wonderful. I can't wait. Love you too.'

She put the phone down and sat for a few moments, staring at it. He still loved her. All was well. Or at least, it would be once she'd smoothed things over with the Admiral.

'NOT AGAIN!' Frankie groaned. 'When are you going to get someone more reliable? It's the second time this week he's been too drunk to do it.'

'There's no one else, Miss. That's why I'm here. The Commodore needs to go now. Can you do it?'

'I'm meant to be behaving myself and not getting involved,' Frankie said with a sigh. 'You're determined not to make it easy for me, aren't you?' Shaking her head, she went to get her coat and let her parents know she was taking Mr Portis' boat out again.

The Commodore was already on board when she arrived, his collar turned up against the wind.

'My thanks, Miss Thompson. I apologise that we've had to call on your skills again. If we could use our own men for this, it would make life so much easier.'

'Why can't you? I've never understood why you had to use a civilian launch to get out to your ships.'

'It's all to do with regulations. We have no jurisdiction in the harbour and it was part of whatever agreement the

Admiralty made that no naval boats would be tied up on the jetty.'

As Frankie pulled her mackintosh closer around her and stepped onto the deck, Mr Portis himself arrived.

'Get your hands off my boat, Missy! I'm perfectly capable of taking her out, thank you very much.'

Raising an eyebrow, Frankie turned to face the irate man. She smiled sweetly at him. 'I'm sorry, Mr Portis, I was told you were indisposed and it was something of an emergency.'

The man swayed as he stepped down onto the deck. 'Well, you can run back to your cleaning now, can't you? I'm here and I'll pilot my own boat, if you don't mind.'

The Commodore frowned but forbore to comment. As the boat lurched out into the channel, Frankie watched it go, worried Mr Portis was going to crash into one of the other boats that were moored up. A wave smashed against the side of the little boat as it turned and she watched in horror as a figure tumbled over the side. It took some time for Mr Portis to understand what the sailors were shouting about and it rapidly became clear the unfortunate man in the water couldn't swim. Shrugging off her coat and shoes, Frankie did a shallow dive off the end of the jetty. In a few strong strokes, she reached the man, wrapped an arm around his upper body and towed him back to the jetty. Hands reached down to help them onto the safety of the platform and Frankie gratefully relinquished her hold on the man.

'Thanks, Miss. Never did manage to learn to swim.'

Frankie peered at him through the water dripping from her fringe. 'One question. If you can't swim, why on earth did you join the Navy?'

The man looked at her, bemused. 'Why would I need to know how to swim? I'm always on a boat!'

Frankie stared at him for a moment, then shook her head, collected her shoes and coat and squelched back along the jetty to the hotel. Her father was in reception as she walked through the door.

'Don't ask,' she said. 'I'm going to get dry and change my clothes.'

When she came back downstairs, there was a young woman in a WRNS uniform waiting for her.

'Can I help you?' Frankie smiled.

'Admiral Ashton would like to speak to you…' she trailed off and a flush spread up her neck and across her face. She cleared her throat. 'When you are sufficiently recovered from your most recent escapade.'

Frankie grinned at the woman's obvious embarrassment. 'Was that a quote?'

The woman nodded gratefully.

'We might as well get it over with,' Frankie muttered. 'Although he might show a bit more gratitude. After all, it was one of his men I rescued. And I have been trying to keep out of trouble recently!'

She followed the Wren to the Admiral's office, trying to project an air of confidence. It rapidly dissolved however, when it became clear the woman was not coming into the office with her. She simply delivered her into the room with a smart salute, then turned on her heel and entered the adjoining room through a door on the opposite side of the suite.

'Miss Thompson.' Admiral Ashton sighed heavily.

'Before you say anything, Admiral, I didn't rush into it – the boat wasn't going to get back in time and I did kick my shoes off first and…' She trailed off as the Admiral gazed placidly at her.

'I was most impressed.'

Frankie wasn't sure she'd heard correctly. 'Impressed?'

Admiral Ashton nodded. 'I was watching from the window. I didn't hear exactly what Mr Portis said, but you

81

kept your temper and then when the accident happened, you assessed the situation and reacted promptly and appropriately.'

Frankie gaped at him. 'You could tell all that from up here? No wonder you're an admiral.'

Admiral Ashton failed to completely suppress a grin. 'Body language tells one a lot. Miss Thompson, one way or another you appear determined to involve yourself in the affairs of this base and I'm of the mind that it might be easier to keep control of you if you have to report directly to me. I understand the boat you originally stowed away on belonged to your parents?'

She nodded.

'Do they have another boat?'

Frankie nodded again.

'In which case, I wonder if I might ask you to fulfil a dual role? Mr Portis has proved himself an unreliable harbour pilot and Mr Nelson cannot work all hours, but it has to be a civilian boat. If your parents agree, we will use theirs from here on and you will pilot it for us. However, I would prefer to have some authority over you – I cannot imagine the havoc you would be capable of causing otherwise – and so I propose to unofficially draft you into the WRNS. The other part of my proposal is that you become our swimming instructor. It occurred to me that many of our men will not have had the opportunity of learning to swim and I cannot help but feel it is a useful skill for a sailor to have. If you are in agreement, I will requisition the Lido and instruct the non-swimmers on the base to have lessons in some of their off-watch time.'

Frankie opened her mouth to answer, then clamped it shut again. 'Admiral, I don't need to tell you that I'm 18 and more than capable of making decisions for myself. However, I promised my parents I would try not to do anything rash and therefore I think it only right to discuss this with them before I give you my answer.'

Admiral Ashton nodded. A slight smile twitched at one corner of his mouth, but otherwise his expression was grave.

'Although I'm sure they'll say yes!' The words burst out of her and she bounced on her toes.

The Admiral burst out laughing as she blushed bright red and fled the room.

FRANKIE LOOKED at herself in the mirror and adjusted her hat so it sat correctly on her head. Even after so many weeks of wearing it, she still felt a thrill run through her every time she caught sight of herself in uniform.

She'd settled into life in the WRNS quickly. Admiral Ashton had been right. Although she sometimes chafed against authority, a part of her felt more settled now she was – albeit unofficially – doing her bit to help the war effort. Being at home meant she was still able to see Mac on the days he wangled some free time and now she had more to write to him about in between. The launch piloting shifts had been relatively uneventful, although Mr Portis had taken to glaring at her every time they passed in the street. She tried not to care; it wasn't her fault he was too drunk to be reliable. If he stayed off the booze he'd have kept the job. A small part of her whispered that she shouldn't be glad, even though his misfortunes had given her exactly what she'd always wanted. Consequently, she always went out of her way to smile at him through the incoherent rants.

The swimming instruction was one of her favourite parts of the job. Although the water in the Lido wasn't the warm-est, she always came out of it with a glow that wasn't entirely the result of a dip in cold water. She took an immense amount of pleasure from seeing the progress the sailors were making and knowing it was down to her coaching. The only downside to it was that it was causing some friction between her and her mother. Once she'd understood Frankie wouldn't be leaving home, Lily had been supportive of her daughter's new job. However, that had only lasted until she realised quite how much time Frankie was going to be spending at the Lido.

When the manager had enlisted, the call had gone out locally for someone to manage the pool in his absence and John Liversidge, newly retired from the docks, had responded. This meant Frankie was now spending a good portion of her time in his company and Lily was not happy about it.

'Mum, I'm doing my job. It's not like I'm there chatting to him all afternoon. I'm polite, he's polite and that's it.'

'And what about his son?'

'Adam's usually at work when I'm there and even if he wasn't, I'm there with a squad of sailors. What do you think is going to happen to me? I understand Mum, really I do, but you're worrying over nothing.'

Frankie had barely even blushed as she told the lie. Adam was increasingly turning up part way through the hour lesson the Navy had the pool booked for, often claiming he was there on dockyard business. *He must think I'm an idiot,* Frankie thought. *What business can the dock have with the Lido that requires him to be here two or three times a week?* Although Adam usually stayed in the office with his father, she had caught him watching her from the big window which overlooked the pool. She wasn't remotely interested in him – how could she be when Mac filled her every waking moment – but it didn't stop her noticing the way his eyes followed her whenever she got out of the pool. On a few occasions she'd bumped into him as she was leaving the changing rooms and he'd complimented her on her teaching.

'They're making good progress. What happens when this lot can swim properly? Do we lose the pleasure of your company in the afternoons?'

Frankie laughed as she tucked her hair back into her hat. 'No chance. Once I get rid of this lot, there's another bunch who can't swim waiting to have me lecture them for a few weeks.'

'I can't imagine any of them mind too much,' Adam said, his eyes fixed firmly on hers. 'I certainly wouldn't mind being taught by you.'

'Tell them that, would you?' She waved an arm as the men emerged from the other changing room. 'According to them I'm a regular tartar.'

Adam rested a hand on her shoulder briefly. 'I'll take on anyone who says you're anything less than a wonderful instructor.'

Frankie froze at his touch. There was nothing untoward in it, but it was the first time he'd made any physical contact with her and she was unsure how to react. It was one thing to enjoy feeling admired, but in touching her he'd crossed a boundary she wasn't even aware she'd erected and she took a step away from him.

'Don't worry,' she said, shouldering her changing bag. 'I can look after myself. Even with this lot.' She softened the words with a grin then hastened towards the exit, aware Adam was watching her all the way.

If she'd told her mother about any of this, Lily would have banned her from taking any more lessons, Admiral or no Admiral and consequently, Frankie kept quiet. She told herself that she didn't tell Mac about it because there was nothing to tell. He had nothing to worry about – Adam had always been a flirt, although it was the first time he'd attempted to charm Frankie. She wasn't interested and therefore there was no need to upset her fiancé.

The next time Adam had arrived at the Lido during a lesson, he'd made no attempt to speak to her until it was almost time for them to leave. He'd tried to leave the office, but his father had blocked his path and although Frankie couldn't hear anything through the closed door, it was clear their voices were raised in anger. She hid a smile. It seemed John Liversidge was about as keen on his son talking to her, as her mother was. Lily clearly had nothing to worry about.

Outside of her duties in the pool and manning the launch whenever she was required to transport officers from ship to shore and back again, her life had a certain regularity about it. Much of her time was spent in the Admiral's office taking notes and then typing them up, or taking dictation and sending letters. On rare occasions, she worked with the more regularly employed Wrens, learning from them what she had missed in training because of her unorthodox introduction to life in the services. Leading Wren Seaton took her under her wing and arranged for her to work with different Wrens to learn the necessary skills. Gradually Frankie picked up the intricacies of signalling and engineering and learnt how to drive and repair a car. They were all useful to know, but she was happiest when she was piloting the launch or in the Lido giving lessons. She'd argued that since her role in the WRNS was technically unofficial, she could continue to pilot the launch boat.

'Not that you'd have listened to us if we'd said no,' Mr Nelson had told her sternly. He had taken over the role of harbourmaster since their return from Dunkirk, as well as continuing his shifts as launch pilot and Frankie knew he found it highly amusing watching her take orders from the Admiral.

'I might have done.' Frankie examined her shoes. When

Mr Nelson didn't immediately reply she risked a glance at his face. His eyes twinkled and she smiled. 'Well maybe not, but you didn't, so can we at least pretend I'd have given it up?'

MR NELSON SHOOK his head as she left the office, watching as she took the path back to the hotel. She was going to get herself into trouble one of these days, but he hoped for her sake it wouldn't be too serious. Her good humour had kept him from sinking into depression during the agonising journey back from the south coast and he was grateful for it. When she'd said she coped by not thinking too closely about her fear, he'd understood the sentiment, having no desire to examine his own thoughts too closely either. He'd believed he'd left scenes like that behind when he was discharged from the army in 1919 but, watching with growing despair as the world moved inexorably closer to another war, he'd been glad he was now too old and his children too young to play a part in the coming conflict. He certainly hadn't expected to be in the middle of enemy action but when the Navy had come calling for his boat, he'd made the immediate decision to sail it for them. There were other owners whose boats were simply commandeered, but the Navy needed people to sail them, so he'd volunteered to go with them. That way, at least the fate of his beloved boat was partially in his own hands.

I wonder how many we left behind. He shook his head. He couldn't think about them. He had to believe they were prisoners and their war was over. *At least they'll come home in the end,* he thought. *There's many we left on that beach that won't.*

FRANKIE CURLED up on the window seat, a mug of tea warming her hands and watched as a boat made slow progress out to sea. Even in the creek, the water roiled and she shivered.

'I'm glad you're not out in it,' Lily observed, coming up behind her and laying a hand on her daughter's shoulder.

Frankie leant into her mother, acknowledging the tremor in her voice. 'Not much chance of that. The officers are all back on land with no plans to go anywhere. The only ships out tonight are the duty patrol boats.' She pointed out of the window. 'That's the *Oceanus* on its way and the *McGrath's* already gone. They're in for a hell of a night of it.'

Thunder rumbled again and Lily's grip tightened, her fingers digging into the hollows of Frankie's shoulder. Frankie unfolded herself from the seat and wrapped her arms around her mother.

'It's okay, Mum. Come away from the window.'

For as long as she could remember, her mother had been terrified of storms. White-faced and shaking, she would sit, trying to make herself as small as possible in the chair, while her husband soothed and reassured her. By contrast, Frankie had always loved the wildness of them. They made her feel free and she would happily have watched the lightning all night as a child. *But then*, she considered, *I didn't lose my father in a storm*. She'd never known her maternal grandparents. Lily's father had died when she was very young, his fishing boat claimed by a storm, his body never recovered. Her mother, unable to cope with life without her husband, had drifted listlessly through the next few years, eking out enough money to keep her daughter from starving, until finally she'd given up on life as well. Lily had been left alone in the world before she'd even left childhood. *There's no wonder storms terrify her.*

'I'll tell you what, why don't we get you into bed with a

cuppa and your book. Take your mind off the weather 'til Dad gets back.'

Lily allowed her daughter to lead her upstairs and once she was settled, Frankie left her and returned to the living room to resume her observation of the storm.

A short while later, her father entered the room, shaking off the worst of the water from his coat and hair.

'What a night!' He crouched in front of the fire, warming his hands for a moment. 'Is Mum alright?'

Frankie nodded. 'She's in bed with tea and a book. I thought it was the best place for her. She was worried about you.'

'I'll nip up and let her know I'm back. Probably best not to tell her about the 'plane that nearly took my head off though.'

Frankie raised her eyebrows.

'Give me a minute to go and see Mum and then I'll tell you about it.'

When he returned with the news that Lily had been reassured, but was staying in bed, Frankie urged him to tell her about the 'plane.

'It came out of the clouds somewhere above me,' Laurence said. 'It was really low – much lower than normal – and I could see it was one of theirs. I threw myself on the floor, thinking it was going to come over the town, but it banked away and headed out over the creek towards St Osyth. Not the most pleasant experience, but it could have been worse.'

'Probably a good idea not to say anything to Mum,' Frankie said. 'It would only make her worry even more about you being out.'

Her father smiled ruefully. 'She doesn't think about my leg when she wants things lifted and carried, but as soon as I said I was joining the LDV my leg became a problem again.

She seems to forget I worked at the docks for over a decade doing manual labour. I might not have been fit enough to serve in the Navy, but I was fit enough to build their ships for them. It kept me out of the last war but it's not keeping me out of this one.'

Frankie burst out laughing. 'And you wonder where I get it from?'

Her father smiled, acknowledging the truth of her words. 'The difference is my darling, I at least think first. I don't jump in with both feet. I know my limitations, whereas you charge through life determined to bend the world to your will.' His expression changed, becoming melancholy. 'I'm afraid that comes from my side of the family. You remind me very much of my...' he trailed off for a moment, as though changing his mind about what he'd been about to say. 'Of my brother, Freddie.'

Frankie jumped from her seat and ran to give her father a hug. She knew all about Freddie and how he'd lied about his age to join the army with his friends. The first day of the Battle of the Somme had been both the first and last time he saw action.

'I have been trying, Dad.'

Laurence ruffled her hair. 'I know, love. But your mum and I will always worry about you and Addie. It comes with the job.'

Later that evening, as she was getting ready for bed, Frankie heard the all too familiar drone of German planes and wondered where was being targeted. Avonstow had been relatively lucky so far, the south of the county had been hit far more often than the north and it was only one or two families who had been forced to find alternative accommodation. Ken's parents had been lucky – they were now living in a house one street over from the bombed-out shell of their old home – but others were still staying with relatives or had been forced to leave the town altogether.

The next morning, Frankie was awake early and she ran downstairs, intending to start on breakfast for the Naval officers before beginning her shift on the launch boat. As she drew the curtains in the front room, however, it was clear something was happening. A group of women were gathered in front of the hotel, clustered around the end of the jetty. Frankie drew her uniform coat on and hurried outside.

'What's going on?' She caught hold of one of the ratings as he evaded the waiting women and tried to slip around the side of the hotel.

'It's the *McGrath*. It didn't come in this morning.'

Frankie let him go. The *McGrath* had come down from Fleetwood as part of the Royal Naval Reserves and many of the crew's wives had come down with their husbands and were lodging at various places in the town. She strode over to the group.

'Good morning, ladies –' She got no further than the greeting: questions were thrown at her from all sides. She held her hands up. 'Please, I understand your concerns and I know how you feel, but I don't have any answers for you. Go home and the Admiral will no doubt be carrying out investigations and questioning the men who were out last night to find out what's happened.'

'What the bleedin' hell do you know about anything?' The speaker was a florid faced woman of middle age, her hair bound up in a scarf. 'You're nowt but a slip of a lass. Go home? Our husbands are out there somewhere and you'll ask questions. What flippin' good will that do? You should be out there looking for them. How can you possibly know how it feels knowing your man's missing and you can do nowt but wait?'

Frankie fixed her eyes on the woman and spoke quietly. 'I

know how it feels because I've done it. My fiancé is in the RAF and he ditched his plane out there. It took them hours to find him, but I was lucky, I got him back. I haven't forgotten those hours in between though, so don't presume to know anything about me. I promise you, the Admiral will be doing everything he can. I'm sure he'll come and speak to you at some point, but please just let him do his job.'

All day, Frankie sat with the Admiral taking notes as the senior officers questioned every single man who'd been out on patrol the previous evening. None of them had seen the *McGrath* after 10 o'clock. They had seen the aeroplanes Frankie had heard and one man said he thought he'd seen something fall from the planes but couldn't be sure. He'd radioed back to the base and told them, but the rest of the patrol had been completed without incident, beyond the usual problems created by stormy weather.

When the patrols went out that night, Frankie passed on the Admiral's instructions to keep a look-out for any sign of the trawler or its fate, then returned to the hotel and collapsed into a chair. She was woken by a gentle shake of her shoulder and a mug of tea was pressed into her hands.

'Thank you.' She smiled at her mother. 'It's been a long day.'

'Is there any news?'

Frankie shook her head. 'Nobody saw or heard anything from her after about 10 o'clock. It's like she just vanished. The wives are still speaking hopefully, but you can see in their eyes they know their men are gone. I felt so helpless today: their representatives have been in and out of the office and every time we told them there was still no news, I watched them crumple a little more into themselves. By now, even if there were any survivors, they'll likely have drowned.'

'Is there anything we can do to help them?'

'Adam came up from the dockyard. Told the Admiral the

men were doing a collection. Most of them are Avonstow families and they've been through this before. They know if a boat doesn't come back when it should, it rarely comes back at all.'

Frankie watched her mother's lips pinch into a thin line. Even when the Liversidges were doing something good she couldn't bear mention of them. Nevertheless, she nodded a grudging approval.

'If they want to come in here, I'll have some money ready for them.'

The next morning, Frankie reported for duty to be told there was still no news of the *McGrath*.

'The Admiral said he wanted to see you in his office the minute you got here,' the Wren going off duty told her.

Frankie knocked on the door and saluted as she entered. Admiral Ashton looked up from the papers on his desk, his eyes red-rimmed with sleeplessness.

'Thompson, good. You're here. I need the launch this morning. We're heading out to look for the *McGrath*. With a low tide and daylight, hopefully we'll find something to tell us what happened to her.'

'I'll get her ready, Sir.' Frankie saluted and headed to the jetty where the launch was moored. Two sailors were already there waiting as she jumped aboard and started the engine. Admiral Ashton was not long behind her and she eased the boat out into the creek, turning it to head for the deeper water of the open sea.

About two hours into the trip a shout came from the lookout in the prow of the boat.

'Over there, Sir,' he handed the binoculars to Admiral Ashton. 'Do you see them?'

The Admiral's face was pale as he handed the binoculars back.

'24 degrees to Starboard, Thompson.'

Frankie turned the wheel, her eyes straining through the cabin window to see exactly what they were heading for. As the launch bobbed and rolled its way through the waves, a sickening feeling settled in the pit of her stomach. Two masts jutted out of the water ahead of them, one still standing tall, the other bent at an unnatural angle. She pulled as close as she dared.

'It's the *McGrath* alright.'

Admiral Ashton removed his hat and bowed his head. The others on board hastily did the same and for a few moments they paid their respects. Then, Frankie pulled the launch around and they headed back towards the town and the women who were now widows.

'What will you tell the wives, Sir?' Frankie spoke quietly as the Admiral joined her in the cabin.

'It was hit by a mine.' The Admiral's lips were taut, his bearing stiff. 'The bloody thing should never have been out there. I told them the trawlers needed de-gaussing[1], but did they listen? Of course they bloody didn't. Insignificant commander of a tin-pot base, what does he know? Well, they'll de-gausse the rest of them now, or they won't leave harbour. I'm not sending more men to their deaths than I have to.'

Frankie kept her eyes firmly fixed on the horizon. She'd never heard the Admiral lose control and for once, she wasn't sure how to react. When he spoke again, it was in his usual measured tone.

'My apologies, Thompson. I would appreciate it if you didn't mention it to anyone. Loose lips and all that.'

'Sorry, Sir. Did you say something? It takes all my concentration to steer this thing.'

Admiral Ashton relaxed and took a seat. 'I'm sorry to ask more of you, Thompson, but I'd like you to be present when I speak to the wives. I don't… I don't deal with crying women very well. Never sure what to say to them.'

'Of course, Sir. Perhaps Leading Wren Seaton could be there as well?'

The Admiral nodded. 'Quite. Quite.'

Frankie held herself together all day as she comforted the women from Fleetwood and absorbed their grief, but at the end of a long and wearying shift, she laid her head on her pillow and wept. Even though the women had been expecting the worst, knowing it was likely and having it confirmed were two different things. Some of them had taken it stoically, simply sitting down and withdrawing into themselves, others had verged on the hysterical. Many had young children and one or two had only been married a short time. All were left devastated, more so because there was no way of retrieving their husbands' bodies. As Frankie wrapped her arms around herself, she could only think of how desperately she needed to speak to Mac, to feel the warmth of him next to her, to be sure he was alive.

A FEW WEEKS later when the *Bagman* sank, not 400 yards from the *McGrath*, Frankie found herself once again bouncing over the waves, this time picking up survivors. If the word lucky could be applied in that situation, the men on the *Bagman* had been so. They had struck the mine in daylight on a calm day and had time to radio for help.

'Should have known there'd be a second one,' one of the men grumbled to Frankie. 'They always drop the bloody things in pairs.'

'Just be grateful you're alive,' Frankie said sharply, then bit her lip. He had no way of knowing she had been re-living

Dunkirk all day. 'I'm sure my parents will have tea waiting when we get back.'

The sailor threw his head back and laughed. 'We don't want tea! You reckon they'll have any whisky?'

Frankie smiled. 'I imagine there'll be a bottle or two they can dig up for you.'

When all the survivors had been brought to shore, there were four more Northern widows in Avonstow. They were supported by the women they had arrived with, none of whom had returned to the north-west town. Frankie couldn't help asking one of them why.

'I don't mean you're not welcome to stay,' she added hastily. 'Of course you are. I just wondered why you preferred to be here rather than going home.'

'What's to go home for, lass? We rented our house and we brought all our stuff with us when he got posted down here. All that's up there is a load of memories I can't face. We've no family to speak of and this is the place he died. With no grave to visit, what else have we got? Besides, some of us have got jobs. At least here we won't starve.'

Frankie went to see Admiral Ashton. 'The thing is, Sir, these women have nothing. I know the shipyard and the Navy have done a collection for them, but money isn't everything. They need to be able to say goodbye properly to their men. I know I'd want to.'

The Admiral studied her for a moment. 'What did you have in mind?'

Frankie looked at her feet. 'I wondered if I might be permitted to take them out on the launch, Sir. Let them lay a wreath on the site. It would need a couple of trips – the boat isn't big enough to get all of them on at once, but I'd be happy to do it on my day off: it wouldn't interfere with my duties.'

'You can take them the day after tomorrow. Give them time to organise the flowers.'

She was clearly dismissed, but Frankie hesitated.

'Was there something else?'

'I… May I speak freely, Sir?'

The Admiral's mouth twitched. 'You don't normally wait to be invited.'

Frankie blushed. 'Sir, the conversation we didn't have after the *McGrath* went down… I only wanted to say that at least now you didn't need to feel as guilty about what happened. The *Bagman* had been de-gaussed and it still blew up. The *McGrath* wasn't your fault.'

Admiral Ashton sighed. 'Not my fault perhaps, but still my responsibility.'

Frankie turned to leave, but the Admiral called her back.

'Thompson? Thank you.'

FRANKIE SPUN the wheel of the boat. The first trip out to the wreck sites had been uneventful, but now she had anxious eyes on the sky. The tides had delayed the trips and it was getting dark. Under normal circumstances she would have used the lights of the towns along the coastline to guide her home, but the blackout made that impossible. She knew the local waters well and in daylight needed no map to know where the shallows and sandbanks were, but at night there was always the danger of miscalculating and running aground, especially in rough seas.

She opened the cabin door and called out. 'It's going to be a bumpy one, ladies. You might want to find something to hold onto.'

Worried faces turned towards her in the gloom and she forced herself to grin reassuringly. 'Don't worry, I'll get you home as quick as I can. You might be a bit damp by the time we get there, but she's a good little ship and she's sound as can be.'

Below the sightline of the window, she crossed her fingers as she spoke. It wasn't an outright lie, she had faith in the launch, but in very rough weather, it did tend to let in water. She just had to hope they'd make port before the worst of it hit.

When the shadow of Frakes' Folly finally loomed large on the port side, Frankie heaved a sigh of relief. She'd wrestled with the wheel for most of the journey home, unable to release it even to check her map. All she'd had to navigate with was a compass clutched between her thumb and forefinger – the only two digits she could spare from steering. She knew her instincts were good when it came to the water, but on a pitch-black stormy night, having to time her turns, trusting she'd gone far enough in the right direction, was not something she wanted to try on a regular basis. The lights and bells on the various buoys helped her to avoid running aground, but it wasn't her favourite way to navigate.

Once she'd tied the launch to the jetty, she helped the women ashore and they hurried towards the hotel, bent double into the wind. As Frankie had hoped they would be, Lily and Laurence were ready with a warm fire and a drink. Leading Wren Seaton had also stayed to lend a hand.

'I'm impressed, Thompson,' she said. 'The ladies have been singing your praises. Getting home in that weather and in the dark, without a map, is some achievement, even when you are familiar with the waters. Well done.'

Frankie smiled. The senior Wren's praise was rarely bestowed and was always genuine. Like Frankie, she had a fiancé serving, but hers was in the army rather than the RAF.

'Everything we do helps to shorten the war,' she had told Frankie at the beginning of her first shift. 'That's what you always have to remember when the duties are boring, or the orders challenging. The sooner we win, the sooner our men come home safely and what's more important than that?'

Alicia Seaton was in her mid-twenties and Frankie had taken an instant liking to the older woman. Her calm, unflappable demeanour reminded Frankie a little of Addie and she was determined not to let her commanding officer down, especially when she'd taken such care to ensure Frankie was well equipped to do all the other aspects of her job.

'THE ROAD in looked a bit different this morning.' Mac stretched his legs out and offered Frankie a chip.

'They've been building them all over the place,' she said, blowing on her burnt fingers. 'I suppose it makes sense to have defences ready just in case, but it makes it feel as though they're expecting an invasion.'

'I'll bet the farmers aren't too happy about it either,' Mac smiled. 'Pillboxes don't exactly enhance the views across the fields, do they?'

'They're doing their best to hide them,' Frankie agreed. 'But once you know they're there, your eyes are drawn to them all the time.'

'They're easy to spot from the air as well. No amount of camouflage can disguise them. It's fairly obvious there's something there, even if you're not a hundred per cent sure what it is.'

Frankie bit off a piece of the now cooled chip. 'No more talk of war,' she said firmly. 'I've only got you for a couple of days and I'm working this afternoon. What do you want to do? Shall we go for a walk tomorrow?'

Mac was silent for a moment, then he put the packet of

chips down on the bench. 'How would you feel about getting married?'

'What? I thought you said there was no need to rush?'

'I heard from home a few days ago and… well, it made me think. We can have a proper ceremony after the war – white dress, bridesmaids, all the trimmings, but at least we'd know we belonged to each other.'

'When did you have in mind? I assume you don't actually mean to get married tomorrow?'

'No, but maybe we could go and see the vicar and make the arrangements. I spoke to the CO and he can't authorise official leave, but given how things are going, he was pretty understanding and said he'd turn a blind eye to me and Ken being off base on our rest day. We could come down as soon as we're off duty, get married the next day and get the last train back that night. The honeymoon would have to wait, but what do you think?'

'I think it's mad, but we should do it. I'll telephone Addie tonight and see if she can get time off to come.'

Mac leant in to kiss her. 'I love you so much, Frankie Thompson. Never forget it.'

'Mrs Alasdair Macmillan.' Frankie sighed, happily. 'I could get used to that.'

JOHN - 1940

'They know where she is, John. They know where she is, and they'll kill her if you don't do as they ask.'

'Who? They know where who is?'

'Alice Thompson. They've found her.'

John slumped into a chair and stared at his father. 'How?'

'I don't know, but they'll kill her and the child if you don't co-operate.'

'Dad, I can't. I don't have the access anymore. Not since I retired.'

'Then you'd best find a way to get it, son, because if you don't, they'll make Alice pay. Or is that what you want? You always swore you'd kill her if you found her.'

'I was an idiot. I wouldn't have harmed a hair on her head. How did they find her? I never could.'

'They have their ways son, as you know better than most. Now. What is it I'm going to be telling them?'

John heaved a sigh. 'What choice do I have? Tell them I'll think of something. They just need to give me some time.'

'If I were you, I'd have a chat with young Adam. He's got a

little side-line going that could get him into a lot of trouble if the authorities were to find out. Now, my friends don't want to cause him any grief, but they reckon he could be quite a useful asset to them. It might be in the boy's best interests to co-operate.'

John looked at his father in disbelief. 'You want me to involve Adam?'

'Ah, I don't think he'll mind. There's more of the Irishman in him than there's ever been in you. He knows what heritage and family mean, even if you don't.'

When his son had left the room, Garrett Liversidge picked up the telephone receiver and dialled a number. When his call was answered, he spoke in a low voice.

'I told you it would work. He bought it completely. He'll play ball now.'

JULY 2017

'So, he never told you he was married?' Ellie shook her head, her features pulled into a disapproving expression. 'And you had no idea?'

Frankie's smile was sad. 'It wasn't like it is nowadays,' she reminded the younger woman. 'We had nothing like the internet, you had to take people at face value. I mean, obviously we were all on the lookout for spies – the whole country was – but Ken introduced Mac to me and I trusted Ken implicitly. I had no reason to think he was anything other than what he said he was.'

Ellie hesitated. 'I assume Ken didn't know he was married either?'

Frankie shook her head. 'He was furious when he found out. Mostly with Mac, but with himself as well, I think. If I'm being honest, a part of me blamed him too, but it didn't take me long to realise how stupid I was being. There was no way Ken would have kept something like that a secret.'

'Was the fear of spies genuine?' Hannah asked. 'You read about how people were convinced there were spies parachuting in all the time.'

Frankie considered for a moment before replying. 'I think we were more aware of it because of the naval base,' she said. 'And also because of the lights.'

Ellie nodded. 'I remember Alice saying about lights flashing like signals during the first war. Was it the same during the second?'

'It was black marketeers mostly. Rationing hit people hard and some couldn't cope with it. If you were desperate enough, there were ways of finding out who could get you what you wanted and there were always those were happy to buy more whenever they could. It drove my mother wild. Avonstow was a town of sailing families. Half the population had people either in the Navy or on the merchant ships and they knew better than most the cost of getting that food into the country. She could never understand why anyone in a town like ours would do something that put our own people at risk.'

'I suppose some people didn't think about it in those terms,' Hannah said. 'They only saw their own need.'

'Need had nothing to do with it!' Frankie scoffed. 'There were some who didn't understand, but mostly they didn't care. People traded in secrets and lies until they were so bound up in them, they couldn't see their way out and by then it was too late and they were trapped. Those that were doing the selling didn't care about anyone beyond themselves and their wallets.'

She fell silent. Ellie opened her mouth to speak, then changed her mind and waited for Frankie to continue.

*J*ohn looked at his son. He looked composed and the arrogant twist of his head reminded the older man of his father. Good looks and a certain amount of charm had carried Adam thus far in life and a part of John envied him the confidence with which he approached everything. His son was concerned with the needs and desires of others only insofar as they coincided with his own. He felt no loyalty to anyone and like his grand-father, viewed his father as weak and easily ignored.

'How could you be so stupid?' John hissed. 'If you get caught, you'll be sent to prison. Is it really worth risking your freedom for a bit of extra cash?'

Adam laughed. 'You're so short-sighted. It's not about the money, it's the power. These days people will do a lot to get their hands on a few extra supplies. Surely you of all people understand how important control is?'

It was his father talking and John was transported back to that awful night twenty years earlier. The body on the floor and all that followed. He'd hoped it would finally bring him his father's approval, but Garret had held him in as much contempt as ever, especially when his marriage had failed. Lily had been outwardly submissive, but she'd never stemmed his need for Alice. She was the only woman he'd ever loved and, in his desperation, he'd driven her out of his life. He'd tried substituting her, but neither of his wives had ever come close.

He tried again. 'Adam, you don't know what you're getting mixed up in. These people are ruthless. If you cross them, they will kill you without a second thought.'

'I can handle them,' Adam said, with a dismissive flick of his hand. 'They're a bunch of old men and they need me more than I need them. Besides, it won't be too difficult. Between the men at the shipyard and their desperate wives and daughters, who need money, meat, or stockings, I've got so many people in this town in the palm of my hand, they can't afford to cross me. The ones who are in the market for extras, are often in the market for a different kind of extra as well, if you take my meaning, so they really can't afford to get on my bad side.'

John felt sick. He was trapped, destined to repeat his mistakes over and over again and there was nothing he could do to break the cycle. Garrett had moulded his grandson in his own image and he would get his way again, just as he always did and it would be John who would bear the burden. His shoulders slumped.

'So, I'm to tell your grandfather you're willing to co-operate?'

Adam grinned. 'If it doesn't affect me and there's money in it, then I'm in. If he wants to talk to me tonight though, tell him to make it quick. I've got a man to meet in Colchester.'

JULY 1940

*F*rankie smothered a yawn and swallowed half her coffee in one gulp. She pulled a face.

'I can't get used to having it black.'

'Well, you don't have a lot of choice, young lady. Unlike some people round here, I'll have no truck with off ration stuff.' Lily banged the coffee pot down on the table.

'Alright, Mum. No need to get in such a tizz. I was only saying!' Frankie started to laugh but stopped when she saw her mother's face. 'What's got you all riled up?'

Lily's lips pressed into a thin line. 'Nothing. You hear things, that's all. All I'm saying is there's a few people in this town who need to think about where all that stuff comes from.'

Frankie shook her head. 'Mum, I don't think anyone would begrudge someone the occasional extra egg or splash of milk. Enough people round here keep their own animals.'

'That's not what I'm talking about, love. Don't worry about it, I'm just a bit flustered this morning.'

Frankie finished her breakfast, then went in search of

Mac. She found him in the front bar, watching the activity on The Hard.

'Wishing you'd joined the Navy instead?' She kissed the top of his head.

'You finally surfaced, then? Is this what married life is going to be like with you? Lazing around in bed until all hours?'

'Oi! I didn't come off watch until late last night and then someone woke me up a few hours later creeping into my bedroom. I had sleep to catch up on.'

Mac grinned and pulled her onto his lap. 'I didn't notice you complaining about being woken up.'

'I couldn't possibly comment.' She wriggled away from him and stood up. 'Come on, we need to go and see Reverend Blissit. He said he could see us at half past and it's gone 10 o'clock already.'

They left the hotel a few minutes later, heading towards the vicarage. Their appointment with the vicar done, they left the vicarage with their wedding date confirmed and all the necessary arrangements put in place. Turning onto the High Street, they met Ken's mother coming the other way. Mac bent to kiss her cheek.

'Hello again, Mrs Ford. Ken was well when I left yesterday.'

She smiled. 'Yes, I had a letter from him this morning, telling me he'd be home on a flying visit soon.' She turned to Frankie. 'I understand congratulations are in order?'

Frankie blushed and nodded. 'We've been to see Reverend Blissit and he's agreed to marry us.'

Meredith Ford gave her a hug. 'We wish you every happiness, my love.'

'You will come, Auntie Meredith, won't you? It's only a quiet ceremony, we're not even having a reception really, only a few sandwiches back at the hotel. Mac and Ken have to get back pretty much as soon as we're married, but it wouldn't feel right without you and Uncle Lionel there. I've spent nearly as much time in your house over the years as I've done in my own!'

'Of course we'll be there, lovely.' Meredith lowered her voice. 'And if you need something blue, you pop in and see me. I've got just the thing.'

As they parted company, Meredith called them back. 'Oh, Frankie, love, I've a memory like a sieve at the moment. I meant to ask if Lily was alright?'

'Mum?' Frankie frowned. 'Why wouldn't she be?'

'I saw her speaking to Eric Warburton this morning and she looked so angry when she walked away from him, I was worried she was going to cry. I'd have gone after her, but I was in a queue at the butcher's and you know what it's like. I thought I'd pop in and see her later, make sure she was alright. I wondered if something had happened with our Addie?'

Frankie laughed. 'They're not back together if that's what you mean. I get the feeling she's quite taken with someone on the farm she's working on.'

'Any details?'

'You know Addie. She won't let on until she's sure. It's just someone who always appears in her letters. I could have got it completely wrong.'

'As long as everyone's well,' Meredith said, smiling.

Frankie said goodbye and she and Mac walked slowly back to The Mermaid.

'That's really strange,' she said. 'Mum was out of sorts this morning. She was angry about something and rambling on about the black market. I wonder if Eric said something about Addie.'

'How on earth did you come to that conclusion? Addie's not even here?'

'Well, it's the only thing I can think of that would make Mum so cross. Addie's working on a farm and her relationship with Eric ended badly. I wonder if he said something about Addie taking advantage of having ready access to off ration food.'

'Why don't you ask your mum?'

Frankie looked appalled. 'That's not how it works,' she said. 'If I ask her directly, she'll dismiss it out of hand. Mum only shares things when she's ready to, if at all. Even with Dad she keeps things pretty close to her chest. She'd make a brilliant spy – you'd never know what she was thinking if she didn't want you to.'

Mac laughed. 'You must take after your dad. You should never play poker – your face would give you away every time.'

Frankie grinned. 'I like to let people think that. Actually, you'd be surprised at what I've hidden over the years.'

'Should I be worried?'

Her grin widened. 'What do you think?'

Mac shook his head.

'Actually,' Frankie continued. 'I probably shouldn't joke about Mum making a good spy. Not at the moment, anyway.'

'I guess not. Especially with your hotel being the base for the Navy.'

'They are a bit twitchy about spies at the moment.'

'That's natural in wartime, isn't it?'

Frankie shook her head. 'I don't mean in general terms. I meant here specifically.' She lowered her voice and glanced around them. 'There're flashing lights up and down the creek again. Somebody is signalling about something, but they don't know what or who. Dad says there were lights all around this area in the last war too and they never found out who was behind them either.'

Mac nodded. 'My dad mentioned that once as well.

Apparently, the reason they never found out who it was, was because the lights kept moving. They never appeared in the same location twice in a row and the Navy was chasing them all over the place, until eventually they seemed to give up.'

'It can't be a coincidence that as soon as we're at war again, the lights re-appear. But we're doing nothing secret here. It's just a normal shipyard and Navy base. Anyway, the Admiral has put the base on high alert for possible invasion and we've had orders that if it comes, we're to blow up the shipyard. In fact,' she giggled. 'Do you remember when you told me you were being trained with a rifle so you could defend the airfield and I got all upset? Well, now all us Wrens are being trained to do exactly the same here. I've got a good eye apparently.'

Mac gripped her hand. 'You will be careful, won't you?'

Frankie smiled and patted his arm. 'You sound like Mum and Dad. I'm in no danger. Hitler's not going to invade and there's no way Avonstow has spies. Everyone knows everyone here. We'd notice a stranger straight away. Those pillboxes we were talking about yesterday? When the men came to build them, within half an hour of them arriving, there was a whole bunch of locals crowded round, asking what they were doing. Jerry's got as much chance of parachuting a spy in here as he has of…oh I don't know, invading America!'

Mac was forced to laugh. 'Come on then, let's go and tell your parents what Reverend Blissit said. We've got a wedding to prepare for.'

'YOU MADE IT!' Frankie threw herself at Addie, as she stepped onto the platform.

'Missed me then?' Addie wrapped her arms around her little sister and hugged her tightly.

'Not in the least, but I'd look pretty daft without a bridesmaid, wouldn't I?'

'Rotter.' Addie laughed. 'When do I get to meet this man of yours, then?'

'He and Ken are coming tonight. They're staying with Aunt Meredith and Uncle Lionel, but everyone is coming to the hotel for dinner, so you'll see him then.'

'It's all a bit quick, Frankie. Are you sure you're doing the right thing?' Adelaide waved an impatient hand. 'Don't jump down my throat, I'm not saying you're not, but I wouldn't be a very good older sister if I didn't ask, would I? We all know what you're like for jumping in with two feet.'

Frankie's eyes clouded for a moment. 'Not this time, Addie. I love him and he loves me, I'm sure of it. There's been loads of quick weddings recently; everything is so much more hurried these days. Besides...' She stretched up and whispered in her sister's ear.

Concern fluttered across Addie's face. 'Are you sure?'

Frankie nodded, a nervous smile playing at the corners of her mouth. 'It's a good thing, Addie.'

Addie drew her sister's arm through her own. 'Come on then, let's go see Mum and Dad. I've some supplies in my bag for them, courtesy of my favourite farmer.'

'Eric?'

Addie stuck her tongue out. 'Drew.'

Frankie's eyebrows shot up.

'Andrew Robinson. It's his father's farm I'm working on.'

Frankie waited, but Addie didn't seem inclined to give her any more details. 'And?' she prompted eventually.

'He's training as a solicitor, but he has poor eyesight so he couldn't join up. When he's not at the office, he helps out on the farm. The family are lovely and when I asked if I could have a couple of days off to come to your wedding, they insisted I bring some food with me so you could have a decent meal afterwards.'

'That was kind. They won't get into trouble though, will they?'

Addie shook her head. 'The sheep broke its leg, so it had to be put down. If that happens it's off ration. The potatoes and the vegetables are all homegrown from the farm.'

'Mum will be delighted. She's been fussing all week about me not having a proper sit-down meal, but I don't care about a big 'do', I just want to marry Mac. The living room would have done if it had been allowed. He's more concerned about it than I am –keeps saying that after the war we'll have another ceremony, do it properly, as he puts it.'

'How's Ken?'

'Quiet. I've barely seen him recently. He writes all the time, but it's not the same.'

'You know why he doesn't come.'

'I do and I don't blame him. I know he finds it difficult, but I miss him. I never wanted to hurt him: he's my best friend. But when I met Mac, I knew.'

'I know, sis. I know.'

When they arrived at The Mermaid, Lily was waiting at the door to greet them. She ushered her daughters inside, then pulled Addie into a hug.

'Let me look at you.' She ran her eyes up and down her eldest child and nodded approvingly. 'Farm life agrees with you.'

Laurence appeared in the doorway and kissed his daughter's cheek warmly. 'It's good to see you, Addie. You look well.' He waved a pile of letters. 'I've just got to run these up to the Navy offices and then we'll have five minutes for a cuppa. Your mum's given me a list of jobs a mile long!' He grinned at his wife, then disappeared before she could respond.

'Ignore your dad,' she told Addie. 'He's giddy as a schoolboy today. Goodness knows what he'll be like by the time tomorrow comes. Anyone would think it was him getting married!'

By the time Mac and Ken arrived with Ken's parents, even Lily had to admit everything was as ready as it could be for the following day.

'Are you sure you don't want to borrow a dress?' Addie asked as she watched Frankie get ready for bed.

'Positive. I want to get married in my uniform, same as Mac. Besides,' her sister's face became wistful. 'I don't know how much longer I'll be able to wear it, so I might as well make the most of it.'

'How are you feeling?'

'Tired mostly. A bit sick. Nothing too bad so far.'

'Still, I'm surprised Mum and Dad haven't noticed. When will you tell them?'

'After the wedding. I haven't even told Mac yet.'

'Whyever not?'

'At first, I couldn't believe I'd been so unlucky as to fall for one. We were careful after the first time, but it was obviously too late. We were planning the wedding anyway, so I decided I'd wait until afterwards to drop that particular bombshell. It's lucky I'm not showing yet.'

Addie shook her head and laughed. 'You can't ever do things like everyone else, can you?'

Frankie smiled ruefully. 'I like to carve my own path, you know that. Plus, I didn't want all the fuss and I'd have had to give up my job.'

'How do you think Mac will take it?'

'He'll be delighted, I expect. I've no reason to think otherwise.'

. . .

THE WEATHER HAD BEEN dreadful in the weeks leading up to the wedding, so it was a relief to Frankie when she arrived at the church to be greeted by a warm sun. She paused under the lychgate and turned to look over her shoulder.'

'Hold still,' Addie told her. 'The sun is catching your hair perfectly.' She raised her camera and took a photograph.

'Your last one as a single woman,' Addie smiled. 'Are you ready?'

Frankie nodded, squeezing her father's arm excitedly. 'Come on, Dad.'

The little party headed into the church, where Mac, Ken, Lily and Ken's parents were waiting for them. Frankie drifted through the service, not really hearing the words. All her attention was on the man at her side. Her partner, her lover, her husband. It was hard to believe they were actually getting married. It had all seemed so unreal until she had found herself in front of the altar. In the space of a few short months, Mac had gone from resisting a relationship, to hastily arranging a wedding. It struck Frankie for the first time that he had never explained what had caused the sudden change of heart. She had been so grateful it had happened that it had never occurred to her to ask why. A slight frown creased her face. Mac squeezed her hand.

'You alright? Not regretting it already, are you?'

She smiled. 'Not in the least. Just thinking about us.'

'And that made you frown?'

'I was thinking, not frowning.' She stretched up and kissed his cheek. 'Let's walk back to the hotel, shall we? Let everyone else go off. There's something I want to talk to you about.'

Mac looked worried but nodded. 'Okay. I'll tell everyone to go ahead.'

When he returned, Frankie linked her arm through his and they set off down the road.

'Frankie, you're worrying me. What's happened? Are you ill?'

Frankie tilted her face up and smiled at him. 'No. I'm pregnant.'

Mac stared at her.

As SOON AS her sister walked through the door of the hotel, Adelaide knew something was wrong. She was smiling, but the smile didn't reach her eyes. She hurried to help Frankie remove her coat.

'What's wrong? Did he not take it well?'

'Not as well as I'd hoped,' Frankie whispered. 'He sort of went quiet at first. Oh, he said he was pleased and made all the right noises, but I don't know... it was like he was going through a list of things he knew he should say.'

'Maybe it was the shock,' Addie said, trying to reassure her.

'Maybe.' Frankie patted her arm and went into the dining room.

Addie met Mac's eyes as he came through the door hung his coat up.

'Don't spoil my sister's wedding day,' she warned him, her fingers digging into his arm.

He grimaced. 'You know as well then.'

Addie nodded.

'I am pleased,' Mac insisted. 'It was just unexpected. I thought maybe after the war we'd have children. It's not that I don't want them, it's a bit soon, that's all. You know what Frankie's like, but I'd hoped motherhood was something she wouldn't rush into.'

Addie raised an eyebrow. 'I hardly think she rushed into it

on her own.' She turned away and left him standing in the cloakroom alone. When she entered the dining room, it was to see Ken observing her sister closely, a thoughtful expression on his face. Their eyes met across the table and then he quickly turned away to speak to her mother.

'I'M SORRY, DARLING.' Mac kissed the top of Frankie's head. 'I hate that we have to rush off and leave you, but duty calls.' He kissed the slim gold band on her hand. 'I love you, Mrs Macmillan.' He brushed a discreet hand across her stomach. 'And I love you too little one.'

He stepped away, Ken taking his place. 'May I?' He opened his arms to Frankie, who threw her arms around him.

'Don't be silly. You always can.' She kissed his cheek. 'You take care of yourself, you hear me?' She glanced at Mac, who was lifting their overnight bags onto the train. 'Both of you.'

Ken squeezed her tightly, then held her at arm's length. 'Look after yourself.'

'I will. Fly safe.'

He nodded, then jumped on the train as it started to pull out of the station. Frankie stood on the platform, waving until the train was nothing more than a green smudge on the horizon. The sun caught the gold band, making it sparkle and she smiled. Everything was going to be alright. She was overemotional. Mac was happy. He'd said so, hadn't he?

She left the station and turned towards home. She had one evening left with her sister before she too went back to her job and Frankie would return to her duties. The next day would bring more swimming lessons. She glanced at the sky. Hopefully it would be another sunny day, otherwise the temperature of the pool would drop. She shivered in anticipation of that first plunge into the water. It would be warm, she told herself. It had to be.

'THOMPSON! THOMPSON!'

Frankie turned and smiled when she saw who was calling her. 'What is it, Hopkins?'

'Admiral Ashton wants to see you.'

'You've never been hauled up in front of him, surely?' Frankie stared at the young man. If there was a more unlikely candidate to be in trouble than George Hopkins, she'd yet to find one. He was quiet and unassuming and unfailingly polite. He'd not been based in Avonstow long, but he'd already made friends with most of the locals,

Hopkins laughed. 'Not at all. All the new ones who can't swim had to go and see him. I gather you're going to be teaching us?'

Frankie nodded. 'That's what the Navy employs me for. That and making sure you lot get to your ships in one piece. Keeping you lot afloat in one way or another seems to be how I'm destined to see out the war. Not the most exciting job, but someone has to do it, I suppose!'

She made her way up the stairs and along the corridor to the Admiral's door. When she entered, he was standing by the window looking out into the small yard at the back of the hotel.

'Sir?' Frankie saluted.

He beckoned her over to the window. 'What do you see, Thompson? Sorry, Macmillan.'

'Thompson is fine, Sir. Nobody remembers, so it's easier not to change it for now.' She looked down into the yard. 'Empty barrels, the garage, the bins.'

'And what if I told you those barrels weren't empty? That there was petrol in them.'

Frankie bristled but held her tongue.

The Admiral chuckled. 'Permission to speak freely, Thompson.'

'I'd tell you that you were a bloody idiot if you thought my parents were dealing in the black market.'

Admiral Ashton laughed again. 'Don't worry, I'm not accusing your parents of anything underhand. The point I'm trying to make is that you wouldn't believe me and neither would anyone else because your parents are honest, upright citizens of the town. It's inconceivable they would be doing anything illegal. In their case, people would be absolutely correct. But that's not to say it's the same for everyone. This goes no further than these four walls, young lady, but we've had fuel stolen from the shipyard. It's not so difficult to hide it, nor is it hard to conceal a lot of black-market goods. Something is wrong in this town and I don't like it.'

'May I still speak freely, Sir?'

The Admiral nodded.

'Why are you telling me? If you genuinely believed my parents were involved, I'd be the last person you'd confide in.'

'Because you know the people here. If you see or hear anything suspicious, even if you think the person couldn't possibly be guilty of anything, I want you to let me know. I spoke to your father a few days ago and as a result, I made some telephone calls, one of which was to my predecessor here. He told me some very interesting stories about his time in service in Avonstow, but I need proof before I can do anything more.'

'And that's what you want me for?'

Admiral Ashton shook his head. 'Not as such, but there is something you could do to help me.' He paused and studied her face for a moment. 'How well do you get on with the management at the Lido?'

'Mr. Liversidge doesn't like me very much. Adam's okay, I guess. We were at school together, but we were never really what you'd call friends.'

'But you might chat to them when you're waiting for the men to get changed after their lesson?'

'Sometimes, yes.'

'Could you drop something into the conversation?'

'Like what?'

'That there are rumours that we've received instructions to the effect that if an invasion comes, we're to send all our ships out to release barrels of fuel into the sea and set fire to it.'

'Are there such rumours?'

'There will be when you start them.'

'To what purpose?'

'That's on a need-to-know basis.'

'And presumably I don't need to know.'

'It's probably best if you don't.'

'I'll see what I can do. Assuming I can, what then?'

'Just let me know you've done it.'

Frankie saluted again and left the room with her orders. She wondered what the Admiral was hoping to achieve with his rumour spreading. It couldn't be anything directly to do with Adam or his father; presumably they'd been vetted along with the rest of the shipyard personnel when the Navy first arrived.

'WELL DONE, Hopkins. You're almost there.' Frankie threw a towel to him as he hauled himself out of the water. 'Another couple of weeks and you'll have cracked it, I reckon.'

He was the last one out of the pool and she followed him towards the changing rooms. Adam stood outside the office, leaning against the wall.

'Morning,' he smirked. 'Frankie Thompson, married. Who'd have believed it.'

'It comes to us all eventually,' she said, laughing slightly. 'Even the tomboys. Don't worry, Adam. Someone will have you one day. You're not on the shelf quite yet.'

His smile became uncertain for a moment, then he seemed to decide to take her words as a joke.

'I've got something for you.' He held out a small package. 'Wedding present.'

Frankie hesitated, then reached out a hand and took it from him. 'What is it?'

Adam rolled his eyes. 'Open it and find out.'

She slid her fingers under the string and unfolded the brown paper. Inside lay a folded pair of stockings. She looked up at Adam, who shrugged.

'Your mum would notice if you turned up with extra sugar. I didn't know what else to give you.'

'You do see it's inappropriate though?'

He shrugged again. 'It's no different to buying them off a man in a shop.'

'Except you can't get these in the shops anymore.'

'I know a man who knows a man.'

Frankie tucked them inside her uniform jacket, then threw a quick glance at the office, where John was visible through the window. His head was down and his attention on whatever was on his desk.

'Well at least it was a nicer surprise than the last one I got,' she said quietly.

Adam leant in. 'What do you mean?'

She glanced around again. 'I shouldn't,' she said, biting her lip. 'Careless talk and all that.'

'How long have we known each other?'

She nodded and lowered her voice further. 'I was tidying up in the Admiral's suite and I think he forgot I was in the bedroom. He was on the phone in the office. Apparently, if we're invaded, the Navy have orders to take the ships out to sea and release all the oil they have and then set fire to it. If Jerry wants to invade, he's going to have to do it through a firestorm all along the coast.'

Adam's eyes widened. 'Rather them than me,' he said. 'I bet you were terrified when you heard.'

Frankie nodded. 'Life in uniform isn't quite what I thought it was going to be. There's a lot of things the public don't know about that would terrify them if they found out, but it's all very hush hush. Sometimes the Admiral tells me things I'm not supposed to know – I think it's because he basically lives with us – and honestly, some of it would turn your hair white!'

The sailors began emerging from the changing rooms and Frankie stepped away from Adam.

'See you next time.' She waved an arm as she followed the men out onto the road. She could sense Adam's gaze following her as she went.

Well, Admiral, she thought. *I delivered your message. I wonder what you think it's going to achieve?*

'HE GAVE ME THESE.' Frankie slid the stockings across the desk.

Admiral Ashton looked at them, a blush crawling from beneath the collar of his shirt. He cleared his throat.

'Well done, Thompson.'

'What should I do with them?'

'I'd put them in a drawer and forget about them.'

'Do you want me to do anything else, Sir?'

'Not for the present, no.'

'If I might ask, Sir? What are you expecting to happen now?'

The Admiral leant back in his chair, steepling his fingers. 'I don't, Thompson. I don't know. Nothing. Or something. One of the two.'

'I don't understand.'

'I'm not sure I do either, Thompson. And I don't like it. I don't like it at all, but those were my orders. Deliver the message, then sit and wait. Henley was very clear about that.'

'Is the Admiral still in service then?' Frankie was surprised. She knew her father had worked for him during the Great War.

'Long retired but keeps himself informed of everything. I just wish I knew what game he was playing.'

'My mum always says there's no use borrowing trouble, there'll be plenty of the real stuff sooner or later,' Frankie said.

'Wise woman, your mother,' Admiral Ashton remarked. 'Well, I shall take her advice for now and wait and see what tomorrow brings.'

*I*t had been a long day already and it was only lunchtime. Frankie had come down to the lounge to eat a hasty lunch and was sitting in her usual position in the window seat when her father came in looking harassed.

'Hello,' Frankie waved a limp hand.

'Is your mother around? I want to top up my Thermos and then I'm going out again.'

'There's no let up today, is there?'

Her father's face was grim. 'The Observers are run off their feet down at the Folly. It's been wave after bloody wave. Those poor people in London...'

'I was meant to go off duty at six. At this rate I'll have been on for 24 hours! Never mind, it's not like I'm the only one and at least I have a rest day tomorrow. There's others have it much worse today.' Her voice wobbled and her father hurried to put a hand on her shoulder.

'Don't be nice to me or I really will bawl.' She put her plate down. 'I've got to get back.'

Her father looked concerned. 'You've barely touched your lunch.'

'I'm not hungry.'

'It's not only about you, sweetheart. Not anymore.'

'I know, Dad. Don't worry, I'll get something later, I promise.'

'Have you told the Admiral yet?'

Frankie shook her head. 'I know I should, but I don't want to give this up yet. It's early days and I can still do my job.'

Laurence frowned but didn't push the matter further. Frankie was grateful. She didn't want to argue with her father – she knew he was right and yet she rebelled against it. She was pregnant not dying and she was still more than capable of piloting the boat to and from the bigger ships. Without work she'd have been driven mad today, watching the formations of bombers flying overhead, knowing they were heading towards Debden. She couldn't dwell on Mac and Ken if she had work to do.

'Speaking of my job, I need to get back to it.' She jumped up and kissed her father's cheek. 'Tell Mum I said goodbye.'

Two minutes later, she was on board the launch and heading out to the ships.

OCTOBER 1940

*F*rankie was heading to bed when the telephone rang. Her father answered it and she watched his face grow paler as he listened to the voice at the other end. His eyes flicked to her then instantly to the floor and a feeling of dread coiled in her stomach. She put a hand on the bannister rail, needing to feel something solid beneath her. Her father replaced the handset.

'What is it?' Her voice sounded as though it were coming from far away and she felt her knees buckle, as she thumped onto the step.

Instead of answering, he ran up the stairs, returning a few moments later with her mother. Lily's eyes were full of compassion as she sat beside her daughter and put an arm around her shoulders. Frankie stared at her parents, full of fear, unable to ask which of the people she loved wasn't coming home.

'Darling...' Her father crouched beside her and put a gentle hand on her knee.

'Please...'

'That was Ken.'

His voice was as gentle as his touch, but Frankie felt as though he'd punched her. Her breath wouldn't come and she shook her head.

'I'm so sorry, my darling girl.' Her mother's arm tightened around her shoulders, but Frankie shrugged her off.

She staggered to her feet, still shaking her head. 'No.' She pushed past her father. 'I'm going out on the boat.'

Her father caught hold of her and pulled her into his arms, pressing her head into the familiar warmth of his cardigan.

'He didn't go down over the water.'

A howl of anguish caught in Frankie's throat and her father's arms tightened around her.

'Tell me.'

Her father hesitated.

'Tell me,' she insisted. 'I need to know.'

'His plane crashed and exploded. Ken saw it happen.'

Frankie took a deep shuddering breath and exhaled slowly, willing her heart to stop racing. Her face, when she lifted it to her father, was pale but composed.

'At least it was quick.'

Laurence attempted to draw her close again, but she resisted. 'I'm okay, Dad. I'm going to bed.'

She climbed the stairs, leaving her father staring after her. She couldn't face his kindness, not at the moment. She didn't bother undressing and crawled into bed, pulling the covers over her head. When she woke it was dark, there was a nagging ache in the pit of her stomach and she felt feverish. Turning her light on, she found a glass of water and a packet of aspirin on her nightstand. Blessing her mother's thoughtfulness, she took one and laid back against the pillow.

A few days later, Ken turned up at The Mermaid. 'I have a 24-hour-pass,' he explained.

Frankie was still in her pyjamas when he arrived and barely lifted her head to acknowledge him.

'Frankie, I need to talk to you. There's something you need to know, but before I tell you, you have to understand I only found out myself the other day. If I'd known...' He picked up her limp hand. 'If I'd known, I would have told you. You have to believe me.'

Frankie looked at him uncomprehendingly. 'Known what?' She didn't really care. Nothing he said would bring Mac back.

'Mac is... was... Frankie, he was married.'

'I know. I was there.'

'No, I mean...' Ken cleared his throat, his expression pained.

Understanding struck and Frankie stared at him. 'You don't mean to me, do you?'

Ken shook his head. 'Frankie, I'm so sorry. I had no idea.'

'How did you find out?'

Ken looked embarrassed. 'When a pilot dies, the rest of us go through his things before they're sent home, to make sure there's nothing in them that his family don't need to see. Mac's locker had... well, it had a photo of his wife and daughter in it, as well as the ones of you. There was a letter addressed to me and one for you.'

He handed her an envelope and she looked at it. Her name in Mac's familiar handwriting was on the outside.

'What did yours say?' Frankie couldn't raise her voice above a whisper.

'He apologised for lying to me. Asked me to pass the other one to you. Said you deserved an explanation, but he'd leave it to your judgement whether or not you shared it with me.'

She stared at him. 'I'd like you to leave.'

Ken stared at her in dismay. 'Frankie, I swear I had no idea. Do you honestly think I'd have let you anywhere near him if I'd known he already had a wife?'

'Please leave. I can't... I can't do this...'

'Frankie, please...'

She turned away from him and a few seconds later she heard the door close behind him. The letter lay heavy in her hands and she threw it away from her. *I don't want to read it. I can't. There's nothing he can say.* She hadn't cried when he died and she wasn't going to cry now. If she started, she feared she would never stop. It wouldn't change anything and it was unproductive. She had to be practical, to think about what she was going to do. She had a baby to take care of. Everything solidified to a cold hard lump inside her. *A baby who no longer has a father.* It was one thing to not care about society when you didn't have to, but Frankie was suddenly afraid. What were the neighbours going to say? *You know exactly what they'll say: the truth. That you were a gullible fool who was taken in by a handsome man. No wonder he was reluctant at first – he played you perfectly.* She had been so certain of his love she'd never pressed him to say what had changed his mind about her. He'd taken her for the fool she undoubtedly was. How could she have been so naïve? Pain lanced across her stomach and, feeling suddenly nauseous, she crumpled to the floor. The last thing she heard was the door opening and her mother screaming her name.

When she woke, it was to find her parents at her bedside, the back of her mother's hand pressed against her forehead.

'Hello sweetheart, how are you feeling?' Lily sounded concerned and Frankie tried to reassure her that she was alright, but the words stuck in her throat and a tear trickled down her cheek. Her father bent over her, but his face swam in and out of focus.

'I think we need to call the doctor out.'

The ache in her stomach was worse and Frankie reached out and gripped her mother's hand, pulling it to her stomach. Lily seemed to understand – her hand twisted round to squeeze Frankie's tightly.

'You go. I'll stay with her.'

Frankie closed her eyes again, trying to block out the pain shooting across her stomach. The doctor was on his way. Everything was going to be okay.

FRANKIE TRIED to sit up but it hurt too much. Everything hurt. Where was Mac? If she was having the baby, he should be here with her. Not in the room, but pacing outside at least. The corridor was silent. Why wasn't he there? Sweat poured down her face and she threw the covers off. She needed to find him. Strong arms pushed her back onto the bed.

'You need to lay still, dear, or you'll do yourself an injury.'

'My husband...' Frankie fought against the arms. 'I have to get to him.'

There was a sharp scratch on her arm and she slid back into unconsciousness. For hours she slept fitfully, one minute restless and thrashing, the next listless and silent. And always there was the pain: sometimes a dull ache, other times a sharp stabbing. Towards morning, she heard her door open and smelt her mother's lavender water.

'Is she awake?'

Frankie opened her eyes. 'Mum?'

The next moment, her mother was on the bed beside her, clutching her hand.

'You're awake. You gave us such a fright.'

'I'm sorry. I didn't mean to worry you.'

'We thought we were going to lose you.' Her mother's voice wobbled.

'The baby?'

Silence.

Frankie turned her face away from her mother's gentle caress.

'It's probably for the best, darling. Under the circumstances.' Her mother's voice whispered in her ear, but the wet cheeks told Frankie that Lily didn't believe it either.

THE NURSE STOOD up and busied herself with something in her bag. She'd heard enough of Frankie's incoherent ramblings the previous night to work out the situation the young woman had found herself in. She didn't judge the girl. Or her mother. She had only done what she believed was best. The nurse was in no position to judge anyway. Thankfully, her husband would be home on leave soon and the dates could be fudged to match. She touched her hair self-consciously. Hopefully her baby would also have red-hair and then there would be no awkward questions.

DEAR FRANKIE,

My dearest little sister, I want so much to come home and be with you. I telephoned, but Mum said you weren't ready to talk to anyone yet. I am so sorry I can't be there to comfort you. Oh, if I could get my hands on that man! How on earth he thought he was going to get away with it after the war, I have no idea. I'm sorry, I've just realised I'm ranting at the very person who needs it the least and I swore I'd stay calm when I wrote to you, but nobody gets to hurt you without having me to answer to and I'm angry. I can't imagine how you must feel, especially about the baby, but if I know you, it's probably a little relief and a lot of sadness and perhaps guilt that you feel relieved. I wish you would talk to me so I knew what to say to you and how to make this better.

I don't know what else to tell you – I don't want to talk about Drew when you're so miserable, but other than the pig escaping from her sty and having to be chased around the farmyard until we could herd her back in, I don't really have any news beyond 'today I milked the cows'.

Please, Frankie, come to the telephone when I next call. I promise not to shout, or even to mention his name, or ask how you are. I want to hear your voice. I miss being there with you all, even though I know what I'm doing is important.

Mum and Dad love you very much, as do I and when you are ready to talk, we'll listen. None of this is your fault, sister of mine.

Much love,
Addie

PS EVEN if you can't talk to him yet, please write to Ken and tell him you don't blame him. The poor boy is beside himself with worry and is convinced you despise him. I've told him you wouldn't be so unreasonable, but he needs to hear it from you.

'KEN TELEPHONED AGAIN.' Lily put the bowl of soup down in front of Frankie. Her daughter didn't respond. 'Frankie, I know you're hurting, but you can't shut him out. None of what happened is his fault.'

'I know.'

'Then why won't you talk to him?'

'I don't want to.'

'He didn't know, love.'

'Why does everyone think they need to keep telling me that? I'm not an idiot.' Of course Ken hadn't known. She didn't want to talk to him because she couldn't bear to hear the sympathy and the pain in his voice.

'Are you going to eat your soup?'

Frankie managed two spoonfuls, then laid the spoon back on the tray. 'I've had enough.'

She didn't need to look at her mother to know there were tears in her eyes, but she couldn't bring herself to care. Mac was gone. The baby was gone. Her chance of motherhood had gone. The doctor had been sympathetic, but firm. There would be no children in her future. He'd tried to be positive – told her she was lucky he'd managed to save her at all – said after the war there would be plenty of motherless children in need of a good home. He assumed she'd marry again. Frankie didn't want to know.

Her eyes drifted to her nightstand. As expected, the letter was back in its usual place. She still hadn't read it. She had no doubt what it would say. He loved her. He hadn't meant to hurt her. But none of it meant anything. Because if he'd loved her, he would have told her the truth.

'The Admiral came again.' Her mother's voice cut through her thoughts. 'He said to take as long as you needed. We haven't told him everything,' she added quickly. 'As far as everyone knows, you lost Mac and the baby and that's all. Ken said there was no need to say anything about the rest of it – he cleared out Mac's locker, so there's only him and his CO who know. Ken says there's no reason to spread it around. Just let everyone think you were widowed. Ken says you were really, so why give people anything to gossip about.'

'Ken has rather a lot to say,' Frankie spat, losing her temper.

'He's only trying to protect you, love.'

'I don't need protecting. And you can tell Admiral Ashton I'll be back at work next week.'

'So soon? Don't you think you ought to–'

'I said next week! Other women carry on after they've lost husbands and children. Why should I be different?'

'But it is different. You–'

'Got taken for a fool. If you really want to keep the truth hidden, then we need to carry on as we were. I'd like to sleep now, please.'

Frankie turned her back on her mother and pulled the covers over her shoulder. Lily picked up the tray and put a hand on her daughter's unyielding shoulder.

'I know you're hurting, but it's not fair to push away the people who love you. We deserve better and so does Ken. You're being unfair, Frankie. I know life probably feels terribly unfair right now, but you're not going to get through this on your own. And Frankie? For what it's worth, I think you should read Mac's letter. If he'd told you while he was still alive, would you have refused to listen to him? Or would you have given him a chance to explain?'

Frankie lay quietly as her mother left the bedroom. *Why should I read it? It will only be excuse after excuse. He had plenty of chances to tell me. He chose not to, so why should I listen to him now?*

ADAM - 1940

'We need someone on the inside. You've not brought anything useful for quite some time.'

'It's not my fault! The Navy have stopped letting my men in. Whatever they need, they come to us now. I don't think they're suspicious, but it pays to be cautious sometimes. If I try to push for access to the base again, they might start to put things together.'

'What we need, is a good little girl.' Garrett's Irish lilt calmed the frayed tempers in the room. 'My grandson's a good-looking lad. Sure, it won't be too difficult for him to find a wee Jenny[1] to woo, there's plenty of 'em in town!'

His contact looked grave. 'That would keep them off your backs for a wee while, but you'd better start producing results soon, or there's other avenues they might pursue.'

John froze, his gaze fixed on his father, who shrugged nonchalantly.

The Irishman continued. 'Who knows, if they find something of interest to the pigs, they might set them sniffing down a particular path that wouldn't be good for you now.'

John's shoulders relaxed, just a fraction.

Adam laughed. 'Tell your bosses not to worry. I've got this covered. Charm's my secret weapon. I have one or two in mind who might fit the bill quite nicely. Just give me a few weeks. If charm doesn't work, maybe information will, so I'll ask a few questions.'

The acknowledgement was terse. 'We don't care how you get the information, what's important is that it's reliable. The big man gets twitchy if we go silent for too long. He has to send regular reports to his bosses and we all know what happens if you cross them. Europe's finding that out on a daily basis. You get busy and everyone stays happy. Know what I mean?'

Adam nodded. His grandfather smiled, the curved mouth thin but approving. By contrast, his father looked terrified. Adam would have liked to think John's concern was for his son, but knew better. He was determined never to give his grandfather the power to control him like that. Garrett Liversidge might think he was in charge of the family, but he was old and Adam was young and unlike his father, he wasn't weak. The time was coming when Garrett would have to acknowledge that his traditional place in the family hierarchy now belonged to his grandson. Adam's expression hardened as he looked at the other men in the room. They'd all know soon enough.

'*H*e married you?' Ellie was incredulous. 'How could he?'

'And the baby?' Hot tears sprang to Hannah's eyes and rolled down her cheeks.

'How did you cope with all that loss?' Hannah whispered. Memories and images flashed across her brain. The clinic. The pain afterwards. The searing hurt every time she saw a child of the same age. Frankie had lived with it so much longer. Did calm come with the passing of time? Hannah didn't think so. She felt Kate's arm go around her shoulder and for a moment allowed herself to draw comfort from her friend before remembering her pain was of her own making. She drew away.

'It must have been awful.'

'It was. They told me afterwards they'd tried to get her out quickly to give her a chance, but in trying to save us both, they caused so much damage I'd never be able to have more children.'

'I don't know what to say.' Ellie sat back in her chair. 'It certainly explains why my grandmother was the way she was. No wonder she didn't want to talk about him.'

'Don't judge him too harshly, dear. It was a very different time and we were all convinced we were going to die sooner rather than later. With seventy years to reflect on it, I'm not as angry as I once was.'

'How could you ever forgive him?' Hannah murmured.

'Forgiving him was the easy part. Forgiving myself took a bit longer.'

'How do you feel, Ellie?' Kate asked gently.

'I'm not sure. The feminist in me is angry, but I also just feel sad that he was so unhappy bigamy felt like his only option. I knew my grandmother was a difficult lady, but I had no idea she'd been so awful to him.'

Frankie smiled sadly. 'She'd had a lot to bear and it's not surprising she lost her way a little.'

'You're very understanding, considering.' Ellie said. 'I'm not sure I'd be as accepting.'

'It was all such a long time ago,' Frankie said. 'I wasn't this accepting when it all came to light, believe me. Much as I liked to pretend I didn't care what people thought of me, deep down I wasn't as brave as my mother and I couldn't bear the idea of people laughing at me, or worse, pitying me. You think everyone knows everyone's business round here now, back then it was much worse. For example, we all knew the nurse was having an affair with the doctor. Nobody said anything – not to their faces anyway – but everyone knew. His wife was an invalid and her husband was a bad-tempered man and they probably believed they were being ever so discreet, but the only people not in the know were their respective spouses. Everyone talked behind their backs and I didn't want it to happen to me. Part of the reason Addie was so keen to join the Land Army was to get away from all the 'well meaning' inquiries about why she'd broken up with Eric Warburton. Not that it mattered much in the end.' She shook her head sadly. 'He ended up getting arrested for dealing on the black market and he never quite recovered from the humiliation. Drank himself into an early grave and the farm went to his sister's boy. You remember Peter, Ellie.'

Ellie nodded. 'He was a nice man. He found Uncle Will's body.'

'He took after his mum, thankfully. She was always nicer than her brother.'

'How did you move on from it all?' Hannah asked. 'How did it not crush you?'

'For a time, I couldn't see a life beyond what I was going through, but I did eventually.' Frankie fixed her gaze on Hannah. 'We all do in the end. We have to. Otherwise, we crumble under the weight of the guilt and the pain. We have to learn to let go.'

'How?' Hannah's voice was barely above a whisper.

'I don't know about other people, but for me someone told me I was still needed, could still be useful.' Frankie's voice grew stronger as she spoke. 'He gave me a purpose, reminded me of the fierce, strong-minded girl I'd once been. It wasn't always the easiest route back, but I got there in the end. What I learnt was that if you want something badly enough, you have to be prepared to fight to get it. So, if you really want to keep this place open, you're going to have to use every trick you can think of to get the council to agree and it's going to take more than four of us to make it happen. We need to get everyone together and talk this through properly.'

'I'll put a post on our Facebook page,' Kate said. 'Let everyone in town know what's happening. That will give us an idea if people actually care or not.'

'I'll speak to Martin Giggleswick – he's still our local councillor, isn't he? See what he's got to say for himself,' Ellie said. 'And whatsisname, the MP fella.'

'Dean Johnson.'

'That's the one. I'll email him as well.'

'*I*'m glad you came, Frankie.' Ken's voice sounded terribly far away and Frankie peered at him, wondering when it had got dark. 'It's good to see you.'

Frankie hiccupped and tightened her grip on her glass. It was from Auntie Meredith and Uncle Lionel's wedding set and was one of the few to survive the bombing of their house.

She studied Ken's face, watching the expressions play across it in the light of the fire. Closing her eyes, she willed the room to stop swirling. She shouldn't have had the last gin. Ken was speaking but the words washed over her, lulling her into a sense of calm. Ken always had that effect on her, soothing away her worries and fears. Good old Ken. Lovely Ken. Opening her eyes, she saw him watching her. A tear leaked from the corner of her eye and he brushed it gently away with his thumb. Frankie leant into his touch and on a sudden impulse, leant forward and kissed him. He jerked back, his face alarmed, but she leant further and kissed him again.

'Frankie, stop.' He pushed her away.

'Why?' She hated that the question came out in such a whining tone. She wouldn't beg. 'You wanted me before.'

'It's different now.'

'Am I damaged goods now? Is that why you don't want me?' Anger rose in her and the challenge flew from her mouth.

'Don't be ridiculous. As if I'd care about that.'

'So you do think I'm damaged, but you'd have me anyway? How magnanimous of you!'

'That's not what I meant and you know it. Frankie you're drunk.'

'Not so drunk I don't know when I'm being insulted.'

'Oh for goodness' sake, I'm not insulting you!'

Frankie wobbled to her feet, her face white, apart from the two spots of colour high on her cheeks. 'Well at least I know where I stand with you,' she spat, tears blurring her vision. 'I'll take my soiled self home now, where I can't corrupt you any further.'

'Frankie –' Ken stretched out a pacifying hand towards her, but she swept past him, trying desperately to hang onto the final shreds of her dignity.

Only when she was curled up in her bed would she give in to the tears. What had she been thinking and what must Ken think of her? His rejection had made it clear he no longer cared for her in that way and try as she might, she couldn't blame anyone but herself. *Why do I even care?* She scowled. *I'm not in love with him so what does it matter?*

The next morning, Frankie came downstairs to find a note at the reception desk with her name on it.

DEAR FRANKIE,

I had to leave very early this morning, so I'm leaving this note by way of explanation for last night. You know I have always accepted and loved you just as you are and I do not know why you think this would have changed in recent times. My feelings and wishes have not altered in the last year – you are as dear to me as you have ever been, but first and foremost, you are my friend. I did not want to leave things between us as they were last night and while you may not like the explanation, I believe you need to hear it. I did not reject you for any reason other than you being drunk. Whatever Mac's sins may have been, you loved him and you are still mourning his loss. For me to have taken advantage of you would have been unforgiveable and had I done so, I have no doubt you would have hated me more this morning than you currently do. I may have hurt you, but please believe it was done with the best of intentions. Do write and let me know you understand.

Always yours,
Ken

FRANKIE REFOLDED the note and returned it to its envelope. Why did he always have the ability to do this to her? She was angry, rightfully angry, with him and in one short note he had swept away her sense of righteous indignation and left her feeling as though she was the lowest form of bug. Of course Ken would try to do what he saw as the right thing. He would have seen it as taking advantage of her inebriated state and she would absolutely have regretted it this morning. So why couldn't she write and tell him so? She knew his note would remain unanswered because to answer it would mean giving an explanation she was unequal to.

DECEMBER 1940

Frankie drifted through the next few weeks in a daze. She piloted the boat through the Creek as expertly as ever, but she no longer engaged in easy conversation with the men she was transporting. At the Lido, her observations and comments for improvement were as incisive as ever and the men under her care continued to improve but gone were the smiles of encouragement and the extra words of praise. Off-duty, she haunted The Mermaid's lounge, an unread book in her hand. Her parents tried to encourage her to go out – there was no lack of opportunity, the Navy put on regular dances and concerts for the Wrens and the men at the base. She wasn't interested.

'I never thought I'd see the day when you'd be afraid of your own shadow.'

Frankie turned away from the window to look at her father. 'I'm not afraid.'

'In that case you're an excellent actress. Perhaps you should consider a career on the stage when the war's over.' Laurence pulled up a chair beside the window seat and sat down. 'Your mother said to give you time, to let you do things at your own pace, but I can't do it, Frankie. I can't watch my girl shrivel away and not say something.'

Frankie gestured to the half-eaten sandwich beside her. 'I've eaten.'

'It's not enough and besides, I wasn't talking about physically – although it wouldn't hurt you to put a few pounds on. I was referring to your mental state. We've let you mope about the house long enough, it's time to face the world again. I know Mac hurt you badly, but you can't shut the world out forever. It might help if you read his letter.' He held a surrendering hand up as Frankie began to protest. 'I know, I know. I won't force you to read it, I'm only saying it might help if you did. But either way, you're not spending the rest of your life sitting in this room. Going to work doesn't count as going out. There's a concert this evening and you're going. No arguments. I won't even make you change out of your uniform if you don't want to, but you're going to that concert if I have to drag you there myself.'

Frankie nodded. 'Okay.'

She pushed her feet back into her slippers and left the room. It was easier to do as she was told. That didn't require her to think and she'd done far too much of that recently. The concert didn't hold any particular appeal, but if attending would make her father happy, then she would sit through it.

HALFWAY THROUGH THE evening she had changed her mind. What had she been thinking? When her father had said it was a concert, she'd assumed he meant classical music. She hadn't been expecting to hear songs which reminded her of Mac. Determined not to embarrass herself by crying, she slipped out of the room. Hidden from the street by the high wall that ran around the hall, she leant against the building breathing in the fresh air and trying to slow her heartbeat. "I'm Nobody's Baby" might have been popular with everyone else, but Frankie hated it almost as much as she hated Frank Sinatra wittering on about never smiling again. She knew how he felt, but she didn't feel the need to warble about it. She bit her lip. She would not cry.

Suddenly aware she was being watched, Frankie opened her eyes. Eric Warburton swayed in front of her. She sighed.

'What do you want, Eric?'

He grinned and she shivered. The wall which had offered shelter now threatened. She stood straighter.

'I was just wondering,' he slurred, 'If it's true what they say about girls in uniform.'

'What do they say?' Frankie didn't really need to ask. 'Up with the lark and to bed with a Wren' was as familiar to her as her own name.

'That you all make a good groundsheet.'

Frankie wrinkled her nose in disgust. 'And you wonder why Addie turned you down?' She turned to leave, but Eric grabbed her shoulder and flung her back against the side of the building.

'Where do you think you're going? I was talking to you. Your bloody sister. Stuck up cow. Thought she was too good for me.' He planted a wet kiss on Frankie's lips. 'I reckon maybe I went for the wrong sister. Maybe you're more like your mum.' He put a rough hand up her skirt.

Frankie slapped him with as much force as she could muster.

'Let go of me,' she hissed.

Eric grabbed her arm, pinning her to the wall again. 'That'll show your bloody sister. Me and you going together. She won't be so bloody high and mighty then, will she?'

Frankie twisted her head away as he tried to kiss her again.

'Eric, stop it. I'm not interested. God, you're pathetic.' She yanked her arm free and pushed him. He staggered backwards.

'Why?' The question came out as a whine. 'All three've you...' he trailed off incoherently. 'Happy to give it out elshwhere. But not here. Why? Not bad looking.'

'You're a drunk and an idiot. Go home.' His words suddenly registered and Frankie stared at him. 'All three of us? You tried it on with Mum?' She screwed her face up. 'What is wrong with you? Why would you do that?'

Eric sneered. 'Ask her. She wasn't above giving it out when she was younger if she got something out of it. Thought I'd offer her the same deal.' He shrugged. 'Issnot like I fancy her or anything. Was just b'sness.'

'You're disgusting.'

Suddenly he lunged at her. 'Don't you dare judge me, Frankie Thompson. You're as bad as your bloody sister.' His words slurred together then he crumpled to the floor.

'What did you do to him?'

Frankie started and looked up. Adam Liversidge stood in front of her.

'Nothing.' She rubbed her knee. 'He was drunk and he tried it on with me. I told him to get lost.' She stooped and peered into Eric's face. 'He's fine, he's just passed out. God knows why he was so drunk, it's a concert not a pub crawl.'

She took the hand Adam offered and stepped over the prostrate body. 'I better head home.'

'I'll walk you there. See nothing else happens – I think your evening has been eventful enough already.'

Frankie started to object, then broke off. She nodded. 'Thanks.'

Outside The Mermaid, Adam said goodbye, then leant in and kissed her cheek. 'It's nice to see you out again, Frankie. I'll see you around.'

. . .

FROM THE UPSTAIRS window of the hotel, Lily watched as Adam walked towards the town. Her brow was furrowed and her eyes stormy. The boy had kissed her daughter and Frankie had allowed it. She continued to watch as his figure grew smaller and eventually disappeared from view. This could not be allowed to happen. What was Frankie thinking?

AUGUST 2017

'*I*t's always the bloody same, round here. You lot couldn't give a monkey's about Avonstow. You're happy to take our Council Tax, but when it comes to providing the town with anything we might actually need, you're nowhere to be seen!' The meeting with the Council representative had been fraught from the beginning and the latest speaker, a florid man in a suit, was no exception. 'We've had to fight to keep the library open, we had to beg to have the public toilets upgraded and now this! Where do you propose people who can't drive go, if they don't want to swim in the sea? Cause we all know there's no bloody bus service to Clacton and not everyone wants to go on water slides!'

Martin Giggleswick raised his hands placatingly. 'I understand you're angry, Sir, but please believe I'm on your side. I will be speaking to the Council when I next meet with them and asking about how this town can best be provided for.'

The speaker glared at him, arms folded, face red. 'That's not quite the same as saying you'll fight the closure, is it?'

Martin Giggleswick had the grace to look abashed, but he turned his gaze elsewhere until he found someone who looked less belligerent. 'You, Madam, on the end of the row?'

Ellie stood up. 'Would the District Council be open to the idea of leasing the Lido to the Town Council or to an independent group of people prepared to take on the running of it?'

Martin opened his mouth and immediately closed it again. 'Erm…' he said eventually. 'I, er, don't know. The question could be asked, I suppose.'

Ellie nodded. 'This is what I propose then. We'll put together a proposal to present to both councils and see if we can find a way to move forward. I think it's fairly clear from the responses tonight that as a community we strongly object to the stripping away of yet another asset from our town. The council have nothing in place either to replace the facility or to ensure the site is not left to simply become an eyesore, so perhaps they might be open to examining other options – alternatives to closing. I think their contempt for this community is clear from the fact that neither other representatives from the council, nor our local MP, could be bothered to come to tonight's meeting, so maybe it's time we showed them we're not going to accept being written off and ignored.'

A visible lump moved in Martin's throat and he nodded desperately. 'Yes, perhaps that would be a sensible option.' He forced a smile. 'Remember my door is always open if I can be of any assistance.'

As he sat down with a thump and loosened his tie, Jack leant over Ellie to address Hugh. 'My little finger would be of more assistance than him. He has trouble distinguishing between his backside and his elbow.'

Hugh snorted as Ellie shushed them. 'I'm not saying you're wrong, just don't say it so loud. We might need his cooperation to get this idea off the ground. Let's get everyone together at the café and get this proposal done. The quicker we move the better our chances, I reckon.'

'Right. We all know why we're here, so let's hear any ideas you have.' Ellie looked around the table in the Lido cafe. Jack and Frankie flanked her. Hugh, Mark, Ken, Hannah, Clem, Kate and her husband Harry made up the rest of the working party.

'Won't the council have thought of everything decent already?' Hannah asked. 'I don't mean to put a downer on things, but the bottom line is that the numbers don't lie. It's a lovely part of the town, but people don't come. I mean, look at it today. It's gorgeous weather and yet there's almost no one here.'

The eyes of everyone around the table followed the direction of her finger as she pointed out of the window. A handful of people sat in deckchairs around the edge of the pool, soaking up the warm August rays, but no one was in the water. It lay still and silent, the deep blue of its painted floor reflecting the jabs of sunlight that darted off its surface. Paint peeled off the walls around the edge and rust pockmarked the greyed fencing. The only things which looked truly alive were the weeds growing along the edge of the pump room. It was as if everything was sleeping, waiting for the handsome prince to come and deliver the fairy-tale ending. Except it wasn't a story and there was no happy ending unless they could find one themselves.

'It has the potential to be so much better than this if the council would just spend some money on it, but if we don't have the cash, I don't see what we can do.' Ellie sighed.

'Well, we can't sit back and let them close it. We can't.' Jack thumped the table.

'I don't see how we can stop them if that's what they decide. They own it after all.' Mark laid a pacifying hand on his friend's arm. 'Jack, we all agree it's a shame, but what else can we do? You saw the figures Giggleswick had. It's been running at a loss for years. Let's face it, people don't want to come to an open-air pool anymore. It's too bloody cold for a start. When was the last time you came here?'

'I was here two days ago.' He bristled at Mark's words and Mark smiled gently.

'In the pool?'

Jack glared at him.

'You know perfectly well I don't like swimming.'

His wife raised her hand. 'I still go most days. I'm not so different to everyone else round here.'

Mark laughed. 'Ellie, you grew up in Australia. You're part fish and even you're blue some days by the time you're done. Face it, the Lido is on its way out.'

'And what will happen if it does close? The same things that happened in every other place that shut their Lidos, that's what. Blackpool was huge by comparison to us – their outdoor swimming pool was stunning – and what did their council do? Closed it and built that monstrosity on the promenade.'

'What monstrosity?' Hannah smiled at the description.

Jack pulled his phone out of his pocket and after a few seconds turned it round to show her the screen. 'The Sandcastle. I mean, I'm sure it's a lot of fun to go to but look at what it replaced.'

He tapped the screen and a series of images flashed up. Hannah could see what he meant. There was nothing wrong with the leisure centre as such: it wasn't a pretty building by any means, but it was functional. But when she saw what it had replaced, she understood Jack's anger. A semi-circular colonnade of elegant white stone embraced the oval pool and a huge glass dome marked the entrance. Bathers could hide in the cool shade or move to the opposite side of the water for the welcome warmth of the sun. *Not,* she thought, *that Blackpool has a lot of that.* Even so, if they could have found a way to heat the water, perhaps it could have survived. She wondered how many love stories had begun there and while she didn't approve of beauty pageants in general, she had to admit, the pictures from the 1960s of the young women lining the edge of the pool were pretty spectacular.

'You get it, don't you?' Jack said quietly, stretching out his hand to take the phone back. 'And it's all gone now. Barry Lido was the same, beautiful chalets, massively popular in its day and then left to go derelict before they pulled it down altogether. You know what it's like round here – if our Lido goes, the next thing you know they'll be building some godawful flats on there or there'll be kids breaking in and we'll end up with graffiti covered hoardings. What will that look like to tourists? What sort of impression will it give of the town? That we're in decline. That we're not worth visiting. What is the point of the council investing money in a new campsite if there's nothing to keep the campers' money in the town once they're here? We'll have a captive audience once that re-opens.' He nodded at Kate and Harry.

'But you have to admit that most people don't want to swim in freezing cold water.' Mark brought them back to the obvious point.

Jack slammed his hand on the table. 'Then we have to find a way to make them want to!'

Mark put a placatory hand on his arm. 'We all want to keep it open, mate, that's why we're here. We just need to work out how. We have to come up with something which means it doesn't necessarily matter if people use the place for swimming or not. The main thing is to make sure it's being used. I've talked to an acquaintance on the council and they're not going to change their minds unless something drastic happens and we get an influx of cash.'

'Might it be worth Hannah having a look at the accounts?' Clem asked. 'There might be somewhere that costs could be cut. It probably wouldn't amount to much, but it might help a bit?'

'That's a good idea,' Ellie said, 'Hannah, would you be prepared to do it?'

'I could give it a go, I suppose. I'm not sure they'll give us access to them though.'

'It would be worth asking though, surely?' Clem said. 'Didn't you say your next-door neighbour works there?'

'I don't know which department she's in, but I'll ask.'

'Good.' Ellie made a note on her pad. 'So. Hannah will investigate the accounts. Hugh will get us some press coverage about fighting the closure and Mark and Jack are going to liaise with the two councils on our behalf. The rest of us need to come up with some decent ideas about what this place could be used for apart from swimming. If we do get the go ahead, it's going to have to support itself – it can't run on goodwill alone.'

'Some of us don't have a lot else to do but think, if we put our heads together, I'm sure we'll be able to come up with something,' Ken said.

'Don't you be doing too much though,' Kate warned, reaching out and squeezing his hand. 'You need to look after yourself.'

'I'm being well taken care of, don't worry.' He tipped his head towards his family. 'This lot are a right bunch of nagging Nellies. It'll give me something to do when they're not bossing me about.'

Hannah felt tears prickle at the backs of her eyes. The

affection in Ken's eyes proved his complaints a lie and again she felt a stab of envy at the easy relationship they all shared. Clem bumped his shoulder against hers and winked at her when he got her attention. She smiled back at him, sitting straighter in her chair.

'We have to save it,' Frankie put in suddenly. 'We simply have to. This place is far too important to lose.' Ken folded his fingers around her shaking hand as she continued. 'It's a part of this town, a part of the community, of our shared history.'

'Do you mean because of being here in the war?' Hannah asked.

'Oh, not only that,' Frankie waved her other hand impatiently. 'It was built by the people of this town and it gave employment to scores of our men, my father included. So many jobs had gone and families were literally starving. Building this place meant more than money, it was about self-respect and doing something for the community. It's so much more than just a building. But yes, it's also about the war. How many of the men who learnt to swim here were saved because they'd had that training? And it wasn't all about the lessons.' She stopped abruptly, clamping a hand over her mouth.

'Is it to do with the death you mentioned?' Kate asked.

Frankie went pale and shook her head. 'Forget I said anything.'

'Frankie?' Hugh's voice was gentle. 'You know the war records are unclassified now, don't you?'

'I still can't talk about it.'

'Even if it would help to save the Lido?'

'We could turn it into a project,' Mark suggested. 'Collecting people's memories of the place. I'm sure we could cobble together enough stories and photos to make a display out of them. It might remind people it's here and encourage them to use it a bit more.'

'That's not a bad idea,' Hugh nodded approvingly. 'We could go into the local care homes. I'm sure there's plenty of people in them who grew up visiting it and I'm pretty sure the school used it for lessons at one point.'

'They did,' Ken confirmed. 'It wasn't built until after we'd learnt, but I remember seeing the kids walking back to school and their mums standing on the corner with hot chocolates to warm them up.'

'We could rebrand some of the menu,' Kate said. 'Use stories like that to come up with names for the stuff we sell. It wouldn't take much work to change a few names, but it would tie it all together nicely.'

'What do you think, Frankie? Would you be up for telling us about your war?'

Frankie shot a quick glance at her husband. Ken smiled and squeezed her hand. 'I think you should do it, love. You can't get into trouble if it's all public knowledge now.'

'I'm not sure all of it is. Certainly not round here. It might do more harm than good.'

'There's not many left who were there,' Ken said, shaking his head. 'Who's going to complain?'

'I don't want to hurt anyone,' Frankie said quietly.

'You mean me.'

'I don't want to drag it all up again.'

'Frances Ford, I told you when I asked you to marry me that I didn't care about your past. I didn't care then and I certainly don't care after seventy odd years of marriage. Tell the bloody story and get it off your chest.'

Frankie laid her head on his shoulder. 'I don't deserve you.'

'I was lucky you said yes, now get on with it woman!'

Frankie chuckled, but her eyes were still sad. 'There isn't

much to tell really. I just did a bit of passing information on to the right people.' She looked over at Ellie. 'I have your grandmother to thank actually. It was getting her letter which finally pushed me into getting on with my life.'

'My grandmother wrote to you? Why would she do that?'

'I don't know,' Frankie shrugged. 'Perhaps as she said, his death made her feel more magnanimous towards your grandfather. Maybe she felt guilty? Whatever the reason, it made me understand Mac a bit more.'

Ken muttered something under his breath then looked guilty. 'No offence, Ellie.'

Ellie smiled. 'None taken, especially as I didn't hear what you said.'

'Probably for the best,' Frankie said, fixing a glare on her husband. 'As I said, it made me understand the situation better and I was grateful to her. She was a woman who had clearly spent much of her life in pain. She didn't have to write to me, but she chose to do it anyway.'

'Possibly she felt she owed you,' Jack said. 'After all, she cost you the chance to marry Mac properly.'

'She had no idea he'd married me anyway,' Frankie said. 'And I didn't see the point in telling her. I simply wrote back and thanked her for the letter and wished her the best for her daughter. It wouldn't have changed anything and I didn't see the point of inflicting more pain on someone who had already suffered so much.'

'And what about the spying? How did that come about?' Harry asked. 'Sorry.' He held his hands up. 'But that's what people are really going to be interested in. It's not every day you find out you have a real-life spy in your community.'

Ellie laughed. 'You say that, but actually it was pretty common around here. After Frankie told us about it the other week, I went and did some research about this place during the Second World War.'

'Of course you did!' Her husband shook his head and grinned affectionately at her.

Were there spies in both wars then?' Hugh asked. "It really annoyed Gran that she never found out who the spy was in her war.'

Frankie glanced at him and then at Ken, her eyes clouded. 'That's a story for another day. I think we need to go home and rest.'

Ellie narrowed her eyes and Frankie looked away. 'Another day, Ellie. I promise.'

ADAM - 1940

'Well done, my lad. The knight in shining armour routine never fails, especially when the knight is a handsome one. Now's your chance to move in and secure your position.' Garrett clapped his grandson on the back.

Adam shook his head. 'Not yet. Don't rush me. I have an eye on the long game. If I try anything now, she'll be suspicious of me stepping in with Eric. Leave it a while and let her remember I acted purely because it was the right thing to do.'

'What if Warburton tells her you paid him to do it?'

'He won't. Not if he knows what's good for him. He's up to his ears in debt to me and he knows I'll call them in if he breathes a word about it. If he wants to inherit the farm, he'll keep his mouth shut. If old man Warburton finds out Eric's gambling again, he'll cut him off and give the farm to his daughter's son instead. Eric can't stand his sister, or Peter. We don't need to worry about him.'

'And you're not worried she might find someone else in the meantime? That boy she was always hanging around with? He was always keen on her, wasn't he?'

'Ken?' Adam scoffed. 'Not a chance. Especially not with him being away. Let me play this my way, it will be worth it in the end, I promise. By all accounts, she has the Admiral's ear and, if you believe the rumours, other parts of him as well.'

'Are you saying they're lovers?'

'More that he'd like them to be. There's talk among the Wrens that he singles her out, has her doing jobs above her rank. They think it's funny – he's old enough to be her father and he's acting like a lovesick schoolboy, desperately trying to get her to notice him.'

'Is she aware of his interest?'

Adam shrugged. 'She blushes when they tease her about it. I'm not worried though.' He grinned. 'I'm confident I'm a more attractive proposition than he is and it won't take much to reel her in, especially when she's so vulnerable. A bit of subtle flattery here and there, show a bit of kindness to the grieving widow and she'll be in my bed before she knows she's even been seduced.'

'Be careful your confidence isn't misplaced. Women can be devious creatures.'

Adam laughed. 'Not this one. Frankie and Addie are open books. If the Thompson girls don't like you, you're not in any doubt about it! Trust me, I know what I'm doing. She'll be putty in my hands soon enough, I guarantee it.'

Garrett raised his whiskey glass. 'I'll drink to that, she's a fine-looking lass alright. It won't be a hardship for you, will it now?'

Adam sniggered. 'I've had worse.'

JANUARY 1941

*F*rankie closed her eyes and sighed as she pulled the last of the reports from the typewriter. The Admiral's usual secretary was ill and he had asked Frankie to spend the day standing in for her. She had taken dictation all morning, then typed the letters and reports up.

'Just put them in the top drawer of my desk, please,' he said, when she re-entered the room with a sheaf of paper in her hand.

Frankie pulled the drawer open, but the sight of a gun made her gasp and she snatched her hand away from it.

'It's not loaded,' Admiral Ashton said, replacing the file he'd been looking at and sliding the cabinet drawer closed. 'The bullets are in a separate box. I'll only need it if the base is invaded and that's looking less and less likely now. Just leave the reports on top of it and I'll sign them all later.'

Frankie did as he asked, then waited to be given her next job.

'Sit down a moment.' He waited while she took a seat. 'How are you?'

The question took Frankie off guard and for a moment she didn't answer, collecting her thoughts.

'I'm okay.' She attempted a smile. 'Just getting on with life, same as everyone does.'

'How are you really?'

'I'm fine.' She didn't know what else to say. Her voice sounded dull, but she couldn't inject more life into it. Nothing roused any emotion in her anymore. She knew her encounter with Eric should have upset her, but beyond a feeling of minor irritation that he had insulted her mother and sister, she couldn't bring herself to care. She knew the emotions she should experience but felt nothing.

The Admiral dismissed her to take the launch out and collect the men coming off duty and she left the office as quietly as she had entered it. However, when she returned to her room that afternoon to collect a clean handkerchief, she saw Mac's letter was again propped up on her lamp. A flash of anger surged through her and she flung the letter into a drawer, slamming it shut. The emotion fizzled out as swiftly as it had appeared and she sank to the bed. This wasn't how her life was meant to be. People kept telling her how strong she was being but she wasn't. They didn't know. Couldn't see.

Her thoughts drifted as she stared at the drawer. She couldn't do this anymore. Couldn't keep up the pretence. Leaving the room, she made her way down the corridor to the Navy's wing of the hotel and let herself into Admiral Ashton's office. Opening the top drawer of his desk, she pulled out the gun and found the box of bullets. Then, unsure what to do, she sat in his chair, swivelling it to face the window and put her feet on the sill, the gun cradled in her hands.

She had no idea how long she sat there, staring unseeing out of the window. When the overhead light turned on, she jumped and the gun clattered to the floor. The Admiral stooped and picked it up.

'I wondered if you might come back for this,' he said quietly.

Frankie didn't respond. She knew she should salute and apologise for being in his office, but really, what was he going to do to her? She didn't care if he punished her and he knew it. He pushed her feet to one side and took a seat on the windowsill.

'You know,' he said casually, 'If you're going to shoot yourself, I'd much prefer you didn't do it in my office. It would take weeks to get the blood out of the carpet. Besides, I think I have a better proposal for you. How would you like to do something that could actually help to win the war?'

Frankie sat up. 'What do you mean?'

'There's a job I need a Wren to do. It's not a nice one and it's not particularly moral, but it would be for a good cause.'

'And you figure I have nothing to lose anyway.'

The Admiral shrugged. 'I'm not the one sitting in someone else's office playing about with a gun.'

Frankie smiled briefly. 'What did you have in mind?'

Admiral Ashton leant back against the window. 'Do you remember I told you I'd had a conversation with my predecessor?'

Frankie nodded and the Admiral leant forwards.

'He had quite a story to tell.'

An hour later, back in her room, Frankie had Mac's letter in her hands. The Admiral's proposal had taken her by surprise, but it held a certain attraction. The old Frankie would have agreed immediately, but the last few months had taught her she couldn't take anything for granted, even her own judgement. Consequently, she'd asked for a few days to consider her answer. The Admiral 'knew people who knew people' and had assured her the request for her help had come from the highest offices in London – straight from the desk of Tar Robertson, in fact. Not that she'd known who he was until the Admiral explained. Now she did, she was flattered but scared. It would mean watching every word, every action and giving away nothing she didn't intend to. *Am I really capable of that?* she wondered. *The Admiral obviously thinks I am.* But the Admiral didn't know her secret shame. Didn't know she didn't even have the courage to read Mac's last letter. Anger flared and she tossed the letter onto the floor. Why did she feel ashamed? She'd done nothing wrong. She wasn't the one keeping secrets. *If you accept this job, you will be.* She silenced the voice in her head. That was different. Her mother would understand eventually. Frankie would make sure of it. She looked down at the letter. It stared back, accusingly. Leaning forward, she picked it up and slid her finger beneath the flap and pulled the paper out. She began to unfold it, then threw it onto the bed and sprang to her feet. Pacing the room, her fingers knotting and unknotting themselves, she stared at the folded pages, her heart pounding. *Breathe, Frankie. Breathe.* She snatched the letter up and unfolded it, tears blurring the familiar handwriting as she smoothed out the creases.

MY DARLING FRANKIE,

If you are reading this, then I am gone somewhere your wrath cannot reach me, but while it is not entirely undeserved, I hope you will read this and find it in yourself to forgive me, even if it is just a little. Perhaps forgiveness is too much to hope for, so instead, I will ask merely for your understanding. You must believe it was never my intention to hurt you and my feelings for you were absolutely as I told you they were. I love you beyond measure, Frances Thompson and in my heart, if not in law, you are my wife. By now, you will have been told I have a wife and daughter in Australia.

With that exception, everything I told you about my life is true. I met Dot when I was modelling for my sister's life drawing class. She offered me a large sum of money to model privately for her and I couldn't turn it down. Would that I had! I was naïve and stupid and did not realise she had a different motive to the one she expressed. I allowed myself to be seduced - I was young, I lacked confidence and I couldn't believe this woman wanted me. None of this excuses my behaviour, I'm only trying to give you an insight into my mind at the time.

When she told me she was pregnant, I was appalled. I felt I had no choice but to propose, though I felt nothing for her beyond a certain physical attraction. I hoped that in time, my feelings would develop and I did my best to be a loving and loyal husband to her. The fact she refused my initial proposal should perhaps have given me an indication of her feelings, but at the time I put it down to natural modesty, or perhaps a desire not to impose further upon me. Nevertheless, as time went on, it became clear, even to me, that Dot did not wish me to be the kind of husband I aspired to be. I was removed to the spare bedroom and treated more as a houseguest than a partner.

When I joined up, I believed time and space might allow us to come to an understanding but I was disabused of this notion on the eve of my departure, when Dot informed me that, should I survive, she would prefer it if I returned to my parents' home instead of ours. She had Margaret, our daughter, and that was all she required from life. Having provided her, I was not required to perform any further function. I was angry. Margaret is my daughter and although I did not want to be a father at first, once she was born, I would have done anything for her. We argued. Dot refused to listen. Margaret was all she had wanted and she did not intend to share her more than she absolutely had to. With the help of my sister (who can be just as stubborn when the mood takes her) I secured an agreement that I would have access to Margaret on my return and I set off for England, feeling I had won a small victory.

I know now, that warning you I was bad news was the worst thing I could have said to you. My darling girl, you are hideously headstrong and although I love you for it, my only hope is that Ken will always be there to extract you from whatever mess you inevitably find yourself in.

By the time I returned to duty after my sick leave, it was too late and I was in love with you. I never intended to propose, but the happiness I felt when you accepted convinced me I could somehow make this mess work. I sent a letter to Dot, telling her I intended to marry you and informing her of my intention to seek a divorce. In reply, she sent a telegram refusing to countenance it. A letter followed, informing me that should I pursue the matter, she would re-consider my access to Margaret on the grounds that I was an unfit father. I was so incensed by the unfairness of the whole thing, I decided I would simply marry you and be damned. There was nothing to prevent me staying in England after the war and I believe my parents and sister would have understood my actions once I explained what had prompted them. If Dot was going to Margaret from me anyway, then it would be easier to bear at a distance and this way, I would have you by my side. I had hoped that, in time, Dot might be brought around and be more reasonable. In that case, I fully intended to marry you again after the war, to make our union legal. Stupidly, I gave no thought to the possibility of you having a baby in the meantime. When you told me you were pregnant, I was delighted, but horrified because it complicated everything further. Nevertheless, I would have loved being a proper father to our child and I dreamt of you and our baby, all the way back to base that day.

I have no idea how I met/will meet my end but know this: I cannot bring myself to regret marrying you, however wrong it was in the eyes of the law. I love you and I believe that had I lived, I would have spent the rest of my life trying to make you as happy as you have made me. For so long, I felt as though I were simply moving through life, living none of it and these last months with you have made me more content than I believed possible. My darling girl, you are the source of every moment of happiness I have experienced in this country and for that, I thank you. I hope, given time, you will believe that I love you and that I am truly sorry for lying to you and your family. I have asked Ken to deliver this to you, but please believe he knows nothing of the contents. I have presented myself throughout as a single man and he knows nothing of my life in Australia. I am sorry for deceiving him. He is a good man and like you, deserved better from me. Who knows, perhaps one day you and he will come together. Strangely, I find some comfort in the idea he may be the man to raise my child with you. If that happens, our child will be the luckiest of creatures.

It's almost time for me to go on duty, so I must bring my letter to a close. I will leave you with this final offering. I wish I had met you first. I wish my life had been different. But wishes mean nothing and life is what it is. I will be forever grateful I met you and loved you and if my life is to end behind the controls of my 'plane, then my final thoughts will be of you and our baby. Tell him or her that their father loved them and their mother very much indeed. I know you will need every ounce of your bravery and spirit in the months to come and I am so sorry to be the cause of it all, but I did love you. I DO love you. Now go and live your life the way it should have been, had I not interrupted it. Become the woman I see in you and remember how very much loved you have been.

All my love, always,
Mac

FRANKIE SAT until the light drained from the sky outside, Mac's words chasing each other through her mind. When she had finished reading the letter, she had laid it down next to her, still feeling nothing. It was much later, when she got up automatically to close the curtains and put the blackout up, that a howl rose within her and she grabbed the nearest object from her dressing table, hurling it at the wall. An ornament followed the hairbrush: its porcelain features split and scattered themselves across the rug.

Moments later, Lily threw open the door and wrapped strong, comforting arms around her. Soothing, non-descript noises surrounded Frankie as her mother gently rocked her and stroked her back. Finally, she tucked her beneath the blankets and picked the letter up, replacing it in the envelope and returning the whole thing to the drawer of the bedside table. She smoothed the hair away from Frankie's face.

'Rest now, my darling. It's time to let him go.'

Frankie put a hand above the covers and closed it around her mother's. 'I'd like you to read the letter,' she whispered. 'It's not right, but I understand now. I want you and Dad to know.'

Lily nodded. Taking the letter from the drawer, she bent and kissed Frankie's forehead.

'Sleep.'

As Frankie drifted into oblivion, she heard the bedroom door click quietly, then there was nothing until her alarm the next morning. When she woke, it was as though the weight pressing her down had been lifted. Nothing had materially changed, but she had other things to think about now. Things that didn't involve berating herself for being a fool. She wasn't the idiot she had believed herself to be. She hadn't missed the signs because there had been none to miss. No one else had suspected Mac was anything more than he claimed to be and this brought her some comfort. Her judgment hadn't been to blame. Drawing her legs to her chest, she laid her cheek on her knees. She was going to say yes to the Admiral, but first she had to work out what she was going to say to her mother. Lily couldn't be told the truth, or at least not much of it, but Frankie couldn't bring herself to cause unnecessary pain to her parents either. She'd already put them through so much. *No*, she thought. *That's not negotiable. If the Admiral wants my help on this, he's going to have to let me give Mum some kind of explanation. And what will Ken think?* Frankie had resumed writing to him, omitting any mention of the ill-fated night she'd kissed him. There was nothing in his letters to indicate he had made any assumptions about the state of her feelings towards him, but it was inevitable he would have questions if he saw her with either the Admiral or Adam. She sighed. Life was going to get complicated, but at least it might make her feel something. Any emotion was better than the numbness that had engulfed her.

ADAM - 1941

'Here's your sugar. I hope that husband of yours appreciates his cake. When does his leave start?'

Elspeth tucked the packet into her shopping basket. 'Next Tuesday. I want him to have a bit of something nice while he's home.'

'Feeling guilty, are we?'

She gave a start. 'What do you mean?'

'Oh nothing, nothing. Just that your life's a bit different to his, that's all.'

'Well, it's the same for everyone, isn't it? He deserves a bit of home comfort after he's been off fighting.'

'Oh, indeed he does. Nothing comes for free these days, does it? Even freedom itself. There's always a price to pay.'

'I almost forgot, didn't I?' The woman dug in her purse and fished out a few coins. She handed them to him.

He took them from her. 'It's not enough. I want more.'

Elspeth flushed. 'I don't have any more.'

'That's alright. It's not money I'm after.' His fingers snaked out to caress the bright auburn hair.

Her blush deepened. 'Not again, Mr Liversidge, I'm a married woman.'

'Doesn't seem to bother your doctor friend. I was surprised when I heard what the pair of you have been getting up to. I thought you liked being wined and dined. Never imagined bombed out buildings were your thing. Still, it takes all sorts I suppose and it does make discovery less likely, doesn't it?'

All the colour drained from her face.

'Don't look so worried,' Adam laughed. 'I've moved on. All I want is some information and then your secret's safe with me. For now.'

He leant forward and whispered in her ear. Elspeth drew back, shocked.

'Patient information is confidential! Anything from when I was attending Mrs Macmillan is private.'

'So there is something.' Adam shrugged. 'Your choice. You can give me one tiny piece of information and live with your conscience. Or, if it's too much to ask, you can keep quiet and hope your husband never finds out what you've been getting up to while he's been out fighting for King and Country.'

Elspeth swallowed hard, tears of shame pricking at her eyes. Leaning forward, she whispered in his ear then hurried away, her heels clicking on the pavement as the tears flowed.

AUGUST 2017

*H*annah breathed in the steam rising from the mug clamped in her hands and allowed it to soothe her. She'd been unsettled ever since the meeting in the café the previous evening. She'd only agreed to stay behind after the café closed to make drinks for everyone, but somehow had found herself drawn into taking part in the meeting itself. The Lido meant nothing to her beyond her pay cheque at the end of the month; she wasn't even local so couldn't claim any kind of emotional attachment to it. *So why did you agree to stay?* She couldn't answer the question.

Kate had called her over and she'd sat down without even thinking about it. She hadn't expected to be asked to do anything beyond make drinks and so the request to look at the accounts had taken her by surprise, not giving her the opportunity to think of an excuse to avoid it. Of course, it wasn't the accounts themselves – she had no problem looking at those – it was the possibility that they might bring her into contact with Richard which worried her. *Look what happened when he came into the cafe. How stupid would you look having a panic attack in the middle of the council offices?* It wasn't just the public humiliation she feared, it was the idea of him knowing how much what had happened still affected her. He wouldn't care – if he had any feelings at all, he would never have pursued her in the first place – but she didn't want to reveal such a weakness to him. In his arrogance, he might think it was because she still harboured feelings for him. Which she didn't. Not romantic ones anyway.

But if I don't do it, who will? None of the others understood how accounts worked and it was important someone had a look at the books if they were going to understand the scale of what they were proposing to take on. *Come on, Hannah. Big girl pants on. You can do this. You don't even have to go into the council. You've only got to ask Sharon if they're available.*

She still didn't understand why she felt compelled to do it. And then it dawned on her. These people were her friends and they were counting on her. She couldn't let them down. Not when they'd been so kind to her. For someone who didn't regard themselves as friend material, she had suddenly found herself surrounded by people who cared about her. Clem had looked after her when she had the panic attack without asking questions, Kate was constantly inviting her to socialise, Frankie had shared her own story when she sensed Hannah was unhappy and even Ellie, whom she barely knew, had drawn her into their family circle. They were important to her. Richard had already taken so much from her: she wasn't going to allow him to take these friends away as well.

Putting her mug down on a coaster, Hannah slipped out of her side door and down the alleyway to Sharon's. She knocked sharply three times.

'Hello, Hannah love. What's up?' Sharon beamed at her and Hannah responded with a tentative smile of her own.

'Hi. I wonder if you could possibly help me with something?'

'Of course, come on in and I'll pop the kettle on.'

Sharon bustled ahead of her through the house, leaving Hannah to close the door and follow her into the kitchen.

'Make yourself comfortable, love. Milk? Sugar?'

'Just milk please.'

'What is it you need?'

'You mentioned you worked at the council and I wondered if you knew anyone in the accounts department?'

'Whatever for?'

'I'd like to have a look at the accounts for the Lido if I can. Do you happen to know if they're available to the public?'

Sharon was quiet for a moment, busying herself with adding milk to the mugs and putting the teabags in the bin. She handed Hannah's across the kitchen island.

'Is this all part of the grand plan to keep it open?'

Hannah nodded. 'They're keen to do it, but like with any business, they need to know what they're letting themselves in for. They asked if I'd have a look for them and see if there's any reason beyond "not enough people are coming swimming" why it's not making any money.'

Sharon looked thoughtful. 'Well, I don't know if they're public record or not, but I reckon I can get hold of them for you. I'm owed a few favours in that department and the guy who's in charge of the Lido accounts isn't popular, which always makes going behind their backs a bit easier. He's a bit handsy, if you know what I mean.'

'Richard Temple?'

'You know him?' Sharon coloured. 'I'm sorry, I didn't mean –'

Hannah cut her off. 'Don't apologise. I know exactly what he's like.'

'Can I assume then that you'd rather keep your name out of it?'

Hannah nodded, only daring to look at Sharon when the

silence grew too long. To her relief, there was no judgement, only understanding. Sharon smiled.

'Leave it with me. Hopefully you'll find something that'll embarrass him as well as saving the Lido.'

The two women laughed and clinked their mugs together in a toast.

'I'm behind you lot 100 per cent,' Sharon told her, draining the last of her tea. 'I grew up in Croydon and they closed our Lido back in the seventies. It's a bloody garden centre now. A garden centre! I ask you. What on earth were they thinking? No forward thinking, that's what's wrong with people today. If it doesn't make a quick buck, let's get rid of it. Idiots. You keep fighting, love and me and the girls'll do what we can to help. If you want placards and picket lines, you let us know.'

Hannah smothered a giggle at the thought of her sixty-year-old neighbour chained to the Lido gates. 'Won't it get you into trouble at work? I mean, with you working for the council.'

Sharon snorted. 'I'd like to see them try to tell me what I can and can't do on my days off. I'm in housing anyway. Different department. I'll be out there with the Lido Ladies.'

'The Lido Ladies?'

'Oh, that's right, you don't often work Sundays, do you? There's a group of us always come on a Sunday. We never arranged it, it just sort of worked out like that. Anyway, we took to all finishing our swim at the same time and then setting the world to rights over a bacon sarnie and a mug of tea. Highlight of my week. Couple of them, I reckon it must be the only time they speak to someone, unless they've done a bit of shopping. They live on their own – no family close by, so it's something to look forward to.'

'I suppose it's like the library, isn't it? Somewhere people can go if they've got no one around and they can guarantee there'll be someone there to talk to.'

'It's always been about the community. You know the story of how it got built, don't you?'

Hannah nodded.

'And during the war it played its part as well. I've a friend who's part of the U3A and they've been looking into the history of it. During the war there were swimming lessons and concerts and all sorts going on there. Mind you,' she looked thoughtful. 'She also said there was a death there during the war, but maybe best not to use that fact to advertise the place, eh?' Sharon laughed, but Hannah was thoughtful. Frankie had mentioned a death and then claimed she'd got confused.

Frankie was right about one thing though, Hannah mused, as she said goodbye to Sharon and unlocked her own side door. The Lido was about more than swimming and the bricks and mortar. That was the message they had to get across to the council and to everyone else, for that matter. Make them see beyond the money and whether or not they liked swimming and get them to recognise the service the Lido provided for the community as a whole.

FEBRUARY 1941

'*H*ello, Frankie.'

Frankie turned at the sound of her name and smiled as Adam fell into step beside her.

'How are you?' He hesitated. 'After Eric, I mean.'

Frankie shrugged. 'I'm alright. He's been avoiding me. Not that I'm complaining, I'm not frightfully keen to speak to him and it is quite funny to watch him dive into the nearest shop when he sees me coming.'

Adam laughed and for a brief moment, rested a hand on her arm. 'I imagine he's worried you're going to hit him again. I wouldn't want to get on the wrong side of you.'

Frankie resisted the urge to brush his hand away and scrub at the spot where he'd touched her. *How could I ever have thought he was charming?* She made herself relax.

'It would serve him right if I told everyone what he tried to do. He won't do it again though. Not if he's got any sense. I might be a widow, but there are still people looking out for me. I'm not unprotected.'

'Your dad doesn't strike me as someone who's handy with his fists.'

Frankie made her expression become dreamy. 'Dad would do anything to protect me, but it wasn't him I was thinking of.'

Adam took her arm with a smile. 'I'm flattered you –'

'Admiral Ashton has been very kind,' Frankie interrupted. 'And I'm very grateful to him.'

Adam fell silent. Frankie slid her eyes sideways, trying to gauge his reaction.

'I see,' he said eventually. His shoulders slumped. 'I know your mother would... but I had hoped...' He trailed off.

Frankie tucked her arm through his and patted his hand sympathetically. 'Why don't you walk me home?'

'What will your mother say? I don't want to get you into trouble.'

'Mum likes the idea of me being taken care of after...' Her voice wobbled on his name and she took a deep breath. 'But I don't know. I suppose I feel... well, the Admiral and Dad get on well, being a similar age, but I want adventure.' She laughed. It was carefree and wild. *Reign it back Frankie. Too much. Just be the person you were.* 'I'm ready to move on now and I want more from life. I want someone who can offer me excitement. I want nice things, I'm tired of rations and make do and mend and while I loved Mac, it made me realise I'm not cut out to be a good little wife.'

Adam released her arm and slid a hand around her waist, tugging her towards him. 'You have no idea how pleased I am to hear that,' he murmured, his breath tickling her ear. 'I think you're exactly what I've been looking for.'

Frankie allowed her body to melt against his for a moment, before feigning modesty and moving away.

'What do we do about your mother though? I wouldn't put it past her to lock you in your room if she got it into her head you were sneaking out to see me.'

'Leave Mum to me.' Frankie gave him a conspiratorial

wink before she tucked her arm into his and they continued walking.

At The Mermaid, Lily was weeding the small vegetable patch when they arrived. Her face darkened when she saw them and her expression became wary as she watched her daughter approach. Frankie gave her an almost imperceptible nod, watching as her mother straightened up and squared her shoulders.

'He's not welcome here.' Lily spoke abruptly, her voice harsh.

'Mum!'

'I said, he's not welcome. Come inside. The Admiral's been asking for you.'

Frankie rolled her eyes. 'Again? It's my day off.' She turned to Adam and grimaced. 'Honestly, I think that man forgets there are other Wrens in Avonstow. I spend more time in his office than I do anywhere else at the moment. There's always something he wants.'

She winked at him. Adam spoke, his voice carrying across to the hotel garden. 'Is he bothering you?'

Frankie glanced at her mother. 'Not really. He's very kind to me. Mum says… well, she thinks it's too good an opportunity to pass up.'

'He's also old enough to be your father.' Adam lowered his voice, looking disgusted.

Frankie sighed but didn't reply.

'Frankie!' Lily shouted again. 'I won't tell you again.' She glared at Adam. 'Leave my daughter alone. She's had enough to cope with, without you sniffing around her.'

'I don't want to cause trouble, Mrs Thompson.' Adam turned to Frankie and whispered, 'I'll go, but if you need anything, leave a message with my dad when you come for the swimming lessons. Anything at all, you just let me know and I'll be there.'

'I will. Thank you.' Frankie crossed to her mother and watched until Adam rounded the corner, then put an arm around Lily's shoulder. 'Well done, Mum.'

Lily laid her head against her daughter's. 'Let's hope it works. I'm going to miss you.'

ASHTON TO HENLEY:
  Undine baited. Awaiting further instruction.

HENLEY TO ASHTON:
  Proceed with caution. Establish line of communication and test strength.

ASHTON TO HENLEY:
  Huldbrand engaged. Fisherman moving into position.

A FEW DAYS LATER, Frankie and Admiral Ashton sat in the corner of the snug in The White Hart public house in Thorrington.

'Are you sure this is where he'll be?'

Admiral Ashton nodded. 'He always comes here for his private business meetings. I hope you're not too uncomfortable.'

'It does feel odd, but I'll have to get used to it if we're going to make it convincing.' Frankie let out a sudden peal of laughter and rested her hand on the Admiral's arm.

He frowned, but she raised an eyebrow and immediately

he captured her hand in his own, leaning across the table to stroke her cheek gently.

'Hello, Frankie. Admiral.'

She raised her face to the figure beside her. 'Hello, Adam.'

'Are you well?'

Frankie blushed. 'Yes, thank you. Just enjoying an evening out. You know Admiral Ashton, don't you?'

'Of course.' Adam nodded towards the older man, who acknowledged him with a return nod.

'Can I get either of you a drink?'

'We've got one thanks.' Frankie gestured to her port and lemon and the pint sitting opposite it. 'Another time, perhaps?'

'Of course. I'll leave to you enjoy your evening.' Adam gave a slight bow then turned and returned to his table on the opposite side of the room.

Frankie slid her arm out and rested her hand on the Admiral's sleeve. 'Is he still watching?'

'He is.'

'How long do you think we should stay?'

'I believe finishing our drinks and then leaving would be the most sensible course of action. No need to over-egg the pudding. Not at this stage.'

Frankie affected to look away, as though embarrassed. Through her lowered lashes she could see Adam across the room. He was clearly observing the couple and she suppressed a smirk of satisfaction, before looking back at the Admiral and returning her hand to his arm. He patted the seat next to him and she slid around the table to sit next to him.

Her every movement was exaggerated: the head thrown back in girlish laughter, the coy expressions and the flirtatious touches of his uniform. The Admiral made no move to stop her behaviour and gave every sign of responding to her interest. It was mortifying.

When she had drained the last of her drink, they stood and the Admiral helped her put her coat on. He pulled the collar up for her and untucked her hair from inside it, then placed his hand on the small of her back and guided her towards the door. As he opened it for her, Frankie turned and caught Adam's eye. The moment she did so, his expression transformed from an attitude of stern observation to a gentle smile. As the door closed behind them, Admiral Ashton turned to her.

'Well, that was an education.'

Frankie hung her head. 'I'm sorry, Sir, but you said it needed to be convincing. That's how Adam is used to girls behaving around him.'

He put a finger under her chin and made her look at him. 'You did brilliantly. I'm certain he was convinced of my interest in you. Well done.'

'Thank you, Sir.'

He opened the car door for her and once inside, he was as business-like as ever. 'I meant to tell you earlier, but they've finally settled on your codename. You're to be known as Undine.'

Frankie looked blankly at him. 'What does that even mean?'

'It doesn't mean anything. It's a name.'

'Never heard of it.'

'Neither had I. Apparently she was a mermaid who drowned her unfaithful husband with her tears.'

'Charming. Isn't that a bit obvious though?'

'Tar likes to play with language. He's confident the connection won't be made.'

Frankie shrugged. If the top brass had approved it, there wasn't much she could do except hope everyone else was as ignorant of the fairy tale as she had been. Back in Avonstow, he parked the car and they walked back to the hotel in near silence. At the foot of the stairs, the Admiral paused.

'Well done, Thompson. Very well done indeed. I think our line is well and truly baited. Let's see what his next move is.'

'Thank you, Sir. Goodnight.'

'WELL DONE, boys. Go and get changed now.' Frankie pushed herself away from the wall of the Lido where she'd been leaning. The sailors hauled themselves out of the pool, shivering their way to the changing rooms and she followed slowly behind them, noting that Adam was in his father's office. He came out to meet her.

'How are things at home?'

Frankie shrugged. 'I'm moving out.'

'What on earth happened?'

'Walter… Admiral Ashton, that is, is concerned about the propriety of us living under the same roof when he's expressed an interest in me. It's bad enough he's an officer, but we could get around that one way or another. If I'm not there, it would make things easier for everyone. Mum is all in favour of it, of course. She thinks it shows he's serious about me, but I think it's a lot of fuss over nothing and I wish she'd stop pushing me towards him. She doesn't seem to understand I'm in no hurry to find another husband. And if I were, I might make different choices to her.' She heaved an exaggerated sigh. 'I wrote to Addie and told her Mum had gone off at the deep end about you walking me home. She said not to worry too much about it, things usually had a way of working themselves out. I thought about what she'd said and I realised if I'm not at home,

Mum can't keep track of my comings and goings or on who I'm seeing.'

Adam raised an eyebrow and she laughed. 'Yes, I know. Avonstow is so small you can't sneeze without someone on the other side of town asking if you're feeling a bit under the weather, but the gossips have to rest at some point.' She gave him a shy smile. 'So, if you wanted to come and say hello one afternoon, that would be perfectly respectable and you wouldn't have Mum glaring at you the whole time.'

Adam trailed a hand down her arm. 'That sounds like it would be very neighbourly and I may just take you up on the offer. Would the Admiral not mind? I wouldn't want to get in his way.'

Frankie grinned. 'What he doesn't know won't hurt him, will it? Anyway, I've made him no promises. I think Mum sometimes forgets I'm a widow, not a little girl anymore. I don't have to put up with being bossed around. Or at least,' she laughed, 'Only by His Majesty's Navy. And only by them when I'm at work!'

'I'm very pleased to hear it,' Adam said. 'And I look forward to helping you explore this new-found freedom.'

'Just keep it quiet for now. I have to keep the Admiral sweet – he could make life difficult for us if he suspects anything.'

'Of course,' Adam smiled. 'I understand. You don't want to risk your position with him.'

'Exactly. Not only that, but he doesn't want the Admiralty to know about us either. That's why we were in The White Hart the other night. He thought that outside of Avonstow we'd be less likely to run into anyone who knew us. He wasn't best pleased to see you but I managed to convince him you wouldn't say anything if I kept you sweet.' She laughed. 'It gives me the perfect excuse if he happens to see us together. I told him you'd been after me for years and if I agreed to a few dates, you'd be more likely to keep quiet about me and him.'

'Clever girl,' Adam nodded approvingly.

Frankie jerked her head towards the office, where John stood watching them.

'Can your dad be trusted not to say anything? And how does he feel about you seeing me? I always got the impression he disliked Mum as much as she does him.'

Adam put a hand on her shoulder, his thumb stroking her collar bone through her cotton shirt. 'Don't worry about Dad. I'm glad you've realised I'm not as bad as your mum seems to think.'

'Well, we all have to grow up sometime, don't we? Start being independent, thinking for ourselves.'

Adam traced a finger along her jawline. 'We do indeed. I like this new Frankie. She sounds like my kind of girl.'

Frankie blushed and looked away as the first of the sailors emerged from the changing rooms. She took a step away from Adam.

'I'll see you soon,' she said, then followed the men to the exit.

AUGUST 2017

'So, your friend said yes?'

'She's not my friend, she's my next-door...' Hannah didn't finish the sentence. Sitting in Sharon's kitchen drinking tea and chatting with her had felt like the beginnings of a friendship. She smiled to herself. 'She was happy to help. Apparently, she's here every Sunday.'

'Oh, is she one of the Lido Ladies?' Kate grinned. 'They're a brilliant group. They come every week, rain or shine and they're always cheerful. I love it when they come through the door – it's utter chaos every time. No one can ever remember what they've ordered, half the time I'm convinced they eat the wrong food, but they don't seem to mind.'

'That sounds like them,' Hannah laughed. 'Sharon said they were a proper mixed bunch.'

'I'll tell you what though, they look out for each other.' Kate became serious. 'If any of them don't turn up and they've not let someone know, one of them goes round on the way home to check they're okay. One time, one of the younger ones turned up with a black eye and a few of them went home with her and kicked the boyfriend out.'

186

'Didn't he just come back when they'd gone?' Hannah's eyes were wide.

'Nah. By the time they'd finished with him I reckon he was too scared. He wasn't a local – if he had been, they'd have been round to see his mum first.'

Hannah frowned. Surely she wasn't serious? Kate laughed at her dubious expression.

'I'm not joking. We used to live by the Legion and one night there was a couple of blokes having a row outside. Obviously, I was listening through the door – who doesn't, right? Eventually, one bloke says to the other, "I've had enough of this. You're pissed and you're being a twat. I'm telling your mum." Five minutes later, the other bloke's mum turns up, gives him a bollocking and marches him home.' By the time she'd finished the anecdote, Kate was almost choking on her laughter.

'That's the sort of thing I can imagine Frankie doing,' Hannah chuckled.

'Absolutely. I'll bet she was a real firecracker when she was younger. I wouldn't want to cross her, even at the age she is now!'

'Me neither. I wish I had half her confidence.' Hannah picked the empty crockery up and took it to stack in the dishwasher.

'You could always practise being confident by asking Clem if he fancies a drink after work?'

'Did I hear someone taking my name in vain?' Clem appeared in the doorway of the kitchen.

'Only me.' Kate grinned at Hannah. 'Hannah was suggesting a drink after work and I said you'd probably need one too after a day defending yourself from flirtatious teenagers.'

'That sounds like a great idea. They're worse than ever today. Where do you suggest? The Station? Maybe not, actually. The same teenagers will all probably be in there.' Clem took a long drink from the bottle of water.

'How about The Ferry?' Kate suggested. 'It's the other side of town so they're less likely to be in there.'

'Good thinking. The Ferryboat Inn it is. We can walk down after we close up.'

'What are you doing?' Hannah hissed, as the door out to the Lido swung shut behind Clem.

'Giving you a nudge in the right direction.'

'I told you I wasn't interested in a relationship.'

'I want you to be happy and I know you and Clem would work if you'd give it a chance.'

'You know next to nothing about me.'

'I know I like you. Whatever it is you're afraid of, I'll bet it's nowhere near as big a deal as you think. Go this afternoon and just relax. You never know, you might even enjoy yourself!'

'This was a brilliant idea.' Clem stretched his feet out and lay back against the plush fabric. His half-drunk pint sat on the table next to the remnants of Hannah's gin and tonic. 'We should do it more often. It's a shame Kate couldn't come though.'

Hannah blushed. *Say something.*

'I'll have to get home to Monty soon. He'll be needing a walk.'

'I noticed he wasn't in his usual spot today. Is he okay?'

Hannah grimaced. 'He's in disgrace. He sneaked into the kitchen last week and jumped up at the counter. Kate wasn't happy about having to make the breakfasts again, so I thought it best to leave him at home for a few days.'

Clem threw his head back with a shout of laughter. 'Did he at least enjoy them?'

Hannah nodded. 'Little so and so looked delighted with himself. Anyway, I need to get home to let him out and take him for his walk.'

'Sorry, you should have said and I wouldn't have kept you so long.'

Marvellous. Well done, Hannah. Now he thinks you don't want to be here.

'It's fine. I didn't mean...' She grabbed her drink and swallowed a large mouthful.

Clem tilted his head. 'Would you and Monty like some company on your walk? I haven't seen him for ages.'

'Oh. Yes. I mean... That would be lovely, thank you. He'd love to see you too.'

Cursing her inability to string a coherent sentence together, Hannah took another mouthful of her drink.

'Maybe next time we could go somewhere that allows dogs and then Monty could come with us?'

Hannah stared at him. *Is he...Does he think this is a date?* She forced a smile and nodded.

'If you'd rather not, it's okay to say so. I'm used to rejection.' Clem laughed gently at the stricken look on her face.

'I'm sorry. I just... I mean...'

'Relax, Hannah. I'm only asking if you'd like to do this again. No strings. No hidden agendas. Just a drink. It's what friends do.'

'Friends?'

'That's what we are, aren't we?'

Hannah nodded, her face aflame. 'I'm not very good at this.'

'I'd noticed,' Clem said drily, giving her a lopsided grin. 'Look, I'll level with you. I know Kate wants something to happen between us, but I also know that for whatever reason, you're not interested and that's okay. I'm not either. I like you as a friend, but I'm not looking for anything more.'

Hannah laughed, relaxing a little. 'Is Kate always so…'

'Forceful? Bossy? Interfering?'

'I was going to go with "determined".'

Clem nodded. 'Always. She means well though. She's adamant she wants to see me settled. But it has to be with someone she approves of. I'm only hoping I get a say too!'

Hannah smiled. It was obvious he was extremely fond of his sister-in-law and wasn't being wholly serious.

'Put it this way,' Clem continued. 'I'm glad she's on my side. She never liked Emmy and Emmy was terrified of her. It made family get togethers interesting.'

Hannah laughed. 'I bet it did! I can imagine her being like Frankie when she's older.'

'Oh absolutely.'

They fell silent for a moment, then Clem turned to face her. 'You know, Hannah, whatever it is you're holding back, you can trust me with it. You probably think it's something really shocking, but the things we build up in our heads are rarely as awful to everyone else as they seem to us. When I found out Emmy was having an affair, I was mortified. I thought it reflected on me somehow: if I'd been a better husband she wouldn't have done it. It was Kate who pointed out I'd done everything Emmy wanted me to and it still hadn't been enough.'

'What do you mean?'

'The port and the docks used to be owned by a man called Simon Liversidge but he sold it all and left Avonstow when I was 12. My mum went with him. They'd been having an affair and Dad knew nothing about it, so he was completely blindsided.'

Hannah put her hand over his. 'Clem, I'm so sorry. That must have been awful.'

'Harry and I have had no contact with her since she left. I was so angry with her I didn't want to see her. She wrote a few times, but I burnt the letters without reading them. I went a bit off the rails for a few years. Ended up leaving school with very few GCSEs and went into an apprenticeship. I bounced around for a few years doing all sorts of different things, picked up loads of skills, but nothing you'd call academic and then I met Emmy. We were in the same pub one night and we got chatting. I asked her out and when we started to get serious, she started suggesting things I could do to "better myself".'

'Like what?'

'A-levels at night school to begin with. Then it moved onto me doing a degree through the Open University.' Clem pulled a face. 'Don't get me wrong, none of it was bad advice and I think in the beginning at least, it was meant well. The problem was, I didn't really know what I wanted to do and so I let Emmy push me into what she thought I should be doing.'

'And what was that?'

'She got me an interview for a Project Manager job up in the City. I was good at it, but I was miserable. She kept pushing me to go for promotions and it meant I was earning decent money, but it still wasn't enough for her.'

'What happened?' Hannah bit her lip. 'I mean, you don't have to tell me if you don't want. Kate told me the basics.'

A short, humourless laugh burst from Clem's lips. 'I'll bet she did.' He shook his head. 'Long story short, Emmy decided a solicitor had better prospects than a Project Manager and had an affair with her boss. He wasn't married and she reckoned if she divorced me, they could conquer the world of business law together. I finished a job early and came home thinking I'd surprise her with dinner when she got home from work. Instead, I found them in bed together. I packed my things, moved out that night and haven't been back since. She knew how messed up I'd been when my mum left but instead of being honest and telling me she didn't love me anymore, she went behind my back. I couldn't forgive her for that. I quit my job the next day, worked out my notice and went freelance. I was struggling a bit, to be honest, so when I saw the council were looking for lifeguards and were offering to train people, I figured it would be an opportunity to do something really different for a few months. It doesn't pay a huge amount, but it's enough to live on while I figure out what I want to do with my life.'

'Sounds like me,' Hannah said. 'Not the getting divorced bit, the not being sure what to do with your life.' She sighed. 'That's what Kate can't seem to understand. Until I figure out what I want to do, I'm not interested in trying to fit anyone else into my life.'

'Not even a friend?' Clem's eyebrow lifted a fraction.

Hannah laughed. 'Perhaps a friend. I'm not sure I'm a very good one of those, but people keep trying to convince me otherwise.'

Clem nodded, his face becoming serious. 'I think you undervalue yourself. How many times have you listened to Frankie talking about her past recently? And today you've listened to me rabbit on about my rubbish love life. I think you're a better friend than you give yourself credit for. And maybe,' he tilted his head to one side and pursed his lips, 'Maybe now you know what a hopeless case I am, one day you might trust me with your story?'

Hannah paled and didn't reply for a moment. 'Maybe. One day,' she whispered eventually.

Clem took her hand, gave it a quick squeeze and let go. 'Only when you're ready. Now,' he said, his tone becoming brisker. 'What about that walk you promised?'

Hannah downed the rest of her drink and jumped to her feet. 'Poor Monty! He'll be crossing his legs by now!' Thrusting her hands into the sleeves of her cardigan, she followed Clem out of the pub and they headed up the road to her house. *Hopefully he's not been in Destructadog mode today.* She grimaced, remembering the last time she'd had to leave him at home alone for the day. Sharon had a day off and had promised to pop in at lunchtime to let him out, but Hannah knew even that wouldn't guarantee Monty's good behaviour.

'Hello, love.' Sharon beamed at Hannah as they met at the end of their shared alleyway. 'I was just on my way out. He's been as good as gold, by the sounds of it. I popped in and let him out for a wee at lunchtime, like we said, but I've not heard a peep out of him all day. I reckon he's been asleep for most of it.'

'Thanks, Sharon.' Hannah smiled gratefully at her, but Sharon's eyes had moved to Clem and there was a gleam in them that Hannah didn't like.

'Clem! Lovely to see you. You had all the girls flocking round again today?'

Clem blushed.

'I knew you would have.' Sharon turned back to Hannah. 'Poor bloke never gets any respite, does he?' She chuckled. 'Proper terrors some of that lot. Mind you,' she sniggered. 'Some of the older ones are no better, are they? How many times you been propositioned this week?'

Clem flushed an even deeper shade of red and mumbled something incoherent.

Taking pity on him, Sharon turned her attention back to Hannah. 'About that other business.' She cleared her throat and Hannah smiled.

'It's okay, Clem knows all about it.'

'Righto. Well, I reckon I should have the goods by the end of next week. My friend reckoned it might take her a few days to put it all together, but as soon as she does, I'll pass it on.'

'Oh brilliant. Tell her I said thank you, will you?'

Sharon nodded. 'Will do.' She paused, then clapped a hand to her head. 'Blimey, I've got a brain like a sieve at the moment. I meant to say the other day and then I went and forgot. If you're looking for something to raise some money, what about a Band Night? I sing in one and we're always pretty popular if I do say so myself. I reckon there's a few other local groups who'd do a good gig for you if you asked them to. Get a couple of 'em booked in and Bob's your uncle. Instant money-maker. I'd best be off anyway. Let me know if you want me to have a word with the boys and I'll see you on Sunday, Clem.' With that she walked off down the road, her shopping bag swinging jauntily alongside her.

'It's not a bad idea at all, is it?' Hannah fitted her key into the lock. Wasn't it Frankie who suggested that the other day? It sounds like it could be a good night and if we can rustle up something different in the kitchen, we could serve food and drinks from there. Do we have an alcohol license?'

Clem shrugged. 'You'd have to check with Kate. I wouldn't have thought so: there's not really a lot of call for booze in the café normally, is there? No reason she couldn't get one though.'

MARCH 1941

*F*rankie wrapped her arms around her knees, reluctant to leave the warmth of her bed. She'd worked late the previous day, but it wasn't only weariness that kept her under the covers. Adam was pressing her to move things along in their relationship and she didn't know how she felt about it.

For months she had pushed thoughts of Mac aside. They had never truly been married, she owed him nothing, and yet... And then there was Ken. He'd been nothing but supportive yet she hadn't written to him for weeks. How could she? The only thing she wanted to talk to him about was the one thing she couldn't mention and when he inevitably found out, he'd be hurt all over again because she hadn't told him herself. Everything was a mess. It wasn't even as though she'd been able to find out anything useful or pass on any proper information. She was still being told to be patient and allow things to take their natural course. Their natural course. It was this which had brought her to her current state of anxiety.

Last night, Adam had taken her to The Royal. The cinema was showing a re-run of 'Broadway Melody of 1940' which she had seen with Mac the previous year. Then, she had listened to 'I've Got My Eyes On You' and felt the warm glow of being loved, this time, the reference to spying had sent a chill down her spine. The entire plot centred around one deception or another and by the end she was shaking uncontrollably. She hadn't even realised she was crying until Adam had wiped the tears away. She'd dismissed his concerns by explaining it had reminded her of Mac but assured him she was feeling quite well. On the way home, he'd taken advantage of the blackout to stop and kiss her as they'd taken a shortcut through the alleyway that led to her lodgings. Actually, she corrected herself, he'd done far more than kiss her. The experience had left a bad taste in her mouth. She didn't feel guilty – she was doing it for a good cause – but it felt sordid. Cheap.

When she'd arrived home, it had been to find a letter had been slipped under her bedroom door with a note from her landlady, explaining that her father had called round to deliver it. The postmark was Australian, the paper thin and threatening. She had assumed Mac's claim of telling his family about her had been a lie, so why would anyone in Australia be writing to her? She put the envelope on her bedside table and went to sleep. In the morning, curiosity got the better of her and she opened it cautiously, sliding out the closely written lines. When she saw who it was from, she was half tempted to throw it into the fire. What could she possibly have to say? And did Frankie really want to hear it? *Be the woman you're pretending to be. What harm can she do you now?* With shaking hands and uncertain breath, she unfolded the letter.

. . .

Dear Miss Thompson,

I find myself strangely compelled to write to you and explain my recent actions. I cannot explain this compulsion, for I feel no guilt and would do the same again, yet I cannot settle until I have put pen to paper.

I do not know whether or not Alasdair told you he was married, but I was aware of your existence, even if you were not aware of mine. I have not had the happiest of lives and it has left me with a somewhat jaded view of the world. I lost my brother in the first war and on receiving Alasdair's possessions, I discovered a photograph of him at the plaque bearing my brother's name. That he had thought of me, even after I had behaved so appallingly, moved me more than you can imagine and it brought back something my brother once said about it costing nothing to be kind. I'm not sure this letter will cost me nothing – I have had to do a lot of pride swallowing in the writing of it – but I know it is the right thing to do. I only hope it reaches you, as I only have your name and the town you live in. I remember my brother telling me how small it was though, so I am hopeful it will be enough.

To the point then. Alasdair loved you enough to want to marry you. As I have already said, I cannot bring myself to regret saying no to the divorce – were he still alive, I would still be refusing to countenance it. However, as he is gone, there can be no harm in telling you of his wishes. I am a selfish creature, life has made me such and I make no apology for it. I do however hope this letter may explain why Mac could not commit himself to you. He did love you. He did not love me. Perhaps there is some comfort to be found in that for us both.

He was a good man who deserved more than I could give him. A part of me is glad he experienced love in the end. It is a pain which must be endured if we are to be surrender ourselves to 'the one'. There is something to be said for a life of love, but I am not sure it is one I would wish to experience again. The pain is too great a burden when one is not free to share it.

. . .

Yours,
Dorothy Macmillan

FRANKIE REMAINED STILL, staring at the letter long after she had finished reading it. It was an odd missive, in parts almost asking for forgiveness, in parts dismissive of the feelings of anyone save its author. Mac's sudden change of heart about the wedding and much of what he had written in his own letter of explanation now made sense. If he had loved her as much as he claimed to (and surely Dot's letter was proof of that) then he must have been devastated to learn he would never be free to marry her openly. It didn't excuse what he had done, Frankie still maintained he should have told her the truth and allowed her to decide, but she now understood he had feared losing her altogether and the bigamous marriage he hoped no one would ever discover must have seemed the perfect solution. Was what she was doing any better? Offering herself to Adam was a deception for the right reasons, but did that make it acceptable? She was too much involved now to withdraw from the plan, she must simply learn to make peace with her part in it. She was doing what was needed, fighting her own private battle on behalf of her country. Her own feelings were unimportant. Others in her position would undoubtedly be required to compromise much more than their peace of mind and ultimately, if it helped end the war sooner, did peace of mind really matter all that much? Others had already sacrificed much more and she owed it to them to do everything she could to continue the fight on their behalf.

She lay back and closed her eyes for a moment, allowing

memories of Mac to resurface from where she'd kept them locked away. Tears pricked at her eyelids and she allowed them to fall, dripping from her cheeks to the pillows beneath. At least there could be no consequences. Things could be worse.

The first walk resulted in shared fish and chips and Hannah was so relieved Clem was happy to talk to the people who stopped to admire Monty, that she tentatively suggested he might like to come out with them more often.

'I don't know how you do it,' she said. 'I get so overwhelmed when they want to chat. I never know what to say to them.'

'You manage alright at the café, don't you? Just pretend you're at work.'

'It's different,' Hannah said. 'When I've got my uniform on, I can pretend I'm someone else. Without it I'm just me and I'm really not that interesting to talk to.'

'So, I should take pity on you and subject myself to your conversation more often, if only to make sure you don't bore half the town to death?' Clem laughed, but stopped when Hannah didn't join in. 'Hannah, you know I'm only joking? I don't find you remotely boring and I'd love to come for more walks with you and Monty.'

Hannah forced herself to smile and pretend she'd known

he was joking. *Truth can be hidden in a joke though, can't it? You know that better than most.* 'Of course. You'll be a local hero if you do. I warn you though, if you start wearing your pants over the top of your jeans, I'm not walking with you.'

Clem grinned. 'Damn. I was looking forward to setting a new fashion trend. Fancy fish and chips again tonight? My treat.'

Hannah smiled. 'Go on then.'

'At least Monty will be more enthusiastic about sharing my company.'

Hannah rolled her eyes. 'You gave him chips last time. Of course he will be.'

As she finished mopping the floor, Clem sat with his feet propped up on a chair.

'I thought we'd wander down to The Hard,' Hannah said, wringing the mop out into the bucket. 'I've walked past what used to be The Mermaid so many times since I moved here and never really looked at it properly. Knowing Frankie used to live there has made me really curious about it.'

'Fine.' Clem's eyes were closed. 'On the way we can call in at the campsite. Harry asked me to drop some paperwork off to him.'

'They're starting to get the work done on it now, aren't they? Kate's been filling me in on the horror story that is the shower block – her words, not mine!'

Clem groaned. 'She bending your ear about it as well? Every time I see her she tells me about a new plan she has for the place. How Harry hasn't killed her by now is beyond me and goodness only knows how he manages to reign her enthusiasm in. I'm surprised she's not pulled the whole thing down singlehandedly yet.'

Hannah laughed. 'She's excited, that's all. It's a new project and she knows what she wants it to look like in the end.'

She put the mop back in the corner of the kitchen, turned the lights off and grabbed her jacket. 'Come on Monty. Walkies!'

Monty rose from beneath the counter, sniffing around the doormat as Clem opened the door and shooed him out into the late afternoon sun.

'Come on boy. This way today.' Hannah locked the door, then rounded the corner of the building and set off back towards the town centre, Monty trotting along happily at her side. Clem strode next to her, his shadow stretching out ahead of him, dwarfing hers.

When they arrived at the campsite, Harry was in the office, his desk piled high with papers. An older man sat on the other side of the desk, a tool bag at his feet.

'It's another job off your list,' he said, as Clem and Hannah walked in.

'Hi Harry. Dad.' Clem waved a hand towards Hannah. 'This is Hannah and Monty. Hannah, you know Harry and this is our dad.'

'Call me Fred.' He wiped his hand down the leg of his overalls before offering it to Hannah, who shook it warmly.

'Pleased to meet you,' she said quietly, trying not to make it too obvious she was attempting to hide herself behind Clem.

Harry smiled a greeting, but his attention was on the paper in his hand. 'Thanks, Dad, but there's so many more still to go. It feels like it's never ending.'

'You'll get there in the end, son. The toilets are sorted and I'll make a start on those showers tomorrow.'

'Ah, the infamous showers.' Clem laughed. 'Kate will be pleased to see them go, won't she?'

Harry's face cracked into a smile. 'Don't get her started about that again! I thought she was going to explode when she saw them.'

'Are they really that bad?' Hannah wondered how bad they had to be to have wound her usually cool-headed boss to boiling point.

'I've never seen anything like it! They're disgusting, but it's typical of the kind of people who usually own these places,' Fred said, 'They're not remotely interested in doing a good job or making it a pleasant stay for people. All they can see is the opportunity to make a quick profit and it all goes straight into their pockets rather than on paying the staff a decent wage so they do their jobs properly. Any caretaker worth their salt would have kept on top of all that and it should never have been allowed to get into such a state. There's no excuse for shoddy management, but when the government does a half-arsed job, how can you expect the country to be any different?'

Clem groaned and rolled his eyes. 'Stop ranting, Dad. It's only a shower block!'

'But that's just it, isn't it? It's all symptomatic of the mess we're in as a country. The government in their infinite wisdom decides everyone needs to get a university education. Well, that's all well and good, but if we end up with a nation of worthless degree holders, but we've no-one to fix the toilets, what kind of mess are we going to be in? You need the common man to do all the crap no one wants to do, but everyone needs. I can't write an essay, but I've yet to meet a plumbing problem I can't solve or a machine I can't get working again. But that lot in Westminster don't see any value in that. Probably cause the plebs like me wouldn't vote for them if they were the only party going.'

Harry burst out laughing. 'Don't worry, Hannah. Dad's a dyed in the wool Labour man and he can turn anything into a debate on politics if he chooses to. You'll soon realise it's all bluster though.'

'Don't talk nonsense,' his father laughed, resuming his

seat. 'You'll scare the poor girl. And besides,' he continued. 'It's not bluster. It makes me genuinely cross. You two were named for good solid leaders and that lot make me ashamed to be British sometimes.'

'Leaders?' Hannah murmured to Clem.

'Harold Wilson and Clement Attlee. Labour Prime Ministers.'

Hannah tried not to giggle. 'Really?'

Clem nodded. 'Him and Mum had talked about names but when we were born, he took himself off to the registry office and put our names down rather than the ones Mum had chosen.'

'He's that passionate about it?'

Clem rolled his eyes and tilted his head towards Fred, who was still ranting at his eldest son. Harry's eyes had glazed over, but as soon as his father took a breath, he jumped into the gap in the conversation.

'Clem, did you bring those forms?'

Clem handed over the folder he'd been carrying. 'Here you go. Signed, sealed and delivered. All boxes ticked and awaiting approval from the council.' He glanced down at Monty, who was sat at Hannah's feet. 'We'd better get going anyway, or this mutt will start causing mayhem.'

'You taking him for a walk?'

'Yes, Dad. Maybe you should do the same, burn off some of that rage against the machine.'

'Don't start quoting songs at me Clement Denton. I'm fine, thank you very much.'

Clem laughed and after saying goodbye to his family, he and Hannah resumed their walk, a fact for which Monty was particularly grateful, if the speed at which he set off was anything to go by.

For a little while, they walked in silence, then Hannah spoke slowly.

'How did your mum react to your dad putting different names down on your birth certificates?'

'By all accounts, not well. I don't think she ever properly forgave him for it. She certainly brought it up enough and although she always made it sound like a joke, I don't think it was one she ever found particularly funny.'

'She didn't share your dad's passion for politics then?'

'Not in the least. According to Dad, she was Tory through and through. He says it made sense when she ran off with Simon Liversidge because he was always campaigning for the Tory candidate. He reckoned they fell in love over poli- tics. I think it's the only excuse that makes sense to him, but I don't think it's true. I think it's simply that she didn't want to be with Dad anymore. Simon offered her a way out and she took it.'

'Hang on. Simon Liversidge?' Hannah frowned. 'I've just made the connection. Liversidge, as in Adam Liversidge? The one Frankie's been telling us about?'

'Simon was Adam's son. Well, still is, I assume. Like I told you the other day, I haven't seen Mum since the day she left.' He laughed, but it was a short, humourless sound. 'Dad always maintained there was something dodgy about the family. Harry and I just put it down to the fact they were all Tory voters but Dad reckoned his parents thought the family were strange too – apparently they always got a bit twitchy when people started talking about the war and when there were events for things like the 50th anniversary of D-Day and VE Day, they were really reluctant to join in. It was notice- able enough for it to be commented on.'

'I don't like speculation.' Hannah shuddered. 'People always take it as the gospel truth and there's rarely much truth in gossip.'

Their conversation had brought them to the building Hannah had wanted to walk to. The hotel formerly known as The Mermaid, had, for years, been an apartment building. The exterior had been kept much as it had always been, but the interior had been divided up into several smaller properties some time in the late 1960s when Lily and Laurence Thompson had retired. Frankie was teaching and Adelaide had her own career plans, which didn't include running a hotel and so they had sold the building to a developer.

'Looks like there's a flat for sale.' Hannah pointed at a For Sale board leaning against the fence that ran around the property. 'Oh wait,' she squinted at the small print. 'It's not a flat, it's the whole building. The landlord must be selling the freehold.' She closed her eyes for a moment, then opened them to find Clem laughing at her. 'What?'

'I just wondered what you were doing.' His eyes crinkled at the corners.

'I was trying to picture what it must have been like being here during the war. The town's so different now to what it once was.' She gestured to the flats behind her. 'I mean, the marina development is beautiful, but it doesn't lend itself to picturing this as docks, does it?'

'I suppose it's the same anywhere these days. Everywhere changes so quickly and even though I've lived here all my life I sometimes forget what it was like when I was a kid. For example, did you know that where the traffic island is up on the High Street, there used to be an underground public toilet?'

'I bet it made for a lovely smell when people were doing their shopping!'

'That's why they closed them in the end. They were so disgusting it was more economical to cover them over than to try and repair them. The docks went the same way. They weren't getting the trade anymore but I suppose we should be grateful we've at least got a half-decent development on it.

It would have been much worse if they'd just left it dilapidated and empty.'

'That's why we have to save the Lido,' Hannah said firmly. 'Otherwise, who knows what we'll end up with.' She turned back to the former hotel and sighed. 'I'd love to have seen what it was like inside before it was divided up. Frankie's told us so much about the war I can almost picture her here. Would the boat have been based here as well?'

Clem took her arm and turned her around to face the creek. 'See where the boats are moored up at the far end? That's where the launch would have set off from.' He gestured to the left. 'The Naval base was down that way and the bigger ships would have been down there.' He pointed the other way. 'They'd have gone out at high tide and out into the river and then to the sea. The patrols went from Harwich down almost to Southend.'

'I know we joke about Frankie being formidable, but she was only 17 when the war started. I'm far older and I can't imagine being out there under fire, or sitting here talking to you and watching planes fly overhead, never totally sure if they were friendly or if they were going to drop bombs on my home. I always associated that kind of thing with London and places like Dover, not a sleepy little town halfway up an estuary.'

'I know what you mean. Looking at it on a day like this, you can't imagine it, can you?'

'She was so brave. Especially when you think how young she was. I don't think I could have held all those secrets in.'

'Oh, I don't know,' Clem mused. 'You don't give much away about yourself.'

'What do you mean?' Prickles of panic raced up Hannah's spine.

'Whenever the conversation is focused on you, you say something to deflect it, to ask someone else a question.'

R.E. LOTEN

Hannah blushed. 'There's nothing to tell. I've lived a very boring life.'

Clem pulled her arm through his. 'I don't believe that for a second. What's your deep dark secret, Hannah?'

He laughed, but Hannah pulled her hand away. 'Why would you assume it's a dark secret? Maybe I'm just a private person and don't appreciate people sticking their nose into my business.'

She tugged Monty's lead and stomped away from him, angry with him for being nosy, but angrier with herself for letting her guard down. For a short blissful time, she'd imagined they were friends, that maybe her efforts to save the Lido counted for something and she might be allowed to be happy, but yet again it had been snatched away from her. She was cross that she had allowed herself to believe it might be different. She should have known better. People with her history didn't deserve to be happy. Why was she even trying to fight the inevitable?

FEBRUARY 1943

'*H*ow was your day today?' Adam's breath was hot on Frankie's neck as he unbuttoned her uniform.

'Routine. Yours?'

'Boring. Lots of paperwork. I could run that place blindfolded if they'd let me.'

'Mmhmm.' Frankie pulled his face to hers. 'Of course you could.'

'I just need them to give me a chance to show what I'm capable of.' He sat up, his face drawn into a scowl.

Frankie sat up and slid a hand under his shirt. 'My landlady's out for the afternoon, I'm off duty and all you can do is sulk about work?' She gave him a slow smile and slid her hand under his belt. 'Is there anything I can do to take your mind off it?'

Adam leant over and laid her back on the bed. 'Tell me about how amazing your day has been.' He kissed her neck again and she arched her back to meet his exploring hand. 'What's happening in the world of the Navy?'

Frankie groaned. 'I spent part of the afternoon learning Greek.'

Adam's fingers stilled for a moment. 'Greek?'

Frankie sought his lips. 'Yes. We had a delivery this morning. Don't stop.' She pressed herself against him. 'I think it was a mistake though. Boxes and boxes of Greek phrase books. Oh yes, that's good. God knows what they're for. The Admiral told me to parcel them back up and return them to London. Mmm, that's it. I had a look through them before I did it.' She fell silent until he'd finished.

Later, when they had re-dressed and she had restored her uniform and hair to a more respectable appearance, she lay with her head on his lap.

'Did it work?' She grinned at his puzzled expression. 'Did I take your mind off work?'

'Very effectively.' There was a long pause and then he continued. 'Do you often get random deliveries? It's much more exciting than the bills and design schematics that land on my desk.'

Frankie considered for a moment. 'Not often. It's usually far more mundane things like letters from home and requisition orders from the ships. Occasionally we get orders from the Admiralty telling us some of our ships are being relocated, but none of it's particularly interesting. We sometimes get muddled instructions though, which can be quite entertaining. We had one the other day requesting a whole fleet's worth of summer uniforms.' She laughed. 'We spent ages trying to work out why the *Heliope*'s crew needed tropical wear when they only go as far as the North Sea and it's still freezing. Turned out it was for the *Hermione* and someone had muddled the ships' names. God knows where they're off to, but it's obviously much warmer than here!' She shook her head. 'Men aren't natural organisers, are they? That's why they need us Wrens. There wouldn't be half so many mistakes if they put us in charge of stores.'

'That's why we find you so very useful,' Adam murmured, bending to kiss her. A moment later, he straightened up. 'I'm sorry, darling, but I have to go.'

'Must you?'

'I'm afraid so. Some of us still have work to do.'

'It's probably for the best. No doubt Mrs Dobbs will be back soon anyway.'

She followed him down the stairs and watched him leave, waving at him from the door. Then, she went back inside and picked up the telephone.

When the call was answered, she simply said, 'Undine cast the spell.' Then she replaced the handset and went to run herself a bath.

ADAM - 1943

'Tell me again what she said.' The Irishman spoke calmly, but his hands twitched, his fingers drumming on the table.

'They got a garbled order for tropical uniforms which should have been requested for the *Hermione*. They were also sent a box full of Greek phrase books.'

'Is there any possibility she was feeding you information?'

Adam laughed. 'Not a chance. The state I had her in, she'd have told me anything I asked. She thought I was stressed because of work and it was mindless chattering to entertain me. She was purring beautifully the whole time. A useful and entertaining afternoon. It's so easy to get things out of her, I almost feel guilty. She might think she's worldly-wise, but she's still the same naïve kid she's always been. Trust me, I have her exactly where I want her.'

He laughed again and this time the others laughed with him.

'Well make sure you keep it that way,' the man said. 'If this proves to be accurate, it will give us the credit we need and convince Uncle Fritz to send us what we've asked for.'

. . .

YOU DID WELL, MY BOY,' Garrett said, as they returned home. 'Keep working on the girl and keep her sweet, but don't get attached. There may come a time when you need to be more persuasive to get the information we need.'

Adam turned to his grandfather, a frown on his face.

'You mean to ask her directly for it? Wouldn't it be risky?'

Garrett's smile was grim. 'Only if you have nothing on her. Find something you can use against her if you need to. If there's nothing obvious, talk to your father about her mother. He could tell you a thing or two about her, things the family wouldn't want made public knowledge.' He considered for a moment before continuing. 'I'd rather not take that risk if we can avoid it: Lily Thompson has secrets of her own to spill and it could backfire if she finds out you've threatened her daughter, but as a last resort...'

'We won't need it.' Adam was confident. 'You know I like to be prepared. I knew eventually we'd need something over her and I already know exactly what she doesn't want the Admiral to find out.' He smiled. 'She'll do exactly what I ask, don't worry.'

AUGUST 2017

a bunch of flowers appeared around the opening into the kitchen and a throat was cleared. Hannah turned round. Leaning back from the grill, she saw Clem looking sheepishly at her.

'Peace offering?'

'What for?' Hannah asked cautiously.

'Being an arse the other day. I was trying to be humorous, but it obviously didn't come off that way and I upset you.'

'I overreacted. I'm sorry too. It's just –'

Clem held up his hand. 'You don't need to explain yourself. You don't owe me anything.'

'It isn't personal, Clem. I promise. It's only that I've trusted people with my life in the past and had it blow up in my face. Do you know what I mean?'

'I do. I hate having to go through all the explanations about why Emmy and I aren't together anymore. It's no one's business but ours and yet everyone feels they have a right to know. Of all people, I should have known better.'

Shyly, Hannah took the flowers from his outstretched

hand and buried her nose in them. 'Thank you. They smell beautiful.'

'Kate asked me to give you this as well.' He handed her a piece of paper. 'She wants to know what you think of it.'

'What is it?'

'They booked your friend's band to play next week and Kate thought it might be a good idea to do a special evening menu.'

Hannah glanced down the typed menu, then handed it back to Clem. 'Wow. That's really ambitious. Will she be able to cook it in here?' She looked around the tiny kitchen uncertainly.

'She seems to think so.'

'Does she want me to work?'

Clem looked abashed. 'She didn't like to ask. They're not sure if the council will cover overtime wages.'

Hannah shook her head. 'I'm starting to think maybe your dad has a point! I'll let Kate know I'm happy to volunteer for the evening if necessary.'

'Any news on the accounts front?' Clem dropped his voice to a whisper.

Hannah grinned. 'Sheila dropped them off yesterday. I'll start going through them as soon as I can.'

'Last message from Kate. She also says, are you free for dinner this evening? If so, she'll expect you at seven thirty with a bottle of white.'

'What's the occasion?'

Clem grinned. 'Kate doesn't need an occasion, just an audience!'

Hannah giggled. 'No seriously. What's it all about?'

'She's got this idea about possibly offering date night dinners on the campsite – you know, if people want a special meal but don't want to go into town – so she's got a couple of new recipes she wants to try out.'

'I'm a guinea pig then.' Hannah laughed properly this time.

'As am I,' Clem said, still grinning. 'She's roped me in too. My instructions were to bring a bottle of red, so goodness knows what concoction she's brewing up!'

HANNAH LOOKED AROUND THE TABLE. Harry was at its head, with his friend Ben and Ben's partner, Elspeth sat across from Hannah and Clem. Kate was at the foot of the table where she had easy access to the kitchen. The requested combination of red and white wine was explained by Kate's decision to provide a tasting menu rather than a full dinner.

'I needed to try all different menu options,' she explained. 'And this was a far easier way of doing it than having four or five separate dinner parties.'

Hannah was impressed. Kate's culinary skills were hardly being tested in the café if the miniature meals she had served up were anything to judge by. Bite sized Beef Wellingtons with Dauphinoise potatoes and asparagus had followed a chicken breast accompanied by sea salted potatoes and carrots, which offset the rich, creamy sauce covering the chicken. A mixed bean cassoulet and garlic bread catered for vegetarians and vegans, as did a vegetable lasagne and salad.

'I'm not normally a fan of vegan stuff,' Ben said, sitting back in his chair with a contented sigh, 'But that was delicious Kate.'

Kate looked embarrassed but it was obvious she was pleased. 'I thought we'd have a bit of a break before desserts,' she said. 'Let everything go down a bit.'

Hannah was grateful. She wouldn't normally eat so much in one go, but she hadn't liked to give Kate the impression she didn't like it. Her boss had been so supportive and it was nice to have a chance to return the favour. Her attention was drawn back to the table when Clem kicked her ankle and she realised she'd been asked a question.

'Sorry.' She laughed to cover her embarrassment. 'I was woolgathering.'

Elspeth smiled. 'I was asking about your job. Harry said you were an accountant in a previous life. I was wondering how you ended up waitressing at the Lido Café.'

'Oh.' Hannah frantically scrabbled for something plausible and settled on a half-truth. 'The firm I worked for was taken over by a bigger one and they didn't need all of the existing staff. I took voluntary redundancy because I was thinking of going freelance anyway. I needed something just to tide me over until I decided whether I wanted to do it or not and the hours suited me.'

Elspeth nodded. 'And have you made a decision yet?'

Hannah hesitated. Why was this woman so interested in her affairs? Elspeth smiled encouragingly.

'Forgive me. I sound terribly nosy, don't I? I don't mean to be. It's only that we're looking for a new accountant as our current one has told us he's retiring and as we have friends who also use him, I thought perhaps we could pass on your details to them if you'd decided to go out on your own.'

Hannah swallowed hard. 'Why would you choose me? You don't even know me.'

Elspeth laughed. 'We like to go on recommendations and Kate said you were going to be doing the accounts for the campsite. If you meet her exacting standards, you must be good.'

Hannah stared at Kate, who blushed, but nodded.

'Sorry.' Elspeth looked over at Kate. 'Did I let the cat out of the bag?'

Kate waved away the apology, instead looking at Hannah. 'I was planning to ask you if you'd consider it.'

Hannah blinked away the tears that sprang to her eyes. 'Of course I will.'

'And us?' Elspeth prompted.

Hannah's laugh was half-strangled and she took a hasty gulp from her wine glass. 'It looks like I'm going into business for myself, so yes!'

Clem picked up his glass and raised it to the table. 'To Hannah and her new venture.' As everyone echoed his toast, he nudged her gently. 'Looks like you'd better get some business cards printed.'

Elspeth and Ben left after dessert, needing to get back to relieve their babysitter but promising to pass on Hannah's phone number to the rest of their friends who shared the same accountant.

WHEN THEY HAD GONE, Kate studied her wine glass sadly and reached for the half-empty bottle. She sloshed a decent amount into her glass, stretched across to top Hannah and Clem's up, then slid the bottle down the table to her husband. The evening hadn't exactly gone as intended. Although her plan to get Hannah some clients had been a roaring success, there had been no hint of a spark between her employee and her brother-in-law. Although Clem's hand had appeared to linger on Hannah's when he passed her the salad bowl, Kate was fairly sure it had been accidental. She heaved a sigh and leant back in her chair.

'What is it, Kate?' Hannah smiled at her boss. 'That was a rueful sigh.'

I was thinking what a lovely couple the two of you would make.' Kate eyed her over the top of the wine glass, a mischievous grin on her face.

'Oh, give it a rest,' Clem said good-naturedly. 'Ever since you got Dad to go on that date, you've decided you were

Cupid in a former life. Some of us are happy being single you know.'

Kate harrumphed and took another mouthful of her wine. 'Yes, well. I understand you being a bit cautious after... whatsername... bitchface. But what about you, Hannah? What makes you so men-averse?'

Hannah coloured, alarm bells suddenly ringing in her head. Between her panic and the effects of the wine, she couldn't think straight. 'I'm not... I... I just...'

'Kate.' Harry's voice held a definite note of warning.

Kate waved a hand at her husband. 'I'm not being nosy, Harry. Hannah's my friend and if some twat of a bloke has upset her this badly, I want to know!'

'Why?'

'So I can...' she paused to think for a moment, then grinned in triumph as she found the words she wanted. 'Duff him up.'

In spite of her panic, a smile tugged at the corners of Hannah's mouth. There might be an escape for her. 'No one needs duffing up, Kate. I'm not men averse, I'm just content on my own.'

Kate looked disbelieving. 'Then what's wrong with Clem?' She waved a hand again. 'Look at him. He's kind, he's good looking. What's not to like?'

'Thinking you married the wrong brother, sweetheart?' Harry laughed.

Kate got unsteadily to her feet and wobbled the length of the table to sit on his knee. She kissed the top of his head. 'Never. I only want your brother to be as happy as we are. And I know him and Hannah would be good together.'

Hannah smiled, but it didn't quite reach her eyes. 'There's nothing wrong with Clem, Kate. I'm just not looking to date anyone at the moment.'

Kate shook her head. 'Don't give me that.' She wagged a

finger at Hannah. 'You've got a secret, Hannah Carmichael and I intend to find out what it is. Friends look out for each other.'

'I think maybe it's time to call it a night,' Clem said, scraping his chair back from the table. 'Thanks for a lovely evening you two. I'll walk you home, Hannah, if you're ready to go?'

As Hannah nodded and rose from her chair, Clem turned back to Kate and grinned. 'I'll see you and your hangover at work tomorrow.'

Hannah walked round the table and hugged Kate. 'Thanks for caring, boss. I'll have a bacon sarnie ready for you when you come in.'

'You mustn't mind Kate,' Clem said, as they walked down the road. 'She'd had a bit too much to drink but she doesn't mean anything by it.'

'I know,' Hannah said. 'But I wish she'd accept I'm not interested.'

'That's a shame.'

At first, Hannah wasn't sure she'd heard him correctly. For a moment she walked along in silence, then her curiosity got the better of her. 'Did you say, "that's a shame"?'

Clem cleared his throat. 'Did I say it out loud?'

'I think you did.'

'Sorry.'

'What did you mean?'

'Nothing.'

'No, go on. If you've got something to say, then say it.' Hannah knew this wasn't a good idea; it was why she didn't normally drink a lot.

Clem shrugged. 'I'm not looking to date anyone, you know that. But you're an extremely attractive woman and

I've had too much to drink and I would very much like to kiss you.'

Hannah bit her lip. This was definitely not a good idea. 'Don't read anything into this.' Then she reached up and kissed him.

JUNE 1943

*F*rankie pulled the sheet up as Adam rolled onto his back, panting.

'You seem distracted today,' he remarked. 'What is it?'

'Nothing,' Frankie said. 'At least... I feel guilty,' she admitted.

'Whatever for?'

'The Admiral's in a terrible mood today: he wanted me to stay after work and I said I couldn't.'

'My poor girl. What was he in such a grouse about?'

'He's been ordered to transfer some of his men. He doesn't like losing them once he's trained them to do things his way, you see. And it doesn't help that this lot are being sent abroad, so to him it feels as though he's sending them off to die.'

'Abroad? That's unusual, isn't it?'

Frankie nodded absently. 'I think extra men are needed for some big push somewhere, so ours have been sent to replace them.'

'Do you know where they're being sent? I mean, if Ashton

is worried he's sending them to their deaths, presumably it must be close to the action.'

Frankie shrugged. 'I can't really remember where he said they were going. It was somewhere hot, I think. The Med, perhaps? Or maybe Greece, given those phrasebooks we got a few months ago? I didn't think Greece was in the Med. I don't know, Geography was never my thing, was it? I think Mr Butterworth despaired of my ever learning where things were. Do you remember when he got so angry with me for putting Blackpool in Wales that he threw the board rubber at me?' She started laughing until she noticed Adam wasn't and stopped abruptly.

'What is it?' she stroked his face, calling his attention back to her.

'What? Oh! Nothing.' He smiled. 'I was thinking about what you said, that's all. It must be tough for the Admiral to give men orders knowing they're likely to see fighting soon. Still, it could be worse. At least in the Mediterranean they'll be warm.'

'You mustn't say anything to anyone,' Frankie said, a sudden pink flush blooming in her cheeks. 'I mean, it's probably not important, but we're not supposed to say anything about troop movements, are we? Loose lips and all that.' She looked guiltily at Adam. 'You won't, will you?'

He kissed the top of her head. 'Don't worry, I won't breathe a word. Anyway,' he laughed. 'Knowing your geography, they're probably heading for the Atlantic!'

Frankie stuck her tongue out at him. 'Rude. Anyway, it's not the only reason I feel guilty about him.'

'What else is there?'

She rolled onto her side, pressing herself against him. 'This.' She kissed him. 'You.' She let out a sigh. 'I don't know if I can do this anymore.'

Adam stroked the curve of her hip, his warm hand

caressing her bare skin. His expression was unreadable as he regarded her steadily.

'Are you saying you want us to stop seeing each other?'

Frankie tilted her head and gently bit his bottom lip, pressing herself closer to him. The invitation was clear and he pulled her closer still, his hand moving to squeeze her breast.

'What do you think?'

He growled and lowered his head to her body, leaving little red marks scattered across her chest.

'You don't want to know what I'm thinking.'

Frankie gave a throaty chuckle and slipped her hand beneath the sheet. 'I think I've a fairly good idea,' she whispered, then kissed him, shifting so her leg was draped over his side.'

His breath caught in his throat for a moment. 'So, if you don't want this to stop –'

'I really don't.' Frankie moved her hips encouragingly and it was some minutes before Adam was able to continue the conversation.

'What is it you're feeling guilty about?'

Frankie propped herself up on one elbow. 'The Admiral himself.'

Adam frowned.

'He'd like there to be more to our relationship than there currently is.'

'Oh. And how do you feel about it?'

'I don't know.' Frankie chewed her lip. 'He doesn't know about you and me and I know Mum would like it, but it feels wrong to let him think I care enough for him to... well, you know.'

Adam stroked her face. 'Does that mean you care for me? This isn't just a fling for you?'

Frankie harrumphed. 'Is that what you think of me? That I'm the kind of girl who –'

'Of course not!' Adam interrupted. 'It's only...' he paused, looking suddenly awkward. 'I hadn't dared hope...I mean, you're...' he trailed off again.

Frankie caught her breath. 'You feel the same?'

Adam nodded and she kissed him.

'I've been widowed for almost three years. Mac...' She broke off as a sob rose in her throat and she swallowed it. 'Mac wouldn't have expected me to remain alone for the rest of my life.'

Adam wiped a tear from the corner of her eye. 'I don't want to lose you, Frankie, but I care too much to stand in your way. The Admiral can offer you far more than I can and if you think you could be happy with him, I'll stand aside.'

Frankie smiled warmly at him. 'You're very sweet.'

Adam fell silent for a moment. When he eventually spoke, he pulled Frankie back into his arms. She couldn't see his face and wondered what form his expression had taken.

'Perhaps you shouldn't tell him about us yet, though,' he said.

'Would it not be kinder?'

'Perhaps. But it could also make things difficult for you at work, couldn't it? You said he trusts you with things that aren't really your responsibility, didn't you? I'd hate for you to lose that position of trust when I know how much it means to you and how much you love your job. I don't want to cause trouble for you.' His arms tightened around her. 'As much as I hate the idea, it might be better for you if you continue letting him think he has a chance with you.'

'And if he does want to take things further?'

Adam hesitated again. 'Then it's your choice what you do.'

'You wouldn't mind?'

Suddenly, Adam flipped her onto her back and attacked

her mouth with his. One hand gripped the back of her head, pressing it firmly against his, the other ran roughly over her body.

'I'd hate it,' he said fiercely. 'I mind dreadfully, but I can make my peace with it as long as you keep coming back to me. I don't want to lose you, Frankie and I'll do whatever it takes to keep you here.'

Frankie's eyes widened and she stroked his back, trying to calm the raging storm she could feel inside him.

'I'm lucky to have you,' she said. 'And I'll do everything I can to avoid that happening. I love you too.'

Is he buying this? The sudden burst of passion had taken her by surprise and alarmed her. Suddenly it had felt as though Adam was no longer simply telling her what he thought she wanted to hear. *Is there a reason why he's blind to how ridiculous he sounds? Surely he can't truly believe I'd be considering sleeping with the Admiral?* They were pushing him too far. At some point he must realise he wasn't as irresistible as he believed. Frankie could only hope the moment didn't come when they were alone together. His reference to Mac had unsettled her, but she forced herself to remain relaxed, though every part of her longed for him to leave so she could scrub herself clean.

Remember why you're doing this, Frankie.

AUGUST 2017

*T*he café door opened and Kate slipped inside, dark glasses covering her eyes. Hannah handed her a bacon sandwich and a mug of coffee.

'How do you look so fresh? I can't be the only one suffering, surely?'

'A pint of water before bed,' Hannah said. 'But I still feel worse than I look, trust me.' She gestured to the sandwich. 'Eat that, it will make you feel better. I had one at home and a second one when I got here.'

Kate groaned but did as instructed and slowly her face gained a little colour. By the time the first customer came in, she looked more like herself, although bending down to load the dishwasher brought on a further bout of nausea. Hannah handed her the packet of ibuprofen they kept on the counter.

'Take a couple of these and I'll make you some more toast.'

Later in the day, Clem came in for his break. 'Any chance of a cup of tea?' he called to Kate.

Kate lifted her head from the side and waved at Hannah. 'Ask her. I'm dying.'

Clem looked at Hannah and went red. She hurried to make the tea, grateful Kate was too hungover to notice their awkwardness.

'How's it been this morning?'

'Not too bad. No one's drowned.'

'Always a good thing.' Hannah handed over the mug of tea.

'Hannah, about last night.' Clem dropped his voice to a whisper.

'I know. We were drunk. It didn't mean anything. It didn't change anything.'

He cleared his throat. 'Good. So we're still friends.'

Hannah glanced at Kate, whose head still rested on the countertop. 'Yes, of course.'

Clem examined his tea. 'Good.'

He headed towards the back of the café then paused and turned. 'Just a heads up, Frankie arrived as I went on my break, so she'll probably pop in when she's done swimming.'

Hannah grinned and filled up the coffee grinder. 'I'll try to wrestle your sister-in-law into a better state then. A hangover and Frankie are not a good combination!'

Clem laughed and the awkwardness fell away. Hannah watched as he rounded the corner and walked back to the office that served as the Lido's reception desk. She touched her fingers to her lips, remembering the previous night. *You were the one who said it meant nothing,* she reminded herself sternly. *So you have no right to be upset when he agrees with you. Take some of your own advice and don't overthink it.* It was easy to tell herself that, but she couldn't deny a part of her was disappointed. *He deserves better than you. He's one of the good guys.*

MARCH 1944

*F*rankie poked her head around the door. Ken lay on the bed, his face pale, his arm and leg encased in plaster casts and a bandage wrapped tightly around his head. She hurried to his side.

'Well, this is a nice pickle you've got yourself into,' she said briskly. 'As a way out of the war, you didn't take an easy route, did you?'

Ken tried to laugh, but it turned into a groan and he clutched at his ribs. 'Not my fault they gave me a duff plane,' he wheezed.

'You know what they say about poor workmen!' Frankie pulled a chair up to the side of the bed and sat down, taking his hand in hers. 'How are you feeling?'

'Like I crashed a plane into a frozen river.'

'Obviously better than you did if you're cracking silly jokes again.' Frankie squeezed his hand. 'If you could not scare us like that again, I'd be grateful.'

'The lady cares,' Ken clasped a dramatic hand over his heart.

'Of course she cares.' Frankie sounded cross. 'Just because I keep saying no to a date doesn't mean I don't care.'

'Frankie, it's been four years and I know you've been seeing someone because Aunt Lily goes tight-lipped every time she sees me. You won't tell me anything you've done outside of work. I'm not stupid, I know there's someone and you don't want to talk about it and that's fine.' He paused. 'Except I know you and I see your expression when you think I can't see you.' He sighed. 'Oh Frankie, why won't you talk to me? Whatever it is, I'll understand. I can't bear it when you look like that.'

'Like what?'

'Like your heart is breaking and you don't know how to fit it back together.'

'Quite the poet today, aren't you?'

'I got the drugs.' Ken smiled.

Frankie pushed her chair back. 'In that case, I'll come back later when you're less silly.' Her face and tone softened as she laid a hand on his forehead. 'You need to rest.'

He reached for her hand. 'Stay with me.'

'Go to sleep.' She leant over the bed and kissed him. For a moment she allowed her lips to linger on his cheek, then she pulled away. She had to put a stop to it. It wasn't fair on Ken.

'There is someone. It's not serious, just a bit of fun and that's fine. It's all I want.' Biting back the tears, she backed away from the bed. 'Get well soon, Ken. I'll write.'

AUGUST 2017

*H*annah carried the plates out to the last table, then returned to the café and dropped into the nearest seat. Kate slid a can of coke across the table to her. 'There's vodka in the fridge if you want to jazz it up a bit. I'm too knackered to get up.'

Hannah clicked the ring pull back and the can opened with a satisfying fizz. She took a long drink from it and rested her head against the wall. 'That was mental. Like, boot sale mental.'

Kate rolled her shoulders and groaned. 'We did it though. All the meals out on time and everyone happy.'

Music drifted through the closed doors, then got louder as Clem appeared on the patio and opened them. He pulled the two of them out of their seats and twirled them under his arms. Laughing, Kate pulled her hand free.

'He's all yours, Hannah. I'm too tired.'

The music stopped briefly, then switched to a less frenetic melody and Sheila's voice came over the microphone.

'All it does in rain,' Clem crooned along with her, out of

tune and grinning as he pulled Hannah closer and danced her round the café.

'You never could sing, could you darling?' A voice in the doorway stopped him mid-twirl and Hannah stepped away from him, suddenly feeling afraid.

Kate frowned and got to her feet. 'What are you doing here?'

'Calm down. I'm a paying guest like everyone else here. I'm simply being considerate and bringing our plates back.' She lifted the empty crockery to make her point, then laid them down on the nearest table. 'Just trying to be helpful.' She smiled at Clem. 'I'm sorry if I interrupted something.' Her eyes flicked over Hannah, instantly dismissing her. Hannah tried to make herself as small as possible as the woman continued. 'Your dancing was always better than your singing.' She held out a hand. 'Dance with me? For old time's sake?'

A look of disgust spread across Clem's face. 'I don't think so. Go back to whoever you're here with. I've got nothing to say to you.'

Her hand dropped and her eyes flicked across to Hannah again. 'As you wish, but I won't let this go, Clem. I told you I still loved you and I meant it. We were good together you and me and we could be again. I made a mistake, I know that now, but we can move past it if you'll just give me a second chance.'

Clem looked at her stonily and didn't reply. Eventually, she sighed and turned to leave, then looked back at Hannah.

'I don't know whether or not you care, but legally, he's still a married man. Then again,' she smiled malevolently, 'Perhaps that's part of the attraction for you.'

Hannah paled, her nails leaving red half-moons on her palms. Getting to her feet, she grabbed the two plates and hurried into the kitchen. In the café she could hear a muttered conversation between Kate and Clem but it was Kate alone who came into the kitchen.

'Just ignore Emmy,' she said gently. 'She wants Clem back but he's not interested. Why would he want to be with someone who cheated?'

'Why indeed?' Hannah murmured.

'And he won't be married once the divorce comes through,' Kate pressed. 'And it will, he's determined to get her to sign the papers.'

Hannah was pleased when Kate let the subject drop and went to start collecting the empty plates from outside. She gripped the edge of the sink, willing her hands to stop shaking as tears pinged against the metal surface. Why had she let her guard down? It was going to happen again. People were going to get hurt because of her. She had to distance herself from them before it was too late. No more dancing, no more dinners and definitely no more kisses.

The next morning, Sheila knocked on her door. 'What did you think?' she asked eagerly when Hannah opened it.

'You were amazing.'

'I know.' Sheila rolled her eyes and laughed. 'That's a given. I meant what did you think of the event as a whole?'

Hannah laughed. 'It went really well. We took over a grand in ticket sales and then there was the raffle and the drinks on the night as well. No idea how much it cost to put it on, but I reckon there should be a decent profit once it's all added up.'

'Excellent.' Sheila grinned. 'And how are you getting on with those accounts?'

'I'm still going through them, but there's definitely something not right. I just haven't figured out quite what it is yet.'

'Have you said anything to the others?'

'I want to make sure I've got all the facts first. The

Council meeting isn't too far off though, is it? When they make the final decision, I mean.'

'Couple of weeks, I think. You got plans for any more events between now and then?'

'They're doing a second-hand clothes sale in a couple of days and we've got a wine tasting booked in as well. I don't know if it will be enough though.'

'Don't forget, you've only got to show them you have the potential to make more money from the place. You don't have to fix all its problems overnight.'

Hannah sighed. 'I know, but we need something. I'm going to take another look at the accounts today and dig a bit deeper into them, see if I can get to the bottom of whatever it is that's nagging at me.'

HANNAH RUBBED HER EYES. The figures on the screen were starting to blur and dance about. *Time for a break.* She finished off her notes and closed her laptop. Elspeth and Ben had been as good as their word and had not only sent over their own accounts to her but had also somehow persuaded other people to move over to her as well. She already had four confirmed new clients and while she'd been working on Elspeth and Ben's tax returns, she'd seen at least three more inquiries drop into her inbox. Once people in Avonstow knew you came recommended, they were happy to go local with whatever services they could. A small smile tugged at the corners of her lips. She was beginning to hope that perhaps she had found the new start she'd been looking for. *Maybe miracles do happen after all.* Then she remembered the other accounts she'd been looking at and the budding smile fell away. There was a decision to be made and she'd been putting it off for long enough. *I'll have a cup of tea first,* she thought. It could keep for a few more minutes. Or days. Or she could pretend she hadn't found anything. She frowned and shook her head. No. That wasn't an option. She was going to have to face him. She poured the milk into her cup as she waited for the one pot teapot to brew and let herself think about Richard for the first time in months.

SHE'D MET him at the library of all places. If she'd been planning to start a mad, passionate affair, Colchester library wouldn't have been top of her list of places to try to meet someone, but that was where it had begun. It had all started innocently enough – they'd reached for the same book and he had graciously allowed her to take it. She had thanked him and in doing so, had opened herself up to a conversation that very nearly destroyed her life for a second time.

'It really isn't a problem. I've read them all before, I can wait a few weeks more to re-read it.' He paused, his head tilted to one side, his grin just as lop-sided. 'I'm Richard, by the way.' He stuck out a hand.

'Hannah,' she replied, shaking it.

'First time reader or are you like me and going back for another round?'

'First time, I'm afraid. It's not an author I've ever heard of, but the cover looked interesting.'

'Oh, you're in for a treat!'

His enthusiasm was infectious and Hannah found herself grinning as well.

'I don't suppose.' He hesitated. 'I mean, it's a bit random but, would you... would you maybe like to grab a coffee or something and I can tell you why it's such an amazing book?'

Hannah found herself nodding and then following him to the desk to check the book out.

'Aren't you going to choose something else?' she asked, sliding the book across the self-scan machine.

Richard looked confused for a moment until she waved the book at him.

'I kind of stole your original choice.'

He laughed quietly. 'I'll come back later and grab something.'

In the café, Hannah found herself opening up to him in a way she rarely did on first meeting someone. At the time she had assumed it was because the coincidence of them both being accountants had fooled her into thinking there was a deeper connection as well. Once they realised he worked for the firm taking over her own, it had felt as though it was somehow meant to be and they had talked about the plans to move the business on. Hannah told him all about Ethan – things she had never told anyone before, including her father – and she'd been so captivated by him, so caught up in the flow of his conversation, that it wasn't until much later in the evening she realised they hadn't talked about the book at all.

Over the next few months, they met regularly for coffee and dinner. Richard said he preferred to keep their relation-ship out of the office and Hannah had agreed, not wanting to fuel gossip. His position was significantly more senior than hers and she knew assumptions would be made. She never wondered why he always came to her flat, while she'd never seen his, never questioned why their dates were always straight after work and he never stayed overnight, even when they began sleeping together. She had been so blinded by the connection she imagined with this gorgeous man, who flattered her at every opportunity and filled her with confidence, that none of the obvious questions occurred to her until it was too late. When he dropped the bombshell on her, it felt as though her world was ending, but it had only been the beginning of the disaster.

'You're leaving?' Hannah felt her throat constrict as though it was trying to trap the words inside.

'It's not a big issue. I'm only going to be in Clacton. We can still see each other.'

'I know, but...'

'You should apply for my job. You're good enough to do it if you wanted to.'

Hannah blushed and shook her head. 'Andy...'

'Andy nothing. You're twice the accountant he is, even if he is your boss.'

Hannah fell silent. It was nice that Richard had faith in her, but she knew the job should be Andy's. Despite what Richard said, he was just as good at the job as she was, plus he had more experience and was far better at motivating others.

'We should celebrate,' she said, determined to appear happy for him. 'Why don't we go out for dinner for a change? My treat.'

Richard frowned, his mouth drawn in tight. 'I don't want to share you. Why don't I come to yours and cook for you? I could make your favourite?'

'I thought it would be a treat. We so rarely go out anywhere, I wanted to do something nice for you.'

Richard ran a finger down her chest. 'If you wanted to do something nice for me...'

Hannah laughed and swatted his hand away. 'Have it your own way. Come round and cook and I'll grab a bottle of champagne and something nice for dessert. Or I could cook for you?'

'You always cook, I'll do it this time. I can't tonight though, but tomorrow? Straight from work?'

Hannah agreed, pushing away the slight hurt she'd felt at his refusal to let her treat him. She shouldn't complain. At least it showed he wasn't with her for what he could get out of her. Even when they should be celebrating his new job, he wanted to do something nice for her instead.

The following day, by the time Richard arrived, Hannah had all the ingredients laid out on the kitchen work surface and she offered him a glass of chilled champagne as he put his car keys down. He pulled her close, kissing her as she held the glasses out to the side, trying not to spill them.

'I'm so lucky to have you.' He bit gently on the spot where her shoulder and neck met. 'Shall we skip dinner and move straight to dessert?'

Hannah giggled as she put one of the glasses down and pushed him gently away. Richard looked affronted.

'Those lines are so corny. Do they ever work?'

'You'd be surprised.' Richard grinned and taking the glass from her he swallowed half of it in one gulp. 'I've had much success with that one over the years.'

'I don't believe you.' Hannah moved away from him. 'But cooking for me will definitely work.'

Richard didn't reply, but he picked up the knife and sliced the plastic packaging open before turning his attention to the vegetables. After dinner, they took the champagne to the bedroom.

'Couldn't you stay over?' Hannah lay against Richard's chest, her head fuzzy.

He groaned. 'I wish I could, you know that, but…'

'I know, I know.' Hannah pushed herself up and pulled the sheet across her chest. 'You can't sleep when it's not your bed. Could you not try it though? You never know, you might be okay here.'

'Don't do this, Hannah. Don't make it harder than it already is. I've told you I can't.'

'I know, but… it feels like…'

'Like what?'

She heaved a sigh. The conversation had suddenly got far

heavier than she had intended it to. 'Like how can there be any future for us if you can't even stay the night?'

'Do you see a future for us?' Richard's voice sounded odd and she looked up at him, confused.

'Don't you?'

'Of course I do.' He looked away and she wondered if he was trying to suppress an emotion. 'It's just…' he turned back to her, his eyes boring into her. 'I wasn't sure if you did.'

She leant over and kissed him, stroking his forehead. 'Well, I do. So, stop worrying and kiss me before you have to leave and get your beauty sleep.'

The next day, Hannah opened an email inviting her to Richard's leaving party. It was nothing fancy: nibbles and a few drinks in the office and partners were invited as well. A small part of her had hoped that now he was leaving, they might be able to tell people they were a couple rather than having to hide it from everyone, but she was disappointed to see the party was being held on an afternoon where she had a dental appointment.

'I know, sweetheart and I'm sorry, really I am. I know you told me you couldn't do that afternoon, but it was the only day next week that all the bosses could do.' Richard's tone was wheedling and in spite of her frustration, Hannah couldn't help forgiving him.

'It's not the end of the world, I suppose,' she conceded. 'It's only that I'd hoped we could, you know, tell people about us now. And it's not like I can change the appointment – my tooth's really sore and I need to get it fixed as soon as possible.'

'I am sorry. You know I'd have loved you to be there, but don't worry. We can tell people about us soon, I promise.'

Hannah swallowed her disappointment and allowed him to kiss away her poor temper. It wasn't his fault the big bosses had insisted on that particular day and it wasn't fair to be cross with him.

THE FOLLOWING WEEK, the receptionist at the dentist phoned to say they'd had a cancellation and, remembering that Hannah had telephoned to try to changer her appointment, had called to ask if she still wanted an earlier appointment. Her tooth newly filled, Hannah headed back to the office, looking forward to surprising Richard with her unexpected attendance. Anticipation coursed through her as she pushed open the conference room door, her eyes immediately searching for the only face she wanted to see.

'Hannah! You made it!' Her boss materialised at her side, drink in hand. He passed her a full glass of champagne.

'Ta. Thankfully the dentist was quick and the traffic gods favoured me today.' She looked around the room. 'They've really pushed the boat out, haven't they?'

'Richard's a popular guy.' Andy shrugged dismissively.

Hannah frowned. 'You don't like him?'

Andy wrinkled his nose. 'There's something about him. He's too…'

'Too what?' Hannah laughed in spite of herself.

'False. You know what it's like. You hear things and you never know whether or not to believe them, but you keep hearing them and you start to wonder. I dunno, he's just too… too nice, I suppose. But not in a good way. It's like he's always trying a bit too hard to come across as everyone's friend to actually be a friend, if you see what I mean.' He nodded a head towards the corner of the room. 'Look at him now. Totally ignoring his wife because he's too busy clapping everyone on the back and telling them how great he thinks they are.'

Hannah felt as though every part of her had suddenly turned to ice. Had she misheard? 'What did you say?'

Her eyes dragged themselves to the corner Andy had gestured to. Just as he had said, Richard was there, laughing, his hand clamped firmly on a colleague's shoulder. As she watched him, he glanced in her direction and his face paled. Hannah started to move towards him and raised her hand to wave, but Richard looked away immediately, not acknowledging her. At his side stood a woman, blond hair swept elegantly off her face to reveal a too tight smile and eyes which darted anxiously about the room, looking at everything except the man at her side. For a moment, they made contact with Hannah's and an odd expression flashed across the taught face.

'Hannah, are you okay? You've gone really pale.'

She felt Andy grip her elbow and draw her towards the door. Something gripped her tightly around the throat, cutting off the supply of air and she stumbled against him as he guided her from the room.

'Hannah?'

Andy's face swam in and out of focus. She could hear him talking but his words were drowned out by the incessant buzzing in her ears.

'Hannah? Hannah, I need you to listen to me.'

Andy shook her and she stared at him, perplexed. He took her hand and put it on his chest. She frowned, straining to hear what he was saying, still struggling to breathe. Her other hand tugged at her throat and Andy captured it, pulling her towards him again.

'Hannah, I want you to focus on my breathing. See if you can match it. In when I do, out when I do.'

She could barely understand him, but gradually worked out what he wanted her to do. The tightness around her throat eased off and air flowed freely into her lungs.

'What did he do to you?' There was an edge to Andy's voice she'd never heard before. Her boss was generally one of the most affable people she'd ever met and rarely raised his voice.

She shook her head. 'Nothing, I...' She hesitated. 'I misunderstood something, that's all.'

Andy looked disgusted. 'Not you as well.'

Hannah frowned.

'Those rumours I mentioned. They were always about women. By the look on your face and your reaction when I mentioned his wife, I'm guessing you didn't know he was married?'

Hannah shook her head. 'I would never...' she trailed off. She couldn't say it, because she had. More than once.

'I know.' Andy put a reassuring hand on her arm. 'I know you wouldn't, Hannah. You're not like that.'

But she was. This wasn't the first time. But she really hadn't suspected. Of course she hadn't. She was an idiot. Everything suddenly fell into blinding clarity: the reason he would never stay over, his preference for quiet, out of the way restaurants. It wasn't because he liked dining in quirky places, he was hiding her away. No wonder he preferred to cook for her at home. How could she have been so naïve again? Her phone buzzed in her handbag. She took it out and looked at the screen.

I CAN EXPLAIN.

SHE BLOCKED THE NUMBER. He probably could, but she didn't want to hear it. Wasn't prepared to listen to the excuses, witness the self-recriminatory tears, forgive the weak male she had dazzled with her beauty. She had heard it all. It changed nothing. It didn't undo the sex, didn't take back the promises of a future together, didn't stop the hurt of betrayal. She had allowed it to happen again. She, who should have known better, who should have been on her guard. She vowed it would not happen a third time. Never again would she allow anyone to get close to her, to let herself think, even for a moment, that she might be allowed to be happy, to be properly loved by anyone just for herself.

'You don't know anything about me,' she told Andy, brushing away the tears that poured down her cheeks.

'I know enough to know this isn't you,' he said gently. 'You're a good person, Hannah, but you have awful taste in men. I told you he was a twat and I was right. You're not the first to be taken in by him and I doubt you'll be the last. Although why his wife puts up with it is anyone's guess.'

'Do you think she knows?' Hannah was horrified by the thought. She couldn't go through all that again.

Andy shrugged. 'About you specifically? No idea. What he's like? Maybe.' He looked at her swollen eyes. 'What I do know is that he's not worth your tears. Come on, I'll drive you home.'

Hannah followed him through the corridors in silence and after giving him her address, fell silent again. When he pulled up outside her flat, Andy unclipped her seatbelt for her and dismissed her thanks for his kindness.

'Not necessary. You're a friend and friends look out for each other. None of this is your fault, Hannah. Men like him are predators and they take in even the cleverest of people. Trust me, I've met plenty like him.'

Hannah looked at him sadly. 'You recognised him for what he is.'

Andy's expression matched her own. 'Only because I've been taken in by men like him in the past. I'm older and more experienced nowadays. I'm lucky – Rob's a lovely guy and I can't believe he chose me, but trust me, in my youth, I was easy pickings for men like Richard. That kind of personality isn't exclusively heterosexual you know.' He squeezed her hand. 'Now. Sharpen up Carmichael. Get yourself inside and into bed. I want you at the office bright and early tomorrow and ready to work. No excuses, understand?'

Hannah smiled weakly. 'Yes boss. Bright and early. Message received.'

She opened the door and slid out of the car, waving from the step as Andy pulled away from the kerb. Numbly, she climbed the stairs and unlocked her front door, before crawling into bed fully clothed and sleeping until her alarm sounded the next morning.

HANNAH APPROACHED her desk to find a post it note stuck to her computer screen. "Top Drawer". Intrigued, she slid the drawer open to find a box of her favourite seashell truffles and another note. "Not going to make a fuss, but you know where I am if you need me. A x" She smiled, feeling the gloom that enveloped her lift, just a little. Her desk telephone rang and she picked up the receiver, wondering who was calling at such an early hour. Most inquiries to the accounts department came later in the day. After a minute or so, she replaced the handle and headed for Andy's office. He smiled when she entered and sat down, but his face became sterner as she explained the reason for her visit.

'What do you think they want?' she asked.

'The only way to find out is to go to the meeting.'

'And what if it's about... you know what?'

'Why would he have told them?'

'If this is a regular thing for him, maybe they worked it out. If they saw me having a panic attack yesterday...'

Hannah trailed off, feeling the thick fingers closing around her throat again.

Andy waved her concern away. 'And if they did, so what? You didn't do anything wrong and he's leaving anyway. Go and have the meeting and come and see me when you're back, but I don't think you have any need to be concerned.'

Hannah headed for the stairs that took her out of their basement offices and up into the main body of the company building, where the bosses had airy, light-filled rooms that were almost as big as the entire accounts department. She rapped on the door, trying to disguise the trembling in her hands and gritted her teeth into a smile as she responded to the command to enter.

'Take a seat.' The instruction was offered with a smile, but the lips were thin.

Hannah perched on the edge of the chair, hands hidden beneath her thighs.

'Thank you for coming so promptly, Hannah. I realise this is very short notice, but we are on something of a tight deadline to get everything organised so time really is of the essence.'

Hannah's fingers twitched and she pressed her legs harder against the seat.

'As you know, we're in the process of restructuring the company after our takeover and Richard Temple's departure has given us the opportunity to promote from within and restructure the team underneath. There will of course be some voluntary redundancies – and compulsory ones if enough people are not forthcoming – and whoever takes over from him will be in charge of that. He has recommended you for the job and we're happy to offer it to you now.'

Hannah stared at him for a moment. Rage bubbled within her, but she suppressed it for the time being. She had told him she didn't want his job. Had made it clear she wasn't right for it. He was still trying to manipulate her.

'Richard recommended me?' She was pleased with the control she heard in her voice.

'He did.'

'And you're offering me the job, just like that. No interview.'

'We are.'

'Forgive me, but… why?'

He looked startled. 'What do you mean?'

'It's a big step up from what I'm doing now. There are other, more senior people, who are equally if not more suited to the role. So, why me?'

'As I said, Richard recommended you. There is a significant renumeration package associated with the job, to reflect the increased responsibility and of course you would be dealing with highly confidential information, so we would expect–'

Hannah interrupted the flow of words. 'Did he tell you why he was recommending me over anyone else?'

He, erm… ah… he felt you were ready for the next step, I believe.'

Hannah's eyes narrowed. 'It wasn't a guilty conscience then?'

'I… I'm afraid I don't quite understand…'

Hannah leant forward in her chair. 'This offer isn't to keep me quiet about how a senior manager in this firm abused his position of trust?'

'Hannah… Miss Carmichael…I…'

Hannah stood up. 'I believe you know exactly what I'm talking about. I made it very clear to Mr Temple I was not interested in the position when he first floated the idea. I am still not interested. If you have any sense at all, you will offer the position to Andrew Mayfield, who has the skills and the experience to do it properly. I may be a fool, Sir, but I am not an avaricious one. I don't want the job and if you will excuse me, I have work to do.'

She turned on her heel and marched out of the office, her back ramrod straight, her head high. Her anger carried her through the maze of corridors but her poise lasted only until she was out of sight in the lift, whereupon her legs wobbled and she sank into the corner of the metal walls. Had she really spoken to her boss like that? What on earth had possessed her? Turning the job down was the right thing to do, but after the way she had delivered her refusal she'd be lucky if she had a job at all tomorrow.

'You did the right thing,' Andy said when she told him what had happened. 'I mean, I'm flattered you told them to offer it to me instead, but that's not what I mean. You could have had a massive promotion and a load more money out of it, but you've been talking about possibly setting up your own business for ages, so maybe this is a sign you should crack on and do it.'

Hannah sighed. 'Maybe. I could take the voluntary redundancy I guess.'

'But equally, if you don't want to leave, you shouldn't let this force you out. He won't be working here for much longer and you're good at your job. If you want to stay, you can definitely ride it out. They obviously want to make sure you're not going to sue them or anything.'

Hannah laughed. 'What on earth could I sue them for? It's not the firm's fault he's the way he is.'

'No, but if you could prove they knew what he was like then you could argue they weren't looking after the welfare of their staff.'

Hannah groaned. 'Why would I put myself through that? I'd gain absolutely nothing except everyone in the office knowing my business and making jokes behind my back.'

'They don't know that though.'

'True. Do you think I should say something?'

'Absolutely not.' Andy was firm. 'Take some time to think about what you really want to do and make a decision that's right for you. Leave them to worry about everything else.'

IN THE END, Hannah had decided to leave and looking back, she reflected that it had definitely been the right choice. Her business was steadily increasing in number and she was happier than she had been at Morgan Peters. She could choose her own hours and she was still fitting everything in around her work in the café, which, she had begun to realise, also made her happy. She had friends and although she still hadn't told them about Richard and Ethan, she was beginning to let her guard down again and to consider telling them what had happened. Perhaps she had been naïve, but also, perhaps neither man had been entirely her fault. She had certainly never intended to hurt anyone and she had been told enough times over the years that Ethan had brought much of his woes on himself. Maybe it was time she started listening.

She looked again at the pages of figures she'd printed out. The paper was covered in highlighted entries and her written comments scribbled at the edges. This was what had led her to think about Richard, but all the reminiscing and recriminations in the world didn't change what she was looking at. The accounts were wrong. Badly wrong. She had to tell someone what had been happening, but if she did and then her history with Richard came out, what would people think? It would look like she was trying to take revenge on him and it really wasn't about that. There were a multitude of ways she could have paid him back for what he'd done, but she had never been interested in revenge. This was wrong and putting it right could help the Lido. That was all there was to it. She had to try something because if she did nothing the Lido would close and it would be her fault. Her friends were relying on her. She drummed her pen on the desk. *Think, Hannah, think. There's a solution to this where nobody gets hurt. There has to be. You've just got to look closely enough.*

JOHN - 1944

'We're risking too much, Dad.' John wiped the sweat from his forehead. 'I know this is important to you, but it's the death penalty for all of us if we're caught.'

'Then we'll have to make sure we don't get caught, won't we?'

Yes, because it's that simple, John thought. Did his father really not understand what they were risking? *Or does he not care? Is the Republican cause something he'd risk his life for? And the lives of his son and grandson?*

'And it's not just important to me, son, is it?' Garrett coughed. 'I'm not the only one with a lot to lose, am I?'

Perhaps it is. John waited for his father to continue. *He'd sacrifice us in a heartbeat if he had to.*

Garrett took something from his pocket and waved it at John. 'This arrived the other day. Can I remind you of what you were told right at the beginning?'

John flicked a switch and the pump room hummed into life, the electric lights buzzing, the pump wheezing in the background. He held out his hand and his father handed over a small photograph. It was blurred and clearly taken some distance from its subjects. He looked at Garrett and shrugged.

'Who's it meant to be?'

'If they say it's Alice, then you'd better believe it's Alice. That's her son with her. RAF, I believe. It would be a shame if his plane was tampered with, wouldn't it?'

John glared at his father. 'You thought highly of her once upon a time.'

'I did. I still do. She's a good woman.'

'And yet you allow your comrades to hold her life in forfeit for my co-operation.'

'The cause comes first.' Garrett made an expression of disgust. 'Our leaders made such a mess of it first time around, we're having to work extra hard to prove we can be a useful ally. If we can convince Jerry to work with us properly, we'll have greater access to weapons again.'

'Dad, it didn't work in '17, it didn't work in '40. What on earth makes you think this time is any different? You're risking all our lives on nothing more than a hope and a prayer.'

'Because this time we have Lernehan. He's been gun-running since before the war. The Germans picked him up in Jersey and he made a deal with them: information for guns to help our own cause. Plus, we have Adam's friendly Wren. If there's information to be had, he'll get it out of her. He's got more of his grandfather in him. We just have to give him time.'

'And what if she doesn't want to co-operate? Look whose daughter she is.'

'Then you'll have to persuade your ex-wife to persuade her daughter, won't you?'

John looked alarmed and his father continued. 'Or maybe you could have a little chat with her husband. Alice is his sister, after all. I'm sure he wouldn't want any harm to come to her.'

Garrett opened the door, whistling jauntily and left the building. John leant against the railings surrounding the pump shaft, willing his legs to stop trembling. How did his father still have the ability to reduce him to this? He looked down. It was at least 10 feet to the base of the pit. He calculated the odds. Not enough to guarantee a swift end, but a decent probability. He put one foot on the lowest rail, then put it firmly back on the floor. *No. There has to be another way. A way that will save us all.*

AUGUST 2017

'*B*efore we retire to consider the case, please can I thank you all again for coming to this extraordinary meeting today. I have to say, you have clearly done a tremendous amount of work in putting your arguments together and I think I speak for all of us when I applaud you on the depth of your commitment to this issue.'

'I bet he still bloody votes against us though,' Jack muttered. His wife dug her elbow into his ribs and he subsided.

'However, unless anyone has anything further to add at this present time, we will close the meeting temporarily to consider your proposals.'

Nobody had anything else to say, so the councillors rose and made their way to the door. Hannah rose to her feet and slipped through the milling crowd into the corridor outside. As Richard appeared, she took a deep breath and, stepping forward, she tapped his arm.

'Might I have a word?'

'Hannah?'

She refused to smile at him.

'What are you doing here?'

'I work in the Lido café.'

'You left Morgan Peters?'

'Obviously.' Hannah didn't elaborate.

He put a hand on her arm. 'Not because of me, I hope? I was surprised to hear you turned down the job I recommended you for.'

'Really?' Hannah ground her teeth together. 'Even after I'd told you I didn't want it?' She barked a laugh. 'It shouldn't surprise me really. I mean, your memory never was very good, was it? How could I expect you to remember a simple conversational exchange, when you can't even remember you're married?'

Richard glared at her. 'Not here, Hannah.'

She looked down the now empty corridor and rolled her eyes. 'Afraid someone will hear? Who is she this time?' She held up her hand. 'No, don't tell me, I really couldn't care less. That's not why I'm here.'

'So why are you here?'

Hannah lowered her voice. 'I know what you've been doing, Richard. I assume this girlfriend likes expensive gifts? That is why you've been stealing money, isn't it?'

Richard grabbed her arm. 'What the fuck are you talking about?'

She shook him off. 'Don't touch me. I'm talking about the money you've been stealing from the Lido accounts, Richard. You hid it well, but not well enough.'

He went pale. 'Is this about revenge? Because if it is, you should know I genuinely cared for you. I never meant to hurt you.'

'Tell it to someone who cares. This isn't about revenge it's about doing the right thing. I don't care that you stole the money and I really don't care what you're spending it on, but you have one chance to sort this out. Get the council to turn the Lido over to the local group and allow them to run it. Put the money back and I won't breathe a word to anyone.'

'And if I don't?' Richard sneered.

'I'll go to the police.'

He shoved her against the wall and pressed himself close to her. 'Give me one good reason why I shouldn't call them myself and have you arrested for blackmail. Why would anyone believe you?'

'Because you know it's true and I have the evidence to prove it.' Willing herself to stay calm, Hannah reached into her pocket and pulled out a folded piece of paper. 'Recognise this?' She handed it to him. 'I'm sure you know your own signature and these accounts can show exactly how much you've stolen.'

'Bitch.'

Richard threw both word and paper at her and stalked away down the corridor, disappearing into the room his colleagues had entered.

Taking a deep breath and rearranging her clothes, Hannah returned the paper to her pocket and slipped back into the main council chamber to wait with the others.

'Where've you been?' Kate asked.

'Toilet.'

Kate nodded sympathetically. 'You should've said. I'd have come with you. Nerves always get me that way too.'

Hannah shoved her hands into her pockets. They had started shaking and she didn't want Kate to see them. 'I think I could do with going again.'

'Come on.' Kate tucked her arm through Hannah's and together they went in search of the bathroom.

Remembering she was meant to have been once already, Hannah was grateful they were well signposted and she steered Kate to the correct door. Once inside the cubicle,

Hannah retched over the bowl, shivers running through her body. She'd known it would be difficult seeing Richard again and speaking to him, but she hadn't anticipated such a physical reaction. Kate knocked on the cubicle door.

'Hannah? You okay in there?'

Hannah wiped her mouth and flushed the toilet. 'I'm okay,' she called. 'Think maybe I'm coming down with something.'

She opened the door to find Kate's sympathetic face waiting for her. 'You need to take tomorrow off?'

Hannah shook her head. 'I'm sure I'll be fine. Let me wash my hands and then we'll go back to the others.'

Leaning over the sink, Hannah could feel Kate's eyes boring into her through the mirror and she kept her own fixed firmly on her hands as she scrubbed them.

Hugh was hovering anxiously in the corridor as they returned. 'Come on,' he said urgently. 'They're back.'

Kate and Hannah jogged the remaining distance as Hugh held the door open and the three of them slipped into their seats, smiling apologetically as they did so. The chairman rose to his feet.

'As you know, the Lido has been running at a loss for a number of years and the Council has a responsibility to ensure its funds are allocated in such a way as to get maximum return on its investments. Therefore, it would be irresponsible of us to continue to subsidise entries in the way we have been for the last few years. We cannot in all conscience allocate funds to a leisure facility which is consistently losing such large amounts of money. Therefore, I regret to say that we still believe our decision to close the Avonstow Lido at the end of the current season, is the correct one. He glanced along the row of chairs to where Richard sat, his face stony. However, my colleagues have been persuaded by your impassioned pleas to take over the running of the pool yourselves and therefore, I am pleased to inform you we have agreed to allow you to take over the running of the pool with immediate effect until the end of the season in October. If, within that time frame, you can prove you have the capability and capacity to run it effectively, then we will grant you the leasehold at a rate of one pound per year for the next five years, subject to approval by a full council meeting. Should the venture be successful, we will then consider whether or not to propose a buy-out of the freehold of the property. Full details of the contract will be forwarded to you within the next few days.'

Kate let out a whoop of delight and hugged Hannah who was sitting next to her. 'We did it!'

Hannah grinned and embraced her friend, trying to distract herself from the expression on Richard's face. She knew he would never forgive her for what she'd done. She didn't care – her days of trying to please him were behind her – but she had threatened to expose him and he was angry. But, she reassured herself, she had moved on and he no longer had the ability to hurt her. He had done his worst and she had survived and moved on with her life. She broadened her smile and reached around Kate to hug Ellie.

'Well done,' she told the older woman. 'Well done.'

'Don't congratulate us too soon,' Ellie grinned. 'We've got to make it work now!'

Hannah laughed. 'We'll do it. You know we will. Jack won't let us fail.'

'HAVE YOU SEEN THIS?' Ellie stormed through the door into the café, brandishing a letter.

'Morning,' Kate grinned. Her joviality disappeared the instant she read Ellie's letter. 'What?' She leant against the wall. 'They can't do this.'

'They can and it appears they have.'

'Do the others know?'

Ellie nodded. 'I texted them all this morning. They're on their way here for a meeting.'

'What's happened?' Hannah leant through the hatch.

'Those money-grubbing bastards at the council happened, that's what.' Ellie took the letter from Kate and handed it to Hannah.

Hannah's eyes widened as she read the contents of it. 'They're refusing to include the money from the band night in the profits? But we organised it, not them.' Her voice bristled with indignation. 'And they're not paying any of us?'

Ellie shook her head. 'Nope. Café staff, lifeguards, front of house, the whole lot gone.'

'Who's going to run it then?'

Ellie ran a hand through her hair. 'I have no idea. I should have picked up on it when he said they were handing it over to us with immediate effect, but I was so pleased we were going to get a chance to take it on that I didn't take in what he meant.'

'You know they've done it on purpose.' Hannah handed the letter back. 'They were deliberately ambiguous in the meeting and then slap this on you with no notice. They know you can't run the place without lifeguards and people can't afford to work for nothing. They're hoping it will be a massive failure so they can prove it's an unsustainable white elephant and close it anyway. Then they can sell the land and build something else on it.'

'Over my dead body.' Jack appeared in the doorway. 'We'll work something out.'

Clem climbed over the little fence which separated the café decking from the pool area. He had a letter too. 'These were waiting for us when we got in this morning.'

'What does yours say?' Kate asked her brother-in-law.

'That as the Lido is now under new management, we're all being reassigned to pools elsewhere in the area. Nobody's happy about it, they know the council are playing dirty tricks, but they need their jobs.'

'They, not we?' Hannah queried.

Clem shrugged. 'I rang them up and told them to stick their job. I figured you'd work out a way to pay my wages.'

'But we need more than one lifeguard.'

'Stick an advert on Facebook. I'm qualified to train people. We can do the training in the evenings and open the pool as normal during the day. I can do the hours myself until we get them trained up. Plus, a couple of the guards have said they're happy to volunteer for a shift each on their days off. We can muddle through for now without risking anyone drowning.'

'Is there any way we could make more money in here?' Jack asked. 'I mean, it's not exactly heaving, is it?'

Kate grinned. 'I did have some ideas about that actually. Hang on a minute.' She disappeared into the kitchen and rummaged around in her bag. 'Here.' She handed a piece of paper to Jack. 'What do you think?'

He looked at her doubtfully. 'Could we manage all this?'

Kate scoffed. 'Of course we can! Did you see what we put together for the band night?'

'I know, but that was a one-off event. This would be every day. Do we even have the equipment for all of this?'

'What we don't have, I can bring from home, but yes, I think we can. I told you I was sick of only offering junk food, drinks, cake and ice-cream. We could do so much more with the place. It needs a fair bit of TLC but I'm happy to do it if you'll give me license to crack on with it.'

'Kate, do what you need to do. At this stage, I'll take on board pretty much any suggestion if it will help us keep the place open. What do you need us to do?'

Kate handed him another list. Jack laughed.

'You don't hang around, do you?'

'No. If you want something done, you've got to crack on and do it.'

He handed the list back. 'Okay, go for it. Let's see if it makes a difference.'

'Should I be worried?' Hannah smiled.

'Only a little bit.'

Hannah rolled her eyes. 'Let me have it then. What am I doing?'

'We're going to start with some painting.'

'That doesn't sound too much of a challenge.'

'I only said we were starting with that.'

Hannah groaned. 'I knew I should never have agreed to this.'

Ellie laughed and pulled Jack over to a table. 'I'll leave you explain the details, Kate. Can we have a couple of coffees when the others get here?'

Kate went back into the kitchen. 'Right. Here's what needs to be done.'

'Frankie! Ken! We haven't seen you for ages. How are you?' The words bubbled out of Hannah. She didn't really need to ask. It was obvious Ken had suddenly grown much frailer and even Frankie appeared less sprightly than usual.

'Muddling along, Hannah love, muddling along.' Ken gave her a thumbs up and she turned away to hide the tears that sprang to her eyes.

'Usual, is it?' She filled the portafilter with coffee grounds and jabbed at the buttons on the machine, as Kate called to say she'd already put their teacake on.

'Yes please.' Frankie held her card over the machine as

Hannah tapped the amount in. 'I hear there's changes afoot in this place.'

Hannah smiled. 'Kate's got a whole new menu planned – paninis, jacket potatoes, homemade cakes – plus she's booked someone to come and do a proper wine and cheese tasting evening.'

'I bet that will do well,' Ken laughed.

'Sold out already.' Kate's head appeared in the hatch. 'Had to put a second date in because there were so many people wanting tickets.'

'And we have another band night coming up. We're doing a hotpot supper for this one. I think that's sold out now as well, isn't it?'

Kate nodded. 'As of yesterday afternoon. One hundred and fifty people all coming to boogie the night away.'

'And hopefully buy plenty of drinks while they're doing it,' Hannah chipped in with a grin.

'And will you still be doing the burgers and chips and the bacon rolls in here?' Ken asked, shuffling to the nearest table. 'Not that I'm allowed to eat them anymore, but I can still enjoy the smell.'

'We are.' Hannah put the two coffees down in front of him, then moved out of the way so Frankie could take her seat. 'This place is built on the back of Kate's breakfasts. I think there'd be a riot if we stopped doing them!'

Kate came out of the kitchen with their teacake. 'How are you really getting on, Ken? We've missed you.'

With a quick glance at his wife, Ken reached out a hand and laid it over hers. 'I'm alright,' he said quietly. 'Doing as well as can be expected. The doctors are happy anyway.'

'He needs to rest more.'

'We've talked about this, love. It's not going to make any difference in the long run and I'm going stir crazy cooped up at home all the time. I've never been one for sitting and watching the telly, you know that.'

'I know you're a stubborn old man who won't do as he's told.' Frankie's eyes glittered, but her lips twisted wryly.

'That's why you fell in love with me, isn't it?' Ken spoke gently and Frankie's smile became a reluctant laugh.

'I suppose so.'

'Well then. Stop looking so woebegone, you two and tell me the rest of your plans for this place.'

'We've got a painting party planned for tomorrow evening.'

'What's one of those?' Ken frowned. 'You're never having kids coming round and firing paint at each other, are you?'

Hannah laughed. 'Not paintball. Hugh and Mark are coming down with Clem and Harry and they're going to repaint the whole place after we close. Between them and us we reckon we can get it done and still be ready to open tomorrow morning. We might just need to open the windows if the smell of paint is really strong.'

Kate waved a dismissive hand. 'Get some bacon on the grill, that'll overpower any other smell.'

'When does the new menu start?'

'Also tomorrow. We've had it on social media that it's coming, but we thought with the new paintjob it would be a good opportunity to promo the new menu at the same time.'

'It will take more than a lick of paint and different food to keep the place open.' Frankie frowned. 'We need to appeal to people's sense of community as well.'

Hannah and Kate exchanged glances. 'Actually, that's something we were going to talk to you about. Out of all of us, you know the most about the history of this place. Would you be prepared to do a talk on it?'

'About the Lido?'

Kate nodded. 'About when it was built – you said your

dad was involved, didn't you – and about coming as a child and then your experiences here in the war. I think it's something people would be really interested in.'

Frankie glanced at Ken. He smiled encouragingly. 'I'll be fine. You should definitely do it. It will give you something else to think about rather than fussing over me all the time.'

'I don't fuss.'

'You do and I love you for it. But you should definitely do this. You've got those boxes of photos from your mum's and I'm sure I remember seeing some of the Lido in there. You could get Ellie to scan them onto her laptop thing for you.' Gesturing at the café's rear doors, he continued, 'You could set some kind of screen up there and project the photos onto it so everyone can see them.'

'That's a great idea. What do you think, Frankie?'

'If you really think people would be interested in hearing me waffle on about ancient history, then I'll do it. Were you thinking of charging people though? Otherwise, I don't see how you're going to make any money out of it.'

'The talk itself would be free, but we'll sell drinks and cakes etc and make the money from them. How long do you think it will take you to get it ready?'

'I should think a week or two would be enough. If I can remember where I put the photos and assuming Ken's right about there being some Lido ones in there.'

'And will you talk about your war?'

Frankie hesitated. 'Some of it. Some parts I can't…' She held up a hand as Ken tried to interrupt her. 'I know what you said. It's not a secret anymore and you're not worried about anything I might have done. That isn't what I meant though.' She sighed. 'You talking about those boxes of photos reminded me of my mum. I learnt so much about her during the war and I know that a lot of what I did must have hurt her badly, but she was always there when I needed her. I still miss her.'

She broke off and wiped her eyes before continuing. 'I don't mind telling you about it all, but I don't want family secrets laid bare, even for the Lido. Do you know, Ken, if it hadn't been for her, I'm not sure I'd ever have had the courage to tell you how I felt. I'd made such a mess of everything. I didn't feel I deserved anyone and especially not you. It was Mum who convinced me it was okay to tell you I loved you. Until I spoke to her, I'd not even properly admitted it to myself.'

'Lily was a good woman,' Ken said. 'Like her daughters.'

Frankie blinked away the tears that threatened again. Ken patted her hand.

'I'm glad she convinced you. You know what I was like when I was younger. After you turned me down the last time, I thought you'd never change your mind. If you hadn't said something, I'd never have guessed how you felt and I wouldn't have missed out on this life for anything.'

A silence fell over the table. Kate and Hannah quietly got up and left the couple to themselves.

MAY 1944

*F*rankie opened the envelope by her breakfast plate and the slid the note out. Reading it, she frowned. Adam usually waited until they were together before trying not-so-subtly to get information out of her. A note urging her to meet him was most unusual. It suggested he was desperate to get inside knowledge on something specific. It was true there had been a lot more confidential telegrams landing on the Admiral's desk recently, but she had no idea what they were about. Contrary to what she had led Adam to believe, Admiral Ashton shared nothing with her beyond what she needed to know. They couldn't risk her inadvertently passing on information she hadn't planned to.

The second letter was from Ken. A smile tugged at the corners of her mouth in anticipation of the contents. His letters had been more frequent of late and always made her feel better. In her darkest moments, they were a place of refuge, words she could retreat to and find comfort in when the scornful voices in her own head grew too loud.

. . .

FRANKIE,

Have you taken leave of your senses? Mother finally confessed she knew who you've been seeing. Adam Liversidge. I told her she must be mistaken, but she assured me that she'd seen him, as she put it, 'sneaking into her lodgings in the middle of the afternoon'. You know she would never say anything against you, so what others must be saying is only to be imagined. Have you no sense of your own worth? I know Mac hurt you badly, but Adam? And so blatantly? Tell me it's none of my business, but as your friend, I am begging you to put an end to this. It cannot and will not end well for you. Is this why you moved out of home? So you could see him? I can't imagine your parents are happy about it. Or does he have some hold over you? Is that it? Is he forcing you into this situation? I cannot fathom why else you would choose him. I had hoped after the last time we were together, you might be coming to care for me, but now I find myself wondering if you were merely amusing your-self at my expense. I don't want to believe you could be so cruel to someone who has always considered himself your friend, but I do not know what else to think. I do not wish to think ill of you, but at the moment you are making it difficult for me to find excuses for your behaviour. Please, Frankie, I am begging you. If there is a rational explanation for all this, then tell me. My feelings for you have never changed, nor have I ever hidden them from you, but it seems you hold me in so little regard you are content to amuse yourself with anyone and everyone except me. Is Adam the reason you ran from the hospital? I am at a loss to square your behaviour with the girl, the woman, I know and love. I no longer know what to think. Perhaps this is the wakeup call I needed and I simply need to let you go, but I cannot bear the thought of a life without you in it. I think it best if you do not visit for a while and would ask that you not write to me, while I think everything over. I do not know what to do.

Yours,

Ken

FRANKIE STARED at the letter until the words blurred. She swiped the back of her hand across her face, angry with herself for crying. She didn't have time for this. Even as her fury with Ken's mother mounted, she knew she was being unfair. Meredith Ford was only trying to protect her son, as any mother would. It wasn't her fault she had misinterpreted the situation. *Except she didn't, did she? She was exactly right about what was happening behind those closed curtains. She just doesn't know why. And she never will. None of them will. They'll take their assumptions and stick with them because I can never tell them the truth. For the rest of my life I'll be the widow who jumped into bed with the next available man. It only confirms what they've always believed about us. About Mum.* She sighed loudly. *I signed up for this and I have to see it through no matter what.*

Draining her last mouthful of bitter tea – the leaves had obviously been reused that morning – Frankie put on her coat and headed straight for the port. It was going to be unpleasant and she would need to draw on every ounce of her acting skills, but how could it possibly be any worse than what she had already done in the name of her country? No matter how many times she reminded herself why she was doing it, she had felt grubby for the last three years. No amount of bathing could remove the stain of her memories or the smell of Adam from her skin. *I'm tired. Tired of the lies. Will I even be able to go back to a normal life after? Who would want me now? Even Ken doesn't.* Tears pricked at her eyes again and she blinked them away. She couldn't afford to get sentimental. Not now. She had a job to do. Clamping her teeth together, she threaded her way through the docks until she reached Adam's office. She took a deep breath and knocked on the door.

'Come in!'

Frankie wiped her hands down her uniform skirt. The door handle was cold to her touch and she shivered. She opened the door, pasting a bright smile onto an unconcerned face.

'I got your note.'

Adam rose as she entered the room, holding his arms open. 'Hello, sweetheart. I'm sorry to drag you all the way over here, but we need to talk.'

Frankie moved into his arms and kissed him deeply, knowing he liked to be greeted that way, to feel as though she'd spent every waking moment waiting to be held by him. She was surprised when he ended the kiss abruptly and moved back behind his desk.

'What is it?'

'Nothing. It's just that I'm at work.'

Frankie glanced at the desk and then at him. 'That doesn't usually stop you.'

He glared at her. 'There was no one here then. There are people around today.'

Frankie pouted. 'Then what did you invite me here for then?'

'I told you. We need to talk.'

'About what?'

'I need to know what's going on in your office. In Ashton's office.'

'I don't understand.'

'I want to know everything you know about where ships are going. Personnel movement. All of it.'

Frankie stared at him in disbelief. That he was suddenly dropping the pretence of not trying to get information out of her had caught her off guard.

'What are you talking about?' she stammered. 'I can't give you that kind of information. For one, I don't have it and for another, it's confidential. You know it is.' She paused, her expression turning to horror. 'Is that what all this has been about? Have you only been courting me because of where I work?' She bit the inside of her mouth and tears sprang to her eyes. 'I… I thought you…'

'Don't be daft, Frankie. You know I love you. How long have we been seeing each other now? I've never asked you for information before, have I? If that was all I wanted, I'd have been asking for it long ago. I wouldn't even be asking now unless it was important.' His tone switched from peremptory to wheedling. 'Sweetheart, you must know something. It's… well you see… I'm in a spot of bother and if I don't get the information they want, then I could be in a lot of trouble.'

'What kind of trouble?' Frankie did her best to look concerned.

'Big trouble. The kind of trouble you don't get out of.'

'What have you done?' she whispered, making her eyes wide.

'I had some stuff that wasn't technically on ration and someone found out and if I don't give them what they want, they'll turn me in to the police. That's not important though. What is important is that you get me the information I need. I have to have it, Frankie. I have to know where on the south coast those ships and men are going.'

'I've told you I don't know!'

'Then find out.' He spoke through gritted teeth and came round the desk to stand in front of her. He gripped her arms and shook her. 'Do you understand, you stupid girl? Find out.'

'Adam, you're hurting me!'

'They'll do more than hurt you, if you don't help me.'

Frankie's breath caught in her throat. 'What has any of this to do with me?'

'Don't be stupid, Frankie. They know you're my girlfriend and they know all about you.'

Frankie froze. 'What's that supposed to mean?'

'Don't play the innocent. We both know you're far from that. They know Mac was already married when he married you. How do you think people around here will react when they find out? Do you think they'll still speak to you? Will they still use The Mermaid? You married another woman's husband, got yourself pregnant by him, then jumped into bed with me. He wasn't even cold in his grave.'

'I didn't!' Frankie protested. 'It was months before we…'

'And do you really think they'll take your word for it? I wouldn't. And I won't be denying it. Might even hint it happened while he was still alive.'

Frankie gulped. 'You wouldn't.'

'Wouldn't I?'

'I thought we… you said…'

'Words mean nothing Frankie, even ones said in the bedroom. They want that information and I don't want to go to prison. I'll do whatever it takes and if you loved me, you'd do the same.'

Frankie threw herself at him and he staggered under the unexpected weight. 'I'll get it,' she sobbed into his shoulder. 'Not because of what you said, but because I love you. I'll do anything as long as you don't push me away. I can't bear it.' She grabbed his face, feverishly kissing him. 'Promise me you'll not send me away. Promise.'

Adam slid an arm around her. 'That's my girl. I'm sorry I had to get rough with you. I'm panicking a bit. I'm in a spot and I need my best girl to get me out of it.'

Frankie sniffed and turned large, watery eyes to him. 'There was no need to be so cruel,' she said reproachfully.

'It's not me, sweetheart. It's them. I had to make you see what they were prepared to do if you wouldn't help. You do understand, don't you.'

Frankie nodded, her lower lip trembling. 'Kiss me,' she said quietly. 'I need to know you care. I need…' she trailed off and bit her lip, her eyes darting to the desk.

Adam followed the direction of her eyes and nodded. He darted over to the door and locked it. 'I understand,' he said, picking her up and placing her on the desk. He slid his hand under her skirt. 'There's something else you should know though. I was told in confidence, but I'll tell you, to prove how much I love you.'

He whispered in her ear. Frankie's throat constricted.

'I don't believe you,' she croaked. 'She wouldn't.'

'She would and she did.'

'How did you find out?'

'I have my sources.' He grinned. 'It's up to you what you do now. In the meantime though, why don't you show me how grateful you are for the information.'

Frankie swallowed her feelings, unfastened the button on his waistband and pulled him towards her.

ON LEAVING ADAM'S OFFICE, Frankie walked slowly, clearing her head. Her mind reeled from what Adam had whispered to her. A part of her was angry, but deep down, she knew Lily had done the right thing. Mind made up, she headed for The Mermaid. Once inside, she went straight to the little office behind the reception desk, where she knew her mother would be.

'Hello, love.' Lily smiled as she walked in. 'What's this in aid of?' she asked, as Frankie came around the side of the desk to hug her.

'Nothing. Just love you.'

'Is anything wrong?' Lily's expression switched in an instant to concern.

'I'm alright,' Frankie sighed, perching on the corner of the desk. 'It's just…'

'Has the Liversidge boy done something to you?'

Frankie grimaced. 'Nothing you need to worry about. You know I can't…'

Lily put her hand over her daughter's. 'I know. You can't talk about it. I remember. You're not a child anymore.'

Frankie smiled. 'You've heard it all before. I know. And I am alright, I promise.' She heaved a sigh. Sometimes I feel old. I'm only 22 but I feel as though I've lived a hundred lives already.'

'War does that to you,' Lily said. 'In 1917, I was the same age as you are now and I'd already lived a lifetime as well.'

'You never really talk about the war. Was it the same then as it is now?'

'It was worse in some ways,' Lily said, after a moment. 'I was a different person then.' She bit her lip. 'I don't talk about my early life because I don't want to remember it. I was a scared little girl who thought she knew everything, thought she could handle whatever life threw at her, because she'd always had to. Your dad showed me I didn't have to do everything on my own.' She squeezed Frankie's hand. 'And you're not alone, darling. I know you can't talk about what-ever it is you're doing, but you don't have to tell me anything. You can just tell me you need me and I'll be there, I promise. I'm always on your side.'

Tears sprang to Frankie's eyes and she squeezed her mother's hand. 'Thank you,' she whispered. 'But there's nothing anyone can do.'

'I don't believe that for a moment,' Lily said. 'There's always something.'

'Not this time, Mum.'

Lily's arms wrapped around her daughter. 'What did we always tell you and Addie when you were small?'

Frankie sniffed. 'That we'd never be alone as long as we had each other. But I am this time. I can't talk to any of you about it.'

'Perhaps not.' Lily stroked Frankie's hair. 'But you can tell me how you feel.'

Frankie considered for a moment. 'Ken is angry with me,' she said. 'I can't tell you why, but he's completely justified. Or at least he would be if what he thinks is happening, was the full story. I know I shouldn't care, but I can't help it.' She looked at her mother, eyes full. 'I wish I was more like you.'

'In what way?'

'You've never cared what people said about you and you always taught us not to be concerned with what society says we should do. I wish… I wish I could be as strong.' Frankie dissolved into tears and Lily's arms tightened.

'My darling girl.' She rocked Frankie gently. 'I didn't care what people thought because I couldn't afford to. There are things I've done in my life that I'm not proud of, but I did them in order to survive. That's what I have to tell myself. Surviving brought me you girls and your father and I can't regret any of you. But it doesn't mean it didn't hurt at the time. That it didn't cut deep when women sneered at me in the street, or when I overheard the names they muttered. What does Ken think is happening?'

'I can't tell you.'

'Why does what he thinks matter to you?'

'I don't know.' Frankie shook her head.

Lily let go of her and stared at her thoughtfully. 'The last time you saw him in hospital, you were upset. Did something happen?'

Frankie laughed. 'I swear sometimes you're a witch. He kissed me.'

'Did you want him to?'

Frankie blushed. 'A bit. Yes.'

'Because it flattered your vanity?'

'No!' The anger that flared in Frankie surprised her and she stared at her mother in shock, then shook her head slowly. 'No. I suppose I... it made me feel less alone and then...' She trailed off under her mother's watchful gaze. 'And then I...' Her cheeks flamed and her hands flew to them. 'I enjoyed it and I felt guilty. I had no right to kiss him when... well, I just didn't, but I... it felt... right.'

'It sounds to me as though you realised you were in love with him,' Lily said gently.

'I am. But I can't be. He can't ever know. Not now.'

Lily took Frankie's hands again. 'Darling, whatever it is you're doing, if Ken truly loves you, he'll understand.' Frankie shook her head, but Lily ignored her and carried on. 'And if he doesn't, you have to find a way to make him understand without betraying whatever secrets you have to keep. Whatever you're doing, it does not define you. Wars take so much from people: you can't let it rob you of the rest of your life.' Lily dropped her voice. 'You know I understand better than most. I might never have had you.'

'I'm sorry, Mum. I didn't mean to bring it all up again.'

'You didn't.' Lily was back to her usual brisk self. 'Just remember you're my daughter, Frankie. You keep your head up and you pretend you don't care until it becomes true. But if you get a chance to put things right, you grab it with both hands and you do not let go, no matter what. You'll find a way through to Ken, I know.'

'Why are you so sure?'

'Because I know you and I have faith in you.' Lily's reply wasn't what Frankie had been hoping for, but she smiled nonetheless. It might not have been 'because I know Ken will love you regardless' but it was nice to have a vote of confidence and her mother was right. Not about Ken – who knew how that was going to turn out – but she wasn't alone. There was one person she could ask for help. It would mean telling him everything, but perhaps he might understand and if everyone was going to find out anyway, she didn't really have anything to lose. Slipping off the desk, she kissed the top of Lily's head and left the room, heading up to the top floor and the Admiral's office.

The frown on Admiral Ashton's face softened into a smile when he saw who had followed the knock on his door.

'Something to report, Thompson?' He gestured to the chair opposite him.

Frankie sat down. 'You said to report anything unusual. Adam asked me to meet him in his office this evening. He very rarely does that, he usually comes to me. And when I got there, he asked me straight out for some information. Actually, demanded would be more accurate. And when I didn't agree straight away, he threatened me.'

'Hmm. That does seem a little odd. I wonder what's rattled his cage?' He drummed his fingers on the desk. 'Let me see...'

Picking up the telephone, he dialled a number, then leant back in his chair.

'Ashton here. Interesting changes to arrangements here. Any info your end?' His eyes widened slightly and he nodded. 'Hmm. Yes, that is interesting. Will do. Thanks.' He replaced the handset.

'Pressure coming from above, I gather. Better be prepared for a different approach from now on, I think. He's desperate. What does he have on you?'

Frankie stared blankly at him.

'What information about you did he threaten to make public?'

Frankie didn't answer.

The Admiral hesitated for a moment, seemingly undecided whether to say what he was thinking. He leant forward in the chair, looking awkward. 'Does he... Has he found out about Mac?'

'What about him?' Frankie blurted the words out, then pressed her lips tightly together. As the silence lengthened, she shifted uncomfortably in the chair, but said nothing further.

'I knew you were the right person for this job,' Admiral Ashton said, 'But protocol says we have to thoroughly investigate each agent and all their known associates. I know Mac was married before he married you but I'm also aware you knew nothing of it until after he died.'

'Why didn't you say anything?' Frankie whispered.

'Because I had no reason to. It had no bearing on your abilities and telling anyone else would have served no purpose. There was no reason for anyone to know you were anything other than a young war widow. However, if Liversidge has found out the truth, and this is what he is using to threaten you with, you have to be prepared for the possibility he may choose to reveal it to everyone else should you not do as he asks.'

Frankie nodded, her throat too dry to speak.

'So,' the Admiral continued. 'We need a plan. Something you can tell him to keep him happy. More importantly, something that will keep Lernehan and his handlers happy. What information did he ask you to get?'

'He wanted to know about the movement of ships and personnel between here and the south coast.'

Admiral Ashton smiled thinly. 'In which case, I have a fair idea what he really wants to know about. Here's what you're going to tell him.'

'I'M sorry it's taken me a few days,' Frankie said, smiling nervously. 'The Admiral's been on the phone in his office quite a lot, so I had to time it carefully for when I could go and look through his files. It wasn't a complete waste though – I overheard some interesting conversations which weren't meant for my ears.'

Adam waved a dismissive hand. 'What did you learn?'

Frankie hesitated. 'Are you sure this is safe? I don't want to risk going to prison. Or worse.'

'I'd never put you at risk, darling. No one will ever find out the information came from you, I promise.'

'And it will definitely get you out of trouble with this man?'

Adam nodded. Frankie looked away, picking at the skin on the side of her fingernail. She sighed.

'Alright. You asked about the south coast, but not all the ships are going there. We've had a couple call in on their way to Portsmouth and Southampton, but that's normal. What isn't usual, is the call the Admiral got yesterday telling him to expect a couple of ships going the other way.'

'The other way?'

Frankie nodded. 'We often get ships calling in on the way down from Scotland after they've been refitted or had new crews or whatever. They've had some running time and occasionally there's a problem which needs to be sorted before they set off properly. Last night though, we had two overnight who were going north. Apparently, they got orders to abort their tour and head straight up to Scotland. They wouldn't normally need to stop, but apparently each of their captains had a diplomatic bag to deliver to Ashton. Whatever it was must have been top secret instructions, otherwise they'd have been sent via telephone or wire, or something. We never get hand delivered orders.'

'Did you see what they were?'

'No. I piloted the boat out to the ships, but he made me wait while he went to collect the bags and speak to the captains and he's been in his office all morning so I wasn't able to have a look at them.'

'Never mind. You did well, sweetheart. I think it will be enough to get me off the hook.' He kissed her cheek. 'I owe you one, Frankie, I really do.'

'You won't ask me to do this again, Adam, will you? I don't like it. I'm not cut out for all this sneaking around.'

'Hopefully I won't need to.' He drew her to him and kissed her. 'But if I do, you'll help me out, won't you? You wouldn't abandon me?'

Frankie sighed and pressed herself against him. 'I couldn't.'

'MISS THOMPSON, this is Major Stephen Dixon.'

Frankie saluted. 'Sir.'

Admiral Ashton handed her a piece of paper. 'Permission to be with an officer, just in case it's needed. Don't want our own chaps picking you up, do we? Not strictly necessary given the different services, but better to be on the safe side, I think. Do you understand what's expected?'

'I think so, Sir. I'll give the Major a tour of the base as cover and then we'll probably head to The Queen's Arms. It's most likely where Adam will be tonight.'

'And I'm to show the lady a good time.' As the Admiral glared at him, Major Dixon swallowed hurriedly and added, 'But I'm aware it's all for show, Sir.'

'Hmm.' Admiral Ashton held his gaze for a few more moments, then turned back to Frankie. 'And you know the information to pass on?'

She nodded. 'I'm a bit confused though, Sir. If an American force is supposed to be here, won't it be fairly obvious there's nothing of the kind in the area?'

It was Major Dixon who replied. 'No need to worry. The area it's meant to be happening in has been completely sealed off to the public and we've taken care of the radio chatter you'd expect for this kind of exercise. Now all we need is to make sure the right people get to know about it.'

Frankie shrugged. It didn't make much sense to her, but she had her instructions. The Admiral dismissed them and she led the American Major out of the hotel to take him on a quick tour of Naval base before heading into town.

'I'll apologise now for being forward this evening, Ma'am.' Major Dixon looked embarrassed. Frankie simply smiled.

'Major, I doubt there's anything you will say or do that would be worse than what I've already done to make this a success. You're providing the icing on a very large cake. Please don't concern yourself.'

The major fell silent and he stopped walking. For a moment, Frankie continued along the path, then stopped when she realised she was alone.

'Major?'

He hurried to catch up with her. 'I may be speaking out of turn here, so you'll have to excuse a plain talking farm boy, but I was brought up to treat a lady right. You don't strike me as anything but a lady, so you'll forgive me if I apologise for being forward.'

Frankie blushed. 'No, Sir. It's me who has to beg forgiveness. It's been… challenging recently and I'm only now beginning to realise quite how much this is going to cost me. It's hard to accept people showing you respect when you know how little you deserve it.'

Major Dixon looked at her gravely. 'You have nothing to be ashamed of.'

Frankie laughed, a harsh, grating sound. 'How would you know?'

Major Dixon leant forward and whispered in her ear. 'Because I'm no more American than you are.'

Frankie's head jerked backwards. The major grabbed her wrists and pulled her close again.

'I work for British Intelligence, same as you do. I've seen every report Admiral Ashton has submitted and I know what you've had to do to get the information to Liversidge and his cronies. I can't tell you what the bigger picture is, but believe me, my bosses are proud of what you've accomplished. As you say, this is just the icing on the cake, but isn't the icing always the final touch?'

Frankie smiled, suddenly feeling shy. 'I suppose so.' She straightened her uniform jacket. 'Let's get on with it then, shall we?'

Major Dixon fell into step beside her and together they entered The Queen's Arms and took their seats at a quiet table. Out of the corner of her eye, Frankie saw Adam look up as they entered, but she didn't acknowledge him. Instead, she gave her full attention to the major, who returned it with interest, allowing his hand to linger on hers when he handed over her drink. When he excused himself to visit the bathroom, Adam quickly took his place.

'What's going on, Frankie?'

'Hello to you too.'

'Don't play games with me. Who's he? I thought access to all coastal areas was banned? We've not been allowed out of the area for days and he's definitely not local.'

'Keep your voice down,' she hissed. 'He's visiting the base on official business. He doesn't count.'

'Well, it certainly looks as if he'd like to count with you.'

'Don't be silly.' Under the table she reached across to squeeze his knee. 'You know I'm not interested in anyone else. Admiral Ashton asked me to look after him. His men are here on exercise, but it's all hush-hush.'

'How hush-hush?' Adam's eyes danced dangerously.

Frankie leant over so her lips brushed his ear. 'Very hush-hush. They're practising landing apparently, then they're on their way down to Dover.'

'Good girl.' Adam squeezed her hand, then left the pub as Major Dixon returned from the bathroom.

'Who was that?' he asked, as the door closed behind Adam.

Frankie smiled. 'That was the delivery boy.'

Major Dixon grinned. 'Then our work is done. Shall we have another drink before we leave?'

Frankie hesitated.

'Just to cement the illusion. I have no designs on you.'

She relaxed. 'That sounds lovely.'

AUGUST 2017

'And of course, my association with the Lido goes back further than most people's!' Frankie gestured to her face and laughed. 'My father helped to build it when he was laid off from the shipyard and before it opened to the public, the families of the people who had helped to build it were allowed in free for an afternoon, as a thank you to the men. There was a bit of a ceremony and they held a ribbon over the top of the slide.

As I was the youngest child, I was chosen to be the first person to go down it and the pool was declared officially open. My parents were very proud, my older sister less so.' She chuckled again. 'Addie was not best pleased at me being centre of attention, but I suspect that had more to do with my gloating than any jealousy on her part.'

Frankie paused and peered at her notes. 'I didn't realise then quite how important the Lido was going to be in my life. Like most people around here, I grew up on the sea and the Lido was more a place to socialise than to actually swim in, but during the war I came here regularly to give swimming lessons to the sailors who had joined the Navy without being able to swim and towards the end of the war, it's where my now-husband proposed to me.'

Placing her notes down on the table in front of her, Frankie took a deep breath. 'What many of you may not be aware of is that this isn't the first time people have tried to close our Lido. In the 1970s the council wanted to shut it down because it wasn't being used as much, but we persuaded them that investing in new changing facilities and turning it from seawater to freshwater, would bring people back and it did. Even further back, the powers that be wanted to close it down because a man died here after an accident in the pump room. In those days Avonstow was a bit more important than it is today so strings were pulled in high places and it was saved.

We can't rely on anyone else now unfortunately, so if we're going to repeat the triumphs of our forebears, we're going to have to do it on our own and the only way to do it is to come together as a community and show them this place is more than a swimming pool. It's part of our heritage, the history of our community. It needs to adapt not close and we intend to make sure it does just that.'

She narrowed her eyes and looked out at the audience. 'So, if anyone else fancies having the spotlight on them and can give a talk that others might find at least vaguely interesting, don't be shy in coming forward. We hope this will be the first in a series of lectures on different topics of interest throughout the winter months when the pool is closed. Thank you all for coming this evening and we hope to see you in the café and the pool over the remaining weeks of the season. Oh, I almost forgot!' Kate's frantic gesturing had caught her eye. 'The café will be closing early tomorrow as it's having a bit of a makeover and there will be a new menu from the following day, so keep an eye on Facebook for the big reveal.'

The assembled crowd began to leave and Kate and Hannah returned the chairs and tables to their usual layout, as Frankie drank a much-needed cup of tea.

'I thought it went really well,' Kate said, stacking a chair on top of its table so she could mop around it. 'Everyone seemed really interested.'

'I'm glad you think so,' Frankie smiled. 'I shall be very grateful to get into my bed tonight! Did anyone offer to do any talks?'

'They did actually,' Hannah consulted her list. 'We've had offers for ones on the changing face of fashion, the life and works of Jane Austen and someone who wanted to do a series of lectures or workshops on an introduction to Classical Music.'

'Do you reckon there'll be an audience for them?' Kate sounded doubtful.

Hannah shrugged. 'Only one way to find out.'

'If it's looking a bit pathetic I'm sure you can twist some arms and get people to make up the numbers,' Frankie said confidently.

Hannah and Kate turned to stare at her.

'What?'

'That's usually your area of expertise,' Kate told her with a smile.

Frankie shook her head but didn't deny it.

'It must be time for another coffee by now, surely?' Clem sighed dramatically and rolled his shoulders, grimacing.

'Beer?' His brother offered him a bottle, cold from the fridge.

'Even better.' Clem held it to his forehead. 'Refreshing in multiple ways.' He removed the cap and took a long swig. 'I don't know how you two manage in here all day in this heat. It's evening. Surely it should be cooling down by now.'

Hannah laughed. 'If you think it's hot now, you should try being in there at lunchtime.' She gestured to the kitchen. 'No need for a fancy spa break, just do a cooking shift, the result is the same.'

Kate emerged from the kitchen, a casserole dish held tightly in her oven gloves. 'It's not much cooler now, to be fair.' She smiled, placing the dish on the tables at the centre of the café. 'Grab that pile of plates, will you Harry. I'll get the salad.'

She returned from the kitchen carrying a huge bowl of

salad and a plate of buttery garlic bread and put them next to the lasagne.

'Shall I be mum?' Without waiting for an answer, she picked up the first plate and ladelled a generous helping onto it before handing it to Hannah. 'Help yourselves to bread and salad.'

'Wow,' Hannah mumbled through her first mouthful. 'This is amazing Kate. What have you done that's different?'

'Cheese sauce,' Kate grinned. 'I know it's meant to be bechamel but I think it tastes nicer with the extra cheese. It gives it a bit of a zing, especially if you use really strong cheddar.'

Hannah nodded and gave her a thumbs up, her mouth too full to reply.

'How are you not the size of a house?' Clem asked Harry. 'If I had this kind of cooking every day, I'd be enormous.'

His brother grinned. 'She only cooks on special occasions. I'm on bread and water most of the time!' He broke off with a yelp as Kate kicked him on the ankle.

Hannah took another mouthful of her beer, wondering when she had suddenly become so lucky. She'd done nothing to deserve the change of fortune, but here she was, surrounded by friends. These people wanted nothing from her except her friendship and they were honest, good people. Slowly but surely, they had drawn her into their circle and made her a part of it. For the first time in ages she felt settled and, dare she say it, happy. Even when she had believed she was building a future with Richard, the spectre of her past had haunted her, but now the memories were fading. Not vanishing exactly, but becoming less important. Less defining. As though she was becoming more than her mistakes and it felt good.

Once they'd all finished, Kate pushed her chair away from

the table. 'Right, I'll get this lot in the dishwasher and then we'll crack on with the second coat.'

'No rest for the wicked.' Harry stood up and stretched. 'Come on then little brother. Back to the grindstone.'

Clem sidled over to Hannah as she crouched on the floor painting the top of a skirting board.

'Can I ask your advice about something?'

'Sure.' Hannah went to straighten up, but Clem put a hand on her shoulder.

'No, don't get up. It's easier if you don't.' Instead, he started painting the wall above her, keeping his voice low. 'It's just... I have a dilemma and I was hoping you could help me untangle it a bit. You know my situation with Emmy – technically still married, but on the cusp of divorce. Well... I wondered if... if it was wrong of me to be thinking about dating again.'

'Hypothetically or actually?'

'Actually. There's this girl I like you see and I was considering asking her out, but I don't want her to think I'm the kind of person who takes marriage lightly. I don't, but emotionally, I've not felt married for a long time and I'm only waiting for it to be official.'

Hannah gripped her paintbrush tightly, willing her hand to stop shaking. For a few moments she didn't reply. When she did, it took all her effort to keep her voice steady.

'If you were anyone else, I'd say you were wrong. But you're not. I do know you and I know there's no doubt your marriage is over and your divorce will go through. However, you have to be honest with her. Tell her you're still married, even if it's only a technicality. It's important, Clem.' She looked up at him, her eyes blazing. 'Really important. You can't tell her you're already divorced. You have to be completely honest if you want her to be more than a fling.' She jabbed her brush into the paint. 'Strike that. Even if it's only a fling you should be honest. Everyone deserves to know the truth before they start any kind of relationship.' Paint splattered across her face as she attacked the wall with the brush and Clem knelt down beside her, laying his hand on hers.

'Hey,' he said quietly. 'I have no intention of lying about my past. I'm not ashamed of it. I wasn't the one who cheated. I was just asking if you thought it was okay for me to be thinking about dating again.'

Hannah took a deep breath, blinking away the angry tears. 'Provided you're honest with her, I don't think it's wrong, no.'

Clem smiled sadly. 'She knows already. It was never a case of hiding anything, only the morality of it. The fact is, I don't know if she wants a relationship. She's a bit of a mystery still.'

'Why don't you ask her?' Hannah's forehead wrinkled. 'What's the worst that could happen?'

Clem bit his lip. Gently he took a cloth from his back pocket and wiped a smear of paint from her cheek. Hannah's eyes widened a little at the unexpected contact and he showed her the smeared cloth.

'I've never been a clean painter,' she shrugged. 'I'll get us some more paint.'

CLEM WATCHED as she poured more paint into their shared tray. 'What's the worst that could happen?' her words echoed in his head. 'The worst that could happen is I lose my friend.'

MAY 1944

*A*shton to Henley: Undine swimming nicely. All packages delivered. Received?

HENLEY TO ASHTON: *Received, not yet acted upon. Almost ready to move. Stand by for further instructions.*

'*T*his is Julian.' Kate waved a hand at the suited man setting out wine glasses on the café's tables. 'Julian, this is Hannah.'

'Pleased to meet you.' The man held out a hand. 'Are you joining us tonight?'

Hannah shook her head. 'Only as a waitress. I don't know much about wine, I'm afraid.'

Julian laughed. 'You should come to one of our nights some time. I guarantee you'll leave knowing far more about wine than you did when you arrived.'

'Do you do a lot of these evenings then?'

'The vineyard is still relatively new, so we're doing a few tasting nights to try and get our name out locally. Kate's helped us out in the past with canapes and things, so it's nice to be able to return the favour and bring our wines to her food for a change. People assume English wines are always poor quality and expensive so you have to get over that prejudice before you have a chance of selling anything. Consequently, I often do nights like this where I use other premises and hidden tastings. We ask people how much they think the wine should cost per bottle and where they think it's come from. At the end of the night, we reveal that all the wines are from our estate, right here in Essex and some of them are as little as seven pounds a bottle. Not quite your supermarket plonk price, but we think it tastes the extra couple of pounds better. Here, see what you think.'

He handed Hannah a glass and she took a sip, her eyes lighting up appreciatively. 'That's really nice.'

'That's our cheapest bottle.' He handed her another glass. 'What about this one?'

Hannah took another mouthful and smiled. 'Even I can taste this is more expensive, but the other one is still lovely and you're right. It is better than the similar ones in the supermarket.'

She put the two glasses in the bag of plastic recycling and went into the kitchen to put her apron on. Kate leant in and murmured.

'Try and sell as much as you can tonight. Julian's agreed to give us 10 per cent of every bottle.'

Hannah's eyes widened. 'Was that part of the deal when you booked him?'

'I always give him a discount on the food I do for them because they're local. He said it was only fair we should make a bit tonight as well. We're sold out in terms of the tickets, so he's expecting some decent sales. I've just got to hope the wine and the food pairings work – if they do, people will be much more inclined to buy a few bottles to take home.'

'Any sign of Clem yet?'

'He's on his way with Harry. They're bringing the last of the pre-prepared bits from home.'

As Kate answered Hannah's question, the café door swung open and several boxes piled high appeared in the doorway, followed by a panting Harry. Hannah hurried to take a couple of them from him.

'Thanks, Hannah,' he huffed. 'I didn't realise quite how heavy they were until I was halfway from the car.' He put the rest of the boxes down on the kitchen then went to return the favour to his brother, who came in staggering under the weight of a similar pile of boxes.

'You serving rocks tonight, Kate?' Clem groaned as his stack teetered on the edge of the work surface. Hannah stuck out a hand to save the top box hitting him on the head.

Kate stuck her tongue out, laying the canapes onto serving platters already decorated with paper doilies. Hannah worked alongside her and they soon had everything ready. Harry took up his position at the door, ready to act as host and Clem hovered in the kitchen entrance looking uncomfortable in his trousers and shirt.

'I don't like being smart,' he groused when he caught Hannah laughing at his expression. 'I'm much happier in my lifeguard uniform.'

'You are not serving at a wine tasting in shorts and t-shirt,' Kate hissed.

Clem rolled his eyes and grinned at Hannah. 'She's such a spoilsport,' he whispered loudly.

Kate kicked his ankle as she handed him one of the platters. 'People are starting to arrive. Go.' She gave him a gentle push. 'Mingle. Offer food. Smile.'

Julian stood by his table, handing out the complimentary glass of sparkling wine included in the price of the ticket for the event, a smile tugging at the corners of his mouth at the overheard compliments to the drink and the speculation as to which brand of Prosecco the guests were drinking.

'How's it going?' Jack, Ellie, Hugh and Mark appeared at the hatch. 'Anything we can do to help?'

'Go enjoy yourselves.' Kate shooed them away. 'You paid for your tickets, you're guests tonight. Just see if you can sign up any more volunteers to come and help out.'

'Or better still, a millionaire or two who fancy being phil-anthropic,' Hannah added, laughing as the two couples walked away to find their table, promising to do their best.

LATER THAT EVENING, Julian handed Kate an envelope and thanked her for a successful evening, before wheeling his trolley of bottles out to his car. When the door had closed behind him, she looked inside and whistled.

'A good night?' Harry asked.

'A very good night. With the money from the tickets and what Julian's given me, even when I take off the cost of the food etc, we've still made over a grand profit.'

'That's amazing. Well done you two!' Clem high-fived them both.

'Thanks for helping out.'

Clem glanced at Hannah. 'Any time.'

THE FOLLOWING DAY, Frankie and Ken were at their usual table; Hannah perched on a chair, chatting to them while the café was quiet. The early morning swim over, Clem had come in for a coffee on his way home.

'I hear last night was a roaring success,' Frankie said.

'It was. It went really well. Kate's food was amazing, as always and the wine guy, Julian, really knew what he was talking about. I'm not remotely interested in wine beyond "does it taste nice" and even I found myself listening to what he was saying.'

'Do I detect a wine convert?' Ken smiled.

Clem laughed and shook his head. 'Not at all but I can see why people enjoyed it.'

'I'm certainly tired enough this morning,' Hannah said,

covering a yawn. 'I feel as though I'd been drinking the wine, rather than serving it.'

'Do you have plans for any more events?' Frankie asked. 'You've not got long to turn a profit if we're going to keep the place open.'

'Mark and Jack said they'd be in this morning to talk through some more ideas, but I don't know what their plans are,' Kate called from the kitchen.

As she spoke, the door opened and they all turned, expecting to see their friends, but it was a slightly built young woman who hesitated in the doorway.

'Excuse me, I'm sorry to bother you. I know the pool isn't open at the moment, but I wondered if it would be possible for me to go in and take some photos?'

'Of the Lido?' Kate asked.

The woman nodded. 'I'd be very grateful. I'm visiting my great-grandmother this afternoon and I thought it would be nice to show her some pictures of what it looks like now.'

'Was she local then?' Hannah inquired.

'Not really. She came here during the war. She was in ENSA – you know, the entertainment people – and she did a concert here.'

'1944,' Frankie murmured. 'I remember it well.'

Ken's hand folded around her. 'Me too. It was a good night.'

Frankie looked at him. 'Was it?'

'It was for me. It was the first time I let myself believe I might actually still have a chance with you.'

'That's not quite how I remember it.'

Ken shrugged. 'You let your guard down. I took it as a positive.'

Kate stifled a laugh and returned her attention to the young woman. 'Do you sing too?'

She coloured a little. 'I do. I'm actually part of a singing trio. We specialise in 1940s music – close harmony, like the Andrews Sisters if you know of them.'

Frankie snorted. 'This lot have never heard of the Andrews Sisters. They wouldn't know good music if it hit them in the face.'

Hannah cleared her throat. 'They sang with Glen Miller.'

Clem threw his head back and laughed. 'Of course you know who they are.'

'I grew up listening to that kind of music,' Hannah said defensively. 'My dad loves it.'

'Your great-grandmother had a beautiful voice,' Frankie said. 'It doesn't surprise me you've followed in her footsteps.'

Clem got to his feet. 'Shall we get your photos then?' He opened the door onto the patio and with a grateful smile, the woman followed him through.

'Angela Williams,' Kate read from the business card the woman had given her. 'And her group is called The Bluebirds.'

Jack and Mark appeared in the doorway and Kate beckoned them over. 'Look at this,' she said, handing them the card. 'She's come in to take some photos, but what about asking if we could book them for an evening?'

Jack looked dubious. 'We only have a few weeks of the season left. Even if they're available, could we sell enough tickets?'

'If we did a bar and food, I'll bet we could,' Frankie said. 'People are always happy to buy drinks and everyone knows how good Kate's food is.'

Kate looked thoughtful. 'What about if we offered picnics? We could do different levels from basic to posh, for people to book in advance. That way we wouldn't need to be cooking on the night. People can bring their own food if they want to, or they can order from us. That way, we'd have a better idea beforehand if we'd made enough money. If we offered cocktails as well, there's even more potential for profit there.'

'We can't do anything if they're fully booked,' Mark said, 'But if you two think we can make it work, let's ask her when she comes back in.'

'We could really push the fact her great-grandmother sang here during the war as well,' Hannah added. 'It makes it even more of a nostalgia evening.'

'I wonder if some of the care homes might be interested in bringing their relatives down.' Ken looked thoughtful. 'I know it's not really their generation of music, but that doesn't necessarily mean they wouldn't be interested.'

'We can certainly ask,' Jack nodded. 'It can't do any harm to try.'

Angela and Clem came back through from the pool area. 'Thank you so much,' Angela smiled at the assembled group. Her eyes were red. 'It was so lovely seeing where Nana sang. I haven't been here since I was a child.'

'It's more run down than we'd like it to be,' Jack smiled, 'But we have plans to improve it.'

'Are you part of the local group who've taken it on?' Angela's face brightened. 'I read about you trying to stop the council closing it. I think it's a wonderful idea.'

'I don't suppose your trio have any availability in the next few weeks, do you? We were thinking it might be nice to have a Forties' Night and it would make it extra-special if one of the singers had a family connection to the Lido.'

Angela thought for a moment, then reached into her pocket and took out her phone. She tapped the screen and when it pinged rapidly a minute later, she smiled. 'We actually had a cancellation this morning,' she said. 'We were meant to be performing at an engagement party, but it's been called off. The others have agreed to do the gig for half our usual fee if the date suits you.'

She named the day and price. Jack and Mark looked at the others.

'It's no good looking at us,' Frankie laughed. 'You two do the finances, you know what we can afford.'

'It's very generous of you,' Jack said eventually. He glanced at Kate. 'Do you honestly think we can pull together an audience at such short notice?'

'I do.' Kate was firm and Hannah nodded her agreement. 'We'll sell tickets in the street if we have to.'

'You'll need another band as well,' Angela said. 'We'll need breaks and this kind of thing always works better if there are two bands playing. Give me a second.' She fired off another text and a moment later her phone pinged again. She smiled. 'I have a friend who runs a swing band and he owes me a favour,' she explained. 'He thinks he can get a small group together to play in between our sets. Because it's not the full band it will be a fraction of the cost. If you're interested, he's up for it.'

She showed them the message and Mark nodded. 'Let's go for it.'

Hannah cleared away the cups as they made plans. She noticed Ken sat quietly observing her and smiled at him. 'Too noisy for you?'

He returned her smile. 'A little. One of the advantages of going deaf is that you can stop listening and then blame your body for failing you.'

Hannah laughed. 'You looked as though you were deep in thought.'

'Actually, I was thinking about you,' Ken said. 'Or at least, about how much you remind me of Frankie.'

Surprised, Hannah waited for him to continue.

'You give almost nothing of yourself away,' Ken explained, 'And yet to anyone who cares enough to watch, it's obvious there's a heavy burden on you. Frankie's the same. Doesn't

297

often open up to people; has this need to prove she can cope with everything on her own. She was always self-reliant, even as a child.' He fixed Hannah with a firm stare. 'Sometimes it's good to share the load, though. When you have someone you can trust with it.'

Hannah bit her lip.

'You'll all look after her, won't you?' Ken's voice suddenly wobbled.

'Of course.' Hannah moved to his side and crouched down. 'Absolutely we will, I promise.'

Ken patted her hand. 'Thank you.' He caught her arm as she moved to stand up. 'And remember what I said. It's not good to bottle everything up – things have a way of escaping whether you want them to or not.'

'I'll bear it in mind,' Hannah promised.

Jack had quickly arranged all the details with Angela while Kate got to work on planning the picnic menus. By the time Frankie and Ken had said goodbye and left to go home with Jack, Mark had arranged for the tickets to be printed the following day and had advertised the event on the Lido's social media pages, as well as the local news sites.

For the next week, the group set to work selling tickets. Every customer who came into either the café or the pool was informed about the forthcoming evening and posters appeared all over town. Hugh managed to get an advert into the local press and a spot on the radio to promote it, which brought another boost to the ticket sales. Each day, one of them would head to the shops which held the tickets to get an updated total of the number sold. Frankie and Mark visited the care homes and secured block bookings from a couple of them.

'How are the picnic sales coming on?' Jack asked when he popped into the café to update Kate and Hannah on the latest sales figures.

Kate took a clipboard down from a hook in the kitchen and handed it to him. Jack glanced at it then looked again, his eyes widening.

'Wow! Can you cater for so many?'

Kate laughed. 'I've had to rope in Clem and Harry to help with boxing them all up, but otherwise Hannah and I have it all under control.'

Hannah waved a knife at him. 'I'm on chopping duty while we're quiet. I get all the glamorous jobs!'

Jack grinned at her. 'It's all in a good cause, Hannah. All in a good cause.'

Hannah let out a mock groan. 'Easy for you to say. You're not the one with a hundred potatoes to peel and chop!'

'I never thought I'd say this, but we're almost sold out. I had no idea old music was so popular.'

'I think it helps that Frankie's been really pushing this one. She's incredibly persuasive when she gets going.' Hannah shook her head. 'I've never seen a sales pitch like it. I wanted to buy a ticket and I'm working!'

'I think she sees the fate of the Lido as the one thing she can influence at the moment. Ken's looking frailer than ever and I think she's finding it tough that she can't fight this battle for him.'

'I'm worried about them both,' Kate said. 'And I don't know what she'll do without him.'

Jack shook his head. 'There's not much we can do, to be honest. She's as stubborn as they come and she won't accept help until she's ready. She knows he can't stay at home much longer, but she's adamant he's not going anywhere until he absolutely has to.'

'Maybe it's her way of coping,' Hannah said quietly. 'If she keeps things normal for as long as she can, she doesn't have to think about the future. She's not deceiving herself about the situation but dealing with a reality is easier.' She shrugged. 'Sometimes your imagination conjures up far worse scenarios than actually happen.'

Kate gave her a curious look but didn't say anything further. Jack gathered his things together.

'I promised Aunt Frankie I'd drive them to the hospital this afternoon, so I'd best get off. I'll see you tomorrow.'

*F*rankie swayed as the notes of 'Moonlight Serenade' soared out over the Lido waters. Around the edge of the pool, tables were dotted about and in between them, the Naval and civilian inhabitants of Avonstow mingled. She leant against the wall of the pump room, grateful for its solid support. Her eyes swam with tears, but whether they were of frustration or humiliation she wasn't sure. She'd been fending Adam off all evening, trying to convince him it wasn't the time or the place for a public display of togetherness. She'd used the excuse of the Admiral's presence and told Adam there had been some awkward questions asked about the nature of their relationship. She'd managed to convince her boss they were nothing more than old school friends finding comfort together with the absence of their peers, but it wouldn't do to make him too suspicious.

Consequently, Adam had spent most of the night with the nurse who had attended Frankie when she had lost the baby. Frankie almost felt sorry for the woman, who looked as though she would rather be with almost anyone else in the Lido. Frankie knew how she felt. She'd spent the whole evening watching as Ken moved from woman to woman to talk, or to dance.

Frankie knew the nurse's eyes would have followed the doctor, who was dancing with his wife, just as much as hers had followed Ken. She couldn't approve of the affair, but she understood it. The doctor's wife wasn't the nicest woman, though possibly not so unpleasant she deserved to be on the wrong end of an affair. Frankie had hoped Ken would ask her for at least one dance, but he had studiously avoided her all evening. *From the amount of dancing he's done, at least his leg doesn't seem to be causing him any pain.* She looked away, towards where the Admiral's party were sitting, wondering whether she should re-join them to cement the illusion the Admiral was still interested in her romantically. Admiral Ashton caught her eye and smiled, gesturing her to join him. When she looked back to where Ken had been standing, he was gone. Reluctantly, she pushed herself away from the wall.

'Psst.' The sound hissed from around the corner of the building.

Frankie turned at the noise. Ken stood, partially concealed, gesturing to her. Wobbling a little, she walked towards him, stumbling, as his arm shot out from inside the structure and pulled her to him.

'What are you playing at?' he hissed, his eyes and tone fierce.

'Don't shout at me,' Frankie crumpled and the tears flowed.

'Oh, for goodness' sake.' Ken handed her a handkerchief. 'You've had far too much to drink tonight. You never drink this much usually. Don't you think it's time you told me what's going on?'

Frankie pulled away from him and walked across the room. 'Don't lecture me! Nothing's going on, except my so-called boyfriend has spent the entire evening with other women.'

Ken's eyes narrowed in the half-light and she turned away from him. He knew her too well. He reached out a tentative hand.

'Frankie, it's me you're talking to. I saw him try to dance with you and you sent him away with a flea in his ear. I don't know what's going on with the two of you, but I know you and you're not happy.' He took a step closer and she could feel his breath on her cheek. 'Please tell me why. I can't bear you to be miserable.'

Slowly, she lifted her head. She had to convince him she was alright. She had to. Then she made the mistake of looking him in the eye. His expression was so tender, so caring she felt the truth trying to worm its way out of her. Something changed in the way he looked at her and she tilted her face to his. His lips were soft against hers and the hand which had been resting on her arm, slid around to her back, gently pressing her close to him. For a moment, she allowed herself to lean into him, to enjoy the sensation of kissing someone she cared about. *Who am I trying to kid? I love him.* Terrified, she pulled away from his embrace.

'Ken, don't. I can't, I...' she trailed off unhappily.

'Frankie, please.' He put a hand out to her and she pushed him away.

For an awful moment, he teetered on the edge of the pump shaft until she reached out and grabbed him, yanking him away from the drop.

'Frankie, I love you. I always have. A few months ago, when I was in hospital, I thought maybe you were beginning to feel the same, but then I found out you were walking out with Adam and I don't know what to think anymore. This isn't you and I've known you long enough to know when you're keeping secrets. I don't know what you're mixed up in but I don't care, I love you.'

Tears welled in Frankie's eyes again. 'You say you know me, but you don't. If you knew the kind of girl I really am, you'd walk away in disgust.'

'Why don't you let me be the judge of that?' Ken's voice was gentle and he refused to let go of her hand. 'Can't you trust me?'

'What's going on here then?' Adam appeared in the doorway, scowling.

'This silly sod wanted to see the pump for the pool and then he went and nearly fell down the bloody shaft is what's going on.' Frankie dashed the tears away, her voice bright once again. 'Frightened the life out of me. It's a good job I've got quick reflexes or you'd have been scraping his brains off the concrete.'

'I hoped perhaps we could have our dance now,' Adam said tightly.

'Of course.' Frankie moved away from Ken without a backwards glance, but then another figure appeared behind Adam.

'There you are, Thompson! I've been looking all over for you.' Admiral Ashton's words were quiet but carried the weight of his authority with them. 'I was hoping we could have that dance you promised me. It's the last one of the evening.'

'Yes, Sir.' Only now did Frankie turn to the other two men with an apologetic smile. 'Excuse me.'

Adam looked furious, Ken merely miserable.

Frankie followed the Admiral to the end of the pool where the dancers had gathered and he took her in his arms for the last waltz.

'Are you well?' he asked quietly, as they moved around the space, weaving in between the other couples.

'Thank you for rescuing me.'

He squeezed her hand sympathetically. 'I saw young Ford whisk you inside the pump room, but Adam also saw. It's a dangerous game you're playing, Frankie.'

'There's no game, Sir. I know what's at stake and I won't jeopardise my position. I'll smooth things over tomorrow. Adam knows Ken has always had feelings for me, but I've never returned them.'

The Admiral fell silent and Frankie was grateful. Something in his silence told her he had guessed the truth but wasn't going to press the issue. *If only Ken would do the same*, she thought. *The only thing that mitigates my behaviour is the truth and it's the one thing I can't tell him.*

SEPTEMBER 2017

'*A*merican Patrol' blasted out across the still waters of the Lido. Hannah smiled happily as she watched people dancing. One couple, who were clearly ballroom dancers, were doing a quickstep around the edge of the big pool.'

'I wish I could dance like that,' she sighed. 'I love the quickstep.'

'I take it you're a fan of Strictly then,' Clem laughed, as he handed over an elaborate looking cocktail to a waiting customer.

'I love it.' Hannah's eyes were dreamy. 'It must feel like floating to move so quickly and gracefully around the floor.'

'Why not give it a go then? There must be some classes in the area.'

Hannah looked embarrassed. 'Who would I go with?'

'I'd go with you.'

Hannah's surprise must have shown in her face because he burst out laughing, then continued. 'I admit it's not really my thing, but it might be fun. I'm up for having a go anyway.'

'Really?'

'Really. Let's find out where the nearest class is.'

Hannah smiled as she turned away to serve the next customer. She really hadn't been hinting, but she blessed Clem for offering. She couldn't understand what had been going through Emmy's head when she'd cheated on him.

'Also,' Clem added with a grin, 'You should totally wear that dress for the lessons.'

Hannah looked down at her outfit. 'I never thought I'd say it, but I actually quite like it now it's on. When Kate turned up with it, I told her she was losing the plot. It's not me at all!'

'It really suits you,' Clem told her. 'As does the Victoria Roll hair do.'

Hannah smothered a laugh. 'Do you mean Victory Roll?'

'Same difference. It reminds me of a Swiss Roll.'

Hannah shook her head 'Hopeless.'

'Well, whatever it's called, you look lovely.'

As the band started playing again, there was a lull in the queue and Hannah giggled as she nudged Clem and gestured to the quickstepping couple who were now jiving to 'In The Mood'. 'That'll be us next year.'

He grinned and nodded towards the other dancers who were attempting to copy the couple's moves with varying degrees of success. 'I hate to break it to you, but I have two left feet. We're more likely to be challenging that lot for the title of least coordinated!'

The band switched to a slower tempo for the last number.

'Fools Rush In,' Hannah sighed, tears pricking at her eyes. 'My dad used to sing this a lot until Mum left.'

Clem glanced at her and took her hand, tugging her around the side of the makeshift bar. 'Come on.'

Hannah resisted. 'What?'

'We're going to give you a better memory for the song. Take your shoes off and tuck your skirt up.'

Hannah frowned, wondering what he was suggesting. Clem gestured to where people had gathered in the shallow pool. 'Come dance with me.'

'I don't know how.'

'Neither do I. We'll shuffle around same as everyone else is.'

Hannah kicked her shoes off and allowed him to lead her into the cool water. 'We must be mad.'

'Then everyone else is too. Maybe it's the music.'

He pulled her in close and she rested her head on his shoulder, allowing the music to wash over her.

'We may not be as good at dancing as them,' Clem whispered in her ear, 'But we can have some fun anyway.'

'Well, I have faith in us,' Hannah declared. 'I think we'll be amazing.'

Clem drew back a little, gave her an odd look, then nodded his head slowly. 'Do you know what? You're right. I think we would be.' His breath tickled the top of her head.

Hannah lifted a hand and gently poked his shoulder blade. 'Have some faith in yourself. We'll make a good team.'

Clem's head shifted slightly on hers and she felt him smile against her hair. 'I know.'

THE MORNING AFTER THE DANCE, the café was packed with people, all talking about how pleasant the previous evening had been. Hannah looked up expectantly as the next customer moved in front of the till.

'What can I get for you?' Her pleasant greeting faltered as the woman glared her into silence.

'You!' the woman hissed. 'If I'd known you worked here, I'd never have come in.' She pulled the two children with her away from the counter, as though afraid Hannah would somehow contaminate them. 'Do they know the kind of person they're employing?'

'I beg your pardon?' Hannah stammered.

'A liar. A slanderer. A slut.' The words hissed out of the woman.

Hannah darted a glance into the kitchen, wondering if she should call Kate out. The woman waved two ice creams at her.

'Be grateful my children are here.' She spoke through gritted teeth and when Hannah told her the price, she threw some coins onto the counter.

'I don't want change from you!'

Hannah picked the coins up and bit back the tears collecting in her eyes.

'If you can't be polite to the staff, perhaps you should go elsewhere,' a cold voice remarked from behind the woman.

'People like her don't deserve politeness,' the woman snapped.

Herding the children, she swept out of the café.

'What got up her nose? Rude baggage, wasn't she?'

Hannah looked up to see Frankie smiling gently at her.

'You okay, love?'

Hannah's voice wobbled when she was eventually able to reply. 'I think so. I've no idea who she is, never seen her before in my life.'

'Maybe she mistook you for someone else.'

Hannah looked doubtful. 'Maybe.'

Frankie shrugged. 'People are strange. They do the oddest things at times.'

'To a total stranger though?' Hannah was perplexed. There had been no hint of doubt in the woman's face. Somehow, she knew exactly who Hannah was, but Hannah had no idea what she had done to deserve such vitriol.

Later that day, when they were mopping the floor, Kate returned to the subject of the mystery woman.

'Are you really okay?' she asked kindly. 'It wasn't pleasant to listen to and I wasn't even on the receiving end of it. I was about to ask her to leave when Frankie stepped in.'

Hannah sighed. 'I'm alright, I guess. I just wish I knew who she was. I can't think of anyone I might have upset so badly, without ever having met them.'

She fell silent and continued mopping the floor, ignoring the voice in her head that reminded her she'd done plenty in her life to hurt people. *Not intentionally*, she muttered under her breath, knowing even as she said it that it didn't matter. She had no idea if Richard's wife knew what he was like, but Hannah had done plenty to cause her harm, though she hadn't been aware of it at the time. She wasn't the woman though.

Suddenly, Hannah froze. There was someone. The memory of rich dark curls and a deep voice whispering how beautiful she was, sprang into her head. She pushed it away, feeling sick. She hadn't thought of him for such a long time, hadn't seen him for even longer and yet the mere memory of him made her anxiety levels soar until they were choking her. The cool calm voice of Madeleine, her second, female, counsellor came back to her, tamping down the other voices to a burble somewhere in the depths of her memory, freeing her throat. *It wasn't my fault,* she reminded herself. She had only half-believed it at the time, although she'd done a good job of pretending otherwise. Now, with the benefit of hindsight and age, she recognised the truth of Madeleine's words. She hadn't been to blame for what had happened. She should have been able to trust him. He was supposed to have been helping her, not taking advantage of her vulnerable state.

Could the woman have been his wife, though? If it had been, would she really have remembered the face of the teenager in the witness stand? Ten years had passed and Hannah couldn't recall the faces of those she had faced in court. His wife had been there though, until she had been removed by the judge who wouldn't tolerate her shouting invectives from the public gallery. Hannah remembered the vile names poured on her head as she gave her evidence, the body contorted with rage as it twisted away from the restraining hand of the court officer. The judge had been surprisingly sympathetic – Hannah had been lucky in that respect – and once her unblemished character and sexual history, or lack thereof, had been established, she had felt he was more or less on her side.

THE NEXT MORNING, Hannah arrived at the café after a sleepless night. Try as she might, thoughts of Ethan had intruded and kept sleep at bay. She had greeted the day with red-rimmed eyes and a degree of self-loathing she hadn't felt for months. Her morning coffee burned and the toast she made didn't make it past the lump in her throat. Kate was standing outside the café, arms folded, staring at the wall. Hannah joined her to see what her boss was staring at. Red letters were scrawled across wall and windows. Kate handed her a folded piece of paper. Hannah opened it and read with increasing horror. The printed capitals danced across the paper, blurred by hot tears of shame.

'Hannah?' Kate put an arm around her shoulders. 'I know it's not true, but do you want to tell me about it? This was put through my letterbox last night. Clem got one too.'

A sob broke from somewhere deep within Hannah and pulling away from Kate, she fled. In the safety of her home, she dropped to the floor and lay there. Monty settled down beside her, pushing his nose under her arm until it lay over his back. Then he fell still, giving her wet cheek an occasional lick. Her phone buzzed, but Hannah couldn't bring herself to look at it. She knew it would be concerned inquiries from Kate and Clem, but she couldn't answer them. She wouldn't lie to them, but she couldn't confess that everything the letter said was true. She had slept with two married men. She had become pregnant and had an abortion at just fifteen. She had destroyed a man's career and his marriage. She was everything the letter called her and more and now, thanks to the scrawled graffiti, the whole town would know.

JUNE 1944

'I'm worried.' Frankie laid Adam's note on Admiral Ashton's desk. 'Why would he suddenly want me to meet him in the Lido pump room? I think he knows, or at least suspects something.'

'I'm inclined to agree. It may be time to retire Undine.'

'What if he follows through on his threat to tell everyone about Mac?'

'Do you want to move away? We can arrange it if it's what you want.'

Frankie shook her head. 'No. I won't be pushed out of my home by him. If he thinks I've been lying to him, he'll be worried. Can we use that against him in some way? Maybe arrest him for all the black-market stuff before he can do anything to me. If I was involved in his arrest in some way, it might discredit him enough for people to believe he's spreading rumours for revenge.'

'I'll make a phone call.' Admiral Ashton reached for the telephone, then paused. 'If I'm correct, it may be that London already have enough on him to close down this entire section of the operation. We have to make sure we can continue to feed information to Lernehan though, so whatever we do, it needs to be done without making their arrest public. Come back in an hour and I'll let you know what London says.'

Frankie hesitated. 'There's one other thing.' She paused again. 'It's something I'd like you to make inquiries about, if possible.'

The Admiral listened as she explained. When she'd finished, he raised an eyebrow. 'Are you sure?'

'That's what he said.'

'And you definitely want to know?'

Frankie swallowed the lump lodged in her throat. 'I need the truth.'

'Have you considered what you'll do?'

Frankie shook her head.

An hour later, she arrived back at the office, to be greeted by a smiling Admiral. 'They've agreed to keep an extra close eye on Lernehan until we can move in on the Liversidges. I'm fairly confident they'll agree to co-operate.' He chuckled. 'It's amazing how many principles disappear when they're confronted by the alternative.'

'Would they really execute them?'

'They did the others.'

Frankie gripped the edge of the desk, feeling suddenly faint. The Admiral jumped up and helped her to the chair.

'What is it?'

Frankie leant over the bin. 'I'm sorry,' she said eventually. 'I hadn't thought...' She shook her head. 'I suppose I didn't really consider that in feeding all that information I was helping Adam to get himself hanged.'

'Frankie, none of this is because of you. If you hadn't helped, the Liversidges would have found someone else to get the information for them and we may not have been able to control what they learnt. The responsibility for their actions lies with them, not you.'

'And the other thing?'

He looked at her gravely.

'Don't give me that look. I know how quickly your people can get information when they want to.'

'It's true.'

A cry choked from somewhere deep within Frankie and tears pricked at her eyes. 'Thank you,' she whispered eventually.

'You haven't done anything to be ashamed of, Frankie.' The Admiral knelt in front of her and took her hand. 'Do you understand? Nothing. And your mother did what she believed was best in the circumstances. Don't be too hard on her.'

Tears pricked at Frankie's eyes but she nodded.

Admiral Ashton returned to his chair. 'Do you want me to come with you to the Lido? There'll be a team arriving soon to search the Liversidge house and they won't need me.'

'I don't think so. Once we make him believe Lernehan's been arrested I think he'll fall apart. Adam likes to think he's in control of everything but take the control away and I think he'll realise quite how vulnerable he is.'

'You will be careful though?'

Frankie smiled ruefully. 'When am I not?'

The Admiral laughed. 'The number of times you were in my office at the start of the war for breaking rules and interfering with Navy business, I would never have guessed what a fine Wren you'd turn out to be. Signing you up was the only way I could think of to control you and the strings I had to pull to keep you here without proper training was ridiculous, but it was the best thing I could have done. I think you're the polar opposite to Adam – he likes to think he's in charge of his life and he can do whatever he wants, whereas you actually can – even when you don't believe it yourself. You are an incredible young woman and I hope that boy of yours knows how lucky he is.'

'Boy?' Frankie frowned. 'You mean Ken?' She shook her head sadly. 'He's not mine. Once upon a time maybe, but not now. How can I explain what I've spent the last three years doing? All he sees is Adam and me together.'

'If anyone can find a way to make it work, it's you. And don't be so sure he's not still in love with you. I've seen the way he looks at you when he thinks no one's looking.'

Frankie wasn't convinced but somewhere inside her, a little spark of hope ignited. Maybe, just maybe, she could find a way out.

OCTOBER 2017

annah tucked the blanket more firmly around her, took a gulp of wine, then picked up her spoon for the last mouthful of ice cream. Aware she was currently a walking cliché she gazed into the bowl, tears threatening once again. She had barely moved from the sofa since the day of the graffiti, leaving her curtains drawn so she could more easily avoid answering the door. Kate had been the first to arrive, the same evening as it had all happened. When Hannah didn't respond, she pushed a note through the letterbox. Hannah had tried to avoid reading it, but couldn't miss the large, scrawled letters telling her to talk to them. Clem had taken even longer to get rid of and she'd had to put her phone on silent when he started leaving voice-mails and texting her. His messages aimed to reassure her they didn't believe a word of the letters and certainly didn't agree with the graffiti, but they made her feel worse. Her friends had sprung to her defence but they didn't know the truth. Didn't know that the words, though crude and cruel, were also accurate.

She had considered calling Madeleine but couldn't bring herself to acknowledge that all their hard work together had been for nothing. She didn't want to admit that although somewhere deep inside her she wanted to accept she was not to blame for the current mess her life was in, there was a bigger part of her shouting that of course it was her fault. She should have known. Should have seen the signs. *This is what happens when you trust people. You let people in and this is the result.*

There was a knock at the door and Hannah froze, willing the person to go away.

Monty sniffed the bottom of the door and barked happily, ignoring Hannah's frantic shushing gestures.

'You may as well open the door, young lady. I'm not leaving until you do.' Frankie's voice was clarion-like as the letterbox flapped open and Hannah couldn't help grinning. 'You might wait out the youngsters, but I was a teacher and I'm retired. I have the patience of a saint and all the time in the world. I've brought my camping chair and I'm not moving until you open the door and let me in.'

Hannah sighed. When she opened the door, it was to find Frankie was indeed sitting on the pavement in a camping chair, a travel mug clamped in her hands.

'That didn't take long, did it?' Frankie beamed up at her. 'I was expecting to at least get to finish my tea!'

'Come in,' Hannah sighed, as Monty bounced around Frankie, licking her fingers. 'I'll put the kettle on and you can have a decent cup of tea. It never tastes the same out of one of those mugs, no matter how nice they look.' She gave Frankie a sharp look. 'But don't think that because I let you in, I'm going to talk to you about anything. I just don't want you collapsing on my doorstep.'

Frankie's eyes danced with merriment. 'I told them you'd

let me in,' she said. 'One of the few advantages of being old is people feel they have to be polite to you even when you don't deserve it.'

Taking a seat, she watched Hannah move around the kitchen, but didn't say anything more until Hannah handed her the hot tea and took a seat opposite her.

'What do you want, Frankie? If it's about the café, I'm not coming back.'

'It's not about the café.' Frankie's bright expression dimmed. 'It's Ken. He's back in hospital.'

Immediately, Hannah reached out and covered the older lady's hand. 'Oh Frankie, I'm so sorry. Is he okay?'

Frankie shook her head. 'He's dying.' She said it matter of factly, but Hannah could hear the effort that went into keeping her voice level. 'He wants to see you.'

'Me? He hardly knows me. Surely, family or…' Hannah trailed off.

'Jack and the girls have been already. So have the rest of the family. He asked for you.'

Hannah could feel Frankie watching her carefully and she nodded slowly. 'If that's what he wants, then of course I'll go. But… do you know why?'

Frankie shrugged. 'Who knows? Silly sod thinks I don't know he's dying. Keeps giving me jobs to do to stop me hanging around the hospital. He thinks if he keeps me busy, I won't notice him slipping away.' She shook her head. 'He doesn't know I was trained to spot a liar at a hundred paces. Daft beggar thinks he was the only one who served in the war.'

Frankie drained her tea. 'Are you ready to go?'

'Now?'

'Well, you'll need to get dressed first,' Frankie said, rolling her eyes in mock exasperation. 'Five minutes?'

Hannah flew up the stairs and threw some clothes on. They were wrinkled, but at least they were clean. Everything still felt muddled and disjointed, but Frankie's news had put her own feelings into perspective. She could refuse to leave the house and continue to wallow in self-pity, but if Ken had asked specifically to see her, how could she refuse?

JUNE 1944

'dam?' Frankie called his name softly, as she pushed open the pump room door. The room was in complete darkness and she fumbled for the light switch. Before she located it, the single bulb flickered into life and she saw Garrett with his finger on the switch. Of Adam, there was no sign.

'He's not here.'

'You sent the note?'

He nodded. 'I'm harder to fool than the rest of my family. I suspected from the start you were a bit too easy to deceive, a bit too willing to soothe my grandson's temper with 'idle' gossip from the base.'

Frankie frowned. 'What are you talking about? I haven't told Adam anything.'

Garrett laughed. 'I know everything Miss Thompson.'

Frankie folded her arms, feeling her heart thump against them. 'Then you know more than I do. Why am I here?'

'You're here because I intend to ensure my family's safety. My idiot grandson may think you're entirely in his thrall and willing to do whatever he asks just for the sheer pleasure of sharing his bed, but I think there's too much of your mother in you for that.'

'What does my mother have to do with anything?'

'You'd have to ask her, but she's not the innocent she claims to be. She made John pay for marrying her and even I underestimated her. I don't intend to make the same mistake with you. You're going to tell me exactly what game you've been playing and then I'll decide what to do with you. You see, Miss Thompson, there's a few interested parties you've managed to upset and I reckon they'd pay handsomely to get their hands on you.'

Frankie held his gaze. 'I imagine they would,' she said calmly. It was clear Garrett did indeed know everything and relief settled across her shoulders. Her part was over. 'But I'm afraid they're not going to get the chance. You see Garrett, you're absolutely right. I've never been in love with Adam, I can't stand the sight of him.'

Garrett turned to the corner of the room that was still shrouded in shadows. 'You see, you fool? The little slut was toying with you all along.'

Adam and John emerged from behind the huge tanks that filtered the pool water. Adam's face was pale with rage and his father's hand was clamped on his shoulder.

A slight smile flickered at the corners of Frankie's mouth. 'I'm sorry, Adam, but you brought it on yourself. You thought I was so desperate for love I didn't care where it came from and you never stopped to consider if I wanted something more from you than a warm bed.'

A choking sound stuttered from Adam's throat. 'You bitch.'

Frankie's smiled broadened. 'Ouch.' She shrugged, the knowledge that she no longer had to pretend, brought with it a sense of detachment. Nothing they said or did could touch her now. 'It's over. For all of you. The black market dealing, the spying. We know everything. Whatever happens to me, all three of you are finished.'

'We?' Adam laughed. 'Since when do you share anything? You've never co-operated with anyone in your life and you expect us to believe that?'

Frankie shrugged. 'Believe what you want. When the news come on the radio, you'll know whether or not I'm telling the truth.'

She headed for the door, but a blow sent her reeling and hands clamped around her throat, slamming her against the wall. The contact sent stars spinning in the air around her and she fought to regain her balance, the toes of her shoes desperately seeking to connect with the ground.

'Give me one good reason why I shouldn't end you now,' Garrett snarled, his face red and contorted.

Frankie was too concerned with trying to breathe to be able to respond, but suddenly, his grip loosened and she slumped to the floor. Massaging her throat, she glanced up through water-bleared eyes to see John wrestling with his father and exchanging blows.

'Don't be an idiot,' he panted. 'Killing her will only make things worse for everyone. I know you couldn't give two hoots about me but think about Adam. If you add murder into the mix, it will only make things worse for him.'

'Do you really think I care?' Garrett's voice rose until it was almost a howl. 'He fucked everything up and I couldn't give a shit if he lives or dies. This was our one chance and he blew it. We could have had the chance to really strike a blow for Ireland and he was so busy thinking with his dick he couldn't see what was in front of him.' He stalked angrily away from his son, towards the back of the room. 'The pair of you are a complete fucking waste of space. You're as pathetic as each other.'

Adam was staring at the fighting pair and Frankie quietly

got to her feet, stumbling to the door. Outside, she breathed in deeply. Her throat was sore and she knew it would be bruised in the morning, but she was alive and free from the pretence of the last three years. Pulling herself together, she straightened up and walked unsteadily along the side of the pool towards the exit. As she reached the office, there was a shout followed immediately by a scream from the pump room. Frankie turned, began to run back the way she had come, then paused, darted into the unlocked office and dialled a number.

'It's me. You need to come immediately.'

T WORKED

KATE LOOKED up from her phone and grinned at her brother-in-law. 'Frankie did it. Hannah's taking her to the hospital.'

Clem looked relieved. 'Thank goodness for that. I didn't know how we were going to get through to her otherwise. Has she told Frankie anything?'

'She didn't say.'

'I reckon Frankie knows more than she's letting on.' Clem looked thoughtful. 'When we said we didn't believe what the letters said about Hannah, she seemed to be hinting there could be some truth to them, even if they didn't tell the whole story.'

Kate shook her head. 'I can't believe Hannah would deliberately break up one marriage, let alone two of them! Does that really sound like the person we know?' She sighed when Clem didn't answer. 'I know it's a sensitive subject for you, but don't let what happened cloud your judgement. Hannah isn't Emmy.'

'I know.' Clem ran a hand through his hair. 'And I agree, it doesn't sound like her. When I was trying to sound her out about dating, she was really firm about telling people I was still married, even if it was only a technicality.'

'It sounds as though she may have been speaking from experience,' Kate said. 'Perhaps that's what Frankie was hinting at.'

'I would ask how on earth Frankie would know, given that Hannah almost never talks about herself, but it's Frankie.' Clem laughed ruefully. 'I'd hate to be the one trying to keep a secret from her.'

'Would that even be possible?' Kate rose from her seat as a woman entered the café. 'Good afternoon, what can I get for you?'

'A cappuccino to take away please.' The woman smiled, fell silent, then spoke again. 'Is Hannah working today?'

Kate shook her head. 'She's taking some time off.'

The woman nodded, looking unsurprised. 'Because of the letters, I presume. Has she actually taken time off or has she been sacked and you don't want to say?'

Kate stared at her and the woman continued. 'Because if it's the latter, I urge you to talk to her. I don't have the full story, but I know my husband and it's highly unlikely to be exactly as he painted it.'

'Your husband sent the letters?' Kate's mouth fell open.

'Why would he do that?' Clem asked, moving to the woman's side.

'Because I finally left him and he blames her. She wasn't the first affair I've dealt with the fallout from, nor even the second or the third. I never blamed the women – I know how charming he can be, I fell for it long enough to marry him and have a child.' Her laugh was bitter. 'And I doubt he advertised the fact he was married. I thought I was doing the right thing by our daughter in staying with him, but then I realised I was only teaching her to accept less than she deserved and I kicked him out. He's done far more than sleep around and Hannah called him out on it, making him confess to me the mess he'd got into. That was the final straw. When I was clearing out his things yesterday, I found a draft version of one of the letters and knowing what a devious, conniving coward he is, I could work out what he'd done.'

'And you came to check on Hannah?' Kate was incredulous. 'I'm not sure I'd have been so magnanimous.'

'She may have been unaware of it, but she gave me the shove I needed to end my marriage. I wanted to return the favour and remind her exactly how worthless a person he is.'

'Can you tell us what happened?' Clem asked.

The woman shook her head. 'It's not my story to tell and like I said, I don't know much, only my part in it. It's up to Hannah what she shares with you. I just wanted to make sure she was given a chance to.'

'She will be,' Kate said with a smile. 'We're working on getting her to trust us with it.'

The woman nodded and collecting her coffee, she left the café. Kate and Clem stared at each other.

'The plot thickens,' Kate said eventually. 'I suppose we'll have to wait and see whether Frankie can convince Hannah to talk to us.'

'I'll bet this is killing you, isn't it?' Clem laughed. 'You hate not knowing what's going on.'

Kate shook her head, her face serious. 'Do you know what? Normally you'd be right, but I'm genuinely worried about Hannah. I think there's something awful in her past and that's why she backs away from getting too close to anyone. That's why she never talks about herself.' Her expression became fierce. 'I'd put money on somebody badly hurting her and her blaming herself for it.'

'It certainly doesn't sound like that woman thinks it was Hannah's fault that her marriage ended,' Clem agreed. 'I hope Frankie can convince her to tell us.' He looked pained rather than angry. 'I can't bear the idea that she believes we think badly of her.'

JOHN - 1944

'You're as pathetic as each other.'

John's arms fell to his side and he stared at his father. 'You can't see it, can you?' He shook his head and laughed. 'This is all because of you. You and your stupid bloody cause. You've dragged me and Adam into this mess because you want a united, independent Ireland. You can't even unite your own bloody family! We don't care about Ireland, Dad. We never have!'

'It's who you are!' Garrett roared.

John flinched but held his ground. 'No, it's not. Adam's never even been there. It's your country not ours and if you hate it so much here, then maybe you should have gone back there after the last war, instead of running round the Essex countryside with your stupid lights and your stupid signalling.'

'Be careful what you say, boy.'

'Or what? What are you going to do to me, Dad? You can't take your belt to me like you did when I was a kid. You're getting old and I'm not a feeble little boy anymore.'

'No, you're a feeble man instead, hiding behind others

your entire life.' Garrett looked at his son steadily. 'But you're forgetting one thing, John. We know where she is. We know where Alice is and –'

'Leave her alone!'

The blow exploded from John's fist, taking him as much by surprise as it did his father. Garrett reeled back from the force of the punch. His heels slipped over the lip of the pump shaft and for a long moment, he teetered on the edge, desperately flailing at his son's arm. His expression shifted from fear to relief, as John grabbed his hand.

'I told you not to threaten her again,' John whispered and let go.

*H*annah fixed a firm eye on Ken's pale face. 'Do you really want me here, or are you using me to avoid speaking to Frankie about what's really going on?'

Ken gave her a lopsided grin. 'Does it matter? You're here aren't you?'

Frankie had delivered Hannah to the door of Ken's room, then left them alone, excusing herself with the need to use the bathroom.

'Wouldn't you rather spend the time with your wife?'

Ken waved his hand. 'Frankie knows I love her and I've got plenty of time to remind her.'

'We both know that's not true.'

'But Frankie doesn't and I'd like to keep it that way. We don't do soppy goodbyes, never have done. It's best for her we carry on as normal.'

'You know she knows, right? She's only pretending because you are. She's stronger than you think.'

'I know.' Ken chuckled, until it turned into a cough. He took the glass Hannah handed him and sipped it, laying back against the pillow with a sigh. 'Frankie's always been the one who tackled everything head on. I've never been able to keep much from her, so I don't know why I thought I'd be able to fool her with this.' He closed his eyes then carried on speaking, his tone becoming carefully casual. 'You know, my Frankie isn't the only one who's stronger than she thinks. You've not had the easiest life, have you? But you're still here, still fighting.'

Hannah stared at him, her heart hammering in her chest. 'What do you mean?' she whispered.

Ken opened one eye, looked briefly at her, then closed it again. 'It's a small town. Frankie knows everyone. You know what she's like.' He pitched his voice a little higher in imitation of his wife. 'That girl's worrying herself over something, Kenneth Ford and I mean to find out what it is.' He chuckled. 'Teachers have long friendships and even longer memories. It wasn't difficult for her to find out all about you.'

'She knows nothing about me,' Hannah whispered, tears gathering in her eyes. 'I don't care what she found out, or who she found out from. They don't know anything.'

'Frankie didn't mean any harm, she was just worried about you.' Ken opened his eyes and took Hannah's hand, giving it a reassuring squeeze. 'You're quite right though, nothing is ever quite as it appears to be, is it?' He beckoned her closer and she leant forward so he could whisper in her ear. Her eyes widened in surprise as he spoke.

'Not a word,' Ken cautioned and she shook her head. 'There's a proper secret for you. Do you still think yours is so awful no one will ever speak to you again?'

'I suppose not.' Hannah still sounded dubious.

'So, tell your story yourself. Make them listen to your side. I'll bet they've been hammering on your door, haven't they? So what makes you think they won't give you the chance to explain?'

'I'm sure they'll listen, but I don't know where to start,' Hannah said, her voice cracking.

'Why not try the beginning? Practise on me.'

Quietly at first and then with growing clarity, Hannah told him about her mother leaving, about the counselling and the fallout from that and then she moved on to Richard and the money. Her eyes were fixed firmly on her feet but at some point, she became aware Frankie had returned. Nevertheless, she continued to pour out her life. As she drew the story to a close, Hannah looked up to see tears streaming down Frankie's face, her eyes resting on her husband's face. Hannah realised the hand she was holding had fallen still.

'Frankie... I...' She was mortified to have robbed Frankie of her last moments with Ken.

'If you're thinking of apologising, don't!' The tone was fierce, but Frankie gave her a weak smile. 'It was what he wanted.' She swallowed. 'He always said I needed to fix people, but he was exactly the same. He knew what people needed even when they couldn't see it themselves, he just went about it in a different way.'

Hannah tried to speak, but tears choked her. Frankie patted her hand. 'He never liked saying goodbye – a hangover from the war – it was too final a word. He always says... said...' The words hung in the air between them and Hannah closed the gap to put her arms around Frankie, who looked suddenly frail. They stood together for a moment, then Frankie stepped back and fixed a stern look on Hannah.

'You want to help me?'

Hannah nodded, wiping her eyes.

'Then make this count,' Frankie said firmly. 'Go and talk to the others. Tell them the truth about you and they might surprise you.'

Hannah's throat constricted at the thought, but her face was determined as she agreed.

JOHN 1944

'So, gentlemen. Here's how this is going to work if you want to avoid facing the death penalty for treason. You're going to continue giving Lernehan the information he wants, but you're going to get all of it direct from me. Is that clear?'

Adam nodded, but John did not react. The Admiral shifted his gaze to focus solely on the older man.

'Mr Liversidge, do you understand what I'm saying?'

John's voice was hoarse. 'I can't.'

Admiral Ashton frowned. 'I don't think you quite understand the position you're in. Either you co-operate with me, or you throw yourself on the mercy of the authorities and take your chances on a charge of spying?'

'Dad, I really think we should –'

'Shut up!' John rounded on his son. 'You don't know what you're asking of me.'

'I'm asking you not to get us killed!' Adam roared. 'For God's sake, is she really more important to you than your own son? You haven't seen her for nearly twenty years; she ran away to get away from you and you still think you have to protect her? He's dead. What can he do now?'

'He is, but they're not. I won't do it, Adam.'

'You're as bad as he was! All he cared about was his precious bloody Ireland and all you care about is her. You're as obsessed as he was, just about different things. It's fucking pathetic! No wonder Mum hates you both.'

'Excuse me.' Admiral Ashton cleared his throat. 'If I might interrupt a moment? Who exactly are you talking about?'

'Alice bloody Morrison. Thompson, before she got married. Frankie's aunt.' It was Adam who replied. He gestured to his father who sat tight-lipped. 'He had a thing for her when they were younger. It ended badly and she ran away and hid from everyone, but for some reason he's still protecting her. I don't know why because nobody's ever allowed to fucking talk about her! I doubt Frankie even knows she exists. Grandad reckoned Lernehan knows where she is and threatened to kill her and her son if Dad didn't co-operate. He knew it was the only thing Dad cared enough about.' His voice was bitter. 'I, on the other hand, couldn't give a fuck about her, so I'm more than happy to do whatever you ask.'

With a roar, John launched himself at his son and it was only the Admiral's intervention which prevented more punches landing.

'That is enough!' He hauled both men back into their respective seats. 'I will make inquiries with regards to Mrs Morrison's whereabouts and we will proceed from there. In the meantime, you will go home and you will stay there. My men will be watching your every move, so I suggest you keep a low profile until I contact you with further instructions. Do I make myself clear?'

Father and son nodded.

'What else can you tell me about her which might help us to find her?'

'Dad said she lived in the Lake District and her son was in the RAF.'

'That's a start a least. Now, get out of my sight and remember, a single word from either of you and you'll be in prison before you can blink.'

'I'll do whatever you ask as long as you guarantee Alice's safety,' John said quietly, not making eye contact with his son.

<u>October, 2017</u>

HANNAH POKED a cautious head around the open door of the café. She sighed with relief when she saw it was empty of customers. Kate was mopping in the kitchen, her head bobbing as music played through the small speakers on the counter. Hannah waited until Kate looked up, watching as her expression changed from shock to pleasure.

'Hannah!' Kate dropped the mop and hurried to embrace her. 'Can I get you a coffee?'

Hannah stood stiffly but accepted the hug. 'Yes please.' Her voice wobbled.

'Or do you want something stronger?' Kate tried to tease a smile out of her.

'Coffee's fine thanks.' Hannah balled her fists and shoved them deep into her pockets, willing them to stop shaking. 'Is Clem around?'

'He's closing up next door. I imagine he'll come through when he's done, as normal.'

Of course he would. He always did. Hannah sat down at the closest table, only looking up briefly when Kate placed the coffee cup in front of her. She put the milk in and stirred it slowly, watching the whirls of white spiral out. Kate left her alone until Clem appeared in the doorway from the pool. He stuttered to a halt when he saw Hannah sitting there but didn't speak to her until Kate had finished tidying up and given him his own drink. Hannah was grateful for the silence that gave her time to collect her thoughts and organise them into something coherent.

Eventually, they joined her at the table and sat silently, waiting for her to speak. When she dared to raise her eyes, Clem smiled at her encouragingly. Kate was clearly trying her best not to ask questions, but Hannah could see she was bursting with them. She bit her lip and wrapped her hands around her cup.

'I...' Hannah hesitated, then took a deep breath and as though the words had been waiting for her to open her mouth, they tumbled out of her. 'You know it's only me and my dad. When I was fifteen, I got it into my head it was somehow my fault Mum left and Dad arranged for me to have some counselling. Ethan, my counsellor, was in his early thirties and he was gorgeous. He was kind and understanding and he made me feel heard for the first time in a long time. That room was a haven and I hung on his every word. I'd have done anything for him because he made me feel loved. He told me I was worth something, that I mattered and I believed he meant that I mattered to him. I flirted and he flirted back. I thought I was in love. When he kissed me, it didn't feel wrong, it was just a natural extension of all the things he'd been saying to me – I was loveable, I deserved to be loved. He told me we had to keep it secret because people wouldn't approve and they'd make me stop seeing him. I lived in fear of that – he was the only person who understood how I felt, who made me feel whole – and so I told no one, not even friends.

'Looking back now, I can see how naïve I was, but at the time I never questioned him. I lost my virginity on the same couch I'd spilled my thoughts on and eventually, the sex replaced the counselling completely. They sent me there to make me happy and for a time, I was. Then I realised I was pregnant. I was horrified, but my reaction was nothing compared to Ethan's. He told me straight away to get rid of it. He was so angry.' Hannah's voice wobbled at the memory and she closed her eyes to trap the tears. Kate's hand closed over hers and she gritted her teeth.

'I had the abortion in the morning and went straight to school from the clinic, trying to make everything seem normal, but I fainted at lunchtime and I had a teacher who wouldn't let it go. She'd been worried about me for a while and my fainting spell was the final straw. Eventually, she got the whole story out of me. She was so calm, but she had the same twitch in her mouth that she got when the class were being really noisy. I tried to tell her it was my fault – I'd flirted with him, I'd been willing, he hadn't forced me to do anything I didn't want to – but it made no difference. She was right, of course, he'd been in a position of responsibility, I'd been vulnerable and it should never have happened, but I was blinded by how I felt about him.

'Social services got involved, so did the police and I had to keep repeating everything, including to my dad. I genuinely thought we'd be together once I left school and I kept insisting he'd done nothing wrong and they didn't under-stand. It took them telling me he was already married and his wife was pregnant, for me to realise our 'relationship' was all in my head. I didn't mean anything to him beyond the time we spent together in his office.

'It went all the way to court – he was charged with statu-tory rape and was banned from working with children and from working as a counsellor – but his wife stuck by him. They tried to claim I'd initiated everything; it had never gone as far as I'd claimed it did; the baby hadn't been his. It didn't work, but it confirmed my belief that everything had been my fault. They got me a second counsellor afterwards and I've seen her on and off ever since.

'When I met Richard, I believed I'd finally found someone decent. I was starting to build some confidence again, to think maybe I could put what had happened with Ethan behind me at last. I told him everything. I didn't want there to be any secrets between us and he was so understanding. He listened, he told me he didn't believe I was to blame, I'd only been a child. I started planning a future again and then of course, I found out he was also married.' She sighed. 'It was like being stuck in a loop, destined to keep playing out the same mistake. I should go back to seeing Madeleine, but I can't bear the thought of telling her I did it again. How many more times am I going to fall for someone's lies?'

'Why on earth didn't you tell us? You were the victim, Hannah. You did nothing wrong.'

'What do you mean?'

'You were fifteen. A child. You were messed up already and he took advantage of you. Whatever he told you, whatever excuses he made, he was in a position of responsibility and he abused that trust.'

'But...' Hannah's eyes filled with tears. 'It keeps happening. 'My mum left me, then Ethan and then Richard. That can't be a coincidence – it's me. It must be.'

Kate took her hand and spoke gently. 'Look at Harry and Clem. Are they nice people?'

Hannah nodded, the tears spilling down her cheeks. 'The best. That's why–'

Kate cut her off. 'Their mum walked out on them and Fred. She had an affair and made her choice. That was nothing to do with them. Her choices don't make them bad people. It's the same with you. Your mum leaving wasn't your fault. Ethan took advantage of you and Richard did the same.

Would you have gone near either of them if you'd known they were married.'

'Of course not!' Hannah knew this at least was true.

'Exactly. Hannah, you're not a bad person, you've just had a rough deal. But things are different now. You're different. And you have a choice. You can either run away again and hide or you can come back to work and see how many shades of right I am.'

'You want me back?' Hannah's voice was barely above a whisper.

Kate rolled her eyes and laughed. 'Well even I need a day off now and again and I'm not leaving Clem in charge again after he nearly flooded the place.'

Hannah raised her eyebrows.

'He left the mop bucket to fill in the sink and forgot to turn the tap off.'

Hannah's laugh was weak, but it was enough for Kate to pull her to her feet and into a hug.

'I'll take that as a yes then, shall I?'

Hannah wrapped her arms around her friend and nodded into her shoulder.

'Hannah, Kate's right. None of this is your fault, you know.' Clem's voice was gentle. 'You can't blame yourself for other people's appalling behaviour. We have to believe we can trust the people in our lives, otherwise what's the point?'

'No wonder you don't like letting people get close,' Kate said, shaking her head. 'What a pair of arseholes.'

A laugh unexpectedly bubbled up inside Hannah and burst out of her. She laughed until her sides ached and tears streamed from her eyes.

'Don't hold back on your opinion, Kate, will you?' Clem looked bemused at Hannah's reaction.

'Well, they are,' Kate said stoutly. 'And Richard's wife clearly thinks the same, even if Ethan's is still deluding herself. I assume it was his wife who was rude to you the other day?'

Hannah stopped laughing. 'I wondered the same thing. It could have been I suppose. She was in court but I don't remember what she looked like. It wouldn't have been hard for her to find out what I looked like if she was really determined. I was on social media, I followed Ethan's work page on them. I'd have been pretty easy to track down.' She paused. 'What do you mean about Richard's wife though? I know what she looks like, I'd have recognised her if she'd come in.'

Kate filled her in on the conversation they'd had with the soon-to-be ex-wife and Hannah looked thoughtful. Clem nudged her elbow.

'Sorry,' she said, shaking her head. 'I was listening. It's just... what you've said makes things easier. I was worried about a decision I'd made, but it sounds as if his wife knows already and if his family won't be dragged into it, I feel less guilty about doing it.'

'You're very mysterious all of a sudden,' Kate said. 'Spill the beans.'

'I will,' Hannah assured her, 'But we need to get everyone together. It's something Jack and the rest need to hear. Frankie too, if she's feeling up to it.'

'Have you spoken to her? Do you know how she is? I dropped a card and some flowers round yesterday and left them with Ellie, but I didn't want to be in the way of the family.' Clem's face clouded. Ken had been dear to all of them and his death, while not unexpected, had affected them badly.

'Not since I took her to Ellie's the day it happened,' Hannah said. 'I know they have more important things to worry about with the funeral and everything else, but they're on the board for this place and I need to speak to them before I act.'

'I hate feeling so useless,' Kate sighed. 'Like Clem said, I don't want to be in the way, but Frankie feels like part of my own family and I wish there was something we could do to help her.'

'I did have an idea about that,' Hannah said. 'I've had a lot of time to think over the last few days and they've all been so kind to me, I wanted to do something.'

She quickly outlined the idea she'd been pondering and was pleased to see smiles spread across both faces as she spoke.

'I think it's a lovely idea,' Clem said. 'I've got a mate who'll do it as a favour for us. I'll give him a ring tonight and get it organised.'

OCTOBER 2017

*H*annah poked a cautious head around the open door of the café. She sighed with relief when she saw it was empty of customers. Kate was mopping in the kitchen, her head bobbing as music played through the small speakers on the counter. Hannah waited until Kate looked up, watching as her expression changed from shock to pleasure.

'Hannah!' Kate dropped the mop and hurried to embrace her. 'Can I get you a coffee?'

Hannah stood stiffly but accepted the hug. 'Yes please.' Her voice wobbled.

'Or do you want something stronger?' Kate tried to tease a smile out of her.

'Coffee's fine thanks.' Hannah balled her fists and shoved them deep into her pockets, willing them to stop shaking. 'Is Clem around?'

'He's closing up next door. I imagine he'll come through when he's done, as normal.'

Of course he would. He always did. Hannah sat down at the closest table, only looking up briefly when Kate placed the coffee cup in front of her. She put the milk in and stirred it slowly, watching the whirls of white spiral out. Kate left her alone until Clem appeared in the doorway from the pool. He stuttered to a halt when he saw Hannah sitting there but didn't speak to her until Kate had finished tidying up and given him his own drink. Hannah was grateful for the silence that gave her time to collect her thoughts and organise them into something coherent.

Eventually, they joined her at the table and sat silently, waiting for her to speak. When she dared to raise her eyes, Clem smiled at her encouragingly. Kate was clearly trying her best not to ask questions, but Hannah could see she was bursting with them. She bit her lip and wrapped her hands around her cup.

'I...' Hannah hesitated, then took a deep breath and as though the words had been waiting for her to open her mouth, they tumbled out of her. 'You know it's only me and my dad. When I was fifteen, I got it into my head it was somehow my fault Mum left and Dad arranged for me to have some counselling. Ethan, my counsellor, was in his early thirties and he was gorgeous. He was kind and under-standing and he made me feel heard for the first time in a long time. That room was a haven and I hung on his every word. I'd have done anything for him because he made me feel loved. He told me I was worth something, that I mattered and I believed he meant that I mattered to him. I flirted and he flirted back. I thought I was in love. When he kissed me, it didn't feel wrong, it was just a natural extension of all the things he'd been saying to me – I was loveable, I deserved to be loved. He told me we had to keep it secret because people wouldn't approve and they'd make me stop seeing him. I lived in fear of that – he was the only person who understood how I felt, who made me feel whole – and so I told no one, not even friends.

'Looking back now, I can see how naïve I was, but at the time I never questioned him. I lost my virginity on the same couch I'd spilled my thoughts on and eventually, the sex replaced the counselling completely. They sent me there to make me happy and for a time, I was. Then I realised I was pregnant. I was horrified, but my reaction was nothing compared to Ethan's. He told me straight away to get rid of it. He was so angry.' Hannah's voice wobbled at the memory and she closed her eyes to trap the tears. Kate's hand closed over hers and she gritted her teeth.

'I had the abortion in the morning and went straight to school from the clinic, trying to make everything seem normal, but I fainted at lunchtime and I had a teacher who wouldn't let it go. She'd been worried about me for a while and my fainting spell was the final straw. Eventually, she got the whole story out of me. She was so calm, but she had the same twitch in her mouth that she got when the class were being really noisy. I tried to tell her it was my fault – I'd flirted with him, I'd been willing, he hadn't forced me to do anything I didn't want to – but it made no difference. She was right, of course, he'd been in a position of responsibility, I'd been vulnerable and it should never have happened, but I was blinded by how I felt about him.

'Social services got involved, so did the police and I had to keep repeating everything, including to my dad. I genuinely thought we'd be together once I left school and I kept insisting he'd done nothing wrong and they didn't understand. It took them telling me he was already married and his wife was pregnant, for me to realise our 'relationship' was all in my head. I didn't mean anything to him beyond the time we spent together in his office.

'It went all the way to court – he was charged with statutory rape and was banned from working with children and from working as a counsellor – but his wife stuck by him.

They tried to claim I'd initiated everything; it had never gone as far as I'd claimed it did; the baby hadn't been his. It didn't work, but it confirmed my belief that everything had been my fault. They got me a second counsellor afterwards and I've seen her on and off ever since.

'When I met Richard, I believed I'd finally found someone decent. I was starting to build some confidence again, to think maybe I could put what had happened with Ethan behind me at last. I told him everything. I didn't want there to be any secrets between us and he was so understanding. He listened, he told me he didn't believe I was to blame, I'd only been a child. I started planning a future again and then of course, I found out he was also married.' She sighed. 'It was like being stuck in a loop, destined to keep playing out the same mistake. I should go back to seeing Madeleine, but I can't bear the thought of telling her I did it again. How many more times am I going to fall for someone's lies?'

'Why on earth didn't you tell us? You were the victim, Hannah. You did nothing wrong.'

'What do you mean?'

'You were fifteen. A child. You were messed up already and he took advantage of you. Whatever he told you, whatever excuses he made, he was in a position of responsibility and he abused that trust.'

'But...' Hannah's eyes filled with tears. 'It keeps happening. 'My mum left me, then Ethan and then Richard. That can't be a coincidence – it's me. It must be.'

Kate took her hand and spoke gently. 'Look at Harry and Clem. Are they nice people?'

Hannah nodded, the tears spilling down her cheeks. 'The best. That's why–'

Kate cut her off. 'Their mum walked out on them and Fred. She had an affair and made her choice. That was nothing to do with them. Her choices don't make them bad people. It's the same with you. Your mum leaving wasn't your fault. Ethan took advantage of you and Richard did the same. Would you have gone near either of them if you'd known they were married.'

'Of course not!' Hannah knew this at least was true.

'Exactly. Hannah, you're not a bad person, you've just had a rough deal. But things are different now. You're different. And you have a choice. You can either run away again and hide or you can come back to work and see how many shades of right I am.'

'You want me back?' Hannah's voice was barely above a whisper.

Kate rolled her eyes and laughed. 'Well even I need a day off now and again and I'm not leaving Clem in charge again after he nearly flooded the place.'

Hannah raised her eyebrows.

'He left the mop bucket to fill in the sink and forgot to turn the tap off.'

Hannah's laugh was weak, but it was enough for Kate to pull her to her feet and into a hug.

'I'll take that as a yes then, shall I?'

Hannah wrapped her arms around her friend and nodded into her shoulder.

'Hannah, Kate's right. None of this is your fault, you know.' Clem's voice was gentle. 'You can't blame yourself for other people's appalling behaviour. We have to believe we can trust the people in our lives, otherwise what's the point?'

'No wonder you don't like letting people get close,' Kate said, shaking her head. 'What a pair of arseholes.'

A laugh unexpectedly bubbled up inside Hannah and burst out of her. She laughed until her sides ached and tears streamed from her eyes.

'Don't hold back on your opinion, Kate, will you?' Clem looked bemused at Hannah's reaction.

'Well, they are,' Kate said stoutly. 'And Richard's wife clearly thinks the same, even if Ethan's is still deluding herself. I assume it was his wife who was rude to you the other day?'

Hannah stopped laughing. 'I wondered the same thing. It could have been I suppose. She was in court but I don't remember what she looked like. It wouldn't have been hard for her to find out what I looked like if she was really determined. I was on social media, I followed Ethan's work page on them. I'd have been pretty easy to track down.' She paused. 'What do you mean about Richard's wife though? I know what she looks like, I'd have recognised her if she'd come in.'

Kate filled her in on the conversation they'd had with the soon-to-be ex-wife and Hannah looked thoughtful. Clem nudged her elbow.

'Sorry,' she said, shaking her head. 'I was listening. It's just... what you've said makes things easier. I was worried about a decision I'd made, but it sounds as if his wife knows already and if his family won't be dragged into it, I feel less guilty about doing it.'

'You're very mysterious all of a sudden,' Kate said. 'Spill the beans.'

'I will,' Hannah assured her, 'But we need to get everyone together. It's something Jack and the rest need to hear. Frankie too, if she's feeling up to it.'

'Have you spoken to her? Do you know how she is? I dropped a card and some flowers round yesterday and left them with Ellie, but I didn't want to be in the way of the family.' Clem's face clouded. Ken had been dear to all of them and his death, while not unexpected, had affected them badly.

'Not since I took her to Ellie's the day it happened,' Hannah said. 'I know they have more important things to worry about with the funeral and everything else, but they're on the board for this place and I need to speak to them before I act.'

'I hate feeling so useless,' Kate sighed. 'Like Clem said, I don't want to be in the way, but Frankie feels like part of my own family and I wish there was something we could do to help her.'

'I did have an idea about that,' Hannah said. 'I've had a lot of time to think over the last few days and they've all been so kind to me, I wanted to do something.'

She outlined the idea she'd been pondering and was pleased to see smiles spread across both faces as she spoke.

'I think it's a lovely idea,' Clem said. 'I've got a mate who'll do it as a favour for us. I'll give him a ring tonight and get it organised.'

JOHN - 1944

'*D*id you find her?' The question burst from John the moment Admiral Ashton walked into the office. 'Is she safe?'

The Admiral held up a hand. 'I did and she is. I spoke to an old colleague of mine and I can safely say the photograph your father showed you was not of Alice.'

'How can you be so sure?'

'Because the person I spoke to helped Alice disappear. She did not go to the Lake District, nor does she have a son. There is nothing to indicate your father's associates have any knowledge of her whereabouts. It was likely nothing more than a way of ensuring your cooperation.'

John's shoulders sagged with relief and he slumped into a chair.

'I'll tell you everything,' he said. 'She's the only reason I didn't report what my father was doing. He coerced Adam into working for him as well.'

'Please don't waste my time making excuses, Mr Liversidge. We know everything already,' Admiral Ashton reminded him. 'That's not why I'm here. As far as everyone else is concerned, I'm here to discuss discontinuing the use of the Lido for swimming lessons for my men. I'm actually here to give you your instructions.'

'My instructions?' John's throat was dry.

'Yes. D-Day may have been a success, but the war is far from over and you and your son still have a part to play in it.' The Admiral pulled up a chair and sat down. 'In return for your co-operation and continued contact with Lernehan, we will list you and your son as having been double agents the entire time. After all, you were very helpful at passing on all the information we wanted your father's associates to have. However,' his face hardened. 'Adam is to stay away from Frances Macmillan. If Mr Lernehan asks any questions, they are simply being more circumspect in light of my continued interest in her. All contact will be made with me and if there is any indication whatsoever that either of you have been compromised… Well, I'm sure I don't have to spell out the consequences. You will continue to pass on the information we give you until such time as we choose to end the arrangement. Is that clear?'

'Perfectly. Admiral, I…' he trailed off as the Admiral stood up.

'Good afternoon, Mr Liversidge. We'll be in touch when we need a message sent.'

OCTOBER 2017

*H*annah looked at the faces arrayed in front of her. She was nervous, but she reminded herself these people were her friends. She had done nothing wrong, she was only there to tell them about wrongdoing she had uncovered.

'Go on then, Hannah,' Jack urged. 'Tell us what you found out.'

She handed out the photocopied and highlighted sheets she'd prepared from the paperwork Sharon had given her. Her neighbour had been gleeful at the prospect of bringing Richard down and made Hannah promise to keep her informed.

'Paperwork's never been my strong suit,' Mark said. 'What is this?'

'Council accounts,' Hannah explained. 'Or at least, a version of them. Do you remember the band night we had that they demanded the money from?'

Mark nodded.

'I know it was transferred to the council because we have a record of it, but it never reached the council accounts.'

Hannah gestured to the rows of figures. 'There's no entry for that money anywhere in the accounts. I went through the figures really carefully and it's simply not there. There are a number of other anomalies as well – he's been skimming money off the Lido ever since he started at the council. He's been clever about it, so I'm not surprised they've not noticed yet, but that's why it looks like the Lido has been running at such a loss recently. In previous years, it was a genuine loss, but this year it's because money has been vanishing into his pocket. We were fighting a losing battle from the start.'

'So, what are we going to do?' Hugh's face was drawn into a scowl. 'I assume you're going to report it to the council and the police?'

'Actually, it depends on you,' Hannah said.

'On us?' Jack looked confused.

'I believe our Hannah has a plan,' Frankie said, a smile spreading across her face.

'I do.' Hannah nodded at her. 'We could do things the right way, or we could try to make it work for us. It might not be strictly ethical, but I could make a case for it being the right thing to do.'

'What do you suggest?' Hugh settled back in his chair, looking intrigued.

'That we use the same tactic I used on Richard to get his support for letting us take over running the Lido in the first place.' Hannah took a deep breath. 'I gave him the chance to put things right by offering to say nothing until he'd had some time to put the money back. I propose that we offer the council a similar deal. We can have Hugh write a scathing article about corrupt council employees defrauding the public. Or, we can let them deal with it internally and quietly and choose when to break the news and in exchange, they hand over the Lido to a Board of Trustees on a permanent basis, give it a grant to get us started and then allow us to keep it open and run it ourselves. Initially we'll pay a nominal lease for it, but ultimately, they'll agree to sell it to us for a small price. What do you think?'

'I think it's risky. Do you reckon they'll go for it?' Ellie asked.

'If they don't, I think we've got a chance the scandal will be so huge they won't be able to close the Lido and they'll have to keep running it themselves. I think they'll be relieved to have it off their hands with relatively little fuss.'

Frankie nodded. 'You'd be surprised the lengths some people are prepared to go to in order to keep a secret.'

'You'd know,' Hannah said quietly, then grinned impishly as Frankie stared at her.

'What do you mean?'

'Ken knew what you did in the war even before you started telling us your story. He worked it out years ago, but never let on. He told me he found your medal, so he knew you'd been involved in something big and he worked out just how big it was, when books started being published about Mincemeat[1] and Fortitude[2]. He was so proud of you.'

Frankie's eyes filled with tears. 'I couldn't tell him. I'd signed the Official Secrets Act.'

Hannah squeezed her hand.

Hugh cleared his throat. 'We think we should try it your way,' he said. 'You're right that it may not be strictly ethical, but sometimes doing what's right for the community involves the sacrifice of individual moral codes.' He laughed. 'That sounds really pompous, but you know what I mean.'

Frankie smiled and patted his hand. 'I know exactly what you mean.'

JOHN - 1944

'What do you want, Liversidge?' Laurence scowled at John as he entered. 'And why did we have to meet in such an out of the way place?'

John glanced around him before scuttling closer to reply in a whisper.

'I assume it was you who helped your sister disappear.'

Laurence looked blankly at him.

'I'm not asking you to tell me where she is, but I must make certain for myself that she's safe. The Admiral said she wasn't in the Lake District, but I don't know if I can trust him or not.'

'You drove my sister out of her home and now you have the gall to come and ask me if she's safe? I know what you did to Lily and if you think for one moment I'm going to tell you anything about my sister, you're a fool.'

'Don't be an idiot, this isn't about me! I told you, I'm not asking to know where she is, I only need to know she's not in danger. Please!'

Laurence sneered. 'Why should I give you the peace of mind you denied to others? You disgust me.'

He turned and walked away, leaving John staring help-lessly after him. John whispered her name, the sound of it sweet torture. He'd never be free of her, never know what had become of her. He could only pray she was safe. If he could only see her again, explain that he still loved her, tell her what he had done for the sake of her niece. That he had tried to make amends for 1917. There was no one else he could talk to about it. Adam hated him for what he had done, almost as much as the boy hated himself for being deceived by Frankie. John wondered if perhaps his son had truly fallen in love with her after all.

And Penny? His wife could never know. Not that she would have cared. She had never been particularly fond of Garrett. John wasn't sure she'd ever been really fond of anyone. Wasn't sure she was capable of it. She'd seen him as a convenient escape and he'd only found out the truth about their marriage long after the ceremony. Perhaps they could have been comfortable together though, if he hadn't been so angry. She'd never forgiven him for Adam and only stayed with him to avoid the scandal if she left. That and the money. Her father had left the port and the dockyard to John. If Penny left, she got nothing, Rockingham's will was explicit about that. But his wife was cleverer than her father had given her credit for and John was just as tied to her. She kept her husband's secrets, as he kept hers and one word from her could ruin him.

As for Alice, it looked as though he was going to have to trust Admiral Ashton's word after all. John felt suddenly old and very very tired. He turned to go home. What else was there to do?

NEW YEAR'S EVE 1944

'Frankie, this is madness. It's freezing!' Ken grimaced as he jumped down from the wall, landing awkwardly on his bad leg.

A giggle floated across the air and he peered into the darkness, trying to see where she had gone.

'Don't be such an old stick in the mud. You used to be fun once upon a time.'

He glared in the direction of her voice. 'And you told me you were less reckless now,' he hissed. 'But the evidence of today would suggest otherwise! Why on earth would you choose to go swimming when it's so cold?'

There was a splash and he hobbled to the edge of the pool. 'Frankie, where are you?'

When there was no answer, he tried again. 'Frankie! Don't play games. Where are you?' He stared at the surface of the water, willing her to float into view, laughing at his anxiety, but there was no sign of her.

'Shit.' He stripped down to his trunks and dived in, the saltwater stinging his eyes. He had no chance of finding her in the dark. He couldn't see above the water, let alone below it, but he had to find her. Relief washed through him as his searching fingers brushed against something solid and he pulled her face clear of the water, strong strokes carrying him to the side of the pool. Pain flared in his leg as he hauled her up the steps and onto the concrete path.

'Frankie? Frankie for God's sake, don't be dead.' He checked her pulse and it was steady, but her eyes were closed and her breathing shallow. He repeated her name. It was a plea. 'Darling, you can't die. Not now. I need you.'

Her eyes fluttered open. 'What did you call me?'

The next moment she was crushed in his arms and he was kissing her as though he were the one drowning. 'I thought I'd lost you,' he muttered against her lips.

'I thought you didn't want me.'

He pulled away and stared at her. 'How can you say that? Frankie, it's always been you.'

She turned away from him. 'I... I don't deserve you, Ken.'

He took her chin in his hand and forced her to look at him. 'I don't want to hear it. I'm not interested in anything that happened in the past. If you don't want me, say the word and I'll leave you alone, but I want to be with you. Not as your friend, as your lover, your husband.'

'You know you're not the first.'

'I'll always walk with a limp. Next.'

Frankie stared at him.

'I thought we were just stating facts about ourselves. Carry on.'

'I'm impulsive and reckless.'

'I like spontaneity.'

'I can never give you children.'

'I couldn't run around after them anyway.'

'There's something else.' She leant over and whispered in his ear, unable to bear looking at him as she confessed her final secret.

He kissed her gently. 'I know. Adam told me.'

'Adam?'

Ken nodded. 'He suspected you had feelings for me that night at the dance and I think he wanted to make sure I wouldn't return them. He said I should know the truth about the baby. So you see sweetheart, I know all of this already and while I love you all the more for giving me all the reasons I shouldn't marry you, will you please, for once in your life, listen to what I'm saying and actually hear it. Frankie Thompson, I am in love with you. I have been in love with you for as long as I can remember and if there is even the slightest chance you love me, I am not letting you go, ever. I want to grow old with you.' He wiped away the tear that had escaped from the corner of her eye. 'Frankie, I love you just as you are and I'm asking... no, I'm begging you, to marry me.'

Frankie laid her head on his shoulder. 'Yes.'

OCTOBER 2017

*H*annah and Jack opened the doors of the café and slipped inside. A sea of expectant faces greeted them and they struggled to keep their expressions neutral.

'Well?' Ellie's hands flew to her hips and she looked exasperated. 'Don't keep us in suspense. What did they say?'

Jack glanced at Hannah, then grinned at his partner. 'They said yes.'

Cheers erupted and the two were swarmed by their friends.

'Well done us,' Hugh declared in satisfaction.

'Well done Hannah for spotting what was going on,' Jack laughed. 'No one else noticed the money was going missing, not even the council!'

'How did they react?' Mark asked, once calm had settled upon them. 'Did they try to fight you on it?'

'They couldn't really,' Hannah said. 'We had all the evidence and they weren't able to argue with it. It was just a matter of whether they took the deal we were offering them.'

'In some ways, I think they were relieved we were happy

to take the place on. If it's off their hands when the story eventually breaks, then I think they're hoping there'll be less of an uproar about it because the Lido is still open and is under new management.'

'Did they say what they were going to do with regards to Richard?' Clem spoke quietly to Hannah, who shook her head.

'Only that their internal affairs people would look into it and take any appropriate action. To be honest, I don't care. He had the chance to put back the money he'd stolen and instead, he took more.'

'Maybe he didn't believe you'd actually do anything with the information. That you still had feelings for him?'

Hannah smiled sadly. 'If he did, he was wrong.' She could see Clem was suppressing the urge to ask whether she meant Richard had been wrong in predicting her inaction or wrong in thinking she still cared for him. She was grateful for his restraint. She wasn't in love with Richard anymore, but her feelings were still complicated. More sessions with Madeleine had helped her to organise her thoughts more clearly, but there was a lot of work still to do. She returned her attention to Clem, who she realised belatedly had continued talking.

'I have some news for you as well, as it happens.' He smiled. 'I've bought a business. Well,' he corrected himself, looking embarrassed. 'The beginnings of one, anyway,'

'That's wonderful.' Hannah smiled, genuinely pleased for him. 'What is it?'

'Do you remember when we saw the old Mermaid building was up for sale?'

'You haven't?' Hannah clapped a hand to her mouth.

Clem grinned and nodded. 'I've got to sort out the planning permission, but I'm going to return it to its former glory and make it a hotel again. I'll carry on freelancing for now so I keep some money coming in until I get it all up and running – I've been offered a 12-month contract with a firm that's mostly done remotely, so the next year is settled and I can set my own hours to a certain extent, so I'll be able to work around the job to get the conversion started.'

'Have you told Frankie? I'll bet she was pleased.'

'Delighted. The thing is… I'll need someone to do the accounts and I wondered if you'd be interested? If you're sticking around, that is.'

Hannah hesitated. She had only planned to stay in Avonstow until she worked out what she wanted to do with her life, but now the time had come to decide where to move to, she found she was reluctant to leave the community she'd become a part of. She glanced over to where Frankie stood, slightly apart from the others and saw that the older woman was watching her. There was a slight nod of encouragement and Hannah took a deep breath, fixing her eyes on her feet.

'I think I'm going to stay,' she said quietly. 'Not forever, but for now at least.'

Clem put a finger under her chin and gently raised her head. 'Maybe it's time to stop running. You have friends here, Hannah. People who care about you. People who would miss you if you left.'

'Madeleine said part of letting everything go was accepting I had a right to be happy,' Hannah told him quietly.

'Madeleine sounds like a good counsellor,' Clem said. 'It took me a long time to accept that what Emmy did was her choice, not mine. Our marriage may not have been perfect, but her affair wasn't my fault. She chose to break our vows and I made the decision not to accept it. You aren't to blame for other people's poor behaviour, especially when you didn't have all the information. You also made the decision to walk away when you found out the truth. You're much stronger than you realise.'

Hannah sighed. 'Ken said much the same thing to me.'

'He was a wise man. You'd do well to listen to him.' Clem squeezed her arm, then changed the subject. 'Speaking of Ken, do you think it's time?'

'Oh yes,' Hannah said, turning to the others. 'Now we know we definitely have something to celebrate, we have something to show Frankie.'

She held an arm out and Frankie took it, looking alarmed. 'What are you doing?' she asked. 'At my age, I'm not big on surprises.'

'You'll like this one, I promise.' Hannah tapped her hand comfortingly.

She led the party through the back of the café and down the steps to the pool area. Ahead of them, on the wall of the pump room, a small curtain had been placed.

'You told us this place always held bad memories for you,' Hannah said to Frankie. 'But Ken told us it was here that he first believed there was a chance you loved him in return and so we thought it was appropriate and hoped it might make your memories a little happier.'

She pulled the cord attached the curtain and it fell away to reveal a shining brass plaque. Frankie gasped, her hand flying to her mouth.

IN MEMORIAM
SQUADRON LEADER KENNETH FORD
1920-2017
REMEMBERED WITH LOVE BY FRIENDS AND FAMILY

FRANKIE RAN her fingers over the engraving, tears collecting in her eyes. 'Thank you,' she whispered.

At a signal from Kate, the others walked slowly back to the café, leaving Frankie alone by the plaque.

'I think she liked it,' Hannah said. 'It won't stop her missing him, but at least he's remembered in a place which meant so much to them both.'

'It was a lovely idea,' Mark agreed.

'This place is going to need a new manager soon,' Kate said, as she handed Hannah a coffee. 'Harry and I got the final lot of permissions today – we're almost ready to open the campsite and I'll be needed to run it. Do you fancy taking this place on?'

Hannah laughed and shook her head. 'I was going to tell you I'm leaving soon too.'

Kate's mouth fell open. 'What? You're never leaving Avonstow? I was so sure you'd stay.'

'I'm not leaving the town, only the café. It's entirely your own fault – you and your friends have sent so much business my way I need to be working full time on accounts! Also,' she flashed a grin at Clem. 'I've just agreed to take on another business and a larger one-off job.'

'And we meant what we said about the campsite,' Kate added quickly. 'We want you to do ours as well.'

Hannah smiled. 'I know. You're on my list, don't worry.'

'What's the other job?' Clem asked.

'The council were so appalled no one had noticed the money was missing from the Lido accounts that they've asked me to do an audit of all their departmental accounts. It's going to take weeks. I said I'd be happy to do it, but they'd have to take their place behind the Lido accounts! Jack's asked me if I'd continue doing them and I agreed of course – no charge for that one though, that's a labour of love.'

Kate raised her coffee cup. 'To us,' she said. 'To friendship and a bright future.'

Hannah tapped her cup against those of her friends and smiled.

AT THE PUMP ROOM, Frankie stared at the plaque through blurred eyes. 'Well, my darling. You were right. All she needed was a gentle push in the right direction. I think our girl is going to be okay now. She's told them everything and they've accepted it, just as we knew they would. I wish I could tell her everything, but I made a promise and you know how much I hate breaking them. I don't know if she would even welcome the truth, especially as she's estranged from her mother. Sometimes a lie is more comforting, isn't it? I wish you'd told me the truth though. I had no idea you'd found my medal and worked out what I did in the war; it would have saved a lot of pain to know that you knew and understood. Oh well, they all know the full story now. No real harm can be done so long after it all.' She paused and laid her fingers on the cold metal. 'Even you didn't find out all my secrets though. I managed to keep one from you.'

FEBRUARY 1945

rankie looked at herself in the mirror. Her mother had done well to create such a beautiful wedding outfit at such short notice and with so few clothing coupons. The cream silk skimmed her knees and she barely recognised herself in the glass. Ken was waiting for her downstairs with the suitcases. Their plans barely constituted a honeymoon but it would do until the war was over and the nightmares appeared to have abated just in time. That night in the pump room had replayed over and over in her head while she slept, her actions haunting her.

FRANKIE PUSHED the door open and put a cautious head through the gap. John and Adam were standing at the rear of the room, looking down the shaft which housed the pump. When she joined them and saw what they were looking at, she swallowed back the bile that rose in her throat.

'We were arguing,' John whispered. 'And then…' he trailed off, his face white.

'He slipped and fell over the edge.'

The two men started in surprise and stared at her.

'It was an accident.'

'But…'

'It was an accident,' Frankie repeated firmly.

'Why would you say…'

'Because that's what happened.' The voice came from the doorway and Frankie's shoulders sagged with relief as Admiral Ashton strode into the room. 'It's what the police will be told, anyway. We were having a meeting about the Navy swimming lessons and we came to inspect the pump. Garrett tripped and fell. There was nothing anyone could do. Come with me gentlemen please. There's a discussion to have before I telephone the police station.'

Frankie hung back as they left the room and as the door closed behind them, she turned and descended the ladder. She looked at the crumpled body as a feeble moan came from it and leant casually against the wall.

'I thought I heard a sound. You know you're dying, don't you, Garrett? I could call an ambulance, but it will be too late by the time they arrive and even if it wouldn't be, I'm not sure you deserve it. Do you know, I actually feel sorry for you. You wanted to be seen as the big patriotic hero, didn't you? Instead, you're slowly bleeding out on a dirty floor. It's quite fitting in a way – you would have been happy to let all those men bleed out on the beaches of Normandy as long as you got the guns you wanted for Ireland, wouldn't you?' She laughed and it made a hollow sound as it echoed around the enclosed space. 'Except it wasn't for Ireland really, was it? You just enjoy the power. You love controlling people and bending them to your will. You would have betrayed your family in a heartbeat if it meant you won. Do you know what your mistake was? You assumed everyone else would be as easily bought and wouldn't think twice about betraying others to get what they wanted. You have no idea what I'd be prepared to do to protect the people I love. That's why I feel sorry for you: not even your own family will mourn your death. We'll carry on feeding false information to your contact and they'll be none the wiser.'

Garrett's eyes flared with rage and contempt, but when he attempted to speak, bubbles of blood formed at the corner of his mouth and slid down his chin. He mouthed the word 'help'. For a moment, Frankie looked at him without speaking. Then she crouched down and gently closed his eyes, before climbing back up the ladder and joining the men in the office.

FRANKIE SAW the tears gathering in the eyes of her reflection and blinked them back. She could not, would not, regret the passing of such a man. His actions had cost her so much, she would not spare him further thought. There was much to regret in recent years – Mac, the loss of their baby, so many deaths and the hurt she had caused Ken – but the passing of Garrett Liversidge would not be one of them. The rest of her life, with Ken at her side, was ahead of her and it was time to look forwards, leaving her regrets behind her.

NOTES

MARCH 1940

1. Australian and New Zealand Army Corps

MAY 1940

1. Reducing the magnetic field of a ship so it was less attracted to magnetic mines.

ADAM - 1940

1. Jenny (Wren) – slang term for WRNS personnel

OCTOBER 2017

1. British intelligence operation to disguise the 1943 Allied invasion of Sicily.
2. Military deception by the Allied nations aimed at misleading Germany about where the D-Day invasion would happen.

AUTHOR'S NOTES AND ACKNOWLEDGMENTS

This book came about because when I was appointed Writer in Residence at Brightlingsea Lido, one of the things I said I would do, was to write a book with the Lido at the heart of the story. I knew I wanted to set part of it during the Second World War but I couldn't find enough information about the Lido during the war to create an authentic story. However, I quickly realised that as I had already created a fictional version of Brightlingsea for 'Folly', it made sense to set the Lido book in the same universe. I was still editing 'Folly' at the time, so went back and added more to Frankie's role, as I knew she was going to be the protagonist of Book 2.

However, the book would never have been written had it not been for the amazing people I've worked with and talked through plot ideas with. Gary Humm went above and beyond – not only did he answer my copious questions about sailing and give me some amazing anecdotes about his life on boats (some of which I adopted for Frankie), but he and his wife Marie actually took me out on their boat so I could experience being out on the Creek myself. I also must thank Ann for her insight into the aftermath of the ANZAC troops leaving Brightlingsea after WW1, as this was where the idea for the turning point of Mac and Frankie's relationship came from.

Once again, I have to thank Olivia Reilly for the stunning cover she has created for me out of a conversation and some very rough sketches. My editors, Sue and Jane worked tirelessly to help ensure the book was the best it could be and I am grateful to them both for putting up with the endless backwards and forwards as I worked through their notes and suggestions

In researching for 'The Mermaid' I found out so much more about the town I live in and I have tried to be as faithful as I could be to the real history of Brightlingsea – the ships in Avonstow have a link to the real ships that were based at HMS Nemo – please get in touch if you work out which ships they refer to and what the connection is between the real name and the fictional one! Where history has been changed, this is deliberate and was done solely for the purposes of the plot and the same applies to the liberties I have taken with the workings of local councils. Obviously, none of the characters bear any relationship to real people.

If reading 'The Mermaid' has sparked an interest in Brightlingsea and this period of history, then below is a list of books and other resources I found useful.

Under the White Ensign – J P Foynes

One Hurricane One Raid – Geoff Rayner

Operation Mincemeat – Ben Macintyre

Double Cross: The True Story of The D-Day Spies – Ben Macintyre

The Girls Who Went To War – Duncan Barrett

Britannia's Daughters: the story of the WRNS - Ursula Stuart Mason

Wingspan: A History of RAF Debden – Keith Braybrooke

RAF Duxford – Michael Evans

Liquid Assets: The lidos and open air swimming pools of Britain – Janet Smith

Brightlingsea: Memories of Childhood in the 1930s and 1940s – Brightlingsea U3A

https://brightlingseaanzacsorg.wordpress.com

Brightlingsea Museum

The Day That Decided The Battle of Britain – Retold Documentary

Mendelssohn's Hebrides Suite

ABOUT THE AUTHOR

Ruth's first writing memory is for her writer's badge in Brownies but her MA in Creative Writing probably trumps that. Ruth is the co-founder and director of the publishing company Castle Priory Press and has been Writer In Residence at Brightlingsea Lido since 2021. She also helps to organise and run the Brightlingsea Literary Festival.

Ruth publishes adult books under her own name and children's books under the pen name Henrietta Edwards. Ruth has also been published in various anthologies, helping to edit many of them as well. Ruth's next book for children, 'The Quest of the Summer King' is planned for release later in 2024.

ALSO BY R.E. LOTEN

FOLLY (AVONSTOW BOOK ONE)

1917

Avonstow is at war, but it's a friendly invasion that forces deeply held secrets to emerge. The arrival of the Australian engineers upsets the equilibrium of the wartime village, while the commander of the village's naval base is convinced a spy is lurking in their midst. The consequences are far greater than anyone might have imagined.

1995

Ellie Whitemore travels to Avonstow after her great-uncle's body is discovered on the salt marshes near the town. She sets about unravelling her family's past and finds that their fortunes are inextricably linked with those of the town itself. But there is always a price to pay when secrets are unearthed.

UNFORGETTABLE

There are first loves and there are last loves. But what happens when they overlap?

Tom Blythe falls in love quickly. He fell for Olivia the first time they met. The same thing happens when he meets Grace. The problem is: Tom is still in love with Olivia.

Pulled in two different directions, Tom has a choice to make. He knows he's unhappy, but is that enough for him to forget the vows he made? Both women have difficult pasts and Tom is desperate to help them, but at what cost?

Can he let Olivia go and commit his future to Grace? Or will the pull of the past prove too strong?

AS HENRIETTA EDWARDS

MAX, THE BRIGHTLINGSEA CAT
LILIBET THE LOBSTER

THE REIGN OF THE WINTER KING (THE COURTS BOOK ONE)

Everyone knows the stories of Robin Hood and King Arthur.

Everyone knows they're just legends.

But what if everyone is wrong?

While Sam, Henry and Arthur think they're going to spend their summer holiday with Uncle Alan, their adventurous relative has other plans. The Silver Arrow has gone missing, and Robin has been kidnapped.

The race is on to find the arrow and rescue Robin, before others beat them to it. Who can be trusted? One wrong move and disaster is sure to follow!

This series is perfect for fans of Susan Cooper's 'The Dark Is Rising' series.

Printed in Great Britain
by Amazon

36889111R00219